Chapter 1

Kingdom of Glenmuir
Scottish Highlands
A.D. 626

As night settled on the king's village, lights blazed in the Great Hall. The people celebrated. Yesterday they and their allies had defeated the evil tyrant who had usurped control of the kingdom. At battle's end amid great rejoicing, the Glenmuirians had restored to the High Seat its rightful king and queen, Michael Langssonn and his wife, Cait nea Sholto.

Among those warriors who had fought in the battle and who now joined in the festivities was Brian mac Logan, Highland warlord. An honored guest, Brian dined at the royal table. He sat to the left of his liege, High King Malcolm mac Duncan of Northern Scotland. Although Brian would have been happy sitting on a hard bench along with his comrades-in-arms, he was grateful to have been honored with one of the four cushioned chairs in the building. Leaning back into the pillowed softness, he gave himself over to a pleasant lethargy created by the imported wine, the glowing warmth of the room, and the aroma of cooking food. At peace with the world, he let his gaze slide lazily around the room.

1

Glenmuir was a small but rich kingdom, its wealth reflected in the furnishings of the Great Hall. Colorful tapestries bedecked the walls and hung over the interior doors. Shields and weapons covered the remaining walls, their gold, silver, and jeweled decorations glistening in the flickering light. Tables, covered in fabric as brightly colored and as skillfully woven as the tapestries, fanned out in a semicircle from the king's dais, on which stood the high table. Extending on either side of the dais was a long table reserved for honored guests. Large cauldron lamps were interspersed throughout the room, their flames dancing brightly; gold and silver bowls and tankards twinkled richly in the lamplight.

An oval hearth, waist-high and curbed in stone, dominated the center of the room. Golden-red flames helped to illuminate the room and to provide heat for cooking. Servants busily served the evening meal. Vegetables, fruits, and nuts. Beef and boar steaks braised in butter and herbs; roasted leg of lamb and deer; spit-roasted mutton; veal stew. Warm loaves of golden-brown bread, slathered in butter or cheese.

Aye, Brian thought, picking up his tankard and taking a swallow of the fine wine, tonight he was a contented man, enjoying the hospitality of the Glenmuirian monarchs. Then he heard deep, husky laughter, *her* laughter. Gwynneth the seafarer. Brian leaned back in his chair and stared contemptuously at the woman who sat six people down from him. He didn't like her and hadn't from the first moment they had met.

As if she felt his gaze on her, she turned her head and returned his stare. A cool smile played on her full lips; her blue-gray eyes mocked him.

Her hair, hanging down her back in a long, thick braid, glimmered golden in the firelight.

Nay, Brian thought, he didn't like her, but she *was* beautiful, and during the recent battle she had proved herself useful. He was forced to admire her prowess as a warrior.

Soon she would be out of his life. He and his liege and their warriors would be returning home to their kingdom of Northern Scotland. The thought of home . . . of Sorcha, his wife, and his four children . . . warmed Brian. No doubt he was a Highland warrior; as surely, he was a man who loved his family.

Behind him on wrought-iron standards, banners representing four kingdoms fluttered in the evening breeze. They seemed to ripple together, as if they were one. And indeed this past week, Glenmuirians, Northlanders, Highlanders, and Scottish seafarers had fought side by side as one army. The decisive victory the day before had chased away any battle fatigue the warriors might have felt. They celebrated with the same relish and intensity with which they had fought.

Again and again they saluted Michael and Cait, high king and queen of Glenmuir. They saluted others who had supported the Glenmuirian king in regaining the High Seat: Malcolm mac Duncan, Michael's identical twin brother; Lady Gwynneth the seafarer, seated to the left of the Glenmuirian monarchs; and Lord Lang, Earl of Ulfsbaer, Northland, who sat at the table to the right of the king.

Long into the night, the people reveled. As they dined on succulent food, bards sang of great deeds done by their liege. Afterward warriors bragged of their bravery and cunning against the enemy. Musicians played; couples danced. Amid great laughter, Michael distinguished himself—against

his own brother—as the champion arm wrestler.
No one outdid Malcolm on the throwing of the
dirk, however, and he was declared champion
sword dancer.

After the sword dance the musicians returned
to their tables, but Malcolm remained in the center
of the room. He received his mantle from one of
the serving maids and tossed it negligently over
one shoulder. His eyes, the same shade of blue as
his tunic, sparkled with vitality. His gaze fastened
on the high table, he raked a hand through his
dark hair.

"Headman," he called out to Brian, "all you've
done this evening is eat and drink. It's time to
demonstrate your skill."

Brian smiled at his liege, who was also his close
friend and trusted comrade-in-arms. "I'm content
to be lazy, my liege."

"But I'm not content that you are," Malcolm
returned.

"Many valiant warriors have competed tonight,
lord," Brian argued, "among them you and your
brother, Michael. Surely that is enough entertain-
ment for one night."

"Nay, headman," Malcolm said. "I have been
forced to compete. So shall you."

Brian set down his tankard. "What do you
suggest?"

"Show us how you wield the cateia, the Highland throwing spear." Malcolm circled the hearth.
"Warriors and villagers of Glenmuir, do you wish
to see Brian mac Logan demonstrate his skill?"

The people shouted, "Aye!" and clapped their
hands.

Slowly Brian rose, stepped down from the dais,
and reached for the spear that leaned against the
wall immediately behind him. He slipped his right

hand through the leather loop attached to the center of the long, cylindrical shaft; he ran his left thumb along the edge of the leaf-shaped head. As he walked to the spot vacated by Malcolm, the silver head glinted ominously in the flickering light. The cateia was a weapon of war, Brian mac Logan a man of war.

Thorfinn, champion of the drinking contest, staggered to his feet. He pushed the hood of his short leather cape from his head so that it bunched around his neck. His words slurred, he declared, "I am a champion spear thrower."

"Not with a cateia," said Malcolm, now seated at the high table beside his brother.

"With any spear, my lord," Thorfinn boasted.

Brian and Malcolm exchanged amused looks. Malcolm shrugged.

Grinning, Brian handed the Northlander the spear and said, "Let us compete."

"Aye, Highlander," Thorfinn growled, then shouted to one of the serving boys. "Lad, close the entrance door. I shall throw the spear into its center panel."

The boy raced to do Thorfinn's bidding.

"Northlander," Brian said, "perhaps you should let me show you how to hold the cateia."

Thorfinn scowled. "I don't need anyone to show me how to hold or throw a spear. I was throwing one when you were in swaddling."

"So be it," Brian muttered and stepped back.

Disregarding the leather loop—a great error in judgment—Thorfinn clasped the shaft. Flexing his fingers, he rolled the spear in his hand, getting the feel of it.

Finally he shouted, "Count off the paces, lad."

The serving boy starting walking. When he reached Thorfinn, he said, "Fifty, sire."

The Northlander nodded. Waving Brian and the lad out of the way, he positioned himself. He straddled his feet and drew back his arm. With a shout he spun around, bringing his arm forward and releasing the shaft. It sailed through the air. The metal head sliced low into the door with a thud.

The warriors clapped their hands and laughed.

Thorfinn's scowl deepened as he turned to Brian. "See if you can outdo me, Highlander."

Without a word Brian walked slowly to the door and pulled out the cateia. As he had done earlier, he slipped his right hand through the loop and with the left brushed wood dust from the blade. He returned to his spot below the high table.

"I shall hit the same spot that you did, Northlander," he announced.

Thorfinn laughed.

Clasping the spear, Brian pulled back his arm, and with a smooth motion born of years of practice, he released the weapon. Again it sailed through the air, thudding into the door.

The lad raced to the target. Kneeling, he examined it and shouted excitedly, "You did it, my lord! Your spear landed in the same spot as the Northlander's."

Amid loud cheers, Thorfinn shouted, " 'Twas luck, nothing more." Grumbling beneath his breath, he pulled his hood over his head and staggered back to his table.

"Let me show you luck, Northlander," Brian said. "Although you look better with your head covered, I shall uncover it for you. Without moving from this spot."

Thorfinn stopped, turned, and squinted at Brian.

Brian loosed the spear. As it flew past Thorfinn's head, the silver head nipped the edge of the hood and pushed it from his head, then thudded into the wall behind the Northlander. Reflexively he raised his hand to his temple.

"If you drew blood, Highlander—" he warned angrily.

"Nay, I did you no harm," Brian answered. "I only removed your hood."

Laughing, another Northlander, Kolby of Apelstadt, rose. "Admit it, Thorfinn, Brian has gotten the best of you."

Bringing down his hand and seeing no blood, Thorfinn relaxed. He didn't smile, but he picked up his tankard and held it aloft. He saluted: "Brian mac Logan, champion cateia thrower."

When the toast was finished and the reveling crowd had quieted, Thorfinn called out, "Kolby, we've seen how the Highlander handles the cateia. Let's show them what a Northlander can do. Wield that fancy bow of yours."

"Aye," Brian shouted, his cry echoed by the crowd. "Show us, Northlander."

Reaching for his bow and quiver, Kolby walked to the center of the room. He laid the quiver on a nearby table and held out his bow, acquired during his travels to the far countries of the east. Called a built-bow, it was made of several pieces of smooth wood glued together; its cross section elliptical in design. Lacquered in black and trimmed in gold, the bow was a work of art. But those who had fought alongside Kolby knew that he had wielded it like a mighty battle weapon. The people gazed in awe.

"End the evening's revelry in a feat that cannot be challenged, my friend," Brian said, playfully cuffing the Northlander on the shoulder.

"Aye, headman," Kolby answered as Brian returned to his place at the high table. "I shall." He turned and looked at the closed door.

"Ten arrows to the center panel," someone shouted.

"Ten arrows to the center panel at fifty paces," Kolby murmured, then nodded. " 'Tis a short distance but it will have to do. It's too dark to go outside." Looking at the warrior who had declared the feat, he said, "To make it challenging, let's lay a wager. For every arrow that lands outside the center of the panel, I shall give each of you a piece of gold."

When the chorus of exuberant "ayes" died down, Kolby added softly, "If all ten hit the center, each of you will give me a piece of gold."

There was a moment of silence before shouts of "Done!" echoed throughout the room.

Focusing on the target, Kolby raised his bow, nocked an arrow, and released it from the bowstring. It sang through the air straight and sure. One after the other, his shots hit the center of the door panel. Breath was held; anticipation ran high. When the last arrow thudded into the target, it seemed as if the room itself let out a sigh. Cheers resounded. Women clapped their hands; men clanged their weapons. All stamped their feet.

The serving lad pulled out the arrows. Holding them in both hands, he cried out, "Ten in a row in the center panel of the door."

Hurrahs filled the room. Tankards were raised in salute.

"Does anyone contest that Kolby of Apelstadt is the champion archer?" Brian shouted.

"No one! None!" came shouts from all corners of the room. Slapping their hands against the tabletops, the people began to chant, "Hail, Kolby the Northlander!"

"Champion archer!" Brian shouted.

Taking off one of his gold armbands, he tossed it to the floor. One by one others did the same. Soon a pile of jewelry glittered around the Northlander's feet. High King Michael motioned, and a servant collected the bounty and put it in a chest.

From the minute Kolby had answered his challenge, Brian had known that he would lose a piece of jewelry. During the recent campaign to liberate Glenmuir from its evil tyrant, Brian had seen several demonstrations of Kolby's expertise with the bow and arrow. Had it not been for one of Kolby's well-timed, well-aimed arrows, Brian himself would have been killed. He owed Kolby a debt of gratitude for having saved his life. The two warriors had met only recently, had fought in only one battle together, yet already they were more than comrades-in-arms. They were friends.

High King Michael rose from the high seat between his wife and brother and moved around the table. When he reached Kolby, he unfastened his torque and took it off.

Holding it out, he said, "None is better with the bow than you, Kolby of Apelstadt."

Cheers punctuated his declaration.

Michael slipped the golden band around Kolby's neck and fastened it. "Truly you are a champion, and we shall salute you as one."

A serving maiden rushed up, handing Michael and Kolby tankards of ale. Michael held his aloft, and the people began to stand.

Before Michael could speak, a rusty voice shouted from one of the tables on the far left. "Indeed Kolby of Apelstadt, Northland, is a champion. But there is another here who is also a champion archer."

Silence fell on the Great Hall. One by one, tankards were lowered; heads turned and eyes searched the crowd for the challenger.

"Mayhap better than the Northlander." The speaker rose, moved around the table, and stepped into the aisle. His leather clothes identified him as one of the mariners who had sailed with Gwynneth, commonly called Wynne the seafarer.

"Who are you, mariner?" asked Michael.

"Ian."

"Is the person of whom you speak here in the Great Hall?" Michael asked.

"Aye, lord."

A slight smile playing on his lips, Ian walked slowly up the aisle, pausing now and then to stare at one of his fellow seafarers. Each time Ian shook his head and moved on. No one in the Great Hall demanded he tell them who the champion was; they allowed him to make the revelation in his own time. They took pleasure in the growing suspense. Heads dipped together; whispers rippled through the crowd.

Finally Ian, standing next to Michael, stopped in front of the head table located to the left of the royal family. He pointed at Wynne. "She is a champion archer, my lord high king."

Brian stared at her in disgust. A woman dared to challenge a warrior. It was an insult. She was ruining a pleasant evening.

"You think Lady Gwynneth is a better archer than the Northlander?" Michael's voice lashed through the now silent hall.

"I don't *think* she shoots a truer arrow than Kolby of Apelstadt, my lord high king," the mariner said, his quiet voice carrying easily so that all could hear. "I *know* she does."

Wynne glanced over at Brian and winked.

"Damnation!" Brian growled softly, leaning his head close to Malcolm's. "Must we forever endure this cursed woman? Today we fought beside the seafarer. Now we'll be competing with her. Always she tries to be a man."

Michael stepped closer to Wynne's table. "My lady, what have you to say about the matter?"

"*My lady!*" Brian muttered sarcastically, his comment once again directed to his liege. "The seafarer may be a woman, but she is no lady."

Nay, the seafarer was no lady! Ladies were soft, gentle creatures, like Brian's wife, Sorcha, who tended to home and hearth, who bore and raised children, who loved and cared for their menfolk. Not so the seafarer. Had she lent a hand in preparing the banquet tonight? Absolutely not! She had been here in the Great Hall, celebrating with the warriors, competing with them . . . and as much as Brian hated to admit it, making a good show of herself. Just as Michael's and Malcolm's bards had sung deeds of their valor, Wynne's bard had sung of hers.

"An answer, lady," Michael demanded.

"Nay, my lord high king," she answered, "I do not wish to compete with Kolby."

"'Twould add some spice to the evening," Michael pointed out.

She smiled. "Not tonight. I'm battle-weary and wish only to relax."

Laughing loudly, Brian leaned forward to stare at her. "Or is it, seafarer," he taunted, "that you don't think you can outshoot the Northlander?"

Wynne's expression hardened, yet her voice was soft when she said, "Whether I choose to compete or not, mac Logan, I am a champion archer. But tonight belongs to High King Michael and his Northland warriors. It is they who declared themselves champions of Glenmuir; they led the fight to liberate the kingdom. It is Michael, their liege, who has married the heir to the High Seat and has taken his place as king. I won't take the glory from him or his warriors."

Brian snorted. "As if you could."

Seafarer and Highlander glared at each other. Wynne pushed back her chair and rose, an indication of her agreement to compete. Michael returned to his seat.

Dressed in tunic, trousers, and boots, Wynne strode to the center of the room. Her red mantle fell to her ankles and swirled around her tall, slender body, billowing out to expose the sword and dirk strapped at her waist.

When she reached Kolby, she said, "My lord Northlander, I left my bow and arrows aboard my ship. May I borrow yours?"

"With pleasure, my lady."

Laying the arrows on the table next to his quiver, Kolby handed her the bow. Wynne ran her fingers lightly up and down the stave; then she clutched the grip, flexing her fist about it. She looked at the target. Finally she held the bow up, aligning it with her body, and plucked the string. When she released it, the twang echoed throughout the room. With her right hand, Wynne picked up one of the arrows, her fingers lightly brushing over the fletching and down the shaft. She rubbed the metal head.

"A wager, my lady," someone called out.

"Nay," she replied.

Murmurs of disappointment ran through the crowd. Much of the excitement of the game was in the laying of bets.

"State your feat," Michael called out.

"Two arrows."

Guffaws greeted her announcement. Brian joined in the laughter. No wonder she hadn't issued a challenge or laid a wager! Two arrows compared to Kolby's ten!

When the levity died down, Wynne continued, "The first arrow to the center door panel. The second will split the first."

Brian's laughter stopped as quickly as it had begun. He leaned back in his chair. He had not been prepared for this. Gasps of surprise were followed by frenzied whispers as individual wagers were laid. Wynne nocked the arrow and held it for a moment before releasing it. It flew straight to the target . . . straight to the center panel. As quickly another arrow followed, this one slicing the shaft of the first one in two, thudding when metal head encountered metal head.

At first silent disbelief embraced the crowd; then it gave way to shouts and cheers. Brian slid to the edge of the chair. Kolby raised his brows in surprise. As quickly Wynne shot two more arrows, again the second splitting the first.

Glancing over her shoulder, Wynne gave Brian a mocking smile. When he glowered at her, she chuckled softly. She then turned to Kolby.

"Your turn, my lord."

Laughing, Kolby shook his head. "Nay, I am not so proficient. I concede that you are indeed champion archer. But one day, lady, I shall challenge you again, and I shall win."

"I look forward to that day, my lord."

Brian shook his head. "Champion swordsman," he growled in an undertone. "Champion seafarer. Now champion archer. What will she do next, Malcolm? Drink us men under the table?"

Malcolm chuckled. "I have no doubt she could do it."

Brian had spoken so low, he figured the seafarer could not hear him; yet she turned and gave him a long, measured stare.

"Nor I," Brian grumbled. It was her damned arrogance and proficiency that angered him.

"My lady," Kolby said, "I have fought by your side and have seen you wield both sword and dirk with expertise. How did you come to be such a valiant warrior?"

"My father taught me," she answered. "I was the son he never had."

"He taught you how to use the bow and arrow also?" Kolby pressed.

"Nay, that is not a weapon of choice here in the Highlands," Wynne replied. " 'Tis reserved for hunting. Like you, my lord, I became more familiar with it during my travels. One day the bow shall be a battle weapon as well as a hunting implement."

This was more than Brian could tolerate. "Nay, seafarer. A warrior needs nothing but his strength and valor and his skill with both sword and dirk."

Wynne stepped in front of Brian's table. "Yesterday in battle, mac Logan, neither your strength nor your valor nor your skill with sword and dirk were enough to save you. 'Twas an arrow that felled the man who would have plunged his dirk into your back."

Brian's eyes narrowed. "Aye, seafarer," he admitted. "Had it not been for Kolby and his bow—"

" 'Twas my arrow, mac Logan."

Warmth suffused Brian's face; he tensed and leaned forward.

" 'Twas I who saved you." She raised her voice so that all could hear.

"You?"

She nodded. "Aye. You had your hands full, my

lord, fighting two warriors at once. You could not watch your back also." A cool smile touched her lips. "I think, my lord Highlander, that you owe your life to me."

Brian's hand curled so tightly around his tankard, the metal bit into his palm. Kolby chuckled softly, as did Malcolm and Michael. Ordinarily Brian would have laughed at himself, but not tonight. He couldn't bear the idea that *this woman* had saved him, that she jeered him as she boasted of the deed.

"Since I have no intention of ever seeing you again, seafarer," he said, "I want to repay my debt now."

"That is good, lord."

"Perhaps we can agree on a monetary value," he said, then added sarcastically, "I believe you pride yourself on being a woman of business, and you do enjoy your booty, *my lady*."

She hiked a brow.

His lips curled into a derisive smile. "I know how much you charged Michael to transport him and his warriors to Glenmuir. It was I who measured the booty. Two chests full of gold, one of silver."

Her eyes narrowed. "The situation was dangerous and warranted more than the usual fare. The quickest route to Glenmuir required that we sail down one of Scotland's most treacherous rivers. I was the only mariner who was skilled enough . . ." She paused. "And courageous enough to do so."

The arrogant bitch! "I am convinced, seafarer, that no matter what the circumstances, you would have demanded a high booty."

"I have been taught, mac Logan, that a laborer is worthy of his hire."

"Since your hire is so high," he said, "I am fortunate that I am a wealthy man. Ask what you will."

"I never ask for more than what a task is worth," she returned. "Tonight is no different."

"State your price," Brian ordered impatiently.

"Nothing, mac Logan." She smiled slightly. "Your life is worth nothing to me. Absolutely nothing."

In unison the crowd gasped. Humiliation burned through Brian. Slowly he rose and glowered down at her.

"You have insulted me, seafarer."

"Nay, mac Logan, you have done that to yourself. I have fought as valiantly as any other warrior, yet you have managed to belittle everything I did. Most of all, you belittle the fact that I am a woman and a warrior. Consider your debt paid in full."

She stared defiantly into the dark countenance of the Highland warrior. His eyes narrowed until they were silver slits. A strand of black hair fell across his forehead. He reached up and brushed it from his face with an impatient jerk of his hand.

Inside Wynne trembled . . . not because she feared the man or the consequences of his anger. She trembled because she was confused and angry with herself. For the first time in many winters, since she had first been attracted to her divorced husband Alba, she was attracted to a man. To this man, Brian mac Logan, who was married and who made no pretense of his dislike of her. Even when so long ago she had been infatuated with Alba, she had not trembled as she did now. Never!

Despising her weakness, but determined that none should know of it, she calmly addressed Michael. "My lord high king, with your permission, I shall retire to my ship."

As if she had issued a command, Wynne's crewmen rose and clustered around her.

"You're not leaving?" Michael asked.

"Nay, I shall fulfill my bargain," she answered. "You paid me to sail you here and to return Malcolm mac Duncan and his warriors back to the kingdom of Northern Scotland. I honor my word. If you have need of me, lord, you know where to find me."

He nodded.

Her head high, her back straight, she shouted, "One last toast before I leave."

"Here! Here!" The crowd complied happily.

Wynne picked up an empty drinking horn, an extremely large one, and held it out. Brows arched and murmurs raced through the crowd. She had issued a silent challenge. For her to retain her dignity and honor, custom demanded that once the horn touched her lips, she could not remove it until it was drained. Wagers were laid.

"To victory!" she shouted and raised the horn to her mouth.

Everyone watched in fascination. To see a man drink like this was commonplace. To see a woman was different and exciting. When she finished, she wiped her sleeve across her mouth and moved until she stood directly before Brian. Turning the horn bottom side up, she thumped it on the table. Again the Great Hall resounded with cheers and clanging weapons.

"Mac Logan," she said, "if I choose to do so, I can drink my men under the table. In fact, when I was much younger and much more foolish I did so on one or two momentous occasions."

Several of her crewmen, who heard her, grinned and nodded their heads.

"I'm wiser now and don't allow my wits to be

controlled by strong drink." Dismissing Brian, she said to her crewmen, "If you wish, you may stay and celebrate. As for me, I'm retiring."

Without a backward glance, Wynne strode toward the door.

Chapter 2

Irritated with herself for allowing Brian to stir her emotions, Wynne jerked open the door and walked out of the Great Hall toward the inlet where she had moored her ship. Glad to be away from the derisive stares of the Highlander, away from his scathing remarks, she welcomed the cool silence of the night.

She had been acquainted with Brian for only two weeks, but during that time he had wreaked havoc with her life. Her emotions were always at the surface, ready to erupt. From the first moment they met, he had disliked her. He seemed to have taken pleasure in letting everyone know how little he regarded her.

When she reached the shore, she leaned against the trunk of a large tree and listened to the gentle rustle of the river; she watched the silver-shadowed ripples. Ordinarily her mountain cat, Honey, would be with her, purring and rubbing against her legs, but Wynne had left the cat home. Honey had sustained a serious wound in a hunting excursion and needed time to recuperate.

Her solitude pressing in on her, Wynne sighed. She was glad she had embarrassed mac Logan. During the past two weeks he had taken every opportunity he could find to humiliate her. She would be glad to leave, to get away from him.

Ever since she had divorced her husband three years ago, she had prided herself on being in control of her life, especially her emotions. But these past two weeks had taught her a lesson: she had only thought she was in control. She had simply not found a man to whom she was attracted.

Once she was away from here, she consoled herself, away from the excitement of victory, she would forget the Highlander. It was a passing attraction. Besides, she had nothing to fear from him or herself. Mac Logan did not like her, and he was a married man. Although married men were allowed to take bedmates, Wynne had promised herself long ago that she would not become one. She had kept her promise . . . and would continue to keep it.

She heard soft footfalls. Knowing she was hidden within the voluminous folds of her mantle, she closed her gloved hand over the hilt of her sword and slowly eased into the moonlit shadows. A man was walking toward her ship.

"Lady Gwynneth," he called softly in Irish Gaelic, "are you here?"

Not knowing the man and not trusting him, she drew her sword but did not answer.

"I know you are about somewhere, lady. I followed you from the Great Hall."

Wynne stepped out of the darkness.

The stranger turned and glanced down at the sword, its blade gleaming in the moonlight. "Have no fear, my lady, I come as a friend."

When she didn't answer, he continued. "I am Siad, recently from Donegal Bay, Ireland."

He paused; still she did not respond.

"I bring you news of Clan O'Illand of Sligo."

Clan O'Illand! Wynne tensed. Alba, her divorced husband, was a member of this clan. When he had been disgraced by the divorcement, he had taken a blood oath to kill her. Had this man been sent to do the deed?

Anxiety tightened like a vise around Wynne's chest, but she kept her voice low and calm as she said, "I know of no news from Clan O'Illand that would interest me."

"This will, my lady," he said softly. "Alba has died."

"Alba is dead?" she repeated.

"Aye."

Wynne felt as if an iron weight had been lifted from her shoulders. She was no longer a woman of divorcement but a widow. No longer shamed. No longer an outcast.

"Clan O'Illand has renewed their blood oath to find you," the stranger added.

"Are you their champion?" she asked.

"If I were, lady, I would not have announced myself."

Perhaps he was telling the truth, but Wynne decided to reserve judgment. She did not lower her sword.

"You have nothing to fear from me," he continued, "but you do from Clan O'Illand."

"If they are as successful in their attempts to kill me in the future as they have been the past three years," she replied, "I have nothing to fear."

"You do, lady. Now that Alba is dead, his father, King Triath, has lost hope of having an heir. Because of you and what you did to Alba, Clan O'Illand is cursed. During the three years that you and Alba have been divorced, trouble has come on the clan. Pestilence. Plagues. Raids. Their cattle are being stolen. Most important, lady, mothers and babes are dying in childbirth. The clan's numbers are dwindling with each passing season."

Siad paused, peering through the silvered shadows into her face. "All the sons destined for the High Seat are dead."

"Manech?" Wynne asked, referring to Alba's older brother.

Siad nodded. "During his thirty winters on this earth he did not sire a child. He was a cursed man, as was Alba."

Wynne understood the implication. Impotence. Infertility. Shame of the greatest degree. Custom decreed that a physically defective person could not rule a kingdom. This imperfection of the king would transfer itself to the land and the people, who in turn would become diseased and imperfect. For this reason Alba could not take the High Seat either; he could only sire the child who would be the next high king.

"In hopes of cleansing the land, someone killed Manech," Siad continued, "and now Alba is dead. King Triath blames you."

Wynne slipped her sword into the scabbard and turned. Slowly she walked closer to the river, wishing she could undo many things in her past. Wishing she had never met Alba O'Illand of Sligo, Ireland, had never become so infatuated with him. In the foolishness of youth, she had made a mistake that continued to haunt her.

She had been sixteen when she had met Alba. He was so handsome, so valiant ... she had thought. No obstacle would keep Wynne from having him. She had determined to marry him, and she had. It hadn't mattered that her older sister, Raven, had spoken to her father, telling him that she was interested in marrying the Irishman. Or that Raven was the elder and by law should be married first. Or that Raven would be disgraced should Wynne take the man chosen for her and marry first. Nay, Wynne had been so intent on having her own way that she had not measured the consequences of her actions. Not until it was too late.

On her wedding night Wynne had learned how weak and disgusting her husband was. He had come to their marriage bed drunk. When he could not perform, he blamed her. He started beating her. She fought back, but she was no match for his strength. She was almost senseless when Honey, her wildcat kitten, attacked him. The cat sank her claws into both his cheeks, ripping out an eye and leaving him badly scarred.

According to custom, Wynne appealed to the assembly for a bill of divorcement. She received it, but it cost her dearly. Alba lied about her, claiming he had a right to beat her. She had deceived him, he said. She came to him as soiled goods, not as a virgin. Judgment went against her. Her father, following the assembly's decree, disowned her, and she became an outcast.

"Whether you are guilty or not, lady, Triath blames you."

The Irishman's voice intruded upon her thoughts. He stood behind her now. She had been so deeply engrossed in her thoughts, she had not heard him come closer.

"Since both direct heirs to the High Seat are dead, the clanspeople must accept a distant relative from Clan Donnal as their chieftain."

Wynne laughed shortly. " 'Tis better than they deserve."

"They fear this new chieftain's loyalty will be to Clan Donnal rather than to Clan O'Illand. Because the O'Illands are diminishing in size, they also fear they will cease being a clan in themselves and will be forced to become a house within Clan

Donnal. This has driven them to renew their efforts to find you, lady. Triath has vowed to avenge the shame you brought upon both of his sons and on his clan. He has a champion who has sworn before God and the saints to find and bring you back to Ireland."

Once again Wynne felt as if a weight had been laid across her shoulders. Alba had not been a strong man, and she had not feared reprisals from him, but this news was ominous.

"Folloman is the one," Siad announced. "For many winters he has been an outcast from Clan O'Illand and a raider. Wanting to shed the dishonor of being an outcast, wanting to be reunited with his clansmen, he bargained with Triath."

Wynne listened.

"Folloman will be accepted into the clan once more if he marries you, the woman whom Triath and Clan O'Illand consider to be Alba's widow. You shall produce a child who shall inherit the High Seat of Clan O'Illand. Once the child is born, Folloman will have custody of it, and Triath can do with you as he wishes."

"He will kill me," Wynne murmured.

Siad nodded. "His revenge will be complete. You will be dead, and he will have an heir to the High Seat. Forever the name O'Illand will be recorded in the annals of Irish clans."

"Why me?" Wynne asked. "I'm not a member of Clan O'Illand. Surely they have women in the clan who would be willing to marry Folloman and have a child by him. Or Triath could adopt a child."

"Neither choice will avenge the shame you have brought on them or lift the curse. Only you can do that, seafarer. You are the one who should have given them an heir through Alba. Therefore it is your duty to give them an heir now through Folloman."

"I owe them nothing," Wynne said, "and that is exactly what I shall give them." She turned around. "Why have you brought me this news, Irishman? What have you to gain?"

"I too seek revenge, my lady. Folloman wanted my wife. She refused to go with him. He killed her, and this is what he did to me." Siad stepped closer and held out his arm, his right arm. His weapon hand was gone, severed at the wrist. "Dishonored, I can never be headman of a clan house." His voice hardened. "If I can't be part of Clan O'Illand, neither will Folloman. That is my revenge."

"I will compensate you," Wynne said. "Ask what you will."

"Information," he replied. "I have heard that there is a kingdom here in Scotland where outcasts take refuge."

"Athdara," Wynne murmured—the land to which she had fled when her father disowned her three years ago. Memories of that day returned.

Frightened, alone, her only companion her mountain cat, Wynne had made her way to Athdara. When she arrived in the bandit chief's village, the men had thought to take advantage of her. Wynne had surprised them. She had fought them off. Still she had known she was not safe. She would have to find sanctuary elsewhere.

Before she left Athdara, an aged seafarer and his wife had sailed into the harbor. They had taken an immediate liking to Wynne, and she to them. They asked her to sail with them. Treating her as a daughter, they had taught her to sail a ship. Wynne had quickly discovered that she had a natural affinity for the sea and was soon hailed as the best seafarer in all of Scotland. The man died shortly after Wynne joined them; the woman soon followed. The crew had then selected Wynne to be their captain.

"Lady." The Irishman again intruded on Wynne's thoughts. "Please point the way to Athdara. I wish to take refuge there."

As he uttered the words, Wynne knew Athdara was no longer a haven of refuge for her. She was no longer safe from Triath, from Folloman, from anyone in Clan O'Illand. Her past had overtaken her to become her present . . . and it offered a fearful picture. She must find a new home. First, however, she and her crew would sail Malcolm mac Duncan and his warriors back to Northern Scotland.

Several days later, Wynne stood on the deck of her ship. She was transporting Malcolm's war booty and a few of his warriors to Northern Scotland. Among them was the disgruntled Brian mac Logan. When Malcolm had decided that he and a few of his men would travel by pony, taking the longer route, he had ordered Brian to accompany the cargo of riches back to the village. Reluctantly Brian had agreed.

He and Wynne had hardly exchanged a civil word during the trip. Each made a concerted effort to stay out of the other's way. Wynne liked this arrangement. She needed time to think and to plan. Ever since Siad had informed her of Alba's death, she had known she was going to have to leave her village in Athdara, the place that had been home to her and her crewmen and their families for the past two years.

Wynne didn't know if her seafarers would uproot their families and move with her. They had a choice. By sea law mariners volunteered their services, and they had an equal voice in all deci-

sions that were made. As soon as she delivered
Brian with Malcolm's cargo, she would call her
crew together. She would repeat what Siad had
told her, then tell them that she must move to a
safer place.

"Are you deaf, seafarer?" Brian shouted.

Jarred out of her troubled thoughts, Wynne
glanced over her shoulder at the Highlander.

"I've called to you several times," he said, "and
you've ignored me."

"What do you want?"

"Why are we stopping here in this remote harbor in Athdara? You know as well as I that the
entire kingdom is made up of bandits and raiders.
The safest place is the main village, not this . . .
this . . ." He swept his arm around the harbor.

"We need water and provisions," she answered.

"But here?"

"Here. If we were close enough to my village,
we would stop there," she said. "But to go there
would take us out of our way and add two days
to our journey."

"We can do without provisions," Brian said.
"Keep sailing."

"I'm captain of this ship," Wynne snapped,
"and we're stopping."

Highlander and seafarer glared at each other.
Finally Brian turned, and Wynne directed her attention back to sailing.

As soon as the ship was docked, she and several
of her crewmen disembarked and headed for the
storehouses that dotted the shore. Everyone else
remained aboard to protect the ship from plunder-
ers. As soon as Wynne paid for the provisions, her
men started loading them aboard the ship. She
was strolling along the quay when she realized
Brian was walking behind her.

"What are you doing here?" she asked. "You should have remained on the ship."

"Where you go, seafarer, I go," he answered. "I intend to ensure that you return to the ship and get me and the goods back to Malcolm's village."

"You don't trust me, do you?"

"Nay."

"Why?" she asked.

"You wear the shoes of a man," Brian answered. "You have chosen to be a warrior, not a woman."

"A man can be both man and warrior," she said. "Cannot a woman be both woman and warrior?"

"A woman's place is in the village, caring for home and hearth, marrying and having children."

"Taking care of a man who may or may not love her. One who may beat her."

"Many men love their wives."

"As many do not."

From a distance they heard a child cry. At the same moment both turned and looked toward a nearby ship. Five brawny men were tossing a squalling baby from one to the other as if it were a toy. One of sailors picked up his spear and jabbed it in the air.

"Throw the bairn this way, lads," he shouted. "Let's see if I can hook her."

The men guffawed. An older woman, hands on her ample hips, stood laughing.

"I'll kill them for this!" Brian swore.

His face a mask of fury, he pushed past Wynne. Muttering imprecations, he raced down the quay, leaped onto the ship, and caught the squalling child when it was next tossed.

"Seafarer!" Brian shouted.

Drawing her sword, ready to fight beside him, Wynne ran to the ship. He held out the baby. Surprised, she stared at it, then at him.

"Take the baby," he snarled.

"What about the crewmen?"

He shoved the baby at her. "Stay out of this, seafarer. 'Tis my fight. I shall deal with them."

With one arm she took the baby. With the other she resheathed her sword. Startled, the woman and gamesters stood like statues watching the exchange.

"Mac Logan," Wynne said, "what happens aboard a captain's ship—"

"Get the child away from here!" His steely tone brooked no argument; neither did his gray dagger-sharp eyes.

The woman, coming out of her stupor, screamed, "Give me that baby. It belongs to me."

Moving away from the ship, Wynne yelled, "You have broken one of the laws of the sea, mac Logan."

"Give me my child!" the woman screamed. She knelt, picked up a cudgel, and lunged at Brian.

"Give us the baby!" one of the men yelled.

"Watch out!" Wynne shouted.

The woman clubbed Brian across the back. He groaned low and grimaced in pain; his body twisted. He cursed, turned, and caught the assailant by the shoulders. He tossed her aside. She fell to the deck, the club skittering away from her. She snarled, rose to her feet, and was running at him again. He sidestepped, and she hit headlong into the mast, cracking her skull and knocking herself unconscious.

Brian turned. The burly warriors, muttering threats, weapons in hands, slowly circled him.

"You killed her," one of them snarled. "She was my whore, and you killed her."

" 'Twould take more than a bump on the head to kill her," Brian retorted.

The sailors were the ugliest and most ruthless Wynne had ever seen. Although Brian was a hulking man, they seemed to be even larger.

Brian unsheathed his sword. "Now, lads, if you want to play, play with someone your own size."

The sailors converged, and Brian became a one-man army. He was everywhere at once, lunging in, dancing out. His battle cry sounded for all to hear. Metal clashed against metal. Perspiration glistened on his face, darkened his tunic across the shoulders and beneath the arms. He went down, then was up in a bounce, his blade whizzing through the air as it pierced and whacked and sliced. His energy and endurance seemed indefatigable.

Wynne wanted to help him. No matter that she disliked Brian mac Logan, she disliked worse the idea of one warrior being pitted against five. Being a proud and confident warrior, a proven champion, he refused her help. A warrior herself, she understood the code by which he lived and accepted his decision. If this had been her battle, she would have handled it exactly as mac Logan was.

Wynne had seen excellent warriors, but none compared to Brian. He fought like a man obsessed, like one of the Northland berserkers. For a verity, he proved that he did not need her or anyone's help. Man by man, he took the crewmen down while suffering only a few minor cuts and bruises himself. Finally he stood on the deck, his chest heaving.

In back of him a crewman, not one of the five Brian had fought against, crept out from behind the store of provisions in the center of the ship. His sword drawn, he lunged at Brian from behind, knocking him down. Brian's head thwacked against a cargo barrel; he was dazed, and the adversary was rushing in on him.

Wynne pressed the baby into the arms of one of her warriors and leaped onto the ship. Drawing her sword, she faced the man.

He laughed. "You think that because you're a woman I won't fight you," he mocked.

"Nay, that is why you *will* fight me."

He growled at her, lunging with the sword. Wynne circled out of his way. Then she felt a hard hand on her shoulder, and she was pushed out of the way.

"I said this is my fight, seafarer, and I mean it," Brian growled.

Wynne backed up as Brian once again faced his adversary. They lunged; they circled. Then Brian rushed forward and pierced the man's shoulder. He screamed, then cursed. His face twisted in fury, he lashed through the air with his sword. Brian laughed at him, dodging from right to left, backing up, sidestepping.

Perspiration trickled into his eyes; they burned. He raised his arm and wiped his forehead. He felt the dampness down his back. Blade clanged against blade. Brian moved forward; the other man followed. They gave blow for blow. The stranger caught the fabric of Brian's tunic with his blade. Brian tore away, only his clothing damaged.

The man was breathing heavily, sweat slicking his hair and dripping into his eyes. He wiped a dirty hand across his face and grimaced. Taking the opportunity, Brian rushed in. As Brian's sword pricked his shoulder, the man turned, deflecting the brunt of the blow. He screamed his battle cry, gripped his weapon, and charged. Brian also charged, plunging his blade through the man's already wounded shoulder. Surprise on his face, the man dropped his sword and clutched his arm. He fell to the deck.

"Kill my man, will you?" a feminine voice snarled behind Wynne.

Before Wynne could turn, she felt the bite of a cudgel on her shoulder. She fell to the deck of the ship.

"I'll kill you."

Wynne braced on her hands and tried to push up. The woman hit her again. Dazed, Wynne collapsed. She heard more footsteps, heavier ones. She rolled over in time to see Brian knock the woman out. She slumped to the deck. Brian raced to Wynne.

"Are you harmed, lady?"

She felt her shoulder and winced. "A little bruised."

Brian caught her hand and helped her to her feet.

As she straightened her clothing, she said, "I'm in debt to you, mac Logan. You saved my life."

"Aye."

"What would you have?"

"Your life, lady, is worth as much to me as my life was worth to you."

Embarrassment warmed Wynne's cheeks.

"Nothing," Brian said. "*Absolutely nothing!*"

He strode back to the man he had felled. He was severely wounded but not dead. Standing over him, Brian asked, "Who are the child's parents?"

The man didn't answer. Brian kicked him. He grunted.

"I asked you a question."

"The baby's of no account." The sailor groaned. "She's a slave and is sickly. It wouldn't matter if we killed her or not."

Anger contorted Brian's face into an ugly mask. He frightened Wynne. He drew back his sword; she caught his arm. With one sweep, he slung her aside as if she were no heavier than a feather. She leaped to her feet and raced back to him.

"It's over, mac Logan," she said. "Let's be off this ship before more trouble comes. We'll leave the child here and let the people of the village—"

"Nay, I'll take the child with me."

The glazed look was gone from his countenance and his voice was sure.

"She's sickly and no one here wants her," he continued. "But I have a kinswoman who recently lost her child. She will welcome the bairn, sickly or not."

"Who—who will take care of the child until you reach Northern Scotland?" Wynne asked. Taking care of children was not something she did well.

Brian surprised her. "I shall. I have four of my own."

"Warriors do not care for children," she pointed out, gaining a new respect for the Highlander. " 'Tis not in their code."

" 'Tis part of this warrior's code."

She arched her brows, and a tiny smile touched her lips. "You accuse me of wearing a man's boots, mac Logan, yet you seem to be wearing a woman's shoes," Wynne mocked softly.

" 'Tis different circumstances," Brian retaliated.

"Aye."

"Let's be on our way, seafarer." Long strides carried him off the ship onto the quay.

Wynne followed. Hovering close by were her men. "What about the provisions?" she asked.

Ian grinned at her. "We're loaded, my lady, and ready to sail. Food. Water. And baby."

As Wynne and Ian leaped aboard the ship, she

saw Brian take the baby from the sailor and lay it on a pallet. At the steering oar she maneuvered the ship away from the quay. Once they were sailing safely up river, she turned the rudder over to Ian.

She walked to Brian and sat down beside him. The naked, squalling babe flailed the air with her arms and legs.

"She's a little bruised," he announced, raising his head to Wynne, "but mostly she's hungry. We're going to have to feed her."

"Don't look at me," Wynne said. "As much as I would like to, I can't wet-nurse the child."

Brian's visage softened, and his eyes twinkled. He glanced at Wynne's breasts. Although she didn't sense that he was flirting with her, Wynne felt her breasts swell and tighten against her tunic.

"Until we reach the village, we shall have to improvise," Brian said. "Have you a leather glove that hasn't been worn?"

Forgetting their animosity, Wynne and Brian tended to the baby together. She raced to her chest and rummaged until she found a glove and a length of soft, white fabric. It was expensive material that she had selected for a new tunic, but it would be ideal against the baby's tender skin. Fabric and glove in hand, she returned to the pallet.

While Brian made a nipple and filled a beaker with milk, Wynne washed the squirming girl. After she dried her off, she wrapped her in the fabric and laid her on a pallet.

Brian caught the material in his fingers. "This is expensive, seafarer."

Surprised, Wynne glanced from the baby to him.

"I know. I have traded for such for my wife," he answered as he picked up the baby and nestled her in his arms. "This will make a fine tunic for you."

"Aye."

"The babe will ruin it. Have you nothing else in which to clothe her?"

"Let her have it," Wynne replied. "I can always barter for another."

He placed the nipple into the baby's mouth, and Wynne watched as she noisily slurped the milk and cupped the beaker with her little hands.

Watching Brian with the babe disconcerted Wynne. She was having difficulty reconciling the man and the warrior. They were so different from each other, yet she was attracted to both of them. No matter that he was a married man or that he disliked her.

Gazing at the baby, Wynne gently stroked the tiny hand with her fingertip. The little girl continued to slurp, but she fixed beautiful green eyes on Wynne. She clasped Wynne's finger in her hand. Wynne felt the tug to the bottom of her heart. For the first time in her life she missed having a family.

"They have a way of wiggling into your heart," Brian said softly.

"Aye," Wynne murmured, "I can imagine they do."

"Bairns teach you how big your heart is," he continued. "You find that you have more than enough room for each one of them. When my first was born, I thought surely I'd never love another, but the birth of the second proved me wrong. I loved her differently from the firstborn, but just as much."

"You love your family?" Wynne said.

"Aye, lady, I do, and they love me. I can hardly wait to return home to my village."

" 'Twill be soon, Highlander. Two more days."

Wynne gently pulled her fingers from the baby's clasp. She had to get away from Brian mac Logan and the baby as quickly as she could. Both of them were making her aware of a void in her life, a void of which she had been unaware until now.

Brian laid the beaker of milk aside and held the baby over his shoulder. He patted her until she gave a loud burp. Holding the baby close to his chest, he rocked her back and forth until she was asleep. Then he laid her on the pallet.

Uncomfortable with the intimacy generated by man and child, Wynne rose and moved across the ship, taking over the steering oar. The wind caressed her face and flattened her mantle against her body. Water sprayed lightly on her. The afternoon sun warmed her.

This is where she belonged, Wynne thought. The ship was her home, the sea her domain, and there was no room in her life for a husband or a child. In two days she would deliver mac Logan and Malcolm's goods safely in Northern Scotland, and she would turn her attention to her own problems.

Chapter 3

⌒~⌒⌒⌒

Four years later
Isle of Cat
Atlantic coast of Northern Scotland

Silhouetted against the rising sun, Brian mac Logan stood atop a sharp incline. The wind, fresh from the sea, blew warm and briny. As if angry at the world, it lashed about the warrior but did little to alleviate the sweltering heat. It whipped his dark hair across his face and billowed his tartan from his body, revealing a broad, muscular chest and shoulders. The hem slapped against sinewy legs encased in knee-high black leather boots.

The weather was inclement, the land severe. So was Brian mac Logan. Although he had always been a warrior, a loyal vassal to his liege, he had also been a warm and loving man, able to see the lighter side of most situations. That had changed three years ago when his wife, Sorcha, had died.

Brian often swore that he too had died on that day. Others shared the same sentiment. His laughter gone, he had dedicated himself to raising his four children and to obeying his liege. He had become hard and austere. Seldom did a smile touch his lips. At times his warriors accused him of being overbearing.

This was one such time. Relentlessly he had been chasing bandits who had raided his village, robbing and pilfering, taking innocent lives. They had stolen a sacred belt, and Brian was determined to get it back. A thoughtful frown furrowing his forehead, he rested a gloved hand on the hilt of his sword.

"So this is where the seafarer lives," he murmured as he gazed at the rugged terrain. "The Isle of Cat."

The endless vista of bare rock, combined with the howling wind, created an air of wildness that bordered on desolation. Brian was accustomed to the harsh beauty of the Highlands, but this island was harsher than anything he had ever seen before.

From behind him Brian heard the crunch of boots against pebbles and knew that his comrade-in-arms drew near.

Lachlann mac Niall called out, "The island is as desolate as the stories have described it."

"Aye," Brian replied.

The wind wailed, its ghastly sound joining the splash of treacherous waters that surrounded the island which was so shrouded in mystery and superstition that no one ventured near it. In times past a few brave and adventurous seafarers had, but their legacy was wrecked ruins strung along the barren coastline and lost lives. Those who escaped to tell their tale spoke in hushed tones of demons who lived on the island, who killed any who dared stay.

Brian could easily believe the isle was inhabited by demons. As he had sailed into the harbor, he had had misgivings about landing. He had never seen such desolation. Set against a gleaming sea, the dark island had stood like a sentinel. Rising above the long, deep inlets were heather-covered hills. Behind them mountains towered into the sky. Along the wild coastal shores water pounded against the rocks and sent spray high into the air.

" 'Tis a shame Kolby could not sail us to Ireland himself," Lachlann said.

"Aye, but it could not be. He had to return to Northland as quickly as possible. His liege, his adopted father, is ill unto death and sent for him."

Both warriors understood Kolby's haste. A liege's word was law, to be obeyed to the death. A father's need was even more important than that.

"I'm grateful he brought us this far before he sailed homeward," Brian said.

"Leaving behind two-and-twenty warriors, ponies, and equipage, that we must worry about getting off this island," Lachlann grumbled.

"It will be her worry, not ours," Brian said.

"What if she refuses to sail us to Ireland or to return us to the mainland?"

"She'll do one or the other. She loves her booty."

"I hope you know what you're talking about, Brian."

"I do." After a lengthy pause Brian added, "There's not a mariner alive, Lachlann, who'll deny that Gwynneth the seafarer is the best pilot in all of Scotland. Few can navigate a ship through these treacherous waterways around this isle. Only she would dare live here and negotiate them day in and day out."

"That may be true," Lachlann replied, "but these aren't the waterways you want to sail on. You want to cross the Irish Sea and sail down the west coast of Ireland to Donegal Bay. She has not sailed to Ireland in four springs. No price was great enough to entice her."

"Aye," Brian replied pensively. "But she is the one I want to carry us there. When she and I fought in the battle of Glenmuir, I sailed with her on one of the most treacherous rivers in all of Scotland. Other seamen said it was too dangerous and wouldn't try it. She did. Not only is she a skilled pilot, Lachlann, she is a courageous woman. Even if it has been four springs since she has sailed to Ireland, I know she's the person to get me to Beathan's village."

"Let's hope so," Lachlann replied. "And let's hope it's soon. The men are tired and weary. They've been away from their homes and families for a long time."

"Aye. Eight weeks on the trading journey, and four weeks to find the seafarer."

Brian would never forget the day he and his weary warriors had returned home to their village in the small kingdom of Northern Scotland. Their ponies and carts had been laden with goods, and they had received a hero's welcome. That evening while they were celebrating in the Great Hall, bandits attacked the village.

Although Brian and his warriors were exhausted, they fought valiantly, finally driving the bandits away and saving the village and its people. But many of the houses had been sacked, possessions stolen. To Brian's joy, his three daughters and son had been unharmed.

His household had not gone unscathed. Among the goods stolen was his eldest daughter's legacy, a sacred girdle handed down from generation to generation within the family. This particular belt, the Mayo Girdle, was even more important to Brian now that Sorcha, his wife, was deceased. Since it was Sorcha's last gift to their daughter, it

held sentimental as well as religious and political
significance.

Many of the bandits had been taken prisoner,
and from one of them Brian had learned that the
massacre had been led by an Irishman named Beathan. Brian had sworn he would find the man and
exact revenge, that he would reclaim the Mayo
Girdle. Today, four weeks later, he was even more
committed to his oath of vengeance than the day
he had sworn it.

"I'll find the man, Lachlann, and repay him in
kind for what he did to my village and my people.
I'll get the girdle back by summer solstice. I swear
I will." He curled his hand into a fist. "Elspeth
will not be cheated out of her inheritance."

The girdle—a nondescript belt made of small
gold links and interspersed with beads carved
from the sacred yew trees of Ireland—was one of
five in all of Eire and Scotland. Each belt belonged
to one of the five branches of the túath of Forest
Glen, one of the largest clans in Eire, and was
passed from mother to eldest daughter. If there
was no daughter, it was passed on to the nearest
female relative.

During her lifetime, a woman wore the girdle
only once—during her sixteenth year when she
represented her branch of the clan in the sacred
Ceremony of Life. From the five maidens who
joined in the celebration, one was chosen by the
blessed sisters of the Cloister of the Yew to become
the Lady of the Yew and to reside at the cloister
as the secular spokesperson for the sisters. Eventually she would become adviser to all the branch
chieftains and to the túath king.

Those not chosen to be the Lady of the Yew
were invited to join the Court of the Yew. If they
chose to enter the order, they were educated and

trained to be herbalists and spiritual leaders. They were revered and honored as women of great wisdom, and their counsel was sought by all.

Since Sorcha had died before she could formally present the girdle to her heir, Elspeth and her father were required to attend the Court of the Yew, where Brian would be entrusted with the belt. When Elspeth reached her sixteenth year, he would make the formal presentation. If Elspeth and Brian did not do this, the Court would choose another family through which the belt would be handed down.

Without the girdle Elspeth would not be allowed to participate in the ceremony. She would have no opportunity to be chosen either as Lady of the Yew or as a member of the court. Her mother's family name would be stricken from the roster of the celebrants. They would miss their special blessing and would not be among the honored families of the Yew.

"I will not allow my daughter to suffer disgrace," Brian swore.

As an innocent child, he had suffered such dishonor. He swore that none of his children would undergo the same kind of indignity.

"Nay, my friend," Lachlann said, "you will not."

The wind gained momentum, whining around the rocks. Several pebbles spilled to the ground at Brian's feet, and his attention was immediately brought back to his surroundings. He squinted against the glare of the sun as he searched for and memorized landmarks, as he looked for signs of hostile forces. Thus far, the only ones he had encountered since he and his men had landed on the far side of the island had been those posed by the land itself.

They resumed walking, and the path was soon enveloped by brambles. In the lead Lachlann cautiously pushed the thorned vines aside.

"Is the seafarer as beautiful as Kolby claims?" Lachlann asked.

Brian could see Gwynneth in his imagination as clearly today as if she were standing in front of him. Although it had been four winters since he had seen her, since he had fought by her side in the fierce battle to liberate Glenmuir, he remembered her sparkling blue-gray eyes, golden hair, husky laughter . . . and smile. He had never forgotten her smile. While it was beautiful, it was also cool and cynical, touching only her lips, never seeming to radiate from her heart or soul.

"I've seen prettier," Brian replied.

"Kolby was smitten by the woman," Lachlann said. "He told me she outfought many of Malcolm's warriors."

Malcolm, about the same age as Brian and Lachlann, was liege to both and was also one of their most trusted friends and comrades-in-arms.

"Aye, that she did," Brian agreed.

"He also said that she was better with the bow and arrow than he was."

" 'Tis true. She saved my life."

The memory of her confession in the Great Hall of Glenmuir had been branded into Brian's memory. He still felt the fire of humiliation he had suffered when she told him his life was worth nothing. Everyone in the building had heard her, had shared in Brian's shame. Later, on the way home, he had saved her life, had redeemed himself, but few had witnessed it.

"Kolby said she will make some man a worthy bride."

Angry at the memories that assailed him, Brian

snapped, "I really don't give a damn what Kolby thinks of the seafarer. If he wants her for his bride, he's welcome to her. As for me, I don't want a woman, especially not Gwynneth the seafarer, and I don't want to talk about her."

They walked further before Lachlann ventured softly, "Sorcha died three winters ago, Brian. 'Tis time you put the past behind you and thought of the future."

"Aye, that's what Malcolm thinks. He has been pressing me to remarry."

Malcolm was also determined to unify all the tribes of Scotland, and Brian's widowerhood seemed to be a godsend. Political marriages were one of the best ways to cement relations between two kingdoms.

The woman Malcolm had in mind for Brian was a Pict princess, daughter of the chieftain of a Pict tribe to the south of the kingdom of Northern Scotland. Having an alliance with this tribe was important for Malcolm because it provided a buffer for his kingdom. Although Malcolm would not insist on the marriage if Brian was opposed, Brian would agree to it.

There was no reason not to. He had loved Sorcha, but she was dead. He had been so numbed since her death that he had not been interested in another woman. He didn't believe he could ever love anyone as he had loved Sorcha.

"I'll not go so far as to say you should be wed again," Lachlann began.

"Thank you for such generosity," Brian quipped.

"Don't mock me, Brian," Lachlann said. "I understand your feelings. I've walked this pathway before you. Like you, I lost my wife. Unlike you, I also lost our bairn."

Brian remembered the grief Lachlann had suffered when his young wife, Gerda, and the babe had died from a flux. Knowing Lachlann meant well, Brian sighed.

"I love you like a brother, Lachlann, but I don't need a mother or a nursemaid."

" 'Tis as a friend and brother that I'm speaking to you," Lachlann said. "How long has it been since you mated?"

"Damnation!" Brian exclaimed. "Can't some aspects of my life be private?"

"I'll wager you have not had a woman since Sorcha died. 'Tis time you had a woman. You don't have to wed her, Brian, just take a bedmate."

Brian shrugged. "Probably you're right, and I should give your counsel consideration."

Unbidden thoughts of Gwynneth returned. He tried to push them away, but they were relentless in their pursuit of him. Readily he admitted that there was no person he would rather have at his side during battle than Gwynneth, no other person he would want to captain a ship for him on the vilest of waterways. But he did not want her in his bed! The gods forbid! Gwynneth was everything Sorcha was not, and everything in a woman that he deplored. All he wanted from her was her piloting skills.

He and Lachlann followed a narrow path through outcroppings of rocks. They climbed a steep incline and rounded a huge boulder. Brian stopped short and caught his breath in surprise as the scene before him turned from desolation into paradise. Below lay a fertile river valley covered in grass and dotted with colorful flowers. Heather swayed in the breeze. Along the shores of the river the village of Cat sprawled lazily, much like its feline namesake.

He heard the tinkling splash of water to his left. Turning, he gazed at a stand of trees, heavy with spring foliage. Through the dappled leaves he saw the shimmer of the pool. And then he saw her. She was swimming in the deepest portion of the pool quite a ways from the shore where he stood. It would be easy for him to take her unawares. And she prided herself on being a warrior!

Smiling to himself, he nudged Lachlann with his elbow, and both men stopped walking. In a low voice Brian said, "Return to the men. Make sure they're watching for my signal. Remember my orders."

Lachlann's brow furrowed, his brown eyes dark with concern. "Are you sure you want to do this?"

"Aye. The seafarer will take me to Ireland, either as a free woman or as a captive."

The two warriors stared long and hard at each other.

Brian shook his head in answer to Lachlann's silent plea. "I won't change my mind. You may leave any time you wish. I'll not hold it against you. I release you from your obligation."

"Nay, my friend. As I promised, I'll stay with you until you're sailing to Ireland. Then I shall return to your village and watch over your children."

"Thank you, Lachlann. I know Malcolm and his queen will insist on taking care of them. But I also know my three daughters and son. While they love Malcolm and his wife, Jarvia, and would enjoy visiting in the king's village for a while, they'll be happier in their own home. And they are closer to you. If something should happen to me—"

"I love your children as if they were my own," Lachlann assured him. "I pledge before the gods that if something happens to you I shall become guardian to them and champion of your household. If the Mayo Girdle is not returned to your eldest daughter, I shall avenge the shame heaped on House Logan." Lachlann held out his hand. "I swear by the gods, Brian, Elspeth will have the girdle when she makes her presentation at the Cloister of the Yew at the summer solstice. At the Ceremony of Life she will represent Sorcha's family and receive the blessing for them. She will have the opportunity to be chosen as the Lady of the Yew."

To seal the pledge Brian lightly slapped his palm against Lachlann's. Giving him a last searching look, Lachlann turned and was gone.

Brian stepped closer to the trees, surprised to find how thickly they grew. He was again overwhelmed by the sheer beauty that lay before him. Judging from the austerity of the coastline, he would never have guessed that such a place could exist on this island.

He had walked along the craggy seaboard, over jagged hills and around stony outcrops. As the island had given new meaning to barren, it now gave new definition to beauty, Brian thought as he gazed into the thick forest. Then he stepped into it, following the *boreen*, the path, into another world.

Huge trees loomed around him, their branches twining together to form a thick canopy to shelter the plants that grew below. Before him Brian saw the forest's end; it gleamed like a golden portal that allowed him entry into a magical land.

Where thorns and brambles had attacked him before, now green plants and flowers brushed against his legs in a gentle caress. He reached the clearing before he stepped into the brilliance of full sunlight and gazed about.

The water itself was clear, like precious glass, and looked like a verdant meadow in the spring. In its deepest parts it was emerald-green, shading into blue at the shallows. The morning breeze danced across the surface, leaving a trail of soft ripples. Arching over it was a soft, iridescent rainbow.

Feeling as if he were indeed in a magical world, Brian stepped out of the maze of trees. He heard soft splashes and knew Gwynneth was somewhere around, but he couldn't see her. He squinted and looked through the bushes that grew along the shore. Still he couldn't find her.

Then he saw a glimmer of gold shoot through the pool. Long, slender arms moved gracefully in and out of the water, her head turning from side to side while she swam. He had found the seafarer.

Like a translucent dress, the water slid seductively over her naked body as she glided through its depths. Her mane of golden hair, a smooth and silky curtain, floated behind her.

She saw him. If she was surprised, she didn't show it. Her expression never changed. "So, mac Logan, you have finally found me." Her voice was husky—as he had remembered it.

"You knew I would."

"I figured we would meet eventually, but not on my island." She never looked at him. "How did you get here?"

"Kolby brought me."

"Where is he?"

"His liege in Northland is ill unto death and has sent for him. He sailed me this far before he departed for his homeland."

"Only a Northlander would risk sailing the waters that surround this island."

"You risked it."

"I had no other choice," she replied. She laughed softly, her husky voice taunting Brian. "Wild man that you are, I should have known you would find someone to bring you here."

"I am not a wild man, my lady."

"Aye, mac Logan, you are. I fought by your side during the Glenmuirian battle. I also watched you fell six warriors in order to save a sickly babe."

" 'Twas the act of a father, not a wild man," he retorted.

"I have often wondered about the child," Wynne said. "How is she?"

"She's well," Brian answered. "With a shock of curly red hair and green eyes, she's the pride and joy of her mother and father. They named her Millicent. Although she has seen only the passing of about five winters, she rules the house."

"I fought with you in battle," Wynne murmured, "but that day, mac Logan, I witnessed a fury in you that I had never seen before. You were as ferocious as the Northland warriors whom they call berserkers."

"I take that as a compliment, seafarer."

"It wasn't meant as such," Wynne replied.

"Since we're reminiscing about the past," Brian said, "whatever happened to Ian? I have often wondered about him."

"I'll wager you have." Wynne laughed. "He is no longer with me. While we were in Glenmuir, he met a young lady, whom he wed. They live there now." Treading water, she added, "You're trespassing, mac Logan. It's only a matter of time before my people take you prisoner."

"Nay, seafarer, my men have surrounded your

island and village. At my signal all your people will be taken captive." He smiled at the look of surprise that darted across her face.

"I wouldn't be so sure of that." She slid through the water, away from Brian.

Beneath the ripples of the water, he saw the hint of flesh, the round firmness of her buttocks.

"I'm sure. In the future, madam, you and your people should not rely solely on natural barriers for your protection." When she did not answer he said, "You didn't reply to my messages."

"I answered the first one. I said no. And since I had not changed my mind, I ignored the others."

Thinking that perhaps she did not understand the significance of his visit, of his request that she hire out to him, he said, "An Irish bandit called Beathan raided my village and stole a sacred girdle."

"Aye, that's what your messenger said." She ducked under the water, rose, and held her head back, letting the water slick her hair to her scalp. Her golden tresses trailed in the water behind her. "What is so important about you or your village that an Irishman would travel so far to raid it?"

"I don't know," Brian replied. "We followed the raiders, but they traveled down the river on a ship and escaped. We managed to capture several prisoners, one of whom told us they were sailing to Donegal Bay, Ireland."

"Why is the girdle so important to you?"

"It's my eldest daughter's legacy," Brian replied. He gave a succinct history of the sacred belt. "Just before my wife, Sorcha, died, she presented it to Elspeth. Now the child and I must attend the summer solstice so that the belt can be entrusted to me until Elspeth reaches her sixteenth year."

He paused. "Summer solstice, lady, is only a few full moons away."

"Aye, mac Logan, I can tell the changing of the times."

Frustrated with her, biting back a retort, Brian said, "Without the girdle, Elspeth will lose her inheritance. Without it, neither she nor any of her direct descendants can participate in the Ceremony of Life."

"Losing one's birthright is painful and fills you with shame," Wynne agreed. "At the time you think it will kill you, but it doesn't."

"Losing *enech*, madam, is the most heinous thing that can happen to a man."

Aye, he had known the sorrow and anguish as well as the shame of being an outcast. The memory had not diminished with the passing of the years. Every time Brian thought of his father so callously refusing to hold him when he was born, refusing to name him, and setting him out in the worst of winter to die, he felt as if someone had put an iron band around his chest and was squeezing the air out of his lungs. He understood what it was to have no honor or *enech*, face. "Yes, losing face is terrible for a man," he repeated.

"And for a woman!" Wynne exclaimed.

He had always disliked the seafarer's audacity, and her conviction that she was equal to men in intellect and matters of business. He was glad that none of his men was here to witness this show of arrogance and disrespect. He knew full well that she would have acted the same if he had been flanked by hundreds of warriors. She cared not a shred what man's reputation she damaged when she behaved in a manner unfitting for a woman.

"I know what I'm talking about, woman. Do you?"

"Aye, *man*, I do," Wynne replied softly. "Like your daughter, I am also a chosen daughter by birth. A princess."

As quickly as she said the words, Brian remembered.

"When I became a woman of divorcement my legacy was stripped from me. My father disowned me, and I became an outcast. I lost face, lord, but it wasn't reckoned to be so difficult for me because I was merely a woman."

"Aye," he murmured, "but your situation is different from that of my daughter. Elspeth is a child, innocent of wrongdoing. You knew the consequences when you decided to divorce your husband."

For a moment he saw a flash of defiance in her eyes, but as quickly it disappeared.

"Aye, lord, you're right," she said quietly. "In divorcing my husband, I did choose my lot in life. I sympathize with the grief you're suffering, and I'm flattered that you have come to me, but you'll have to get someone else to help you regain the girdle."

Brian stepped closer to the pool, the water lapping against the toes of his boots. In his desperation to save his daughter's reputation, her future, he forgot pride and begged. "You're the only one who can help me. I must reclaim Elspeth's legacy."

"Is it the child's legacy you're concerned about saving, mac Logan, or your own honor?"

By all that was holy, he wanted to save his honor. He understood shame and wanted never again to walk its pathway. But this time he was more concerned for his daughter than he was for himself. He would *not* allow her to suffer shame as he had been made to suffer.

"You're the one who has been most greatly

shamed because you were unable to protect your daughter's inheritance."

"Forget *me*, woman," Brian snapped. "Think about a lass who has seen only nine winters. Her legacy, the girdle, is all she has left now that her mother is dead. 'Tis my daughter's claim as Lady of the Yew or as a member of the court. 'Tis her future."

Wynne swam closer to shore, so close that he could see water droplets on the tips of her lashes, on her nose and chin. "I'll give you the name of other seafarers who have traveled the Irish Sea more recently than I have, men who for a price will help you."

"I must have the girdle so that the Court of the Yew can formally entrust it to me. As I have pointed out several times, this must be done at the summer solstice, and it's now the spring equinox. I don't have time to traipse around trying to find someone else, only to have them decline so that I must start the search over again."

Wynne said nothing.

"As much as I wish it were different, seafarer," he said, "and believe me I *do* wish it were different, you're the only person who can help me."

She shook her head.

He undid the leather purse at his waist and loosened the thong that cinched it. Opening it, he dumped the contents to the ground. Gold and silver studded with precious jewels scattered about his feet.

"I know where your loyalty lies, Lady Gwynneth, and I know it can be bought. I don't know your price, but rest assured, I shall find out, and I shall buy you."

Chapter 4

Deep, white-hot anger boiled through Wynne, temporarily stunning her. Never had she despised anyone as much as she despised Brian mac Logan. Softly she said, "You think you can buy *me*, Highlander? You really think that *I* am for sale?"

"I don't think it, madam," he replied. "I *know* it. I know I can buy you, just as others before me have bought you." He smiled sardonically.

"I cannot be bought," she said. "You may buy my services, but you do not buy me. Is that clear?"

He rocked back on his heels and folded his arms over his broad chest. "So tell me, woman of business, how much do you want for your ... er ... *services?*"

Gazing at the gold and silver scattered about Brian's feet, Wynne was carried back in time to the day when she had first met him. That day he had also been dispensing gold and silver. He was weighing the measures paid to her for delivering him and his men to Glenmuir.

"If this isn't enough," Brian said, "I have plenty more that I'm willing to pay you."

She glanced first at the elaborate gold torque around his neck, then at the gold jewel-studded armbands on both his upper arms and wrists. "Aye, mac Logan, I remember. You're a wealthy man."

"*Very* wealthy," he said, "so price is not a factor."

He glared down at her. Wynne had seen that look before. It had frightened her then; it did so now. But even his thunderous countenance did not diminish his rugged handsomeness. A shock of black hair fell over his forehead, and his gray eyes, ringed in midnight, were pinned to her. When he brushed his hand over his forehead, she saw the glint of silver hair at his temples, silver hair that had not been there four years ago. It added to his virility, she decided.

"Now if you'll get out of the water, we'll discuss terms. I'll send your handmaiden to help you dry off. You'll be more comfortable if you're dressed when we discuss our business."

He walked away. Wynne seized the moment. As he had pointed out earlier, she had been remiss in her defense of the isle. It was her duty to save her people. She had to take the chance that he wouldn't turn around.

But he did.

He gaped at her, his mouth slack, his eyes wide. She gaped at him.

Brian would have sworn that a nymph was rising from the sea and moving toward him. Water sluiced sensuously down her body. Like a long veil, her wet hair flowed behind her. Her eyes, glistening like precious gray-blue gemstones and framed by long thick lashes, caught and held his gaze. In the burst of sunlight she was golden.

As he stared at her, Brian's throat went dry. Unlike his deceased wife, who had been a petite and voluptuous beauty, Wynne was tall and slender, her breasts and hips gentle curves. Water droplets glazed her in sparkling brilliance. Like a man dying of thirst, he drank in her beauty: the small, firm breasts; the narrow waist; and the glimmer of golden curls at the juncture of her thighs.

Four years ago Brian had sailed aboard her ship, had fought at her side. He had seen her expertly handle the ship, the sword and dirk, the bow and arrow, but he had never thought of her as a desirable woman ... until now. All he had said about her to Lachlann earlier was now reduced to a lie.

The woman stirred sensations in him that he had thought long dead. Discomfited by her blatant display, by the physical response of his lower body, he raised his head and gazed squarely into her face.

"What is the meaning of your brazenness, madam?"

Wynne couldn't answer. Shock had struck her dumb. She had known Brian was a large man, but not until she was standing before him stripped of her clothing and her weapons did she realize how tall and masculine he was. He towered over her, dwarfing her. It was a new experience.

Her nudity seemed to diminish her in size. She was at a definite disadvantage and had to do something to balance the odds. Out of the corner of her eye, she glanced at her clothing, toward her weapon lying hidden beneath them. Then she looked back at Brian.

"One of my comrades-in-arms pointed out earlier, madam, that it has been a long time since I enjoyed the pleasure of a woman. At the time I thought he was speaking foolishly. Now that I see your lovely body, I know I was the fool."

Brian's dark gaze disconcerted Wynne so much that she wanted to retreat beneath the water. But she wouldn't give him the satisfaction of knowing he unsettled her.

"How much?" he asked.

Nonplussed, not understanding his question, Wynne glanced down at the gold and silver scattered at her feet. She looked up at him again and murmured, "How much?"

"Aye, seafarer, I'm willing to pay for your services. How much do you want for mating with me?"

Fury swept through her, and she straightened her shoulders, the movement thrusting her breasts forward. Even so, Brian was taller than she; he loomed like a giant before her.

"You're despicable!"

"Aye, many have made the same charge." He grinned at her. "But I'm also honest, madam."

Before, Wynne had wished for her clothing. Now she wished only for her sword or dirk. She would wipe the smug grin from the Highlander's face. But he stood between her and her dagger.

His gaze resting on the taut nipples of her breasts, he said, "If you were not just in the water, I would say that you are aroused also."

"It would take a better man than you to arouse me, mac Logan," she retorted.

His eyes narrowed to silver slits, and Wynne inwardly smiled, knowing she had scored another point.

"If you're not offering to mate with me," he said, "why are you flaunting your nakedness?"

Flaunting my nakedness! she thought indignantly. As quickly her indignation fled. That was what it looked as if she were doing. And that was what she must pretend to be doing if she intended to get the dagger.

"*Flaunting* is a vulgar word, my lord." She deliberately lowered the timbre of her voice. "I think *enticing* is a better choice."

The warrior swept his dark gaze over her once again, down, then up. Wynne felt her body grow warm and willed herself not to flush from embarrassment. Inwardly she cringed, but outwardly she maintained her composure, feigning indifference, pretending she didn't care what he, or anyone else, thought about her—something she had grown adroit at doing since her divorce from Alba of Ireland seven years ago.

Again wishing she was fully covered, Wynne gave him a demure smile, one that hinted at flirtation and masked her true purpose. "For all my boldness, sire, I am a shy maiden."

Brian laughed. "For a verity, you are a tease, madam."

"Ah, lord"—she looked beyond him to her weapon—"that I am."

She edged toward the brush, each step bringing her closer to her dagger, closer to freedom from this Highlander. Feeling self-conscious about her nudity, she crouched behind some bushes, her hand slipping beneath her clothes. As her fingers curled around the hilt of her dagger, self-confidence replaced self-consciousness. She whipped it out, but a heavy boot clamped over her hand. She bit back a scream and held tightly to the dagger.

"Did you think to fool me, lady?"

He moved his foot. Disregarding the prick of twigs and pebbles to her naked body, Wynne rolled away and leaped to her feet, her weapon gleaming dangerously in the sunlight.

"Aye, Highlander."

He stepped closer.

"Don't." Her soft voice was firm.

"You may stand a chance with a sword," Brian said, taking another step, "but not with a dirk. You're not strong enough."

She stared into Brian's darkened visage. She was a trained warrior, an expert with the sword and dagger, but he was right. In sheer strength Brian mac Logan clearly outdid her. He was also a man who gave no quarter and asked for no mercy. He had a wild, savage streak in him that had always unsettled her. Still she would not surrender to him without a fight.

"In the end you may win," Wynne conceded, "but by the time you do, you'll be all cut up. That I promise."

Unmindful of her nudity, she moved back, trying to reach the pathway that led to the village. Undaunted by her weapon, by her threats, Brian continued to advance.

Then, before she realized what was happening, he lunged toward her, his arms banding around her body as he knocked her off her feet. She didn't fall on the ground. He twisted so that she landed on top of him. She flailed her arms and legs; she grunted, but she could not escape the iron band of his arms.

"Cease your fighting," he ordered.

"Never!" She kicked her legs, hitting his calves with her feet.

He slung a leg over hers. She was totally imprisoned and could not move. Only now, as her flailing stopped, did she become aware of her nudity, of Brian's body cupping hers. She felt his warm breath fanning her neck and shoulders. She shivered.

Her stomach tightened, and her lower body throbbed. Disconcerted by these new sensations, Wynne knew she must put distance between her and the Highlander. She had created the kind of life she desired, and she didn't want it disturbed.

Most of all, she didn't want to be hurt again as she had been by Alba.

"Let me go," she said. "I won't fight you."

His grip loosened tentatively. A gloved hand took the dirk from her. She tried to free herself from his embrace; his arms tightened again.

"I said I wasn't going to fight you," she snapped.

Brian rolled over so that she lay on her back atop her pile of clothing. Keeping a leg across hers, he braced himself on an elbow and leaned over her. "You promised to carve me up."

"Aye."

Holding the knife out, turning it over in his hand so that sunlight glinted on the blade, he said softly, "Perhaps, my lady, I shall do the same to you."

Although her heart pounded erratically, Wynne kept her gaze on the blade. Slowly he lowered it until he lightly touched the tip of her nose. Frightened, Wynne looked at him.

"A man would be a fool, lady, to ruin such beauty, and I am not a fool." His voice seduced her, as did the smile that eased across his lips. "I love beautiful things."

He ran the tip of the blade lightly around her face, down her neck to her collarbone. Sensation shot through Wynne's body, taking residence in her pelvis. She wanted to cry out, to beg him to stop, but she wouldn't shame herself by begging.

He traced the blade over the swell of her breast to the nipple. It hardened. Wynne forced herself to remain still, to breathe slowly, deeply. Gently the knife blade circled her areola.

"Before, madam, I thought it was the water that had affected your body." His gaze captured hers. Passion, hot and molten, rushed through her.

"Now I think perhaps it is I who have affected you."

"Aye, and the dirk."

He lowered his gaze and softly slid the flat of the blade down her stomach, around her navel. The fire within her spread; it threatened to consume her. Quickly she was losing the struggle to remain calm, in control of her senses, of her body.

"My arousal has nothing to do with passion, lord, only fear."

Brian ceased moving the dirk and lifted his head to look into her face. She stared into eyes smoldering with passion, and shivered anew. Before she realized what was happening, he lowered his head again and kissed her navel, brushing his tongue around the tender flesh. Wynne trembled beneath the caress and dug her fingers into his thick hair. She tried to pull him away, but he was stronger than she.

"Are you frightened, lady?" His breath splayed over her stomach.

"Aye, mac Logan, I have always feared you."

He lifted his head and looked at her.

"Even more now. You have violated the sanctity of my home . . . and my body."

Roughly Brian pushed away from her. Rising, he said, "When I have violated your body, lady, you will know it." He tossed the dagger to the ground. "Let's cease playing games. Put your clothes on."

Feeling his heated gaze on her, Wynne was self-conscious about her nudity, but she pretended to ignore him. She picked up her long tunic, a luxury she allowed herself when she was in the village, and slipped it over her head.

She straightened it about her hips, then leaned down and picked up her necklace, a gold medallion inset with a large red gemstone. She slipped it over her head and bent to retrieve her overtunic and girdle. Before she could reach them, Brian caught her arm, pulled her aside, and gathered up the articles of clothing himself. He draped them over his arm and kicked her shoes toward her.

"Put those on. The rest of your clothes can wait. Right now let's go to the Great Hall and discuss the journey. I'm eager to be on my way to Ireland."

Ignoring her shoes, Wynne jerked loose from his grasp and glared at him. "We shall go to the Great Hall, and you may talk all you wish, mac Logan. But I won't be going on any journey to Eire with you. No threat will persuade me. If you had inquired of other captains, you would have learned that I have not sailed to Ireland in four winters."

"But you will this time, seafarer." Brian grabbed her by the shoulders and dragged her close to him. His face was a mask of anger. His fingers bit into her flesh. "If not for me, then for my daughter."

"What you can't buy, you take by force," she taunted, thinking how like her divorced husband Brian mac Logan was. But Brian was stronger and smarter than Alba, and she was frightened of him. "I think you're using the child to win my sympathy, that you're more interested in avenging your honor than in ensuring your daughter's future."

"Lady, you can taunt and mock me all you like, I will not change my mind. I am a desperate man"—his grip tightened; his voice lowered—"who is willing to take desperate measures."

"Does that include physically overpowering a woman?"

She glanced down at her arms. So did Brian. Her whitened flesh, a contrast to the dark gloves he wore, swelled around his tightly banded fingers. She looked up into his face, unable to read his expression.

"You're hurting me."

Releasing her, dropping her overtunic and girdle to the ground, he stepped back and brushed his hand over his forehead. "I apologize." He sounded tired. "I was mistaken in thinking that you would hire out to me. I considered forcing you to take me, but you're not worth the effort." He turned and moved away. "I'll leave you to your island and be on my way."

Rubbing her arms where he had gripped her so tightly, Wynne watched as he walked out of her life. It was what she had said she wanted, but she was oddly disappointed to see him leave.

"One moment," she called, feeling guilty about Elspeth, who, as Brian had pointed out, was truly an innocent victim. "I'll give you the names of—"

"I don't want your help." He waved his hand. Long strides carried him closer to the forest. "As you pointed out, it is my problem. I'll take care of it. I'll trouble you no longer."

"Elspeth—"

"Is my daughter. I'll take care of her too."

Wynne had been sixteen, seven winters older than Elspeth, when her father had disowned her, when her birthright had been stripped from her. But even today Wynne remembered the pain she had suffered, the loneliness that came of not belonging to anyone but herself. Through the years the pain had diminished and the solitude had become her strength.

But Elspeth had seen only nine winters. She was a babe. Wynne had to help her. Even if it meant confronting her greatest fear, sailing to Ireland, to the land where her deceased husband's family still lived. No one had helped Wynne, and she knew how abandonment felt.

Besides, Brian wanted to sail to Donegal Bay, which lay to the north of Sligo where the O'Illands lived. If she was careful to hide the ship, Triath would not know of her presence there until she was gone . . . if he learned of it at all. Pushing aside reason, trying not to think about the blood oath, about Triath's vow to force her to produce an heir for Clan O'Illand, she decided to help Elspeth.

Elspeth, not Brian.

Wynne ran after Brian, grimacing as pebbles cut into her bare feet. "My—my ship was damaged during a storm. If you can wait until my men repair it—"

At the edge of the clearing, he stopped but didn't turn around. Morning sunlight blazed down on him, burnishing his hair until it glistened as black as a raven. It glinted on his gold armbands as the breeze billowed his mantle from his body.

Wynne sighed. "I'll take you if you can wait until I repair my ship and until I deliver a special cargo to the Cloister of the Grove."

Brian spun around, his colorful tartan swirling about him. "Not only take," he specified, "but bring me back."

"That means I shall have to return later—"

"Or remain in Ireland while I tend to my business."

"After I let you ashore in Eire," Wynne said, "we shall determine how long I will wait. If you have not returned in the specified time, I shall leave without you."

"Agreed."

"How many men do you want me to transport?"

"Two-and-twenty warriors, including me, five-and-twenty ponies, and our equipment."

She nodded. "The *Honeycomb*, my largest ship, will easily accommodate you."

"Then we are in agreement, madam."

"You haven't heard my price."

"I told you earlier, seafarer, price is not a factor."

"Two pounds of gold and three of silver. I shall select each piece individually."

Knowing that he thought she was greedy and that she had overvalued her services, Wynne tensed and waited for his sarcastic comment.

"How soon can we sail?" he asked.

"The repairs can be made within three sunrises," she said, "and the delivery to the cloister—"

"Can it not wait?"

"No, I must deliver some herbs to the Cloister of the Grove, located to the north of us, so that the Dryads can make medicines and potions."

"These are the reclusive priestesses famed for being goldsmiths?" Brian said.

"Aye. They are also known as Grove priestesses," Wynne answered, her gaze inadvertently going to the beautifully designed and crafted torque he wore. "But they don't disassociate themselves from people entirely. The Dryads at the Cloister of the Grove are great healers. The herbs are very important to them."

"I understand that. But surely they can wait. I'll pay you more, if you'll—"

"My price is set," Wynne said softly. "And I won't take you until I have made the delivery. That's final."

Silence stretched between them. Finally Brian nodded.

"The journey to the cloister and back will take three sunrises. We shall be sailing southward toward the Irish Sea in no less than four days."

One hand resting on the hilt of his sword, Brian strode back, stopping when he stood before her. "Assemble your crew, seafarer. I want to speak to them about their duties when they sail under me."

"They won't be sailing under you," Wynne countered. "They'll be sailing under *me*."

Steely gray eyes stared into hers, reminding her of the dark side of Brian mac Logan, headman of one of the major houses of Clan Duncan. Despite the silver at his temples, he was a young warrior, a hard man who had been taught to fight for his integrity and that of his people. He was a man of extremes. One moment he could be laughing; the next ready to run a man through with his sword.

"Your men are sailing under you, madam, but *you* are sailing under me." Wynne had never heard such authority in softly spoken words. "Never forget that you are in my hire. I'm paying for your services."

"I won't forget."

She knew that the only way she could be in Brian's employ and retain her individuality was to stand her ground. He would accept no less from her; she would accept no less from herself.

"And you, sire, never forget that I, and I alone, am captain of my ship. You tell me where to go, and I'll see that you get there, but you will not give orders to my crew."

Her resolve as strong as his, she returned his gaze. Finally he grunted his acquiescence. Wynne felt as if she had won the battle, but she knew a full-scale war lay ahead.

She bent and retrieved her clothing. "While repairs are being made to the *Honeycomb*," she said, her voice muffled as she slipped into her overtunic, "I'll take one of the smaller ships and deliver my cargo to the Cloister of the Grove." She cinched her girdle about her waist and sat down to put on her shoes. "You and your men may stay at the lodges."

"My men shall stay at the lodges," Brian said, "but I shall go wherever you go, seafarer."

Standing, Wynne glared at him. "Wynne."

His puzzled look did not diminish the beauty of his eyes. Lines radiated from their corners, and creases formed on either side of his sensuous mouth. He lowered his lids, and for an eye's blink she saw the crescent of dark lashes lying on his sun-bronzed skin. When he raised them, one lone lash remained on his cheek. She wanted to brush it away . . . she wanted to touch him.

"I don't understand," he said, jarring her out of her reverie.

Irritated with herself for fantasizing about him, she said, "My name is Wynne, and that's what I want you to call me. Seafaring is my trade, not my name."

They stared at each other.

"Say it," Wynne commanded. "I want to hear you say my name. I've known you for four winters, mac Logan, and not once have you called me by my name."

"When we were fighting for the kingdom of Glenmuir," he said, "you didn't seem to mind me calling you *seafarer*."

"I didn't then. We were in the heat of battle," Wynne answered. "But I do now."

"Why?"

"We're going to be confined to a ship for a long time as we cross the Irish Sea. Much too long for you to be calling me *seafarer* and *woman*. Whether it's true or not, I want my crew to believe that you and I have an amicable relationship. It makes for a much more pleasant journey."

A breeze blew, picking up wisps of dried hair and fanning them across her face. Before she could remove them, Brian lifted his hand—a big hand—and with breathtaking gentleness, he brushed the strands aside. His eyes had gone as gentle as his touch, and Wynne lost herself in the downy depths.

He cupped her face, the soft, worn gloves caressing her skin, the musky odor of leather filling her nostrils. His face was so close she noted the texture of his skin, weathered and browned by the sun.

"Gwynneth," he murmured.

Gwynneth! He had called her Gwynneth.

It had been a long time since Wynne had heard her name spoken like a caress instead of with a harshness that reminded her of the day of her greatest humiliation. The day her father had publicly stripped her of her identity and integrity. For a while she thought he had succeeded, then she realized that these were innate qualities in her, given to her by God. No one but she had the power or the authority to touch and affect them. The day she made that discovery she learned that she was strong enough and determined enough to survive.

"You have decided to go against anything I say, have you not, lord?"

"Wynne is a pretty diminutive of your name, but Gwynneth is beautiful and it suits you." He reached out and caught one of the curls that wisped about her temple.

She dodged her head, wincing when she tugged her hair loose. She stepped away from him. Although she took pleasure in Brian's touch, the gentle strength of his hand brushing against her face, she was unsettled by the sensations he had awakened in her.

He was a hard warrior, fiery and impulsive. Like lightning, he might strike anywhere. She never knew what would set off his blind fury. Although he had many redeeming qualities, and she had only witnessed his fighting for good, Brian mac Logan reminded her too much of her deceased husband. She resented that Brian had stirred a spark of fire in her, and was determined to squelch the spark before it burst into flames.

"Your name means 'white' and 'blessed one,' does it not?" he said.

She nodded. "When my father disowned me, he—he took my name from me. That's when I started calling myself by the diminutive."

"But he has since publicly reclaimed you," Brian said.

"Four years ago, after my divorced husband died." For a moment Wynne felt a return of the bitterness she had experienced when her father forgave her and opened his arms and home to her once again. "While a public apology is a balm to injured pride, lord, it cannot undo the pain of the past." Lost in thought, she added, "My father wanted me to return to our village and to his home to live, but I had been my own mistress for too long."

"Was that when you came here?"

"Aye," she answered, still not willing to share her reasons for having moved here. "People had begun to flock into Athdara, most of them bandits and raiders. I no longer had privacy or safety. I deliberately sought an inaccessible place so I would not be bothered."

"A solitary existence," Brian said.

"Quiet, but hardly solitary," Wynne answered. "I have a village full of loyal friends."

She took several steps, leaned down, and picked up her dagger where it had landed when Brian kicked it out of her hand. Slipping it into her girdle, she followed the path that ran alongside the river through the forest. Brian fell into step beside her.

"The Isle of Cat is my world," she said. "I love it here."

"Most of your island is desolate, my lady," Brian said, "but this spot is beautiful."

Large trees towered above them, their branches overspread to form a canopy. The sun gleamed through, casting its golden rays across the pathway. Flowers, a profusion of color, bloomed all around them.

Brian stopped next to a bed of harebells, bent, and gently touched several of the lavender blossoms. "Sorcha loved flowers," he murmured.

For a long time neither spoke. Finally he picked one of the harebells and held it to his nose. Removing the flower, he looked at Wynne.

She grinned. "Your nose is covered in pollen dust."

He returned her grin. "Honey from the goddess. Sorcha told me . . ." His voice trailed into silence.

When it was clear he wasn't going to say more, Wynne asked softly, "What did she tell you, sire?"

He raised his head, his eyes bright. "She said it was an Irish custom for the lover to kiss the honey of the goddess. It made for . . . for . . ."

He looked a little discomfited.

"Made for what?" she coaxed.

He shrugged. "It blessed the lovers with passion and promised a conception when they mated."

Against Wynne's will and better judgment, his
words sent a shiver of anticipation through her.
She wondered what it would be like to have Brian
mac Logan as her lover, to know his fiery passion
and to return it. Thinking about it left her breathless. She felt as dangerously excited as she did
when she climbed to the top of the cliffs and
walked along the edge.

"A myth, lord?"

Brian handed Wynne the blossom. "I'm not
sure, lady."

She brought it up to her face and inhaled
deeply.

He said, "Each time Sorcha conceived, it was
after we had found our flower and had tasted the
honey of the goddess."

Not knowing whether to believe him, Wynne
lowered the flower and gazed at him.

His gray eyes twinkled. "Of course, lady, I'm
not going to tell you how many flowers we
smelled or how much pollen dust we kissed off
each other's noses or what else we did before we
conceived each of our children."

He laughed, and for the first time Wynne heard
its rich spontaneity. Pleasure gently flowed all
over her. Earlier she had thought him handsome,
but it was a hard, chiseled handsomeness. Now
he was warm and friendly. Gone was the primitive warrior.

This man appealed to her. She wanted to lower
her guard and respond to his flirtation. She
wanted to flirt back with him. But a part of her
was leery of him, of any man; she was frightened
of this sudden change from warrior to lover. He
had used his daughter to cajole her into sailing
him to Ireland. He wouldn't be above using any

means at hand to persuade her to his way of thinking, whatever it might involve.

She had to be careful of Brian mac Logan!

He stepped closer to her, out of the sunlight into the cool shade. He lifted his hand to her face. She jumped away.

"Pollen dust," he said. "On your nose."

"Oh!" She reached up to brush it off. He caught her hand. As warmth seeped slowly through her, her resolve of a moment ago was completely forgotten.

"According to legend, madam, the lover is supposed to kiss the dust off." The color of his eyes deepened, and his gaze intensified.

Wynne's legs felt like melted wax. "But we are not lovers." Molten desire might be flowing through her veins, but she kept it out of her voice.

"Nay," he said.

"If legend is true, sire, I wouldn't want you to kiss the pollen from my face. Else I should find myself with child . . . and I am unwed, and not likely to be wed soon."

"For a verity." He brushed the tip of her nose. "The pollen is gone, madam. And I would still like to kiss your nose."

Seduced by his words and touch, Wynne brought her hand up to cover her nose, inadvertently crushing the blossom against her face.

A second time he caught and lowered her hand. His voice still deep and seductive, he said, "Please don't. Your nose is beautiful and kissable, with or without the pollen dust."

Wynne glanced down to see her crushed flower. The flower he had picked for her.

Following the line of her vision, Brian laughed softly. "There are more flowers, lady." He plucked another and handed it to her.

Taking it, she said, "I shall be more careful this time."

"Of what, lady?"

He was teasing her. She heard the unspoken question that underlay the spoken one. Her throat had gone dry; yet her heart was beating furiously, her blood roaring through her veins. *Of you!*

"Careful not to crush my blossom."

But it wasn't the flower that she was going to have to be careful about. It was herself. In a short time she had seen Brian mac Logan change tactics. He had gone from the demanding warlord to the charming nobleman. Knowing this, she had encouraged him to flirt with her; she had flirted back. She wasn't sure what he wanted; she only knew that she must not let her guard down where he was concerned. When she was young, she had been easily deceived by Alba. She was older and wiser now.

"Soon it will be time for the morning meal," she said. "We should be getting on to the village."

Marshaling her emotions, she resumed walking. From the corner of her eye, she peeked over at Brian. As if the previous incident was of no consequence, he strolled beside her at a leisurely pace.

" 'Tis indeed a peaceful place," he admitted.

"Aye. My people and I live as we please." She glanced down at the flower in her hand and smiled. "We don't worry about social restrictions and judgments of the outside world."

Even as she spoke the words, she lowered the flower, forgot her fantasies, and thought about what was happening to her world. Brian was the first to penetrate the solitude of her island, to invade her sanctuary. Forever the isle would be changed by his coming, and the thought unsettled her.

"Is it Isle of Cat," Brian murmured, "or Isle of *the* Cat?"

"As in Wynne the cat?" she asked, then laughed softly. " 'Tis Isle of Cat."

"Did you name it or was it named after you?"

"I named it."

"For a particular cat or cats in general?"

"Both. I love the Highland wildcats and have one as a pet."

Brian frowned and looked around.

"She's not here," Wynne said. "When we return from a long trip—"

"You take her with you on your ship?"

"Most of the time."

"I didn't see her when you were in Glenmuir."

"She was here recovering from a nasty cut."

"The cat is not going to Ireland with us," Brian said firmly.

"She's a pet, sire," Wynne explained. "As tame as any dog one might have as a lap pet."

"I don't have lap dogs, madam, and I hate cats, no matter how tame or fierce they might be."

"You and Honey have something in common," Wynne said.

"I doubt it."

"You hate cats, and she hates men."

Brian hiked a brow. "She hates people?"

"Not people, men," Wynne clarified. "In the past they have not been kind to either of us, and we've decided that our lives are much better without them. We deal with them strictly on a business basis, nothing intimate or personal."

Brian gazed somberly at her before he grinned widely. "I look forward to a prosperous alliance with you, Gwynneth. I promise you need not fear I have designs on your body."

His confession irritated her. "You seemed to earlier."

"Aye, you've a lovely body, lady, and I did ... do ... lust for you. But lust is just a physical reaction. Any woman will do to assuage my carnal desires. Once I've mated with someone, anyone, I shan't be attracted to you."

Wynne couldn't believe what she was hearing! How quickly he relegated her to a woman of no consequence. Although it was what she had been demanding, she was disappointed that he had given up his pursuit of her so easily.

"Just as you have no wish for men in your life," Brian went on, "I don't wish to be encumbered by women. I want only a business arrangement between us." He held out his hand.

Wynne stared at it. She had struck bargains with countless men, but Brian's words rankled her. She didn't understand why. After all, she was the one who had told him she didn't want a personal or intimate involvement with a man. And now that he had agreed and had gone on to define in explicit terms the limits of his attraction to her, she was aggravated.

"To a prosperous business agreement." She lightly struck her palm to his, sealing their agreement.

Still pondering her disappointment and finally concluding that all had been decided for the best, she pushed her troubling thoughts aside.

They rounded the bend and stepped out of the forest onto stony terrain. Wynne looked down the steep incline at the small village that clung to the shore. Unlike most villages, this one was laid out along one side of the river. The sheer cliffs that rose on the opposite shore formed a natural barrier. Most of the buildings, built of stone with thatched roofs, fanned out in a long line down the river on either side of the Great Hall of Cat.

"The village of Cat," Brian said.

As always when she gazed at her home, Wynne was filled with pride. "Aye," she murmured, *"my* village."

Chapter 5

"More than a village," Wynne said, taking several steps and moving closer to the edge of the hill. She remembered when she and her villagers had uprooted themselves from Athdara and had come to this desolate island. "It's my home. I planned it all, the quays and the two streets, the lodges and the Great Hall."

Brian stood so close behind her that she felt his breath on her cheek and shoulder. His nearness, his virility awakened in Wynne a fresh awareness of her femininity, reminded her of the absence of lovers in her life. Before, she had been safe from intimate involvement with him. His marriage had been a barrier between them. Now he was single. Disconcerted by the direction of her thoughts, irritated because she was unable to keep her resolve where Brian mac Logan was concerned, Wynne edged forward a little more.

"Did you plan the village so that it's reminiscent of a cat?" he asked.

He moved closer to her; she felt his chest brush against her back; his breath warmed her neck.

"Nay," she said, her voice breathy. "I didn't know it looked like a cat."

"Aye. Look how it sprawls lazily along the river."

Taking several steps away from him, she looked

at the village anew, as if seeing it through Brian's eyes. The quay and storehouses built around the dock looked like a cat's head, the village itself like its stomach. Smaller buildings, sheds, and cart houses dotted a long line to form its tail.

"It does look like a cat."

"Aye."

"I didn't plan it to look like one. But—" She grinned, turning her head toward him. "I'm glad."

Their gazes locked, Brian said, "The sheer cliffs on the other side of the river, facing the village— were they also part of your grand architectural scheme?"

His smile, and the teasing lilt of his voice wrapped around Wynne like a gentle caress. His eyes were beautiful, soft gray, yet with an underlying sharpness. They also reflected a haunting melancholy. Grief for his deceased wife, she imagined. Would any woman he made love to be a substitute for her?

"In a manner of speaking," she answered.

In a gesture that she was growing to know, one that she liked, he hiked a brow in question.

Reluctantly she turned her attention from him to the cliffs. In the blending of golden sun and morning mist, cliffs jutted sharply into the heavens like the smooth, polished blade of a sword.

"They're beautiful," she murmured.

"Deadly," Brian murmured.

"Only if you don't respect them. They're our guardian sentinels and the reason I chose this spot for the village."

"Evidently the guardian sentinels were not on duty today, my lady," he pointed out. "My men and I had no difficulty getting in."

His declaration chafed her. "Be careful of your

boast, Highlander. You have gotten in, but you haven't gotten out."

"Are you saying we couldn't get out?"

She grinned. "I've said all I'm going to say on the matter."

She had taken a couple of steps, moving closer to the edge of the cliff, when he shouted, "Watch out."

Startled, she whirled around, her heels slipping. She flailed her arms, and Brian caught her, drawing her against his chest. She tried to jerk away from him, but he held her tightly. She felt his heart hammering against hers.

"God help us, lady! You frightened me."

Trying to break free of his embrace, she said, "And you frightened me. I was fine until you shouted."

As if she were a child, he cradled the back of her head with his hand and pressed her cheek against his chest. "It's all right," he murmured. "I have you."

She stopped fighting him, not caring that his gentleness was at odds with the warrior she knew him to be. She fitted against him so well, she didn't want to move away from him. She felt protected and warm and safe. Brian lowered his face and laid his cheek on top of her head. He brushed it against her silky hair.

He held her . . . tightly . . . and she didn't mind. In fact, she liked it. She knew she would never relinquish her claim to independence, but there were times when she wanted someone special in her life, someone she could lean on for support and advice. Who better than a warrior of Brian mac Logan's renown?

"I was frightened. Afraid that you would fall and hurt yourself on the sharp rocks," he said.

She gently pushed out of his arms.

"I thought you were falling, and it reminded me of Elspeth. She fell down an incline once and toppled over onto the shelf of the cliff below. She was unconscious and couldn't answer our cries. We weren't sure if she was alive or dead."

He shuddered, and now Wynne understood his concern for her.

"Others wanted to crawl down and get her," Brian continued, "but I insisted that I do it. They kept telling me a lighter man would be better. They could hoist him up with her more easily."

"But you were her father and wanted to rescue her," Wynne said.

"Aye, but that didn't stop my warriors from arguing with me."

Wynne smiled. "I can't imagine your villagers arguing with you, Brian mac Logan."

"It hasn't stopped *you*," he replied dryly.

"That's different," she retorted. "We're on my island, and I'm mistress here. You're master of your village."

"Seafarer, you argue and bark orders no matter where you are."

He put his arm around her shoulder and hugged her against him. She felt his strength, the bulge of flexed muscles. Again, moving away from him, she looked into his face.

"I knew you were a big man, mac Logan, but I didn't realize how big until now."

"Aye."

"And tall."

"Aye."

"I seldom find a man who is bigger than I am," she confessed.

He gazed at her for a long time, stared into her eyes as if he were reading all the messages of her heart and soul. "You say that as if you think tall and big are ugly."

"They can be."

"And you're only tall, madam, not big." He caught her by the shoulders and held her gently. "You're so fragile, I shall have to be careful lest I hurt you."

Pleasure warmed her cheeks.

"You're such a small thing, madam, that I can easily sweep you into my arms."

He lifted her, swinging her around. Wynne laughed and locked her arms around his neck, touching his torque. Her hair spun about them, and soon they were laughing, joyously and freely. He took several deep breaths when he set her on her feet, but he kept her in a loose embrace.

"No one has ever called me fragile before," she murmured. Light-headed, she caught his tunic in both hands and gazed at him. "You make me feel—"

Then she realized what she was saying, what she was revealing to him about herself. Unable to look at him for fear he would read her heart and know her vulnerability, she lowered her head.

Softly he asked, "How do I make you feel, lady?"

He caught her chin and tipped her face up to his. She stared into eyes that were soft and wonderful, eyes that compelled an answer.

"As I imagined other, smaller women feel," she whispered. "Beautiful. Cherished."

"Has no man ever made you feel that way?"

"Alba—my deceased husband—did when we first met." She spoke tentatively, amazed that she was confessing it. "Once we were married, that changed."

Ugly, painful memories returned, and Wynne

pushed away from Brian. "He was shorter than I was, and didn't like it. He started to make fun of my height."

"For a verity, my lady, being tall isn't bad or ugly," Brian repeated firmly. "My Elspeth is going to be a tall and big woman. Like you, she's self-conscious, and I have to tell her all the time that she's a beautiful girl."

Brian's words again reinforced that he had been thinking of Wynne as a child, not as a woman. She swallowed her disappointment, raised her head and gave Brian a brilliant smile.

"Besides"—she forced herself to speak lightly— "being tall comes in handy at times."

He hiked a brow.

"When a roof needs thatching or the fruit at the top of the tree needs picking."

The soft-caring expression in his eyes never changed, but he returned her smile. "That's exactly what I was thinking, my lady Wynne. I was going to suggest that after we get the Mayo Girdle I hire you to return to my village. The houses should be rebuilt by that time, but we're going to need a master thatcher."

Glad that he had followed her lead, she said, "I'll give your suggestion some thought."

She took several steps away from him, returning to the pathway that led to the village.

"Seriously, Gwynneth," he said.

She paused. Her heart lurched, and a bitter taste came to her mouth. She thought for sure he was going to return to their previous conversation, and she knew she could not stand it.

"Beathan and his warriors burned down many of our houses. Perhaps you would help us rebuild them."

Pleased with his compliment, Wynne spun around. "Are you jesting, sire?"

"Nay," he said. "I admire what you've done here. The village is exceptionally well laid out."

As they walked down the pathway, Wynne told him about her plans for enlarging the village. Brian listened, adding comments, asking questions. Then they launched into a discussion of the rebuilding of his village.

When they neared Wynne's village, he said, "Did you plan these grazing pastures for the sheep and cattle?"

"I wish I could take credit for them," Wynne said, "but if I do, I'm afraid Mother Earth will seek revenge. She designed them and the meadows for hay. We built around them."

Again through Brian's eyes, Wynne saw the village of Cat anew. Barns. Stables and corrals. Sheds for carts and equipment. Storehouses. Covered yards for the sheep.

Aye, she was proud of her handiwork.

The houses were made of stone, filled with wattle and daub, and each was surrounded by neatly laid pens for their domestic animals. Beyond them lay cultivated fields. Built into the river were three long, wide quays, a ship moored at each. Two main streets ran through the village, one parallel to the river leading to the Great Hall, the other to the docks.

"You have three ships," Brian said.

"Aye," she replied. "The largest one is the *Honeycomb*. The smaller ones are the *Honeysuckle* and the *Honeydew*." Gazing in pride at her ships, she said, "We shall be taking the *Honeycomb* to Ireland. As you can see, it will provide us with ample cargo space for your warriors, ponies, and equipment."

As they continued to walk, moving deeper into the village, Wynne pointed to a row of stone huts. "Those lodges are the first buildings that we constructed. We lived there while we laid out the village and raised the other buildings."

"We?" Brian asked.

"My crew and I at first," Wynne replied. "But soon others joined us."

"By choice or force?" he asked.

"By choice," she replied. "They're outcasts like me."

"So you're a fisherman of people?"

She wasn't sure if he mocked her or not.

"Nay, we happened to meet at the right times in our lives, when we needed one another. Through the years we've become each other's families."

Brian was quiet for a moment, then said, "You're a mysterious woman, Gwynneth."

She was surprised by his statement.

"Just when I think I understand you, I see something that suggests I haven't begun to fathom you. You're a bundle of contradictions."

"Is that good or bad?"

"Neither, I suppose," he replied. "You're a woman whose life is predicated on receiving payment for services rendered, yet you rescue unfortunates and provide them with new lives."

"I think you're seeing this wrong," Wynne said. "I didn't rescue them. They rescued *me* and gave me a new life, a reason for living."

"You're happy here," he said.

"Aye, happier here than I'd be anywhere else. This is my village and these are my people."

Brian looked around. A group of boys was playing on the green; several men pushed carts up the street toward the grazing land. Four women stood talking in front of one of the cottages.

"We don't live together because we are kindred by blood," Wynne continued, "but because we are kindred by choice and by heart. We want to be together."

Brian realized that he was arousing the villagers' curiosity. Carts had stopped, the men edging closer to him and Wynne. The women were staring.

"Wynne!" called a dark-haired boy of about twelve winters. "Watch me."

Brian turned to see the group of youngsters on the green engaging in a sling competition. News of his arrival had spread through the village, Brian thought. People were peering out of windows; doors were opening.

"That's Keith," Wynne told Brian. "We call him our miracle child."

"Are you looking lady?" the boy shouted.

"Aye, Keith, I am."

"I've hit the target every time."

Brian glanced at the sapling they had skinned and set in a hole. It was so thin, he was surprised that any of them would hit it with the rocks in their slings.

"I'm the champion," Keith yelled.

"How many times have you hit it?" Brian asked.

"Five out of five tries," the lad said and pointed. "I'm hitting the red mark, sire."

Brian squinted but still couldn't see the mark.

"You'll have to get closer," the boy informed him. " 'Tis too little for you to see at that distance. I know where it is."

Keith reached into the leather pouch fastened about his waist and pulled out an object which he inserted into the cradle of the sling. He drew back his arm, rotating it in a circle above his head. His arm moved rhythmically, the sling whirling so fast, it was a blur of color. Even from where Brian stood, he heard the whir of leather slicing the air.

Keith drew back his arm, stiffened, and flexed his wrist, and the stone sailed through the air. *Thwack!* The sapling vibrated. The boys ran to the tree.

"You hit the mark again, Keith."

"I know you hit the tree," Brian said, "but how do you know you hit your mark?"

Keith came running over. He opened his stone bag, and extracted a metal missile with sharp points. "They stick in the sapling," he explained.

Brian took one of them and examined it. "This could be deadly."

"'Tis, sire," Keith answered. "The blacksmith made them for me out of scrap iron. He also showed me how to settle them into my sling so that I can throw them better."

"You are a champion," Brian said.

"Thank you, sire." The boy beamed. "I'm also a champion in wrestling, aren't I, my lady?"

"Aye, you are, and I'm proud of you."

Although they kept their distance, the villagers were circling Brian and Wynne. The door of the Small Hall opened, and warriors clad in mail, their swords drawn, rushed toward Wynne. She didn't seem to notice. She was more interested in Keith at the moment. Brian wasn't worried; his men surrounded the village, although he wasn't sure where Lachlann was.

"How's that foot of yours?" she asked the lad.

"Fine." Grinning, he hopped about on one foot and swung the other back and forth.

"Let me see it," she said.

"Aw," he muttered.

"Keith."

"All right."

Wynne knelt, and he held out his foot.

"What happened to it?" Brian asked, bending over her.

Wynne pulled up the lad's trouser leg and ran her fingers around the healing wound. It had been highly inflamed, leaving a large, ugly scar. "Leg bands."

"He was a slave," Brian guessed.

"Aye. By the time I rescued him, the inflammation was so bad, we thought we might have to amputate."

"Mother Barbara at the Cloister of the Grove healed it," Keith said, "but she said she couldn't have done it if my lady hadn't been such a good dresser of wounds."

"One of the cloister mothers taught me how to mix herbs and apply dressings, but my knowledge of healing is limited," Wynne explained.

"My leg doesn't even hurt anymore," Keith said, "And I don't limp. I shall be a warrior, sire."

"It's healing well," Wynne agreed, patting his foot before she set it down and rose. "Are you following the good mother's instructions for taking care of it?"

He nodded and brushed a thatch of hair from his face. He looked all around him, and as the villagers closed ranks, he suddenly realized that something was amiss, that Brian was a stranger. Wariness replaced friendliness.

"Who's he, lady?"

Wynne looked at Brian. "A visitor from the mainland."

The boy's eyes narrowed.

"Lord Brian mac Logan," she said.

A man pressed closer. "We don't have many

visitors from the mainland," he snarled, suspicion coloring his words. "What's he doing here on our island?"

"He's come to ask for our help," Wynne replied, her gaze scanning the group around them.

Keith said, "Is somebody hurting him like they did my sister and me?"

Morning meal forgotten, the circle of onlookers tightened.

"Aye, Keith," Wynne replied, "you might say that. An evil man stole a legacy belonging to my lord's eldest daughter."

Keith's eyes rounded. "And you're going to get it back for him?"

"She's going to sail me to the land where the man lives," Brian said. "I shall get my daughter's legacy back."

Keith gave Brian a thorough look, his expression clearly one of disbelief.

The villagers also gazed suspiciously at Brian. Wynne understood that they had gathered out of more than curiosity. They were frightened.

"Don't be afraid," she said. "Lord Brian is a friend. He's not here to hurt any of us."

In the distance Brian saw Lachlann hurrying up the street, coming from the direction of the quay. Brian was glad to see his friend; the crowd looked unfriendly, and he wasn't sure Wynne could control them or her warriors.

Her men pushed forward. She held up her hand and shook her head at them. " 'Tis a friendly visit, lads."

They stopped, but they kept their swords drawn and glared at Brian. Wynne spoke quietly, setting their fears to rest. When Lachlann reached the ring of warriors, he tried to push his way through them, but one of them knocked him back. The villagers, whispering among themselves, continued to stare and didn't break the circle.

"Brian!" he called out.

"I'm fine," Brian assured him.

"Let him pass," Wynne commanded her men. "He's with Lord Brian."

The crowd did not move.

"Let Lord Brian's warrior through." Wynne's voice was firmer this time.

The warriors and people did not step aside, but neither did they hinder Lachlann from pushing past them to reach Brian. Although Wynne had tried to allay their fears, everyone was clearly perplexed. Lachlann, ready for a fight, stood at Brian's side.

Not wanting to strike even greater fear into her people's hearts, needing to convince them that Brian was not from Clan O'Illand and had no designs on her life, Wynne announced, "Please believe me. Lord Brian is not here to hurt me. He has come on a peaceful mission."

"The only company we've had here are the people you brought in your ship." A young woman with dark brown hair edged close to Wynne and the boy. Her green eyes round with fear, she laid her hand protectively on Keith's shoulder.

"It's all right, Erinn," Wynne assured her, "no one is going to hurt you or Keith. I promise."

But Wynne's assurance did not seem to mollify Erinn.

"This time it's different, Erinn," Wynne returned. "Lord Brian hired a ship to bring him to the other side of the isle." Raising her voice, Wynne spoke to all those who had encircled her and Brian. "Don't worry. Everything is fine. The captain who brought him is a trusted friend. He won't be coming back to trouble us. And Lord

Brian and his warriors will be staying with us until we finish repairs on the *Honeycomb*. Then I shall take them away."

The villagers, whispering among themselves, continued to stare.

"All of you go about your business."

No one moved.

"Now!" she added.

Slowly they disbanded and moved away.

Keith turned to his sister. "Shall I get us some water, Erinn?"

"Nay." She glanced fearfully back and forth between Brian and Lachlann. "I'll get the water, Keith. You be scooting to the house. The morning meal is ready."

"Madam," Lachlann said, reaching for the jug, "I shall be most happy to get the water for you. If you will show me—"

"I'll get my own water!" Erinn drew up to her full height, which was a good head shorter than Wynne, and glared at the Highlander. Her eyes flashed. "You stay away from me and my brother."

"My lady," Lachlann said, clearly surprised by her behavior, "I meant you no insult."

Erinn caught Keith's tunic. "Come along, little brother." Giving Lachlann one last smoldering glance over her shoulder, she and Keith scurried toward her cottage.

"It's all right, Erinn," Wynne called to the retreating figures.

"Why is she so frightened?" Lachlann asked.

"She and Keith are Irish. When Keith was a tiny babe, Erinn no older than five winters, they were stolen from their village and enslaved. They escaped their master, who offered a large bounty for their capture. He let it be known that he intended to kill them when they were returned. Drawn and quartered! He wanted to provide a lesson for his other slaves."

Lachlann grimaced.

"They were caught by a mercenary who put them in leg irons and hired a ship to transport them to the village of their imprisonment. I arrived in time to save them. They are fearful because the mercenary promised to kill me because I kept him from getting his bounty. He also promised that he would return them to their master, and draw and quarter them himself."

"Saving them was a worthy cause, my lady," Brian said. "Now both of them belong to you. I can understand why you were so solicitous of the boy's health."

"I'm solicitous because I care, and they don't belong to me. Humans should belong to no one but themselves. I gave them their freedom. I offered to return them to their home, but they had been gone so long, they chose to live here with me." She turned to Lachlann. "Who are you?"

"He is Lachlann mac Niall, my friend and comrade-in-arms," Brian answered. "He is also bestman to High King Malcolm of the kingdom of Northern Scotland, and headman to House Duncan."

"Lord Lachlann," Wynne said, "I'm glad to have met you. I heard a great deal about you when mac Logan and I were fighting for Glenmuir."

"I wish I could have been there with you," Lachlann said, "but at the time I was in the south chasing cattle raiders." He smiled. "The bards sing songs of praise about you in the mead halls, lady."

She smiled.

"Perhaps I shall hear them singing about your

rescue of Erinn. Erinn." He repeated her name, looking at Wynne. "She is called only 'from Ireland'?"

"Aye. She was young when she was stolen and remembers little about her childhood in that land. Her master called her Erinn, and that is what she answers to."

Looking over his shoulder at her, Lachlann said, "She's beautiful."

"In a haunting way," Brian agreed. "Not the kind of woman most men would be interested in."

"But then," Lachlann said quietly, "she would not be interested in most men."

"For a verity," Brian murmured. He also looked over his shoulder at the two who were disappearing into their cottage. "Keith reminds me of my children. Don't you think so, Lachlann?"

"Other than the sex being different from the three older ones," Lachlann teased, "and your son having seen only five winters."

Brian grinned at him. Wynne said nothing.

Lapsing into silence, the three of them walked toward the Great Hall. Men and women scurried around, some of them transferring goods from the larger ship to the nearest small ones. Others transported the cargo into a large storehouse nearby. Still others had already begun repairing the *Honeycomb*.

"Wynne!" a deep masculine voice called.

Brian turned at the same time Wynne did to see a large, older man rushing toward them. He was almost as tall as Brian, one of the largest men Brian had ever seen. Flaming red hair and a beard liberally streaked with white framed his ruddy face. A thick pelt of it formed a shelf over his sky-blue eyes. Long strides brought him even with Brian and Wynne. He scowled.

"My lord," Wynne said to Brian, "this is Cathmor of Eire, my bestman."

Ignoring the introduction, Cathmor demanded, in a voice heavy with concern, "Are you all right, lady?"

She nodded, yet his gaze searched her face.

"I'm fine, Cathmor," she assured him.

"I would have been here sooner, but I was down below the quay at the foodstores. I caught this one"—he nodded toward Lachlann—"snooping around. He told me that you were being held captive and that we were surrounded by Highlanders. At first I didn't believe him, but when he told me how they had made their way to the village, I knew he had to be telling the truth."

"I wasn't being held captive," Wynne replied, "but my lord swears to me that his men do have our village surrounded."

Eyes narrowed, the older man gazed at Brian.

"This is Lord Brian mac Logan of Northern Scotland, Cathmor. He wants to hire our services."

"My lord." Cathmor inclined his head, but his voice showed no respect for Brian's title.

"We are in agreement, mac Logan," Wynne said. "Call your men and let's settle them in lodges."

Brian lifted his hand and beckoned expansively. Twenty warriors, the most valiant of the mac Logan kindred, rose from their hiding places in the hills. Wearing mail and helmets, their weapons drawn, they were ready to attack on command. Wynne and Cathmor slowly turned around to see the village surrounded. The banner of mac Logan fluttered from a wooden standard.

As the Highlanders moved steadily closer, Lachlann said, "Show me where the lodges are, lady.

I'll take care of my kindred while you and Brian tend to business."

She pointed to a row of cottages. Lachlann nodded and moved away from Brian toward the group of Highland warriors who were congregating on the village green.

"You *are* hiring out to mac Logan?" Cathmor said.

"Aye."

"What about the cargo for the Cloister of the Grove?" Cathmor asked.

"I will deliver it first. I promised the priestesses."

He nodded. "They need it for their infirmary."

"See that the goods are transferred to the *Honeysuckle*," Wynne instructed.

"'Tis our smallest ship," Cathmor reminded her. "Do we need more than ten pairs?"

"We will be shorthanded," Wynne said, "but it will leave more men here to work on the *Honeycomb*. While repairs are being made, I'll sail the cargo over to the cloister."

"What are ten pairs?" Brian asked.

"The number of oars on each ship," Wynne explained. "Two men are assigned to each oar, one to row, one to spell. My largest ship, the *Honeycomb*, has twenty double oars, the *Honeydew* fifteen, and the *Honeysuckle* ten."

Warming to her subject, Wynne talked to Brian about her ships as Cathmor ambled toward the green. She described the frame system and pointed out the rudder, the steering oar, on the right side of the boat. Because of the location of the rudder, this side of the ship was called the steering side. He listened as she described the stern. Mast. Rigging block. Strake or plank.

Not interested in the working of the ship, but

interested in Wynne herself, Brian listened. He was fascinated with the sound of her husky voice, impassioned with a love of her subject. Thoroughly enjoying this moment when he could gaze openly at her, Brian studied her movements, her expressions. He listened to each inflection of her voice.

As if she were aware that he was staring at her rather than at the ship, Wynne stopped talking and gazed into his face. Her eyes sparkled, and her lips curved in a soft smile.

"What are you thinking?" she asked.

"This is a beautiful sight, lady."

Wynne brushed an errant curl behind her ear. "Aye, mac Logan, my ships are beautiful."

"I was talking about you, madam."

Gentle color shaded her cheeks. "Thank you, lord, but I think it will be of more benefit to you to learn about the ships than to flatter me. You shall have to depend on the ships for your safety and survival."

"I was complimenting you," he replied.

"Then, lord, keep your compliments to yourself."

"Brian!" Lachlann called out.

Over Wynne's shoulder Brian saw Lachlann coming toward them. The Irishman also started back.

"Earlier, seafarer, I promised that this would be only a business relationship, that I would not mate with you," Brian said. "I shall not go back on my word, but I shall do everything within my power to convince you to release me from the bargain."

"Why?" Wynne asked. "Earlier you said that any woman would do to assuage your lust."

"That's what I thought at the time," Brian said, "but now I'm convinced that you are the woman

I want to mate with. I want you, lady, and I shall have you even if I must wait until after I have settled my business with the Irish raider. That I promise."

"My services are for hire," she repeated, "but I am not. I am not available to you for the wanting or the taking, mac Logan. We shall not leave this island until you understand and agree."

"You can determine whether I take you," Brian murmured, "but you cannot stop me from wanting you."

Just then Lachlann and Cathmor joined them.

Breaking the silence that encompassed Brian and Wynne, Lachlann said, "The men are settled, but we're all wondering when we shall set sail for Ireland."

"*Ireland!*" Cathmor exclaimed, and rounded on Wynne. "Do my ears prove me false, my lady?"

"Nay," she answered softly, taking no offense that Cathmor spoke so openly to her.

Since she had rescued him one and a half winters ago, when he was almost dead from wounds inflicted by a boar, and had nursed him back to health, he had declared himself her personal guardian.

He had also saved her from being raped by a gang of warlords when she was in port in the southern part of Scotland. The two of them had escaped, but if Cathmor had been caught, he would have been hanged for harming a lord who was taking his pleasure with a "whore," as they had called her. Wynne had always figured they would have hanged him because an old man who had seen at least fifty winters had gotten the best of men twenty or thirty winters younger.

For the most part Wynne enjoyed having

Cathmor at her side. He kept other men from making advances, and he gave her sound, wise advice.

"Aye, Cathmor, we shall be sailing Brian mac Logan to Ireland."

Chapter 6

"Nay, lady, you cannot," Cathmor said. "Let Lord Brian find another seafarer to take him."

"I've struck a bargain."

Cathmor's shaggy brows lifted in surprise. "Without discussing it with us first?"

"Those of you who don't wish to sail with me—"

"Lady," Cathmor interrupted, "there is no question of our loyalty to you. All of us will fight to the death for you. I'm surprised that you violated a law of the sea. Mariners are volunteers who have equal say."

The truth stung, but Wynne did not back down. "This trip is one I have to make, Cathmor."

"For *him*?"

"Nay, for myself and for the child. For his daughter." Wynne quietly explained about the raid on Brian's village and the theft of Elspeth's legacy.

When she was finished, Cathmor said, "Crossing the Irish Sea is dangerous for you, lady, and you are liege of the village. Let me take him. I know the waters and the coastline. If something should happen to me, it would not matter to the people as much as if something happened to you."

"Thank you, Cathmor, but I cannot let you take

my place," She smiled at him. "The *Honeycomb* is my ship. I am her captain."

A bell tolled.

" 'Tis the calling for the morning meal," Wynne said. "My lords, please join me."

The four of them headed toward the Great Hall. When the small group reached the building, an elderly woman greeted them at the door. Like the villagers before her, she glared suspiciously at Brian and Lachlann.

"Keith told me about them," she said.

"She's hiring out to the Highlander, Mistress Sheila," Cathmor growled. "Going to sail him to Ireland, she is."

Her mouth agape, the woman's eyes rounded.

"Don't say a word, Sheila," Wynne warned.

"But, my lady—"

"She won't be a'listening, Mistress Sheila," Cathmor said. "I have argued the point with her already. Her mind is set."

"I shall be leaving three sunrises from today," Wynne said.

She entered the house, Brian at her side, the others behind them.

"Did you rescue Mistress Sheila also?" he asked.

"Nay, she's been my personal maid since I was a baby." Wynne looked straight ahead. "When I was declared an outcast, she chose to come with me rather than stay at my father's Great Hall."

"You've been away from your parents, but you've not been without parents," Brian said.

"Nay." She sighed and added, "Only my father is alive. My mother died when I was a small child. I was raised by Mother Melanthe, a Dryad."

"I'm sorry," Brian said. "I know how much my children miss their mother. I can imagine how you must have—must still—miss yours."

"Aye, she was wonderful. My father and I missed . . . miss her." Pushing sad memories aside, she said, "But Mother Melanthe was also a good mother to me."

"What does your father think of your living here?" Brian asked.

"Living here on this desolate and deserted island?" Wynne countered.

"Aye."

"He doesn't like it. He doesn't believe Princess Gwynneth of Ailean should be living in such a place or with such people. As the second heir to the High Seat, her place is in the Great Hall of Ailean."

"He's right," Brian pointed out.

"*Right!*" Wynne whirled on him. "Aye, you would think so. But I don't. When he believed I had disgraced him and his kingdom, he was quick to disown me. He claimed to love me, yet he abandoned me."

"He had no other choice," Brian said. " 'Twas his duty by the people and the land."

"Aye, mac Logan, so he said," she replied bitterly. "But once the stigma had been lifted from me, my father was willing for me to return to Ailean and resume my place as second heir to the High Seat." Her voice grew louder and more heated. "Before my villagers and I moved here, my father came to see us in Athdara. He begged me to return to Ailean. Like you, he pointed out my duty."

" 'Tis your duty to return, madam," Brian said, "and not live here as a warrior outcast."

"You do your duty as you see it, Highlander," Wynne snapped, irritated with Brian's lack of understanding, "and I'll do mine as I see it."

"What does Mother Melanthe think about your decision?"

"She believes the choice is mine," Wynne returned.

"Is Lord Brian to sleep in the guest chamber, my lady?" Mistress Sheila called from the hearth, where she stirred a cauldron of porridge.

Glad to be saved from further discussion with Brian on the subject of her father, Wynne said, "Nay, he'll be sailing to the cloister with me. His men shall be quartered at the workmen's lodges. See to their needs."

"Aye, mistress," Sheila said.

"Now, my lords," Wynne said, "we shall enjoy the morning meal. You have a treat in store for you. Sheila is one of the best cooks in all of Scotland."

Wynne waved her hand at a small table set to the side of the dais on which rested the High Seat of the Isle of Cat. Hanging on the wall behind the dais was a beautiful tapestry, woven in bright colors and embellished with gemstones and gold and silver threads. On one side of the High Seat was a window, on the other a door. Curtains pulled to the side hung over both. More tapestries hung on walls throughout the hall. Torches, attached to the walls in wrought-iron corbels, burned throughout the Great Hall.

As Lachlann and Cathmor strode to the table, Brian gazed around the room. The island had held nothing but surprises for him since he had arrived, and the interior of the Great Hall was no exception. Although smaller than those Brian was accustomed to, it was far more luxurious.

The furniture was finer, the materials more costly. Bracken and heather covered the floor, but on top of these lay pieces of woven cloth, imported floor coverings, Brian imagined, since he had never seen any like them before. Shields and swords made of gold and silver and studded with jewels hung on the walls. Beside one of the shields was a wooden carving of a prow dragon, evidently a gift from a Northland sea captain.

An unusual statue stood at one end of the hall. Brian walked closer to inspect it.

Wynne followed him. "Do you like it?"

" 'Tis different."

"I traded for it. It came from a country in the far east."

"Gold?" Brian touched the statue as Wynne walked to the fire pit and lit a piece of kindling.

Aye, 'tis a statue of their god, Buddha." Returning, she touched the lighter stick to the tip of a long reed. " 'Tis the fragrance they offer to their gods."

The aroma of incense filled the room.

"You worship their god?"

"Nay, but the workmanship is beautiful, the design clever. I like it."

Brian's gaze swept past the statue to mosaic plaques embedded on the wall.

"Those came from eastern lands also, lord."

"You have bartered for many beautiful things for your home," Brian said.

"Thank you."

"The meal is served, my lady," Mistress Sheila announced.

Brian and Wynne moved back to the table. As Brian gazed at the food and inhaled its tantalizing aroma, he realized he was famished.

"My lords, please be seated. The table is small and is not elevated and set apart like the ones you are used to in other villages," Wynne said. "Things are different here. As mistress of the village, elected by my people, I keep the High Seat, but I don't eat apart from them."

She walked over to a spiral wrought-iron rack on which rested drying clothes and several bowls of water. She washed and dried her hands. After removing their gloves and tucking them into their leathern girdles, the men did the same. Since she was mistress of the Great Hall, the men waited for her to sit down. Cathmor sat to her right, Brian and Lachlann opposite her.

Ornately carved silver dishes, each filled with a slice of coarse brown bread called a trencher, were set in front of them. Sheila poured a steaming stew of meat and vegetables over the bread. She also served each one a tankard of hot grape wine, pungent with spices. With little persuasion Brian and Lachlann ate their meal and were grateful for the unsolicited second helping.

When Wynne saw Lachlann eyeing the trencher, she said, "Elsewhere the bread is fed to the poor, lord. Since we have none on the isle, we eat the trencher."

Without a second urging, Lachlann began to pull the bread apart and to sop up his plate, as did the others.

"Mistress Sheila," Brian said, pushing back and sighing his pleasure, "I have not tasted food this good since . . . since . . ." he paused, then added softly, "Since my wife died."

Sheila beamed. "Thank you for such a fine compliment, sire." She winked. "I have even more for you. A subtlety, if you please."

"We please," Lachlann said before Brian could answer.

Brian chuckled and clapped his friend on the shoulder. "He has always had a fondness for sweet pastry."

Sheila's eyes twinkled. "Pastry. Marzipan. And honey."

"Good lady," Lachlann said, "my mouth is watering. I can hardly wait."

"If you'll excuse me, gentlemen"—Wynne rose, as did the men—"I shall not partake of the subtlety."

"You're leaving?" Brian exclaimed more than asked. Surely she could see that Cathmor and Lachlann had not finished eating.

She smiled. "Please continue your meal."

"You insult me, madam!"

"Nay, lord."

" 'Tis your duty to stay until all have finished."

How dare the Highlander to remind her of her duty! His challenge hung between them, but Wynne did not respond. She wouldn't allow him to force her into a defensive position.

"You know full well that the departure of the hostess from the table signals the end of the meal," Brian explained, "yet my man and yours are still eating and have expressed a desire to have their subtlety."

"I apologize," Wynne said quietly, resolved in her decision not to allow the Highlander to rile her. Neither did she intend to let him act as if he were lord of the hall. "I meant no offense. We have our own customs here on the Isle of Cat. 'Tis customary for me to slip away to my bower after the meal. The meal continues until all are finished." She smiled. "Now, my lords, if you'll excuse me."

She crossed the room, her rustling tunic accentuating the length of her legs, the sway of her hips. Then she stepped through the door and out of sight.

"Do not think harshly of her, my lord," Cathmor said. "She has a small bower at the back of the Great Hall. After she eats, she retreats there and meditates."

"No matter what she does or why," Brian said, " 'tis poor manners to leave her company."

To leave him! He didn't want to admit that he was piqued because she was no longer there to visit with him. He enjoyed being around her. She stimulated him, made him feel alive again. Whether she inspired pain or pleasure, anger or joy, she made him feel.

It was a refreshing change for Brian. Since Sorcha had died, his emotions had been numbed. He had gone through all the motions of living, but he had not lived. He felt as if he had died with his wife, left to roam the earth like a lost soul.

Today he had felt the deep prick of anger and irritation, of frustration. He had lusted for the seafarer, had wanted to mate with her. At one point he had told her that any woman could assuage his sexual appetite, but even as he had spoken the words, he had known them to be false. He was attracted to Wynne the seafarer, the woman he had thought he disliked. She was the only woman he wanted.

Strangely, Brian wanted more, and without Wynne's knowing this, she had given it to him. She had gone beyond the physical and had touched his soul. She had released it from its prison of numbness. He had laughed, truly laughed.

"She's an unusual woman," Lachlann said.

"Aye," Cathmor replied. "That she is, lad."

Aye, Brian silently agreed, *most unusual.*

He moved to the window to gaze at the one-room bower set off from the Great Hall. Through the open door he saw Wynne sitting on a stool in front of a large harp. She drew her fingers across the strings, and soft music floated into the Great Hall.

"She always plays after the meal," Cathmor

said. " 'Tis an Irish harp. I gave it to her. I believe every angel should have one."

Angel, Brian thought as he contemplated Wynne. It was a word he would never have used to describe her. But with the morning sun shining on her golden hair, she did look ethereal, so different from the warrior he knew her to be. Calling her an angel put her in a realm far beyond that of mere mortals. The thought that she was unattainable disconcerted Brian. Nay, he didn't want her to be an angel.

"Aye, my lords, my lady is truly an angel." Finishing the last of his bread, Cathmor washed it down with wine. Then he wiped his arm across his mouth. "Once I was wounded by a boar that I brought down. I killed him, but my hunting companions thought that he had killed me as well. Wanting him more than me, they left me to die. I managed to crawl to the edge of the river before I lapsed into unconsciousness."

As the Irishman talked, Brian stared at Wynne who worked her magic on the harp strings. Her hands were beautiful, her fingers long and graceful. She filled the room with a soft, haunting melody that wrapped itself around Brian's heart.

"When I regained my senses," Cathmor said, "a lovely young angel was administering to my needs. At first I thought I was in heaven. Soon I learned that I was aboard Wynne's ship. She nursed me back to health and I've been with her ever since. She's saved all of us."

Someone tapped Brian on the arm. Startled, he turned to look at Lachlann. He had been so engrossed in Wynne that he had not heard his friend approach. Nor did he realize that Mistress Sheila was refilling the tankards and serving the dessert.

Lachlann whispered, "She is beautiful, isn't she, my friend?"

"Aye." Brian's voice was thick.

"As I gaze at her, sitting there in the sunlight and playing the harp, I know why she's called the Lady of Summer." Lachlann took a long swallow of wine. "I understand why you are infatuated with her."

Brian scowled at Lachlann. "You don't know what you're talking about."

Lachlann grinned and winked.

Brian's scowl deepened. Quickly, resolutely, he pushed errant thoughts of the seafarer aside so he could focus on what he must do to save Elspeth's honor.

Lachlann was right. Brian had been far too long without a woman, else he wouldn't be having these fancies about a warrior like Gwynneth. He would be thinking about a woman who was soft and warm and willing.

Cathmor set his tankard on the table with a thud at the same time that Brian looked over at him. As Brian took a swallow of his own wine, he studied Cathmor over the rim of the tankard.

When he lowered it, he asked, "Why don't you want her to take me to Ireland?"

"That's not for me to say, Highlander," Cathmor replied. " 'Tis my lady's story."

Chapter 7

~~~~ ⌒♥♥⌒ ~~~~

Cathmor rose, the bench grating across the floor. "Now I must return to the ship and see to the transfer of goods and the repairs. Else we won't be sailing for Ireland three sunrises from now."

Long strides carried him from the Great Hall.

"I shall be on my way also," Lachlann said. He drained his tankard and rose. "If it's all right with you, Brian, I shall sail with you as far as the Cloister of the Grove, and from there make my way home by pony."

" 'Tis fine with me," Brian said, "but I hate for you to depart, Lachlann."

"I feel the same way, my friend, but it is time to go. Since the cloister is located on the northwestern coast of Scotland, 'twill be an easy ride from there home."

"Aye," Brian murmured, thinking about his children. He was glad Lachlann would be fostering them during his absence, but he would miss his friend. "There is none other I would rather have fighting by my side, none I trust more."

"And I would rather be fighting at your side than fighting with four children ranging in ages from five to nine."

Brian laughed good-naturedly. "They're a bit spirited, Lachlann, but they are good bairns."

"Aye, I know. On my way to your home I shall stop by Malcolm's village and tell him what is happening."

The two men spoke a little longer, Brian giving Lachlann instructions for the men and messages for friends and associates. Eventually Lachlann departed, and Brian was alone.

He left the Great Hall and went straight to the bower. For a moment he looked around the room, dazed by its splendor. Wynne must have collected the furniture during her sea travels. Gold and bronze figurines. Delicate glass dishes. Tiles painted with flowers, animals, and birds.

The wall tapestries were beautiful, as were the delicate bed linens. The floor was covered with thick rugs, and pillows and bolsters were scattered around. A low brazier, resembling a bowl, sat in the center of the room. To one side was a low table. The harp stood before the only window in the room.

Brian felt as if he had been transported to another land.

Wynne looked over at him and smiled but did not stop playing. He sat down in a beautifully carved chair, the color of polished ebony. Leaning back into the thick cushions, he closed his eyes and once more gave himself up to the music. For the first time since Sorcha had died he felt at peace with himself.

When the last note died away he said, "That was beautiful."

"Thank you." Wynne ran her hand over the arched neck of the resonator.

"I would never have guessed you could play the harp."

"I have played only for one and a half seasons, since Cathmor gave it to me."

Fascinated, Brian gazed at her hands, at her long fingers as they traced the intricate carvings. He imagined her hands touching him, caressing him. Dear God, he thought in disgust, closing his eyes. He was thinking like a randy youth, consumed with lust. Ever since he had seen Gwynneth swimming he had yearned for her. With each passing moment his desire for her became more of an obsession.

"Cathmor says I am so accomplished because it's a magical harp."

The husky tones of her voice washed sweetly over him. Again he was seeing a new aspect of the seafarer, one that he would once have considered totally alien to her. Although he had always admitted that she was beautiful, he had also thought she was tough and callous like a warrior. Now she was soft and feminine and sensual—everything he admired in a woman. There was no denying that Gwynneth was a woman.

"This harp was carved from sacred apple trees that grew in an ancient orchard of the Druids in Eire." She leaned back and looked up at Brian, her blue eyes shadowed. "I have no knowledge of music, yet the moment I saw the harp, I knew I could play. And I did."

"I have never heard the melody before," Brian said.

"Nay, I create my own."

"Do you also create words?"

"Sometimes." Smiling, she rose, as did Brian. "But enough idle talk, my lord. I must change my clothes so that you and I can be on our way to the cloister."

Brian realized that he had touched a tender chord within Wynne, a secret she didn't wish to share with him . . . perhaps not with anyone. She walked past him, her hair wisping against his arm.

"Why doesn't Cathmor want you to sail to Ireland?"

She stopped, and Brian glanced down at his arm. Strands of her hair gleamed like golden threads on the sleeve of his tunic.

"That's where he was abandoned by his companions."

"Don't treat me like a fool, lady," Brian said softly. "The Irishman is not fearful for himself but for you."

She turned, and with disappointment, Brian watched the golden threads slide from his arm.

"My husband was Irish," she said, returning to the window and standing next to her harp. "Alba O'Illand of Sligo, Ireland, a younger son, who had come to Scotland to find his fortune."

"And he found you." Brian also walked over to the window, leaning against the frame, gazing at her.

"Aye, his *mis*fortune."

"How?"

She hesitated before she said, "On our wedding night, he was drunk and beat me senseless. Had it not been for Honey, my wildcat kitten, he might have killed me. Honey sank her claws into both his cheeks. He was badly scarred and lost an eye."

"Most men are drunk on their wedding night, lady, and wife beating and scarring are not uncommon." He paused. "There is more to your story, else you would not have been cast out."

"Aye." Wynne ran a finger lightly across the strings, the soft sound thrumming through the hall. "According to custom, I asked for a bill of divorcement. I received it, but judgment went against me. Alba lied. He claimed he had a right to beat me. I had deceived him, he said. I wasn't a virgin. The rest you know. I chose disgrace to a life of misery with a man whom I had grown to despise."

"Is it because of him that you're afraid to go to Ireland?"

"Partly," she replied. "Because of Alba's lies, his clan, Clan O'Illand, blames me for his maiming and for his disgraceful marriage. Alba's father, High King Triath, has sworn a blood oath to kill me. Even Alba's death did not release Triath from the blood oath, since he believes I have cursed the clan by not providing Alba with an heir."

"Is that why you live here?"

She nodded. "When I learned of Alba's death four winters ago, I also learned that Triath had hired a champion to find me and bring me back to Ireland. That's when my villagers and I moved from Athdara to the Isle of Cat. Until today I felt safe here."

"No one has been as desperate to find you as I was," Brian answered.

"Folloman is, and when word gets out that you came here, others will try. I'm no longer safe."

"You could return to the protection of your father."

She said nothing.

"And you ought to."

"I belong here with my villagers."

A breeze picked up strands of her hair and blew them across his face. Soft, silky, they caressed his skin. He drew in a deep breath, his nostrils filled with her clean scent. He felt himself grow hard. He wanted to sweep her into his arms, carry her to the sleeping chamber, and make love to her.

"My lady!" Keith shouted from outside the

bower. "Cathmor sent me to tell you that the *Honeysuckle* is loaded and ready to set sail."

"Tell him I'll be there as soon as I've changed clothes," Wynne called out.

"Aye," Keith answered. "May I go to the cloister with you?"

"Not this time."

"Please, my lady. I want to visit Mother Barbara."

"Keith . . ."

"Perhaps, my lady, she wants to see my wound again."

"Go do your chores, Keith!" Wynne ordered.

"Yes, my lady."

"He's a persistent lad," Brian observed.

"Aye, lord, and it may be my undoing. He knows I have a softness in my heart for him." She laughed as she moved to the large trunk at the foot of her bed. She lifted the lid. "You and Lachlann meet me on the quay. We'll set sail shortly."

"My lady," Brian said, "since you have told me about the blood oath, I am concerned."

Wynne paused in rummaging through the clothing.

"I'm concerned about the safety of my warriors."

Holding a short white tunic in her hand, she faced him. "The oath was sworn against me," she said. "Why should it concern you?"

"Because you are afraid, lady, and your fear has forced you to hide here for the past four years."

"I have known valiant warriors, *men*, who have moved their villages for the same reason that I did—to protect themselves and their villagers," Wynne said. "None of those whom I know have been accused of cowardice. In Great Halls throughout the lands, they have been extolled as

wise men and great leaders." She tossed the shirt
over the chest lid. "But my decision to move here
is not considered a wise one, or my leadership
outstanding because I am a woman."

" 'Tis a fact, madam, that women are emotional
creatures—"

"Any warrior, man or woman, would do well
to be worried about such a vow," Wynne cut in.
"But let me reassure you, my *womanly emotion* will
not endanger you or your warriors. Before I
agreed to transport you, mac Logan"—her words
were clipped—"I was aware that Donegal Bay,
where we shall be mooring, is not as far south as
Sligo where the O'Illands have their home. I figure
that we shall sail in and out before Triath or Folloman has any idea that we have been there."

Gone was the vulnerable woman of moments
ago. An invisible shutter covered her eyes. They
gleamed like blue-gray metal, the kind a blacksmith crafted into a sword. Had they been dagger
or sword, they would have sliced him to pieces.

After a moment Brian said, "Cathmor is from
Ireland and understands the ways of the sea, like
you. Perhaps in this situation, seafarer, it would
be better if he were to pilot the ship."

Anger blazed in Wynne's eyes, but her voice
was calm. "He doesn't have a ship to pilot."

"He could use yours."

A cool smile played over her lips. "Do you loan
out your sword or dagger? Nay. Neither do I let
anyone else pilot my ship."

Now Brian remembered why he disliked the
seafarer. She was unreasonable, a hard woman
who refused to yield an inch. He conveniently ignored the logic of her argument, forgot that he
would have used any means to get her to agree
to sail him to Ireland. He refused to see that he

and she had many similar qualities. Both were determined to have their way.

Wynne's quiet voice broke through the strained silence. "You came to this island and begged for my help, mac Logan. Against my better judgment I allowed myself to be persuaded, and we have sealed our bargain. You'll not get out of it so easily. You sail with me or not at all."

"It's the booty, isn't it?" Brian sneered. "Already you have the chests full of gold and silver in your coffer, and you're unwilling to give them up."

"Aye, I want the booty," Wynne admitted. "But there's more. I've worked long and hard to acquire my ships and to establish my reputation. When one of my ships sails, I sail with it. I'm the captain."

"Then, captain, we shall change our agreement. I'll not endanger the lives of my men because of an emotional woman."

"Once a deal is struck, mac Logan, it is sealed. There will be no breaking it now. I'll not have my livelihood jeopardized because of an emotional *man*." Her back straight, her shoulders squared, she looked him straight in the eyes and never flinched. "Good morrow," Wynne said. "I shall see you aboard the ship."

Summarily dismissing Brian, she once again bent over her clothing trunk. "I must change clothes, mac Logan. Please leave."

Biting back his anger, realizing that he had no alternative but to sail with the seafarer, Brian whirled and strode across the bower, untied the loop that snagged the door covering, and let it fall into place. Scooping it aside with one hand, he walked out. He had taken several steps away from the bower when she called after him.

"Tell Cathmor that I have a trunk in here that needs to be loaded on the *Honeysuckle* before we sail."

"Since I'm going that way, I might as well carry it for you."

"Suit yourself," she answered. "Wait there until I've finished dressing."

Brian returned to the door. Folding his arms over his chest, he leaned against the frame. That the seafarer had unsettled personal problems with the O'Illands still worried him, but he reminded himself that Wynne was a courageous captain, reputed to be the best seafarer in all of Scotland. She would not enjoy such a reputation if she allowed herself to be ruled by her feelings . . . as did most women. Besides, said a voice of reason, he would be there, and she was in his employ. Aye, he thought, all would be well.

The fragrance of the flowers, the warmth of the sun, and the promise of sailing to Ireland all dispelled the last of his reservations.

Standing there, relaxing, he heard the soft swish of material as she changed clothes. The sound seduced his senses, and he forgot his argument with her and remembered only that she was a beautiful woman. Remembering the magic the room had woven about him, he once again gave himself up to his imagination.

Whereas before he had fantasized about the tantalizing things she could do to his body, now he began to think about the wonderful things he would like to do to hers.

"By the time we return from the cloister," Wynne said, "you will have gotten your sea legs."

His sea legs! All he could think about were *her* legs. Long. Shapely. Graceful. Naked!

"Since you don't have a seaman's chest, I'll loan

you one of mine," she went on. "The clothes you'll have to get from Cathmor. The two of you look to be about the same size. For the long journey you're going to need some oiled clothing, trousers, tunic, boots, and a sleeping bag."

He heard a soft thud, a crash, and a yelp.

Responding with a warrior's instinct, Brian whipped his sword from the scabbard, jerked the curtain aside, and rushed into the bower. He didn't see Gwynneth, but he heard a tussle. A boot flew through the air, landing at his feet.

"My lady!"

Disheveled, she rose from the other side of the bed, one boot on, one off. Although her hair was plaited into a single braid, tousled tendrils curled about her face. Her white tunic had pulled loose from her brown seafaring trousers.

Brian couldn't take his eyes off her ... off her shapely hips and long legs encased in the tight-fitting leather. She stood, brushing her hand over her buttocks and down her thighs. She stuffed the tunic into her trousers. Brian watched each movement, his blood boiling hot through his veins. By all that was holy, he wanted to mate with her!

He heard a meow, then a shuffle. He looked around. Rising beside Wynne was a huge golden-brown cat with black stripes. The cat leaped onto the bed, her teeth bared.

She hissed at Brian. He stiffened. This was the cat that hated men! And Brian had to admit she frightened him.

"It's Honey!" Wynne jumped over the bed, throwing herself between him and the cat. Honey spit at Brian; she struggled to free herself from Wynne's embrace. "Don't hurt her."

"Hurt her!" Brian exclaimed. "I'm afraid the damned animal is going to hurt *me*. The Highland wildcat is one of the most ferocious of all animals."

"You've drawn a sword on her," Wynne said.

Still hissing, Honey fastened her tawny eyes on Brian.

"She hates men, so you said."

"Aye, but she won't hurt you ... unless you hurt me." She murmured into the cat's bristly fur.

"Does she understand, madam"—Brian eyed the cat suspiciously—"that if I put my sword away, she is to cease hissing?"

"Aye, lord, she understands."

Cautiously Brian resheathed his weapon, but Honey was not as quickly disarmed. She continued to hiss and to bat her paw at him. Wynne crooned to her, rubbing her behind the ears. Finally Honey purred, though she still didn't completely relax.

"This cat isn't going with us to Ireland," Brian said.

Honey hissed.

"When she's well, she always travels with me," Wynne replied.

"Not this time, lady. I have no desire to be mauled during my sleep ... or at any other time."

By now Honey had lain down on the bed and was purring as Wynne rubbed her stomach. She patted the mattress with the other hand. "Come here, my lord. Let her get acquainted with you."

"I don't want to know her," he said. Nevertheless Brian moved to the bed and sat down gingerly. Honey lifted her head, bared her fangs, and hissed.

"Rub her," Wynne ordered.

Brian reached out tentatively, but Honey hunched up and hissed louder. She swatted at his hand.

"It's all right," Wynne cooed to the cat, pressing her cheek against Honey's neck. "He's our friend. He's going to be sailing with us all the way to Ireland."

Honey didn't relax, nor did she take her eyes off Brian.

"Try it again," Wynne said.

Brian shook his head. "Lady, it's fine with me if the cat and I continue to dislike each other." Yet he slowly slid his hand over the bed linens toward Honey. The mattress shook as she stretched out, her paws extended. She laid her face between them and watched his hands. "Do you intend to take her with us to the cloister?"

"Nay, she's been on ship too long already. She needs some time on land. I'll leave her here with Sheila." Wynne rose and moved to the stool on the other side of the room. Picking up her second boot, she slipped her foot into it. Then she patted the trunk beside her. "This is my extra sea trunk. I'm going to let you use it."

"Is this the one you want carried to the ship?" Brian asked.

"That one." She pointed toward the door.

Brian twisted to see a much larger trunk. Then he felt the mattress give, and he swayed backward. Before he knew what had happened, Honey was standing in front of him, purring into his face. An abrasive tongue lapped Brian's cheek.

"Ugh!" He grimaced and shut his eyes.

Wide-eyed, Wynne stared at him. "She likes you!" she exclaimed. "I have never seen her take to anyone so quickly. Especially not a man!" She laughed. "Honey likes you, my lord."

"I don't like her."

Honey sprawled out, toppling Brian over and

lying partially on top of him. Playfully she swatted him with a sheathed paw. She meowed.

"She'll grow on you," Wynne promised, a mischievous glint in her eyes.

"She's grown on me as much as I want her to," he said dryly. "That worries me."

Giggling, Wynne reached down and picked up a soft ball made of rags. "Here, Honey." Wynne tossed it on the bed.

Honey reared up, lunged, and batted the ball as it flew through the air. She flopped down on Brian's stomach. He gasped and grunted. Honey stretched out, swatting for the ball that kept rolling out of reach.

"Get her off me," Brian demanded in a muffled voice.

Honey wiggled more. Brian grunted. He caught Honey around the stomach and tried to move her. Yowling, she wrapped her paws around him in a cat hug.

"*Gwynneth!*"

Laughing so hard that tears ran down her cheeks, Wynne moved to the bed. She looped her hands around the cat's neck and tried to pull her off, but she was too weak from laughter. Honey had fallen in love with her new playmate and refused to budge. The more Brian fussed and fumed, the more Wynne laughed, and the more loving Honey became.

Then Honey tensed. Her ears perked; she swished her tail and looked around. Moving her head from side to side, she sniffed. She rose on all fours, straddling Brian and weighing the mattress down. Wynne and Brian lay there, hardly breathing as Honey leaped to the floor. Her support gone, Wynne rolled across the bed, landing against Brian. Honey yowled and ran through the door.

"By the holy saints! She's gone!"

"Food," Wynne whispered. "I'll wager Sheila's put her food out."

Brian shifted at the same time that Wynne did, and she realized that their heads were touching.

They were alone and on the bed ... together.

Brian turned his head slightly, their cheeks touching. He moved, and Wynne felt his entire length against hers. Both lay still, the only sound in the room their ragged breathing.

The wispy vapor of incense spiraled through the air; its fragrance blended with the leather of Brian's gloves, his belts and scabbards, with the clean herbal scent of him. His breath flowed warmly over her flushed skin. All of this wove a mystical web around them, separating them from the austerity and harshness of the outside world.

"Gwynneth," he murmured, his wine-scented breath fanning over her already sensitized skin.

For the first time in her life Wynne's body was burning with pleasurable sensation. She enjoyed lying beside Brian, hearing him breathe, feeling the warmth of his body, absorbing his strength and vitality.

He didn't move, didn't try to touch her in any other way. Instinctively she breathed deeply and closed her eyes. Here in her bower she felt safe and protected. This was her magical world, and nothing bad could happen to her while she was in it. She was surrounded by all the gods of the world, and they protected her.

He brushed a knuckle across her nose. She jumped, opened her eyes, and stared at him. He smiled but removed his hand from her face.

"You have a splattering of freckles, madam."

He was so ruggedly handsome, so virile, that

Wynne caught her breath. Never had she been so enamored of a man.

"Elspeth has freckles on her cheeks also."

The gentle smile, the quiet voice, and the talk of his daughter relaxed Wynne, and she let down her guard.

"She hated them," he went on.

"So do I."

"Until I told her that they were only kisses from the sun."

He moved so cautiously that Wynne didn't realize he had caught her chin until she felt the gentle touch. It tugged at her heartstrings, reminding her of the emptiness inside her. As she gazed into his face, she saw the beard stubble shadowing his cheeks, the texture of his sun-browned skin. In fascination she stared at the tiny crinkles at the corner of his eyes.

"You're so beautiful, Gwynneth."

He laid his hand on her abdomen below her breast. She drew a sharp breath, but his hand didn't go any higher. The caress itself seemed innocent, but when she gazed into his eyes, into flames of desire, she knew his true intent. The heat of his passion transferred to her, and she trembled. Her desire was elemental. Sensual. Intense. He was setting her on fire. From head to toe, she burned for him as she had never burned for a man, had not even known it was possible to burn. While Brian's desire enticed her, drew her to him, it also frightened her.

Brian lowered his head. The morning breeze ruffled his hair, and black strands, burnished in the sunlight, fell across his forehead. "I've wanted to do this since I saw you swimming in the pool."

He lightly kissed one corner of her mouth, along the line of her bottom lip, then the upper. She moaned softly as wave after wave of pleasure washed through her. The intoxicating warmth of his mouth drove her to distraction.

When he lifted his head he murmured, "I must thank your cat for bringing us together."

He cupped her breast and moved even closer to her, their desire merging to become one. Her nipples tightened and strained against the tunic. Wynne gasped.

"If it had not been for her," he went on in that low, seductive thrum meant to obliterate Wynne's resistance, "no telling how long it would have been before we . . . became this close."

He shifted only slightly, but enough for Wynne to feel the weight of him along her entire body. He was hot and pleasantly heavy against her. Her yearning intensified, and suddenly she realized Brian was no longer teasing her, no longer regaling her with stories of Elspeth. He was seducing her . . . and she was allowing it.

The playful lightness was gone; sensuality, hot and intense, suffocated her. It frightened her.

"Nay," she whispered.

"You don't like this?"

Aye, she liked it! Liked it too much!

"Please don't."

"I must." His lips clamped down on hers in a hot, fierce kiss.

Wynne fought, but his huge body pressed her into the mattress. Not knowing what to do, knowing that she must somehow protect herself, she twisted her face from his and instinctively brought up her knee. Before she could kick him in the groin, his leg locked over hers, his grip forceful.

Breathing deeply, he glared at her, his face hard and unyielding. "Lady, if you did that, I should punish you severely."

"Then leave me alone."

Puzzled, he stared at her. "Why did you encourage me?"

"I didn't—"

He hiked a brow.

"I didn't mean to."

Brian laughed bitterly. "Perhaps, lady, you thought you could control the situation, but I proved to be stronger than the men with whom you are accustomed to mating. Being a strong woman and a warrior, you would want a weaker man you could dominate."

He was despicable. "You don't know what kind of men I mate with or what kind of relationship I desire," she flung at him.

"Nay, seafarer." His eyes mocked her. "But I do know that you are as sorely in need of a man as I am in need of a woman."

Wynne brought up her hand to slap him. He caught it, clasping her fingers so tightly they hurt.

A derisive smile curled his lips. "Your mouth is saying one thing, seafarer, your body another. And I think it is your body that speaks the truth."

"You would believe that, Highlander, because it is what you wish to believe." She twisted her hand out of his clasp. "I do not want a man in my life."

"Perhaps you don't want one," Brian said, "but you need one." Lifting his leg off her, he slid from the bed.

"Why?" She also rose. After crossing the room to her dressing alcove, she picked up her comb. "Because you're a man, and your pride can't survive a woman who doesn't want you?"

Long strides carried Brian to her. He grabbed her by the shoulders and pushed her against the wall, imprisoning her there with his body, clamping his hands on either side of her. His eyes glittered dangerously. Wynne's heart pumped furiously; excitement rushed through her.

"Lie to yourself all you want, seafarer," he snarled, "but don't lie to me."

Her breath was labored. Brian looked down to see the rise and fall of her breasts.

"You wanted me."

As if on cue, her nipple peaked and pressed against her shirt. Still holding her prisoner, he bent his head and capped the tip of her breast with his mouth. Wynne's stomach convulsed with desire. He blew against the fabric, and tidal waves of sensation washed over her.

"You still want me."

Wynne twisted, but he did not release her. He did not raise his head.

"Desire is nothing to be ashamed of." He straightened. "I want you also, and I shall have you."

Glad for the support of the wall behind her, Wynne trembled. No other man had unsettled her as much as he did. Never before had she been so unsure of herself, of her emotions.

"Are you going to take me by force?"

"Nay." Removing his hands from the wall, he stepped back.

Wynne ducked around him, crossed the room, and stood in front of the window. She stared out.

"But I shall entice you, lady, and wait for you to come into my arms because it is what you want also."

Fearing he told the truth, Wynne crossed her arms over her chest and hugged herself tightly, as if the gesture could ward him off and protect her. "How long are you prepared to wait?" she demanded.

"Not long. I'm an impatient man."

"Then I shall try your patience."

"Nay, lady. From the way you responded you shall be in my bed shortly."

Brian had aroused her emotions to a fine pitch, and she was hungry for more; she wanted to fill the void of emptiness within herself. But Brian mac Logan was a Highlander, a warlord who was accustoming to taking what he wanted, when he wanted it. Brian had accused her of wanting a weaker man, one whom she could dominate, but she had no desire for a weak man. For her first mating with a man, Wynne wanted someone who cared about her, someone who was gentle.

"Even if I should want to mate with you," she confessed softly, "I would not. You frighten me. You always have."

He frowned; his eyes narrowed. "Aye, seafarer, you were frightened." He paused. "But not of me. You were frightened of yourself. Of your feelings for me."

She heard his footsteps as he moved to stand behind her.

"When you cease fighting yourself, you will come to me willingly," he said.

Wynne believed him, and her fear of his hold over her increased. "Only time knows the answer to that, mac Logan," she replied.

"Wynne!" Cathmor shouted from outside the bower. "Keith said you needed help with your trunk."

"Nay, good man," Brian answered, as if he were lord of the village, "I'll bring it for her. You may return to the ship, Cathmor. On your way, stop by the lodges and get Lachlann. By the time you are on board, Lady Gwynneth and I shall be there."

Silence prevailed.

Not knowing what Cathmor would do, but knowing how protective he was of her, Wynne worried. He would die fighting for her. Brian's stance, his tone, his expression brooked no argument. Cathmor was equally stubborn, equally powerful. Moreover, he was dedicated to her. But Brian was the younger of the two warriors. That alone would give him an edge over her friend.

Earlier Wynne had trembled from Brian's passion, frightened of her response to him. Now she trembled in fear of his anger. Earlier she had confronted Brian and had won. Now she wasn't so sure she could. The Highlander's pride was suffering from her rebuff. For the moment the expedient thing would be to defuse the situation.

"Obey him, Cathmor."

A long pause preceded the dull "Aye."

Wynne turned to Brian. "You are liege to your warriors," she said, "not to mine. By giving Cathmor an order you undermined my authority, provoking doubts and questions that might undermine the trust and loyalty between me and my crew. For less than that, mac Logan, a man would have called you out." She laughed bitterly. "Had I been a man, you would not have presumed to behave as arrogantly and pompously as you have in regard to my status on my isle."

"You are right, seafarer," he said. "I did overstep the bounds of my authority. I apologize."

"Your apology is not enough because the damage has been done. Don't do it again, mac Logan." Venting her anger, letting him know how she felt about him and the situation, made her feel better. "Leave and take the chest with you."

"Aye, madam captain," he murmured. "First, since you are determined to make me wait for our mating, I shall take a memento."

He leaned over and, without embracing her, touched his lips to hers. Like a newly hatched butterfly, his mouth tenderly brushed back and forth across hers. Sensation delicately wafted through her body. Fight and resolve forgotten, she whimpered. When his hands cupped her face she closed her eyes. She felt his fingers slide into her hair.

She knew how to fight with sword and dirk, bow and arrow. She could pilot a ship, command warriors, but she knew nothing about affairs of the heart . . . about mating.

As the warmth of his touch pervaded every inch of her body, Wynne realized that she truly did want to experience passion . . . with Brian mac Logan.

Then he lifted his mouth from hers. Feeling bereft, Wynne opened her eyes and stared at him.

"Someday, madam," he said softly, "the woman in you will overcome the warrior, and you'll admit that you are as attracted to me as I am to you."

"Aye, mac Logan, I am," Wynne said, surprising herself as well as Brian. "But no matter how much I may want to mate with you, I shall not. I control my emotions. That is a lesson I have learned well since my divorce from Alba. A lesson you evidently have yet to learn."

Amusement danced in his eyes, and his lips twitched at the corners. "Perhaps, madam, since you control your emotions so well, you will teach the skill to me."

Chapter 8

At sunset of that same day, Wynne stood at the tiller of the *Honeysuckle*. The gods of the sea were with them. The wind was up, the yellow and brown striped sail taut. Quickly the ship sliced the water, sailing eastward from the Isle of Cat, past the small and remote island of St. Kilda. From there they would sail around the Western Isles to the northwestern coast of Scotland, to the Highlands where the Cloister of the Grove was located. If the gods continued to bless them and they maintained their present speed, Wynne thought, they would reach the Grove around dawn.

She swept her gaze across the ship. With a precision that came from having worked together for years, the crew moved economically in carrying out the functions of the ship. Some worked the sails and rigging. Others saw to the oars. Still others cleaned and repaired equipment. As the men worked, they talked and laughed among themselves.

Then she saw mac Logan, a passenger not by her choice but through his insistence. He and Lachlann were leaning against the ship's rail, talking and gazing out to sea. Intrigued with the oiled clothing Wynne and her sailors wore when they were at sea, Brian had changed into similar attire.

His muscular legs were covered with beige water-proof trousers and knee-high brown boots. His tunic, the same color as the boots, accented the bronzed column of his throat and stone-hewn face. The wind played against his hair and billowed his mantle.

Big, burly crewmen worked all around him, but Brian was taller than all of them, his shoulders broader. Even among the many, he was a man set apart. And it was not only his height and powerful build that distinguished him. He emanated a vitality that charged the air.

Was it only that morning that he had arrived at her home with his demand that she sail him to Donegal Bay, Ireland? Wynne wondered. Aye, it was. Without much resistance she had agreed to the demand. But she was not doing it for him, she reminded herself, not for the first time. She was doing it for the child.

The reason she was going didn't really matter. She was going, and she and Brian would be to-gether for days and nights in the close confines of a ship. This concerned Wynne; she was too at-tracted to the Highlander. Thoughts of them to-gether in the bower earlier that day returned to haunt Wynne. Brian had been right. She said she didn't want a man, didn't need one, yet she re-sponded to Brian's every touch.

She was acutely aware of him; she could feel his presence even when she couldn't see or hear him. That morning he had awakened a yearning in her that she had never known before, had stirred sen-sations she had heard about but never experi-enced.

She was uncomfortable with these feelings; they unsettled her. Even now when she needed to be clearheaded, she was thinking about Brian. She was consumed with him. She could not allow her thoughts to be divided. She was captain of this ship, and the safety of her crew and her passengers depended on her. She had to push intimate and personal thoughts of Brian mac Logan from her mind. And she would!

Brian turned and caught her staring.

A slow smile creased his face. She caught her breath at its beauty, feeling as if he had reached across the ship to touch her. She wanted to smile back but didn't. The moment was bittersweet. She was more frightened now than she had been earlier in the day. Their journey to Donegal Bay had not even begun, and already she was allowing the Highlander too much power over her.

Lachlann leaned closer to Brian and spoke. Brian answered but did not take his gaze off Wynne. She knew she should break the spell between them, but she did not, could not. As she stared into Brian's eyes, everyone else seemed to vanish, and she was alone with him. His eyes compelled her to go to a special world with him, one that only the two of them could enter . . .

Wynne took a step toward him. Brian took a step toward her.

"Wynne!" Cathmor called out.

She stopped, and so did Brian, their gazes fixed on each other.

The Irishman rounded the cargo hold and moved toward the tiller. "We're making excellent time," the old man said, stepping between Wynne and Brian. Still, by looking over Cathmor's shoulder, Wynne could see Brian.

"We should put into port at the cloister much sooner than we expected." The Irishman moved to stand in front of her, his huge frame blocking Brian entirely from her view.

"Aye," she murmured, feeling let down.

She gripped the tiller more tightly and tried to give the ship her full attention. But thoughts of the Highlander inundated all others.

"I love the *Honeycomb*," Cathmor said, "but it is good to be aboard the little ship again." He crossed his hands behind his back and lifted his face to catch the salted mist.

"Aye," Wynne murmured.

"My lady," he said, gazing toward the open sea, "your private life is none of my business."

"Aye, Cathmor, it is not." Wynne kept her gaze straight ahead.

"But I am worried about you . . . and the High-lander."

He had a right to be worried, she thought. So was she.

"Please don't concern yourself about me."

Cathmor was a vassal, and Wynne owed him no explanation for her behavior. But he was also her friend. She said, "I have hired out to sail him to Ireland and back. Nothing more."

She hoped that by saying the words she could alleviate her own fears as much as Cathmor's, but the same foreboding came over her now as it had that morning when she had seen mac Logan walk-ing toward the pool where she swam. She had allowed Brian to caress her in the bower. Only moments ago she had allowed him to caress her with his eyes, to enter her mind, and to seduce her senses. She feared that next she would allow him to mate with her . . . and that her life would be forever changed.

"Once the Highlander's mission is completed, Cathmor," she said, "and I have returned him to his home, our life shall go back to normal."

"Nay, my lady." Cathmor sighed. "Our lives

will never be the same again. I fear you are soft where this man is concerned."

How wise was her old and trusted friend. While she did not deny his assertion, she refused to give it strength by agreeing aloud.

"I am soft where his daughter is concerned," she replied. "I know what it's like to lose your inheritance, to be stripped of your honor. 'Tis for Elspeth's sake that I am sailing mac Logan to Donegal Bay."

Saying no more, Cathmor gazed at the sea.

"You don't like mac Logan?" she asked.

"Aye, as a warrior and a father who is going to avenge the wrongs done to his house. But I don't trust him where your feelings are concerned, lady. Many men think that since you are a woman of divorcement, you are also a woman of easy virtue. Perhaps this is the case with mac Logan. Just be careful." After a moment he asked, "Do you wish me to spell you?"

"Nay."

"Then I shall light the torches. 'Tis getting dark."

Wynne watched him walk to the right side of the stern platform, where he was soon shouting commands. At various places around the ship torches flared to life. Glancing around, she saw Brian down in the cargo hold with Lachlann, the two of them examining the hooves of one of the ponies. She stared for a long time, willing Brian to look at her, but this time he didn't notice her.

Finally Wynne turned her attention back to the sea. One minute it was moving hills and valleys. The next it was a solid sheet of crystal, its color as varied as its temperament; how quickly it could change from green to blue to silver and back again. This was the sea she knew and loved. The silver necklace of Mother Earth, the bards called it.

Closing her eyes, she listened to it speak to her, make love to her. The seductive hum of wind in the rigging. The whisper of the gold and brown striped sails. The swish of the water. The rustle of the banner as it fluttered in the wind.

"The sea is beautiful at night," Brian said.

Surprised, she opened her eyes. She had not heard him approach and wished he had not.

"Aye," she said.

The wind whipped through the rigging; the sail popped.

"One of your mariners said we might be in for a storm."

Wynne grinned. "He knows that you and Lord Lachlann are land warriors, lord, and was jesting with you. Tonight will be calm."

Suddenly the ship lurched to one side. Although Brian stood braced against the deck like a seasoned sailor, he raised his brows. "Calm, madam?"

Wynne smiled. "As calm as the sea ever is."

He stepped closer to her. Not willing to let him know how much he unnerved her, she never moved, but her grip on the tiller tightened. She gazed straight ahead into the darkened shadows.

"The sea, madam, is like a woman." His voice was soft and velvety. Like gentle night shadows, it caressed her. Brian intended to caress and seduce her.

A shiver of pleasure ran through her. "How so?" She kept her voice calm.

"Unpredictable."

Wynne clung to the tiller and continued to stare ahead. She felt his gaze on her. As if he were a lodestone, she slowly turned to him.

"And beautiful," he murmured. "And mysterious."

Wynne's heart beat so erratically, she thought she would die.

"Like the sea, you are complex. There is always another secret to be discovered."

Wynne forced herself to look away from him. She yearned for Brian mac Logan; true to his word, he was enticing her. Her body clamored for his touch; she ached for the release that his desire promised.

Or perhaps, she told herself, she was attracted not to Brian, but simply to a man. She was curious and wanted to know for herself the secrets of mating, the feelings experienced by a man and a woman when they shared intimacy.

Earlier in the day Brian had accused her of wanting to mate with a weaker man than he. How wrong he was! She had had a weaker man and had found him disgusting. She wanted a man she could respect and admire, a man who was as strong as she was. Surely it was Brian's strength and honor that attracted her. Who better than he to awaken her to her womanly emotions?

"Aye, mac Logan," she said, breaking out of the sensual web he was spinning around her, "the sea has many secrets. That is one reason that I cannot give it up. I want to discover all of them. The ship is my life, the sea my blood."

"Feeling the way you do, lady, you'll have to wed someone who is a seafarer like yourself."

"One marriage was enough for me," she replied.

"So now you're content with lovers?"

Wynne had never taken a lover, but she did not confess this to Brian. The less he knew about her, the better. "If I remarried, mac Logan, I would be giving up my independence. My husband would be my master."

"Aye, lady, that's the way the gods mean for it to be."

"Perhaps the gods mean it that way," she answered, "but I don't."

"You do not care to be womanly at all, do you?"

"I'm proud of being a woman," Wynne replied. "But as a man enjoys being master of his fate, I want to be mistress of mine." Wanting to know what Brian considered womanly, Wynne asked, "What was Sorcha like?"

He hesitated before he said, "She was a small woman with dark eyes and hair." Wynne heard the sorrow in his voice. " 'Twas her laughter that touched me. After a trading expedition or a battle, I was always eager to return home to her."

As Wynne listened to him describe Sorcha, she realized that the woman was very different from her. Sorcha had loved home, hearth, and family. She had been content to be a wife and a mother. Perhaps at one time that had been Wynne's dream too, but no longer. Destiny had changed her. Even if she should remarry, she would never be happy remaining home while her warrior was away fighting. She would want to be with him, riding with him and fighting at his side. She would demand to be part of the adventure of his life.

"Sorcha was sickly after our son, our last child, was born," Brian said, "but she kept assuring me that she was getting better. When Malcolm asked me to march with him and fight with the Glenmuirians, I thought she was well." He paused. "But when I returned home, she was very sick. Feich, the healer, had done all she could. Sorcha died shortly afterward."

"She was waiting to tell you goodbye," Wynne said.

"Perhaps."

"The priestesses at the cloister have told me stories of people who willed themselves to live long enough to say goodbye to someone special or to do something they felt they must do before they crossed to the otherworld."

"I hope that's the case," Brian said. "Sorcha was special to me, and I'd like to believe I was special to her."

Lapsing into silence, Wynne lifted her face to the wind. The sail billowed tightly, and the ship sliced through the silver water.

"We're making good time," she finally said. "We shall arrive sooner than I expected. By the first light of day."

"Any of your crew could have delivered herbs to the cloister," Brian said, gazing at the star-studded sky. "Why is it so important that you do it yourself?"

"I've told—"

"You told me you are bringing herbs for the Dryads, but not why *you* must make the delivery."

She shrugged.

"Cathmor said you make an annual pilgrimage to the cloister whether you have anything to deliver or not."

"Aye, one of the Dryads is Mother Melanthe."

"The woman who raised you?"

Wynne nodded. "When my education was completed, she returned to the secluded life of the cloister. I like to visit her. I also like to go to the cloister because I feel close to the gods there. It's one of the most serene places I've ever been. The village itself is surrounded by beautiful apple orchards. And the priestesses are gentle women who dedicate their lives to helping others."

"You sound as if you envy them."

"In a way I do," she answered. "They seem to have found a peace that most people search for all their lives and never find."

Brian leaned his back against the side of the ship and studied Wynne. "But in finding this peace," he said, "have they missed out on many of the adventures that make life exciting?"

"Perhaps, lord, they have eliminated the pain of hurt and disillusionment from their lives."

"Perhaps." He straightened. "I've always believed that pain and hurt are part of life, lady. When we no longer experience them, we can no longer experience joy and happiness. We're no longer alive."

The ship lurched. A crash sounded in the cargo hold.

"A line broke!" a sailor shouted.

Trunks, chests, and sacks of food slid wildly about. Barrels rolled from side to side.

"Secure the cargo!" Wynne shouted as she and Brian dashed to the hold.

"My pony!" Lachlann yelled. He rushed from the railing to the center of the ship.

Brian leaped into the storage area amid the barrels. Wynne followed him.

"Get out of here," he shouted.

"You need me to help you save the pony," Wynne answered.

"Lachlann will do it."

"We need a walking plank," Wynne shouted.

The words were hardly out of her mouth before Cathmor grabbed Lachlann and pulled him way.

"Here, sire," he said. "I know what to do."

Kneeling on the main floor of the deck, the Irishman lowered the graded plank into the hold. As Brian led the pony to the plank, several sailors leaped into the hold and began to gather the scattered goods. Before they could fasten them with a new rope, the ship heaved again. The cargo broke loose once more. Wynne placed herself in front of one of the smaller trunks and stopped it from sliding. The ship dipped; the trunk slid forward, knocking Wynne off balance.

"The water barrel!" Cathmor yelled.

Wynne looked back to see the huge barrel teetering on its base. She tried to jump out of the way, but her mantle was caught beneath the trunk. She jerked, but it wouldn't come loose. She clawed at the brooch that closed her mantle about her neck.

"Wynne," Brian shouted, winding through the casks and chests, "unfasten your mantle."

"I can't," she yelled and tugged at the material. "The fall bent the pin."

As the barrel fell and careened across the hold, Brian threw himself between it and Wynne. "Why didn't you get out of here when I told you to?" he snapped.

"Because it's my ship." Her words were muffled, as he drew her tightly into his arms, protecting her with his body.

He tensed, waiting for the blow. He heard the grate of wood and metal on the planking; the swish of a rope.

"It's all right, mac Logan." Cathmor's voice rang out. "We have the barrel."

After Brian pushed the trunk off Wynne's mantle, he jerked her to her feet. Yanking his dirk from the scabbard, he cut the mantle from her shoulders and let it and the weapon drop to the floor. He anxiously ran his hands over her face, her shoulders, her arms. She winced.

"What is it?" he demanded.

"A scratch, I think."

"Let me see."

"I'm all right, mac Logan," she protested.

Ignoring her, he dragged her close to an overhead torch and examined her arm.

"It's not bad," he said, "but several long splinters have pierced the flesh. I'm going to have to remove them, else they'll become inflamed."

Her arm throbbing, Wynne nodded. She turned toward the walking plank, but Brian swept her into his arms and carried her out of the hold.

"Someone bring me a physician's chest," he said as he placed her on the deck.

Cathmor came running. "Here." He shoved a small herb chest close to Brian then he disappeared, returning shortly with another torch, which he handed to one of the crewmen.

"Hold it close to her arm, so the Highlander can see better," he said.

"Get me a sharp needle and some tweezers," Brian ordered.

For a man with big, callused hands, Cathmor had the lid of the chest unfastened and raised in record time. "Needle." He held it out for Brian.

"This is going to hurt," Brian said. "The splinters are big and deep. I'm going to have to dig them out."

"Go ahead and be done with it."

"Hold her upper arm, Lachlann," Brian said.

"That's not necessary," Wynne exclaimed.

"Not for you perhaps," Brian said, "but for me."

Lachlann clamped his hand around Wynne's

arm, and Brian began to probe. Wynne gritted her teeth together.

"I'm sorry," Brian murmured. "I know this must hurt, but they are deep."

"It feels as if the needle is digging into my bone."

"Tweezers," Brian ordered.

Tears stung her eyes as he pulled out the first splinter, then the second one.

"Ointment," he said.

Cathmor opened a large-necked jar and handed it to Brian. He dipped in a finger and spread a thick salve over her arm. Then he put a small bandage over the cuts.

After he tied it off, he pulled back and smiled. "There, lady, you're going to be all right."

"Thank you, lord. You're adept with the physician's instruments."

"I've pulled more splinters out of my children than you can imagine."

Brian was always a father first, Wynne thought. While the thought pleased her, it also left her with a sense of loss.

Having replaced the tweezers and needle back in the chest, Cathmor rose. "I'll take over the tiller, my lady," he said. "You need to rest."

"Aye."

"I'll lay out your sleeping bag."

Gathering the herb chest, Cathmor rose and moved to the stern. Wynne smiled wearily at Brian and leaned against the hull of the ship. He brushed a strand of hair from her face.

"You gave me a fright, lady."

"I gave myself one too." She covered his hands with hers, then leaned forward and pressed her mouth to his. Her lips moving against his, she whispered, "Thank you for saving me, lord."

She would have drawn back, but Brian's hands on her face kept her mouth against his.

"If this is the way you reward me for saving you, lady, I shall have to make sure that I save you again." His lips brushed hers. "And again."

Aware of her sailors watching them, Wynne caught Brian's hands and removed them from her face. "Enough, my lord Highlander. A maiden bestows one kiss only for each brave deed."

"What about a kiss for each of the splinters I pulled out?" Brian asked. "And one for the ointment—"

Wynne laughed softly. "No more kisses, lord. You have had sufficient."

"Nay, lady." His voice was husky.

"Your bed is laid," Cathmor snapped, and Wynne jumped. She hadn't realized he was so close.

Bracing herself on a palm, Wynne started to push to her feet. Already standing, Brian scooped her into his arms a second time. In the distance Cathmor frowned in disapproval.

" 'Tis time to tuck you in," Brian said.

Too tired to fight him, she murmured, "I'm not a child."

"I'm very much aware of that, lady."

Pleasure flowed warmly through Wynne. "It's been a long time since I've been tucked into bed."

" 'Tis a chore I shall enjoy performing." His breath wisped over her face. "If you will allow me to tuck myself in with you, I promise you a delightful night."

"Mac Logan—" Like a whip, Cathmor's voice lashed across the ship. "You and Lachlann will be sleeping over here."

Brian looked over his shoulder. With a sweep of his hand, the Irishman indicated that Brian's sleeping place was on the opposite side of the ship from Wynne.

Brian grinned tenderly as he tucked her into the sleeping bag. "Good night, lady." He kissed the tip of her nose. "May the angels watch over you during your sleep."

"May they also watch over you, lord."

As Brian walked away, Wynne sat up and gazed across the deck at him. Attached to the hull close by his sleeping bag was a torch, its light flickering over him. After he arranged his sleeping bag, he unfastened his mantle, draping it across his seamen's chest. Wynne propped herself on her uninjured arm and watched him undress. His weapon belts. Armbands. Torque.

He tugged the tunic from his breeches, and as he caught the hem with both hands to pull it over his head, he looked at Wynne. For a moment he stood still, his arms crisscrossed. She watched the play of emotion on his face, quick and ephemeral as firelight. He smiled at her, then slowly pulled the garment over his head.

Black hair swirled over his broad, muscular chest, down the hard plane of his stomach, and below the waistband of his trousers. He unfastened his girdle and dropped it to his feet. His trousers parted. They slid low on his hips. Wynne's breath caught in her chest. Brian stood staring across the ship at her. Still she did not lie down. He threw her a kiss; she caught it. His trousers slid over his hips, bunching at his feet and leaving him clad only in his leggings. Her gaze was riveted to his groin; she stared at the bulge of his arousal.

He held out his hand in silent invitation for her to join him. She licked her lips. He crooked his fingers. She wanted to go to him. Since Brian had touched her that morning, a fire of desire had been burning in her, growing to a fevered pitch. She must assuage it. And she could. All she had to do was rise and walk over to him. By all the gods, she wanted to . . . but she could not.

Marshaling all her willpower, she shook her head. He laughed softly, a rich, warm laughter devoid of mockery.

She lay down, thinking of Brian mac Logan until she went to sleep. And even then she dreamed about him.

Chapter 9

At dawn the next morning Wynne and the crew moored the *Honeysuckle* in the harbor at the Cloister of the Grove. In the distance the morning sun pushed up behind the Highland mountains, casting a golden glow over the community. Everyone had been awake for several hours; the crew was eager to unload the ship. Afterward they would take the morning meal with the priestesses.

While the crewmen, supervised by Cathmor and Wynne, quietly and efficiently went about their work, Brian helped Lachlann unload his pony and equipment. The two warriors walked up the quay, along a pathway, and away from the village. They stopped at the edge of the forest. They said goodbye, then Lachlann mounted and rode off.

Brian retraced his steps until he stood on the pathway beside the village gate. Shrouded in a silver-white mist, colored by the fragile light of breaking morn, the cloistered community looked mystical. The whitewashed dwellings had a pristine radiance; the straw on the roofs gleamed golden. Circular in design, the village radiated outward from a single round edifice with four doors. All other structures were laid out along four main streets.

The beginning point of three of the streets, those originating in the north, south, and west, were

large rectangular buildings situated close to the
village wall. One of these had several ovens in
front of it. A cooking house, Brian thought. The
fourth street, much wider than the other three, had
its starting point in the east with a U-shaped
building. All four streets converged at the round
edifice in the center of the village.

Activity had begun in the religious commune,
and as the day became brighter, shadows turned
into discernible shapes. Robed and cowled figures—priestesses, Brian figured—were moving
briskly up and down the streets, some going out
to the fields and orchards that surrounded the village. Others tended to the domestic animals within
the village walls, and yet others started fires in the
ovens. Two figures moved into the huge central
building.

One dryad, a tall woman in a long white tunic
with a sleeveless and flowing overrobe of vibrant
green, walked through a gate into the orchard. Although the hood and robe concealed her face, her
commanding presence arrested Brian's attention.
She seemed somehow familiar.

Earlier Wynne had explained the divisions
within the cloister to him, and he recognized that
this was the high priestess. Bards, or poets, wore
blue robes; the ovates, compilers of knowledge,
wore green; and the priestesses, philosophers,
judges, and advisers to tribal leaders wore white.
The high priestess was distinctive from all the others. A green girdle cinched her white tunic, and
she wore a green overrobe.

The high priestess had disappeared into the orchard. The apple trees were in full bloom, their
tiny white buds glistening with morning dew and
reflecting the golden light of early day. The wind
blew, and a gentle fragrance permeated the air.

The rustle of apple leaves sounded like the tinkle of tiny bells.

Brian saw a movement in the orchard and thought it was the green-robed figure. Instead, an older woman stepped off the pathway, through the gate. Stoop-shouldered, she shuffled slowly and used a walking staff. A satchel strapped over both shoulders rested on her back. Her white hair was grizzled, and her tunic was woven of a coarse, drab brown material. She reminded Brian of Feich, the healer and seer of the kingdom of Northern Scotland. Of course, he knew it couldn't be Feich. She was too elderly to have traveled so far. Brian was amazed at how familiar people and villages seemed.

The door to one of the smaller lodges opened. Another elderly lady stepped out, holding the cowl of her white robe on her head. She grabbed a walking stick leaning against the exterior wall of the house and started toward the quay. When she reached Brian, she stopped and looked him over, her gaze lingering on his sword and dagger.

"Who are you?" she demanded, her blue eyes piercing.

"Brian mac Logan of the kingdom of Northern Scotland."

"This is a cloister for priestesses," she said in an aggravated tone. "What are you doing here?" Before Brian could reply, she added, "Don't tell me, sire, that our high priestess has engaged your services?"

"Nay, good mother," Brian replied. "I came with the seafarer."

He glanced over at the quay to see Wynne walking back and forth among huge jars, barrels, sacks, and trunks of goods. She had taken off her mantle and her weapons and wore only her oiled-leather

clothing. Her hair, braided in a single plait, hung
down her back. She had tied a red scarf around
her forehead to form a sweat band. The ends fluttered in the breeze.

"Aye." The priestess nodded, then yelled,
"Gwynneth!"

Gwynneth turned and waved, but she remained
where she was, helping the crewmen unload the
ships. At the moment her attention was directed
toward a large trunk. When she rested her hands
on her waist, Brian's attention was drawn to her
hips and long legs, enhanced by the leather trousers. The longer he was around her, the stronger
his desire grew.

That he was so infatuated with the seafarer irritated him. He was behaving like a lad who had
just discovered his manhood. Earlier Brian had
criticized Wynne for giving in to her womanly
emotions, and here he was a prisoner of his own
emotions. Thoughts of Wynne had taken over his
mind.

"Brian mac Logan," the priestess snapped,
bringing Brian's attention back to her. "Your name
is familiar, Highlander." She smiled abruptly and
cited the genealogy of the Logan name. When she
was finished, she said, "Aye, I remember you,
Highlander. You're one of High King Malcolm's
headmen. An Irishman raided your village and
stole the sacred Girdle of Mayo."

"Aye," he replied.

Hearing footsteps, he turned to see Wynne approaching. Smiling, she waved at him and the
priestess. When she drew abreast of them she said,
"Good morrow, Mother Barbara. 'Tis good to see
you looking so well."

"Gwynneth, 'tis good to see you. Thanks be to
the gods, you have arrived not a moment too

soon!" The priestess moved toward Wynne, her robe swishing about her ankles. Recalcitrant strands of hair escaped the cowl. "You have the herbs?"

"Aye," Wynne replied, waving a hand toward the ship. "They're on the quay now. We'll have them in your storehouse shortly."

"Wynne!" another woman shouted.

Brian turned. A young priestess, robed in pale blue, ran out of the village gate, down the pathway to the quay. Her cowl had fallen back to reveal shining black hair and a glowing face. Breathless, she said, "The fabric, Wynne. Did you get the fabric we requested?"

"Aye," Wynne replied. "And the imported wine."

"Imported wine!" Mother Barbara exclaimed. Horrified, she rounded on the young nun. "Agnes, you're a novitiate. Who gave you the authority to order imported wine?"

Agnes stumbled back. "The superior mother."

"I do declare!" Mother Barbara shook her head disapprovingly. "Raven is entirely too young to be the superior mother of this order. Only this morning she was in the sacred grove rather than in her apartment praying."

"Perhaps, kind mother," Wynne said, "she was praying in the orchard."

"That's not where the high priestess prays," Barbara exclaimed. "She has no regard for tradition. Ordering wine! For shame! I shall have to speak to the other members of the Council of the Grove."

"Sacred mother," Agnes said, her countenance downcast, "we didn't order much. Just enough to have a glass with our meals and every once in a while when we celebrate a special occasion. Raven is a wonderful superior mother. You're jealous because—"

"Not jealous," the elderly priestess interjected, thumping her walking stick on the ground for emphasis. "Concerned. You younger women are changing the order so much that soon I won't know why I joined. And you never ask us older ones. Because you're young, you assume you know what is best."

"Now, Barbara, what's the matter?" Another priestess, also wearing a white robe, joined them. Although she was mature, she wasn't nearly as old as the sacred mother.

Barbara turned. "Melanthe! Oh, Melanthe, I'm so glad to see you. Agnes said Raven ordered imported wine. Can you believe it?"

"Aye, sacred one, I do." Melanthe spoke quietly. "I was one of the councilwomen who advised her to do so."

As if she were a waterskin suddenly emptied, Barbara wilted. "You—you did?"

"When I was a young novitiate, a wise ovate told me that a little wine is good for the body. It cleanses the heart and purifies the blood." Melanthe's brown eyes twinkled. "And you were that ovate."

"Er . . . well . . ." Barbara's cheeks turned scarlet. "Aye, wine does have medicinal qualities."

"Then, sacred mother," Melanthe said, "would you consider letting us keep the wine?"

Barbara thought for a moment, then nodded. "Aye, Melanthe, I think this would be a wise decision. But . . ." Her eyes gleamed with resolve. "I shall speak to Raven about the changes she is bringing about. They worry me."

Melanthe looked at Wynne and Brian. "Holy

mother, we shouldn't be discussing our personal business in front of our guests."

Barbara gave them a cursory look, then sighed. "Nay, we shouldn't."

Melanthe, turning her attention to Wynne, smiled.

"Good morrow, Mother Melanthe," Wynne said softly. She held out her hands.

Melanthe clasped them. "Good morrow to you, Wynne. I'm glad you're here. I always look forward to your visits."

"Melanthe—" Barbara spoke sharply. "You and Gwynneth may talk later. At the moment I need to start my new potions. Gwynneth, let's see to getting my herbs moved to the storehouse."

Grinning, Wynne said, "Aye, good mother."

Melanthe turned loose of Wynne's hands, but she looked at her longer before she settled her gaze on Brian. Having seen only her profile, Brian was startled by Melanthe's haunting beauty. Her golden-brown eyes seemed to be wellsprings of deep-seated sorrow.

"This is Lord Brian mac Logan, bestman to High King Malcolm of the kingdom of Northern Scotland and headman of House Logan," Wynne said. "And Lord Brian, this is Mother Melanthe, one of the superior mothers of the Council of the Grove."

"My lord," Melanthe murmured with a slight nod. " 'Tis a pleasure to meet you."

"Likewise, my lady," Brian said. Taking her hand, he kissed it and bowed low.

Melanthe's brow furrowed for a moment as if she were deep in thought. Then her eyes widened. "You're the headman of the village that was raided by the Irishmen."

"Aye."

"What are you doing here with Gwynneth?" Before Brian could answer, Melanthe turned to Wynne. As if she were praying the words were not true, she said, "He's hired you to take him to Ireland?"

"Aye," Wynne replied. "To Donegal Bay, mother, which is north of Sligo. I shan't be sailing into O'Illand country."

"Come, Agnes," Mother Barbara said, "let's you and I show them where to take our goods." Leaning heavily on her staff, she walked down the pathway to the quay, the young novitiate following.

Leading Wynne in the opposite direction, away from Brian and closer to the village gate, Melanthe said, "You can't go, Gwynneth."

"I've already had this argument with Cathmor, my mother. I'm not going to repeat it with you. I *am* going."

Melanthe stared at Wynne for a moment before she said, "We'll see, my daughter."

The two women continued to engage in a silent duel of wills before Wynne turned and walked down the pathway back to the quay and her work. She shouted a few instructions, and soon several young men, carrying chests and satchels of goods on their shoulders, were following Barbara and Agnes to the village. One of them brought Wynne's cloak to her.

Slipping it over her shoulders, Wynne asked Melanthe, "How is Raven?"

"She's as fine as can be expected," Melanthe replied. "Many in the cloister are unhappy with her appointment as high priestess. They claim she is too young. Naturally Raven is sad because they don't trust her." Melanthe smiled. "But she's a strong-willed woman, and will prevail."

"Aye, she will," Wynne agreed.

"Speaking of Raven's strong will," Melanthe said, "she has decided that we should begin bartering our jewelry. Our first shipment will go to the Shelter Stone Cloister in Glenmuir."

"Your jewelry?" Gwynneth exclaimed. "You're going to trade your beautiful hand-crafted jewelry?"

She clasped the gold necklace she wore around her neck, one that Raven had made many years ago. It was a gold filigree medallion inset with a red gemstone. It held great magic. Raven had also designed and crafted the hilt of Wynne's sword. Like the medallion, it was inset with red gemstones. In addition, Raven had engraved an inscription, a magical *ogham fedha*, on it. Wynne felt that she was indeed protected by the gods.

The dryads of the Cloister of the Grove were renowned goldsmiths, their jewelry some of the most sought-after in all the kingdoms. Considering it sacred to the gods, the priestesses crafted it for their own use and for a few special gifts. It was so costly that only a few people could afford to purchase it. Until now had it never been available for barter.

Melanthe laughed softly. "Aye, Raven finally convinced the Council of the Grove that we must do this for our order to succeed."

"You're not going to barter the special pieces?" Wynne asked.

"Nay, not the ones that have the secret compartments and the sacred messages," Melanthe replied. "Raven believes that we can use the jewelry to trade for items that we cannot grow or produce ourselves."

"I'm glad she has changed her mind," Wynne said. "The jewelry you design is much too beautiful not to be shared."

Melanthe headed toward the village, and Wynne fell into step beside her. Brian followed at a distance.

"When you have finished unloading," Melanthe said, "come by my cell and I'll give you the casket of jewelry that you're to transport. Perhaps you can share the morning meal with us."

"Perhaps."

Melanthe looked over her shoulder at Brian. "He's a handsome warrior. Is he married?"

Knowing the direction of Melanthe's thoughts, Wynne grinned. "His wife is dead."

They took several more steps before Melanthe said dryly, "I haven't blessed your trip to Eire, but perhaps the gods have."

Wynne cut a sideways glance at her. "Mother, please don't misunderstand the situation."

"'Tis time you found a man and married, Wynne. I have been remiss in my duties as your foster mother." She paused and frowned. "I sometimes think it is my fault that you and Raven—"

"Nay," Wynne said. "You were a good mother to me. What I did was not your fault."

"Your father, your sister, I, all of us share the blame," Melanthe said. "You were our child of the summer. We loved you dearly, and whatever you desired we gave to you. We tried to compensate for your mother's death; instead we spoiled you."

"Aye, mother, all of you spoiled me," Wynne said, thinking back seven years ago when she and Raven had been living together and sharing a sleeping chamber in their father's Great Hall. Wynne's selfish behavior had ruined that relationship. "But I knew what I was doing when I chose Alba for my husband, when I begged my father to let me marry him."

"Melanthe," Barbara shouted from inside the village, "I need your help with the herbs."

"I must go now," Melanthe told Wynne. "We'll talk later. I promised Raven I would help her select the jewelry for bartering."

"Tell Raven that I would like a blessing before I sail to Ireland."

A shadow darkening her eyes, Melanthe nodded. " 'Tis good that you are here now. Raven has decided to take a vow of silence."

"*A vow of silence!*" Wynne cried out. "She's already taken a vow of celibacy. Isn't that enough? You must talk to her, Mother. Don't let her do this!"

"I have spoken with her," Melanthe replied, "as I did to you when you chose to become a seafarer rather than join me here at the cloister. I gave Raven the same advice I gave you."

" 'Whatever you decide, weigh the advantage against the disadvantage. Then make your choice,' " Wynne said, repeating Melanthe's words from memory.

"Aye," Melanthe said. "The decision is hers. When you see her later," Melanthe added, "you may talk to her about it."

Heavyhearted, Wynne nodded.

"Now I must go." Melanthe waved to Brian and called over her shoulder, "Good morrow, my lord. I hope to see you again before you leave."

"Aye, good mother." He caught up to Wynne. "Who is Raven?"

"The high priestess of the Cloister of the Grove," she answered, still reeling from Melanthe's announcement.

As if Wynne had summoned her, the high priestess, clad in a green robe, strolled down the pathway through the orchard toward the village gate. She stopped, touched one of the low hanging branches of the tree, then looked up at the hill on which Wynne and Brian stood. Her cowl was pulled forward so that her face was hidden in dark shadows.

Wynne raised her hand and waved. The priestess waved back; then lowered her hands and tucked them into the loose sleeves of the robe. Bowing her head, she once again walked toward the village.

"Are all of these priestesses celibates?" Brian asked.

"Most of those who live here in the cloister are," Wynne replied, "but it's their choice to be."

"Taking a vow of celibacy seems unnatural to me," Brian said.

"You would think so," Wynne said.

"But adding to it a vow not to talk to people—" He shrugged and shook his head in disbelief.

"Once Raven has sworn the oath, she can speak only to her ovate advisory or when she presides over special ceremonial functions for the cloister. For emergency situations, she can converse with the cloister council using their special sign language."

" 'Tis not the life for me, lady."

" 'Tis a harsh one, lord," Wynne agreed.

"One of their own making." Brian was unsympathetic.

"Circumstances forced Raven to make this choice."

"Why?"

"She was betrayed."

"By a man?" Brian guessed.

"By a man and by a woman, her dearest friend. By the man who was promised to her in marriage, and by the woman who stole his affections and married him herself."

"Indeed that must have been a hard blow. So in her pain and weakness she has chosen to hide from life," he said.

"Raven is one of the strongest people I know," Wynne snapped.

Brian's eyes narrowed, and he searched her face. "Who is Raven?" After a moment of silence, he guessed, "She's more than the high priestess of the cloister, isn't she?"

"She's my sister."

Chapter 10

❧

"**Y**our sister," Brian repeated softly.

"Aye, my older sister by three winters."

"She is a mature woman, then."

"Aye, she has seen six and twenty winters."

"And you are three and twenty?" Brian said.

Gwynneth was a mature woman also, Brian realized. Because Sorcha had been several winters older than Gwynneth, he had not thought of age until this moment. Strangely, when he had first met Sorcha, their main concern had been producing an heir to carry on their families' names. Now Brian had his heirs, three daughters and a son, and he no longer gave procreation primary importance.

High King Malcolm did. Brian liked and respected his high king, but of late Malcolm had become high-handed in his demand for Brian to make a political marriage, to produce an heir that would bind their country to another as allies, and to further Malcolm's goal of unifying the kingdoms of Northern Scotland. Although Brian understood and agreed with Malcolm, even shared his goals, he had been reluctant to marry again. Certainly the woman Malcolm had suggested had not interested Brian. Still, Malcolm had pointed out, if Brian did not like his bride, he could take another bedmate.

Until he had seen Wynne swimming yesterday morning, Brian had not even considered the idea of a bedmate. Now he did.

"Melanthe, Raven's mother, was my father's first wife," Wynne said. "Two winters after Raven was born, my father obtained a bill of divorcement from Melanthe and married my mother."

"Your family seems to have a history of divorcement."

"Aye. Once the royal child was born, it was acceptable for him to leave Melanthe, but it wasn't acceptable for me to leave Alba. And Melanthe was a better person than Alba."

Brian and Wynne meandered toward the orchard along the pathway that followed the village wall.

"Have you noticed, lord, that men often beat woman without being punished? Most times they are lauded for being good masters. Women who beat men are severely punished, maimed for life, sometimes executed."

"Aye, lady," Brian answered. "Man is the superior creature. Even nature teaches us that. Always the male of the species is the larger, the more beautiful, and the more cunning. Men are the hunters and warriors, the providers and the protectors. Rather than criticizing us, you should be grateful that we take care of you."

Wynne rounded on Brian. "I can do without the care Alba would have provided." She paused, then asked, "Did you beat your wife, mac Logan?"

"Nay, I had no cause to."

"Were you ever angry with her?" Wynne persisted. "Did she do things that you didn't approve of?"

A small grin tugged at his lips. "Aye, lady, many were the times. Sorcha could push me to the very edge, and she did so regularly. She even took perverse pleasure at times in pushing me *over* the edge."

"And you have a fierce temper, do you not?"

"Very black."

"So you *were* angry at her. Some men might have considered that cause for a beating. Did you beat her?"

Angrily, Brian glared at her. "Nay, I had no desire to hurt her. Besides, seafarer, I love . . . loved Sorcha." He gave Wynne a lopsided smile. "Much to my chagrin, lady, I soon learned that in most cases Sorcha was right."

"I wish all men thought like you, lord. Our world would have one less evil to fight." Almost without taking a breath, she added, "Alba beat me because he was angry at himself. If Honey had not rescued me, I would have been either dead or maimed for life. Alba would have probably gotten a bill of divorcement, remarried, and I would have been left a cripple, a ward of my father for the remainder of my life."

"I think the assembly was wrong in its judgment, Gwynneth," Brian said. "Even if you were not a virgin when Alba came to you, he thought you were. He should have been more gentle with you. Only a cruel man will rupture a maidenhood without tenderness. 'Tis no pleasure for either when a man hurts a woman in the taking." He gazed down at her. "Because of Alba, are you fearful of mating again?"

Wynne stopped walking. Deliberately avoiding his gaze, she stared at the ground. "I have never been mated."

He caught her chin with the tips of his fingers and guided it up so that they were looking at each other.

"I am yet a maiden, lord."

Wynne felt Brian's hand tremble on her chin; she couldn't read the expression on his face.

"No one has mated with you, lady?"

She shook her head.

"Has Alba caused you to fear coupling?"

"I'm not exactly fearful," she confessed, "but I am wary. There are times when I—when my body—" Embarrassed, she broke off.

He spoke for her. "They are times when you want to mate, when need and desire course strongly through you. They build up until you think you'll burst in two, and you get frustrated and angry with yourself, with everyone else."

She nodded.

" 'Tis normal for a man and woman to feel this way, lady, else we would not reproduce." His eyes twinkled. "Else we would miss out on a great pleasure."

Removing his hand from her chin, he caught her hands and held them gently, warmly.

"I am a hardened and seasoned warrior, madam, well into my life."

"Aye." Wynne smiled, her gaze going to his silver temples.

"As the white hair attests," he said dryly.

"I like it," she assured him. "It makes you look even more handsome, my lord."

They shared a deep, open smile.

"As I was saying, my lady, I have not had a woman in my life since Sorcha died, and only Sorcha before that."

His confession reached the deepest part of Wynne's soul.

"I do not wish to ruin our business agreement, madam, and I shall honor my word to keep my distance, but I want to mate with you. I would like to be the first man in your life, to teach you the ways between a man and a woman. I would like you to be the first woman in my life since Sorcha."

"If I—if I were going to mate with someone, mac Logan, I think it would be you, but I'm not."

"Although you want to."

"Aye."

Smiling, he released her hands. "Then, lady, I shall have to keep enticing you until I succeed."

"Or give up."

His smile broadened. "I never give up, lady. Whether a virtue or a fault, tenacity is one of my strongest characteristics. I always get what I want, lady."

His promise excited her.

They resumed walking.

"What happened to your family after your father and Melanthe divorced?" Brian asked.

"Melanthe left, taking Raven with her. She had always been a Dryad, but after the divorcement she chose to live in a cloister. Two winters after my birth, my mother died, and my father asked Melanthe to become his wife again. She refused. If she could have her own home, she said, she would return to the village and raise Raven and me. Of course, Father insisted that Raven and I live in the Great Hall." Smiling, she added, "We shared a bower to ourselves until Raven reached her sixteenth winter. Then Father allowed her to move into the Great Hall. But even after that she would sneak back to the bower, and we would share secrets."

They reached a small brook, and stopped. Brian sat on a large boulder, and Wynne bent, picking up a handful of stones. Choosing one, she skimmed it over the pond.

"You're good," Brian said.

"Aye," she replied. "Melanthe taught me and Raven how to do it. When we were children, we laid wagers on who was the best."

"And you always won," Brian guessed. He picked up a pebble and tossed it. Both watched it skip the water's surface.

"I always thought I won," Wynne answered, "but I never knew if I was better than Raven or not." She tossed another rock. Another, and another. "We were happy, Raven and I." She rubbed her hands down the sides of her trousers. "If only she could have married the man she wanted."

"Do you carry that guilt on your shoulders also?" Brian asked. "Nothing you could have done could have prevented another woman from stealing Raven's betrothed from her."

Wynne threw another rock. "I was the woman who betrayed her, Alba the man."

"By the gods, madam! You did that to your own sister?"

"Aye, lord." Wynne had run out of tears long ago; now all she felt was a deep-seated grief that gnawed at her day and night, a sorrow that had not eased with the passing of time, a guilt that had not been washed away with crying and endless pleas for forgiveness. "I shamed her. I stole her betrothed from her and married before she did."

"That was indeed dishonorable, lady," he said.

"Aye, mac Logan, and there is no way I can undo the harm that I did. Forever our lives have been changed. I was disgraced and made an outcast, and Raven became a recluse." Wynne walked to the edge of the pond and gazed out at the water. "The irony, lord, is that Alba didn't love her, but Raven had already spoken to my father, letting him know that she wanted Alba for her husband. She felt she was quickly passing the marriageable age.''

Wynne snapped a twig from a nearby bush and pulled it through her fingers. Leaves fluttered to the ground.

"I was young and spoiled, lord, accustomed to having my way. Everyone—my father, Melanthe, and Raven—all pampered me. Whatever I wanted, I expected and received. I wanted Alba.''

The wind blew, scattering the leaves, swirling them into a circle at her feet.

"Alba was young, wild, impulsive . . . and very handsome. He was so different from my father's warriors. From the first minute I saw him, I wanted him. I thought he wanted me too.''

She glanced over at Brian. He was staring at the brook, but his expression was set, his lips drawn in a tight line. She stepped closer to the stream, kicking pebbles into the rushing water.

"I went to my father and told him that Alba and I were in love. I demanded that he break Raven's betrothal so we could be wed. Father tried to dissuade me, as did Raven and Melanthe, but I refused." She paused. "Not even when Raven came to me in tears and begged me. She was crying that day, mac Logan, as I had never seen her cry before." Softly she added, "I have never seen her cry since."

Wynne had never shared these painful details with anyone before. She disliked herself at the moment for sharing them with Brian, especially when she knew that he condemned her. Strangely, she wanted him to know. He was the one man to whom she wished to make her confession. Being judged by others had hurt her, but she had learned to live with their disapproval. She didn't want to

be wrongly judged by Brian. His opinion
mattered.

"Raven explained that she was the elder and
should be wed first. I knew it, but in my selfish-
ness I didn't care. She told me that my actions
would humiliate her. Again I brushed her pleas
and arguments aside. She had always given in to
my desires before. I couldn't understand why this
should be any different."

But it was! It had changed Wynne's entire life.
She gazed at the beautiful blue pool and wished
she could shed her clothes and dive in. She
wanted to cleanse herself of the guilt. But no matter how often she bathed or swam, she knew she
could never escape the past. Her burden was
deeply embedded in her heart and could not be
washed away.

"I have no excuse for my actions, lord," Wynne
said, "except I had seen only sixteen winters."

"Nay, lady, that is no excuse. Many women
have borne one or two bairns by that age."

"I was too immature to realize how deeply I
would hurt and humiliate Raven. By the time I
did, it was too late. She had taken refuge in the
Cloister of the Grove." Turning to look at him,
she said, "She's found peace, lord, but I haven't.
Perhaps the only way I will find it is to enter the
cloister like Raven."

He shook his head, his gray eyes holding hers.
"Nay, lady, you don't have to enter ... you're
already there."

Surprised, she stared at him.

"Your bower, madam, is your cloister, your
treasures your gods." He rose and moved toward
her. "And it is all the sanctuary you need." He
waved toward the sequestered village. "This may

be the right life for your stepmother and your sister, but it is not the right life for you."

"You presume to know what I need?"

He caught her hand and pulled her between his legs.

"Nay, but I know what you don't need. You are a lusty woman."

"So you say."

"Aye, you have a passion for life, lady." Again he smiled. "Since I am a lusty man, madam, I recognize the same characteristic in others." Gently he added, "You remind me of myself when I had seen no more winters than you."

"Of yourself?"

Had she seen passion in his eyes, she would have been dubious. But his compassion and understanding touched her.

"My story is different from yours, but I too was rejected."

"How?" she whispered, spellbound by his words.

He guided her over to a boulder and sat down beside her.

"I was born a small and sickly babe. Against my mother's anguished pleas, my father disowned me."

She gasped softly in shock.

"Refusing to bless me or to give me a name, he abandoned me in the dead of winter. His servants carried me from his Great Hall," Brian said, his voice devoid of emotion, "and set me out to die."

His confession shed light on parts of his personality that Wynne had hitherto found perplexing. She now understood his propensity to help children, his blind fury where they were concerned. In her mind's eye she saw him holding the tiny

bairn, now called Millicent, in his arms and giving
her suck from the beaker and glove nipple.

"Feich, the seer, rescued me," Brian went on.
"She kept me in her home until I had seen five
winters. I remember her as a stern woman, but she
was determined that I would live and be strong."

"Not only are you strong, my lord," Wynne said
softly, "but you are one of the biggest men I have
ever seen."

And one of the most thoughtful!

Brian smiled. "Although Feich knew she was
courting death, she returned me to my father's
lodge during my fifth winter. She told my father
the gods had a special mission for me. Then she
appointed me a guardian from among his warriors
and spoke a curse on my father and the warrior
should either not accept me. Fearing the prophet-
ess, they obeyed."

He sighed. "I became one of my father's warriors. Over and over again, as winter followed
winter, I proved myself to be the best and strongest of them all. Everyone acknowledged that I was
the champion of the house, of the clan, of the entire kingdom. . . . Everyone except my father."

The memories rushed in to settle heavily on Brian's shoulders and to prick at his heart. He remembered the years he had spent proving himself,
fighting champions, defeating them, almost being
killed in the process. His reputation grew, and he
was feared by many, respected by most. Others of
less renown and valor were recognized and honored. They received the hero's portion. Not Brian.
He never gained the respect or approval of his
father.

"No matter how I distinguished myself as a
warrior, my father never accepted me, never even
recognized me. He truly hated me and wished that

I had died when he set me out. I was a constant
reminder that he had made a mistake in judgment,
that I was the stronger and wiser son. On his
deathbed, my father declared my younger brother
his heir. He left me no inheritance."

"Yet you became headman of the house."

"Aye, my brother was not a wise man and refused to listen to the counselors my father had
gathered for him. Wanting more land for House
Logan, he waged war with an adjoining kingdom,
a small one indeed, but it was strong and united.
The counselors and I advised him not to fight. He
didn't listen to us. In the ensuing battle he and a
majority of our warriors were killed, and I was
critically wounded. I returned as the only son of
my father, but even then, the house was reluctant
to accept me as their headman because my father
had cast me out."

"But he had accepted you back," Wynne
pointed out.

"Nay, lady. Out of fear of retribution from the
seer's magic, he let me live in his lodge as he did
any other warrior. But he never accepted me as
the child of his loins. To his dying day my father
never recognized me as his son." For a long moment Brian stared at her. "Unlike you, I am still
my father's outcast."

Her own grief forgotten, Wynne leaned closer
to him. She wanted to console him as he had done
her. Now she was beginning to understand Brian
mac Logan. The child in him still sought accep-
tance, approval. The warrior rescued and protected the innocent child. Oddly, while she wanted
to touch his face, his arm, his body, she wanted
to reach his heart and soul, to assuage his grief.

"I am truly sorry, my lord. I had no idea—"

" 'Tis over and done with, lady. I laid it to rest

a long time ago. Feich appealed to the counselors. She told them that she was next in line of succession for the High Seat. Once she was the headwoman, she formally adopted me. Then she stepped down. Through her, my lady, I finally claimed my rightful inheritance."

"You became headman of House Logan."

"Aye, but never son to my father, and my children will never be counted in my mother's genealogy. Always we will be a part of Feich's."

"I'm sorry, lord."

"Don't be, lady. I am proud to be counted as Feich's son. Because of her I have learned to turn loose of the past, as you must learn to do. Running away and hiding are not the answer."

Wynne smiled. "You think a cloistered Dryad hides from life?"

"Aye, my lady, I do. I think it is often fear more than holiness that persuades people to separate themselves from others and associate only with those people who conform to their dictates and judgments."

"I disagree," Wynne said.

"Whether we agree or not," Brian said, "you truly are not meant for a sequestered life. You have much to give the world, my lady. Don't hide your sunshine behind veils and walls."

"You think I am sunshine, my lord?"

He nodded and watched a smile glisten in the depths of her eyes before it trembled on the corners of her mouth. Then it captured her lips to transform her into the beautiful woman whom he knew as the Lady of Summer. A morning breeze blew through the apple orchard, whipping hair loose from her braid and whisking it around her face. As he had done once before, he leaned over and gently removed the strands.

Her creamy skin was smooth and silky. He let his fingers linger. A bolt of desire smashed through him. He felt her tremble, saw her eyes darken, and knew that she returned his desire. But she would not necessarily mate with him.

Yesterday he had thought she was a woman of the world, one of easy virtue upon whom he need only press his suit. Today, after hearing her confession, he knew that Wynne had a right to be frightened, of herself, of men. Alba had done her a great injustice, and if he were not dead, Brian would have killed him himself.

He was beginning to understand this woman who had fought the world single-handedly, and his admiration for her increased. Before, Brian had wanted her body, anticipating a pleasurable mating. Now already his feelings for Gwynneth were undergoing a change. He still felt lust for her, but it was tempered with respect and admiration. He was beginning to understand why she had chosen to be a warrior. Although she had betrayed her sister in a way that some people might consider unforgivable, Brian didn't condemn her.

"Take your solace in your bower, Gwynneth," he said. "You're much too beautiful to hide in one of those hideous cowled robes."

"Do you truly think so, mac Logan?"

"You're more than beautiful, my lady. You're strong and valiant. Good of heart."

Wynne touched his chin. He caught her hands in his, then lowered them and looked at her palms. They were slightly callused from wielding weapons and steering the ship.

"Do you find them ugly?" she asked.

"Nay, lady. They are part of you, part of what you are."

He brought her palm to his mouth and kissed

the pad at the base of each finger. He made her
feel desirable without stripping her of her war-
riorhood. He made her feel cherished. It had been
so from the beginning. Picking the flower for her.
Comforting her when he had feared she was falling over the precipice. Swinging her around in his
arms. Lying with her on the bed. Looking at her
now.

He leaned down and lightly kissed her forehead.
The brush of his lips was tantalizing. Wynne
opened her mouth and held her breath. She felt as
if she were separated from her body. Slowly he
placed light kisses over her face, down her neck,
back and forth across her collarbone.

"So lovely. Your blue-gray eyes have begun to
haunt me day and night."

"My lord." Her voice was husky.

"Such elusive beauty. Sometimes your eyes are
blue, sometimes gray. Always mysterious and
beautiful."

She lifted her face, and he brushed his thumb
over her lips.

"Have you ever truly been kissed, lass, like a
man kisses a woman?"

"You've . . . kissed me."

"Little pecks. Nothing more," he said. "Let me
show you how a man kisses a woman."

"Aye." Her voice trembled.

He put his arms around her and gently pulled
her into his embrace. Tight, warm, and tender. She
felt the thud of his heart, the warmth of his breath.
Already she was trembling, and he was only holding her. His head lowered, his mouth touching
hers. As he lightly brushed his lips back and forth
over hers, he rekindled a slow-burning fire
within Wynne.

She leaned into him, her hands biting into the

hard muscularity of his shoulders. His mouth settled, and his lips, hot and wet, pressed against
hers. Wynne had never tasted anything so wonderful in her entire life. Brian's kisses were a subtlety unlike any that Mistress Sheila had ever
cooked or that Wynne had ever sampled. Heady,
thinking perhaps she would lose consciousness,
she closed her eyes and gave herself up to the
sensation.

"Would you like more pleasure?" Brian asked.

"Is there more?" she asked dreamily.

He chuckled. "Much more."

His tongue ran along the indentation of her
mouth, back and forth, sending more splendid
emotions spiraling through her. It caressed her
lips; it teased them open.

"Wider," he whispered.

She did, and his tongue slipped inside her
mouth. She gasped; she trembled anew. Desire
flickered through her, taking up residence in her
lower body, growing hotter and hotter. His lips
pressed harder on hers; she pressed back. She
clasped him to her, unwilling to let anything come
between them. She felt his tongue as it touched
hers, as it explored her mouth, claiming it for himself, for the passion he had awakened in her.

When he finally raised his head, she looked at
him through star-glazed eyes. "Mac Logan," she
murmured.

His eyes were also glazed, his breathing ragged.
"Perhaps, lady, since we have become intimate
enough to share kisses, you could call me Brian."

"Brian," she said.

"Are you sure you haven't kissed before, lady?"

Her eyes rounded. "Nay."

"You have set me afire with longing, lady."

"You were afire with longing before you met me," Wynne said.

"Nay, lady, I had not thought of mating with a woman until I saw you swimming in your pool."

"I like kissing, lord."

"Then we shall have to kiss many times," he promised.

"Let's do."

With a feral growl, Brian pulled her tightly against him and kissed her again, a long, passionate kiss that seemed to go on forever. Wynne was breathless when they parted. Her eyes glowed, and her lips were pink and swollen. She touched them with her fingers.

"I do like kissing, lord. And I would like to practice often."

"I shall be more than happy to comply, my lady," Brian said, "but I must warn you that kissing leads to mating."

Some of the glow died out of Wynne's eyes.

"I am a man, lady, who is accustomed to assuaging his appetites. I shall be more than happy to teach you to kiss, to teach you the intricacies of mating, as long as you realize that ultimately we shall mate."

She licked her lips. "I—I need to think about this, lord."

"Aye, lady, you do."

Catching her face in his hands, Brian brought it up to his. He slid his fingers over her temples to tangle in her hair. The heel of his hand rested against her chin, the callused palms against her temple. His fingers brushed lightly against her head to send tremors through her.

"You frequently liken me to the fearful warrior of the Northland," he murmured.

"Aye."

His eyes, darkened by passion, searched her face.

"You're trembling. Out of fear or out of—"

"Excitement," she whispered back. "Desire."

"You like the wild barbarian in me, lady."

"I fear the dark side of you, my lord, yet I am drawn to it."

"Perhaps, my lady, there is a wild woman hiding inside you."

"I fear so."

Wynne felt as if she were walking the edge of the cliffs by her village. She had felt this exhilaration before, when he had told her about the legend of the flower pollen, when he had flirted with her. But now the sensation intensified. She was on the very edge of the precipice, swaying . . . wanting to fall. Her blood rushed through her body, roared in her ears.

"I pray that one day this wild woman will come to this wild man and mate with him," Brian said.

"What if this wild woman does, and what if she falls in love and wants to marry the warrior?"

Brian moved away from her. "If the warrior loves her, he will want to take her as his first wife." He paused. "If I am the warrior, lady, I can promise you marriage, but only as a second wife, which would give you my name and my protection."

"But no rights of my own, and my children would not be direct heirs to the High Seat. Why could I not be the first wife?"

"My liege is pressing me into a political marriage."

Although Wynne was disappointed with Brian's answer, she understood political marriages. They were the backbone of kingdoms and alliances. It was in Malcolm's best interests to bond Brian to him in more than friendship.

"I would take you as my second wife or as a bedmate," Brian said.

"Nay, Brian, I would not accept either."

"Malcolm has already suggested a possible bride for me. A Pict princess who will bring prestige and wealth to House Logan."

"Another ally for the kingdom of Northern Scotland," she added softly.

"Aye, but I do not wish to discuss that," Brian said. "You and I are here now, together. We are all that matters."

"I wish we were all that mattered, my lord, but we are not. We have met too late. The fates have already ordained our lives, and I fear our life lines shall not be woven together."

She heard Brian move behind her, felt his hands close on her shoulders. "I too fear as much, lady, and it gives me great sorrow."

She turned. They stood so close that she saw the fine lines at the corners of his eyes. The silver wings in his hair. The mouth that had so recently been kissing her. If she gave in to her desires, she would throw herself into his arms and beg for his kisses again, beg for more. But she would not.

He gazed deeply into her eyes, and Wynne knew he was trying to find the pathway to her heart. She would not allow that. She was far too vulnerable to Brian mac Logan already. If he read her heart, she would have no defense against his amorous assault ... and she knew within the deepest part of her that Brian would continue to pursue her. If she allowed him to, he would possess her ... body, heart, and soul.

Sadly she said, "Let's be going, sire. We have

many things to do before we can set sail for Donegal Bay."

Donegal Bay! The words jarred both of them back to the present, focused their thoughts on their purpose in being there.

"Aye, lady," Brian said briskly.

Each lost in his own thoughts, they walked up the pathway toward the village and the quay.

Chapter 11

As they neared the village, Brian broke the silence. He asked, "Did you design the layout for the cloister?"

She grinned at him. "Why do you ask?"

"It makes me think of your village, especially the quay and the storehouses along the shore."

"The only thing I did," Wynne said, "was to deliver materials. Raven drew the plans and oversaw the building."

"I should have known," he said. "The two of you *are* sisters, more alike than different."

"Nay, lord, Raven and I are quite different."

"Really, madam? Both of you have a penchant for building villages. Yours is occupied with people who are involuntary outcasts; hers is inhabited by voluntary outcasts. Both you and Raven seem to be a high priestess or superior mother over your individual domains."

Wynne laughed softly. "You do seem to be right, lord."

"Is Raven the founder of this cloister?"

"Nay, 'twas founded by a young married couple many years ago."

"Not celibate?" He raised a brow.

Ignoring his sarcasm, Wynne said, "According to legend the woman and her husband were very much in love. He was a Druid priest, she a Dryad

priestess. Both were goldsmiths. Because of their
deep love for each other and their gift for goldsmithing, they created a golden bell. A magical
bell. To give it even more power, they embossed
their own magical talisman on it—the *craebh ciuil*."

"The *craebh ciuil*," Brian repeated softly. "I have
heard of that. 'Tis a silver branch on which hangs
a cluster of three apples. Did the priest and priestess design it for the cloister?"

"Nay, for their home. They were not sequestered; they lived in a village. When, years later,
the priest became ill unto death, he and his wife
traveled here to the sacred apple orchard. They
built the tower and hung the bell. After he died
she remained here. Later other priestesses joined
her, and she established the Cloister of the Grove."

"The bell became its talisman," Brian said.

She nodded. "The bell was used during the winter solstice to remind people to bring the first
fruits to the gods for the Apple Festival. Its peals
symbolized the blessings the gods had poured on
the people. During the spring equinox it rang to
summon the people to the cloister for the feasting
as they began their new planting season."

"You speak of the bell as if it no longer exists,"
he said.

"Irish raiders stole it. Afterward many of the
apple trees died, and the Dryad who was high
priestess at the time took a vow of silence and
celibacy. Since then all high priestesses have taken
the vow of celibacy. A few have also taken a vow
of silence, to be broken only when the bell is
returned."

As they walked past the village gate, a bell
tolled. Brian glanced toward the tower.

"I thought you said they had no bell."

"Nay, I said the original bell, the golden bell of

the *craebh ciuil*, was stolen from the cloister. Soon after it was stolen the Dryads crafted a new one, but they did not emboss their holy symbol on it."

They passed the village gate, turned on the pathway, and walked down to the quay.

"Cathmor," Wynne shouted, "unload my trunk and take it to the—"

Brian pushed around her. "I'll get it."

"Nay," Wynne said. Before she could stop him, he had returned to the ship and hefted the trunk onto his shoulder.

"Lead the way, lady."

"I would rather be by myself," she said.

"Nay, lady. I go where you go."

"I've already made an agreement with you."

"Aye, but too many people are ready to dissuade you from our contract. I don't mind your not bringing me back from Donegal Bay, but I do want you to get me there, lady." He smiled at her. "Besides, my staying with you was part of our agreement."

"Not part of mine," Wynne said.

She walked off the dock, the wind blowing the ends of her head band around her face. She led the way to one of the main buildings of the cloister. Brian easily kept stride with her no matter how fast she walked or how rough the terrain became. They stopped in front of the infirmary, a conical building.

At the portico she said, "You may leave the trunk here."

"You're going inside?"

She nodded.

"It's too heavy for you to be carrying. I'll take it in for you."

"Really, my lord," Wynne said, not unkindly, "I would prefer that you go. I'd like to be alone.

Your friend Lachlann said he would be returning to the kingdom of Northern Scotland from here. Why don't you bid him goodbye?"

"He rode off soon after we landed." Brian shifted the trunk on his shoulder but continued to gaze down at her. "Being gracious is a difficult task for you, isn't it?"

Brian walked past her, pushed the leather curtain aside, and entered a short hallway. Because it was spring, the second set of leather curtains had been pulled away, and he moved into the main hall. Inside the commodious round room a woman watched over a bubbling cauldron suspended on a metal chain from a framework in the center of the roof.

The air was heavy with the aroma of cooking meat and the damp smell of burning fire. Beside the cooking pit was a beehive-shaped clay oven. Extending from the fire pit in several directions were squat tables filled with flagons and jars, bowls and pestles.

"The infirmary," Wynne said softly. "The priestesses here are dedicated to caring for the ill."

Brian set the trunk down, his gaze moving over sleeping platforms situated in enclosed compartments around the outer walls. A tray of medicines in her hand, a white-robed priestess moved from one bed to another, treating patients. When she saw Wynne, she smiled and waved.

"This is where we brought Keith when his foot was so inflamed," Wynne said. "It was Mother Barbara who treated him and insisted that he would get better. No one understands the medicinal qualities of herbs better than she." Wynne smiled. "Although I sometimes think it was her faith that healed him rather than the medicines."

"Probably a combination of both," Brian said.

The empty tray in hand, the priestess walked up to Wynne.

"Good morrow, Susanna," Wynne said. " 'Tis good to see you."

" 'Tis good to see you," the priestess replied. "Mother Barbara came by to say you had delivered the herbs."

"Aye."

After Wynne had introduced Brian, Susanna looked down at the trunk. She smiled. "You didn't forget."

"Nay, Susanna, a promise is a promise."

"Who's there?" a feeble voice called out.

Brian looked over Wynne's shoulder to see a skeletal woman sitting up in bed, staring at her.

"Visitors, grandmother," the priestess answered.

" 'Tis I, Grandmother Cordelia," Wynne said.

"Gwynneth," the woman repeated. " 'Tis you?"

"Aye, grandmother." As Wynne approached the woman's compartment, she told Brian, "She is an elderly ovate, the oldest Dryad of this order yet alive. Religious leaders from all lands come here to seek her wisdom."

Brian followed her with the trunk. At the foot of the bed Wynne knelt, unfastened the trunk, and lifted the lid.

"I knew you would come," the woman said.

Wynne lifted out a beautiful shawl. Folding it over her arm, she sat down on the edge of the bed. "And did you know that I would bring you the shawl you wanted?"

"Aye." Cordelia took the shawl and ran her arthritic hands lovingly over the plaid fabric. Tears ran down her weathered face. " 'Tis the colors of my kindred, Wynne. You remembered."

"Aye, grandmother, I did."

Brian moved to the side of the bed. "Here,

grandmother, let me help you place it around your shoulders." The big warrior gently lifted the frail woman and held her while Wynne arranged the shawl.

Wise, aged eyes gazed at him. "Who are you?"

"Brian mac Logan of the kingdom of Northern Scotland," he answered. "Who are you?"

"I'm Cordelia, the oldest Dryad priestess of the Cloister of the Grove." She cackled. "Probably I've seen more winters than any other person in all the lands."

"Well, Mistress Cordelia," Brian said, "I have a gift for you too. A pin with which to fasten your shawl so it won't slide off your shoulders." He removed the gold pin from his own tartan and held it out. " 'Tis called a safe-pin, good mother, because it latches with a guard over the point so that it won't prick the skin."

The old woman took it and looked at it. She laughed softly. " 'Tis a good pin for the swaddling of babes."

" 'Tis also good for the delicate skin of a beautiful woman." Brian took the pin and secured the shawl.

"Wynne," Cordelia said, "you couldn't ask for a nicer young man."

Wynne's cheeks colored. "He's not my young man, grandmother."

"If he isn't, he should be." Cordelia leaned back against the pillows. Through faded blue eyes she gazed intently at Brian. "I would say he is your man, Wynne. But I may be wrong."

"Wrong about what, Cordelia?" a deep feminine voice asked.

The patient looked beyond Brian. Her face brightened; her eyes sparkled. "Feich, my old friend," she exclaimed. "You have returned!"

"Aye."

"Feich?" Brian murmured, turning to see the visitor. "*'Twas* you I saw earlier!" Concerned about her health after having made such an arduous journey at her age, he asked, "What are you doing here, good mother?"

"Raven made an inquiry of me, and although I could have sent the answer back by messenger, I felt that I should come in person." She smiled. "Besides, I wanted to visit with my old friend here." Lowering her satchel to the floor, she peered up at him. "I heard about your sorrow, my son. I shall offer prayers and sacrifices for the return of the girdle."

"I will find it, holy mother," he said. "I won't let my daughter suffer the shame that I suffered."

"You have learned your lessons well, my son." Feich laid an arthritic hand on his arm. "You'll find the girdle, and you will avenge the wrong done to House Logan. The gods have use of you, Brian mac Logan. You shall do yourself and me proud with your exploits."

Wynne moved from where she had been standing, and Feich saw her. She shuffled closer, scrutinizing her from head to toe. "I've heard about you," she announced. "You're Gwynneth the seafarer."

"Aye," Wynne murmured.

Nodding and clicking her tongue approvingly, Feich gazed at her for a while longer. Then she knelt and unfastened her satchel. "You're sailing Brian to Eire." It was not a question.

"Aye, to Donegal Bay."

"'Tis a dangerous journey," the old lady said as she pulled out smaller sacks, vials, and flagons and set them in a line on the floor where she knelt.

"Let no one dissuade you from going. This trip is destined . . . for both you and Brian."

Surprised, Wynne said, "It is?"

"Aye, both of you have a mission to accomplish. Each of you has darkness in your past that must be cleared away." She leaned back, her hands lying limply on her satchel, and closed her eyes. Her voice dreamy, she said, "You are going to sail beyond the sun and stars, past everything you know and can see to an arc of golden light that stretches as you get closer and becomes a great shining circle."

Opening her eyes, Feich rummaged through her belongings until she found a bowl. Setting it in front of her, she unsheathed her knife and reached for a large root. She began to dice it into the dish.

"You will be frightened," she continued, "but do not turn back. The light will expand and cover everything, extending to the farthest heavens and earth. As it shone in the beginning, it will shine again. Forever."

She stirred the diced root with the blade of her knife. "In the circle of light, Gwynneth the seafarer, you will find your answer."

"'Tis mac Logan who seeks an answer, holy seer."

"Not only Brian, but you also, my daughter," Feich said.

"The answer I seek lies here, grandmother."

"Nay," Feich replied. "Raven is not the answer. The answer lies within you, but you will not see that until you stand in the circle of light. Far too long, Gwynneth, you have searched for the answer in another. Trust in yourself."

She opened one of the vials and measured several drops of brackish liquid onto the roots.

"The gods be with you, my daughter," Feich

said, turning her attention to the herbs. "Visit with the infirm. I have my work to do."

"Thank you for the words of advice, grandmother," Gwynneth said. "I shall take them to heart."

Troubled by what Feich had said, Gwynneth said goodbye to Cordelia and moved to the next bed. Brian dutifully followed her from bed to bed, greeting the sick and helping her dispense gifts. When she had made all the rounds, she walked to the eastern door of the infirmary and stared down the street, lined on both sides with apple trees.

Joining her at the door, Brian gazed at the U-shaped building at the end of the street. "Who lives there?"

"The high priestess," Wynne said.

The door to the building opened, and Melanthe and Raven walked out. Wynne approached them.

"Holy mothers," she said.

"Gwynneth." Raven extended her hand.

Wynne kissed it. Still on her knees, her head bowed, she said, "Superior mother of the Cloister of the Grove, I ask for an audience and a blessing."

"Aye, my little sister," Raven said.

Wynne rose, and she and Raven hugged. When they pulled apart, Wynne turned to Brian.

"My lady Raven, high priestess of the Cloister of the Grove, may I present Lord Brian mac Logan, of the kingdom of Northern Scotland."

"Lord Brian," Raven said, extending her hand.

He didn't kneel before her as Wynne had done, but he lifted her hand and kissed it.

"My lady," he said. "I am glad to have made your acquaintance."

"Thank you, my lord," Raven replied. "What brings you to our cloister?"

"I'm traveling with Wynne," he replied.

Surprised, Raven glanced at her sister and smiled. Wynne felt the heat of embarrassment on her cheeks. "He has hired my ship," she said.

"For a long trip?" Raven teased.

"Not too long," Wynne returned.

"Perhaps, sister, you should reconsider. A long trip might be more enjoyable."

Brian smiled.

"If you don't mind, my lord," Raven said, "I should like to spend some time alone with my sister."

Brian inclined his head.

Her arm around Wynne's shoulder, Raven guided her into the apple orchard. Giving them privacy, Brian and Melanthe followed at a distance, talking between themselves.

"I am glad you are here," Raven said, stepping off the pathway and moving through the trees. "I have a great many things to discuss with you."

"Mother says you are going to take the vow of silence," Wynne said.

"Aye, at Summer Solstice."

"You can't!" Wynne whispered in an anguished voice. She caught Raven's hands and squeezed them tightly. "You are the royal child."

"I have made provision for that," Raven answered. "I spoke to Father about it several moons ago."

"You went to see Father!"

"Nay, I sent for him, and he came here," Raven answered.

"Are you still angry at him for allowing me to marry Alba?"

"Nay, I forgave him a long time ago, just as I forgave you. He's truly sorry about all that happened seven winters ago, Wynne. He's a changed man."

"Pryse of Ailean will never change," Wynne replied.

"He's still very much a warrior king," Raven agreed, "but he's sorry for what has happened to you and to me. 'Tis time, little sister, that you made your peace with Father."

"I have," Wynne answered, "but he's not willing to accept what I have to offer. He wants me to return to Ailean and live my life to suit him."

"Is that so hard to do?"

Wynne chuckled. "You ask me that, sister, when you're not living in the Great Hall of Ailean?"

" 'Tis different for me," Raven said. "I have retreated into religion and philosophy and am not competing with men."

"Father has accepted your taking the vow of silence?" Wynne said.

"Reluctantly," Raven confessed. "I had to make a blood promise to him in front of witnesses. If no other heir shall be born who is acceptable to both branches of the clan, I will, after our father's death, give up my title of high priestess and accept the High Seat of Ailean. I understand that I am the child of peace, and I have promised both branches that I won't renounce my inheritance."

"You would rather be here than in the Great Hall, would you not?" Wynne murmured, her heart going out to her older sister. "Raven," she said tentatively, "you're not doing this because you're still angry with me, are you?"

"No," Raven answered. "I was angry with you, very angry, but I am past that now. I have truly forgiven you, Gwynneth. You have suffered far more than I. I wish before the gods of the Grove that Alba had never entered our lives."

Wynne hugged Raven tightly. "I feel as if I'm losing you, Raven, as if you are going to a faraway land where I shall never see you again."

Raven smiled and brushed tendrils of hair from Wynne's face. " 'Twill not be so bad." Her eyes twinkled. "After all, Melanthe taught you the sign language."

"And I learned it much more quickly than you did," Wynne teased lovingly.

Raven reached up and touched a delicate apple blossom. "Father will be here in a few weeks. I can't say that I'm looking forward to the visit. Despite my promise, he will try to persuade me to leave the cloister."

"Father can be overbearing," Wynne agreed. "The vow of silence that you are taking," she added, "is it forever?"

Raven smiled indulgently. "Nay, only until the *craebh ciuil* has been returned to the Grove."

"Which will be never," Wynne snapped. "We don't even know if such a bell actually exists."

"Whether we have seen it or not, it does exist," Raven said.

"Let's hope so," Wynne said. "Many Dryads have given it great power over their lives."

"We have not empowered the bell," Raven said, "it has empowered us. It is a magical bell." She gazed in the distance at the bell tower. "We still believe the gods will return it to us."

"Believe the gods will return what?" Mother Barbara called out as she rounded the path and approached them.

"That the gods will return the sacred bell to us," Raven answered.

"Aye, they will!" Mother Barbara exclaimed. "Our bell will be returned to the cloister."

Breathing deeply, she dug her staff into the

earth and leaned on it. Transfixed, she stared at
the bell tower. "Our founding mother and her
husband appeared to me in a vision." She nodded
her head. "Aye, they did. Three full moons ago. I
was walking through the orchard meditating. As
bard and warrior priest, they designed and cast
the bell in love. They promised that a bard and
warrior would restore it to the cloister in love."

Barbara sighed contentedly, giving Brian and
Melanthe a cursory glance as they approached.

"After the vision disappeared," Barbara went
on, "I remained in the orchard. The sun shining
through the trees made one of the branches appear
to be silver. Clustered on it were three apples."

"The *craebh ciuil*," Wynne whispered.

"Aye." Barbara never took her gaze from the
tower, and her voice throbbed with excitement.
"As I began to ponder the return of the bell, I
talked with Raven. She also believes my vision."

She glanced at the high priestess who nodded.

"Since that time I have spoken with all the ancient ones who have any knowledge of the bell,
including Mother Eilann and Grandmother Cordelia. 'Twas Cordelia who advised Raven to send for
Great-Grandmother Feich, the seer of the kingdom
of Northern Scotland."

"Feich made this trip because of that bell?"
Brian exclaimed.

"Aye. All our lives we have lived in the bell's
shadow, have thought of it and prayed for its return, but we know nothing about it," she replied,
as only one who lives by faith can. "One morning
I awakened from my nightly slumber wondering
how we were going to know the bell when it
was returned."

"Aye," Melanthe said. "The more we thought
about the bell, the more concerned we became.

Anyone can cast a cauldron bell with a *craebh ciuil* on it. Someone might present this to us saying that it was the ancient bell, and we would accept it."

"We would have no way of knowing any differently," Barbara said. "That's why we needed Feich. To find out if the bell had a mark that distinguished it from all other bells."

"And?" Wynne demanded.

"There is such a mark," Barbara answered. "Great-Grandmother Feich remembered hearing about it. 'Tis the three-pointed knot. The three circles of existence are symbolized by the three golden apples."

"The innermost circle is *abred*, where life springs from," Melanthe said. "Here the human soul must perfect itself."

Barbara murmured, "The next circle is *gwynedd*, or purity, where the life spark finally triumphs over evil and can rest forever from reincarnation."

"The outermost circle, *ceugant*, or infinity, is the dwelling place of the ultimate power of creation," Wynne said. "Do they know where the mark has been placed on the bell?"

"Feich remembers hearing about an ancient runestave that is kept at the Shelter Stone Cloister; it records the making of the bell and the placement of its identifying mark," Melanthe replied. "The goldsmith, our sacred mother-founder who created the bell, recorded the secret hiding place of her mark on the stave."

"I have sent word to the Ancient of Days and Nights, High Priest Sholto, asking if there is such a stave," Raven said. "If so, I have requested that the Council of the Grove and I be permitted to read the inscription."

"When you return to the cloister next," Barbara said to Wynne, "you will bring back his reply. We are excited, Gwynneth. Our summer solstice will be special this year."

Wynne didn't want to diminish their happiness, but she also didn't want them to be disappointed if the bell was not returned. "It has been gone so long, my mothers," she said. "Do you think the bell really exists?"

"Aye," all three of them answered.

"I have heard stories about its magical and healing powers," Melanthe said. "I pray that the bell is returned in time for the Summer Festival celebrated at the solstice."

In time to prevent Raven from taking the vow of silence!

"Feich seems to think it will be," Barbara said. "She has been stirring the water, and the three apple blossoms floated to the top of the brew."

" 'Tis a good sign," Melanthe agreed.

" 'Tis *the* sign!" Barbara exclaimed.

Slowly as the group moved out of the orchard and into the village, Melanthe and Barbara entertained them with stories about the lovers who had designed and cast the bell. They talked about the conflict that later arose between the Druids of Ireland, who had established a monastery of the Grove, and the Dryads of the Scottish Cloister of the Grove. Both orders claimed the sacred bell as their talisman. The Druids built their monastery in honor of the husband. The Dryads dedicated their cloister to the wife. Eventually the Irish Druids stole the bell. The Dryads searched for it during the intervening years, but never found it.

"And now we cannot even find signs that such a monastery ever existed in Ireland," Melanthe said. "We have sent missionaries there many times, but they found no such order."

What if the bell did exist and was somewhere in

Ireland? Wynne wondered. While she was sailing along the coastline, she would look for signs of a monastery. She would question Cathmor, who in turn could question the inhabitants they met. She could think of no greater honor than to find and return the ancient bell to its rightful home.

Chapter 12

By the time Melanthe and Barbara had completed their storytelling, the group had reached the U-shaped building at the end of the east street. Melanthe led the way through the arched entryway, then pushed open a heavy oak gate. They moved into a walled courtyard filled with colorful and well-laid gardens. Pathways wound through them, with benches set beneath willow trees. The refectory and eight rooms opened into the courtyard; these were the private quarters for each of the seven members of the Council of the Grove and the high priestess.

The courtyard with its cloister walk was the Inner Sanctum, a private retreat for the members of the Council of the Grove. Others who wished to enter could do so only by special invitation from the council members. Wynne had been there several times at her stepmother's request, but she was always thrilled anew at its beauty.

"Good morrow, my children," Barbara said. "I must leave you. I promised Susanna I would bring more medicine to the infirmary."

"Please excuse me," Raven said, "but I must also go. I have work to complete before the morning meal." From the shadows of the cowl, she looked at Brian. "My lord, I am glad to have made your acquaintance. Perhaps you and Wynne will join us for the morning meal."

"Aye, my lady," Brian said, "I should enjoy that very much. Thank you for inviting us. We have eaten ship rations since we left the Isle of Cat. While the fare is nourishing and filling, I would appreciate a freshly cooked meal."

"Then you shall have one," Raven promised and headed toward the refectory. "I shall see you later."

"Our cook is one of the best in the land," Melanthe said. "Well"—her eyes twinkled—"she's almost as good as Mistress Sheila."

"Ah, madam," Brian said, "Mistress Sheila is a fine cook, and she turns quite a hand with the subtlety."

"If you enjoy subtleties," Melanthe said, "you will enjoy ours, my lord." She twined her arms through both Brian's and Wynne's, guiding them to the cloister walk. "We have time before the second bell to get the jewelry you are to transport to the Shelter Stone Shrine, Gwynneth. Shall we?"

"Aye," Wynne murmured, but her attention was centered on her sister, strolling across the courtyard, clad in all her cloister regalia. At the moment she had stopped to admire a flower bed. Raven had always loved flowers. Moving to her right, she touched a tall bush, full of colorful blossoms.

Seven years, Wynne thought, watching as Raven cupped one of the blooms and brought it into the depths of the cowl that hid her face. Seven long years since she had closed herself within this community. And at summer solstice she would be taking the vow of silence. Wynne would never hear Raven talk again, never hear her laughter. The only time she would hear her voice was when Raven was chanting at cloister rituals.

"Here we are," Melanthe announced.

Still Wynne watched Raven. Several priestesses joined her; then they walked into the refectory.

"Let's see," Melanthe murmured. "Where could it be?"

Still gazing over her shoulder, Wynne stepped across the threshold into the chamber. Only when her eyes became accustomed to the subdued interior lighting did she realize they had entered her sister's quarters.

"Why here?" Wynne asked as she noticed the sparsely furnished room.

"Raven has more items she wants to add to the collection we intend to barter. I told her I would come by and pick up the casket later."

"Her room is so different from yours, Gwynneth," Brian said. He stood at the doorway, looking around. "But the fragrance is the same."

Wynne followed his gaze to the squat bronze figure of a horse on which burned an incense stick. He stepped fully into the room, brushing his hand over a plain table in front of the open window.

"She lives an austere life," Wynne said.

Against one wall stood a narrow bed with a thin mattress and plain white linens. Next to it was a beautifully carved wooden trunk elevated on four legs.

"I bought her that," Wynne said. "It was so elaborate, she almost didn't keep it."

"But I persuaded her," Melanthe said.

"It's unusual," Brian said. Moving to the trunk, he ran his fingers over the inset jewels, the metal inlays, and the intricate carvings.

"Those are runic *fedha*," Wynne said. "Runic inscriptions."

She watched Brian outline the Norse writing as she interpreted. *"To my beloved.* 'Twas intended as a betrothal gift."

He quickly raised his head. "For whom?"

"For some young maiden of Northland who died before the wedding. They never even engraved her name. I bartered for it because I thought Raven would like it." She laughed softly. "I had to fight with her to accept it. Again Melanthe interceded."

"She has always loved the brazier that you gave her," Melanthe reminded her.

Wynne gazed at the tall, cylindrical brazier in the center of the room. Its highly polished metal glinted golden in the sunlight. The rounded belly easily accommodated wood or coal, and a top shelf served as a food warmer.

Wynne walked over and touched the blue and white porcelain knob at the top. She saw a blur of color and looked down to see her reflection in the polished metal. She heard the soft thud of Brian's boots on the planked floor as he joined her where she stood.

His presence was so strong, it was like an embrace. She was surrounded by his heat and vitality. She closed her eyes and breathed in deeply. When she lifted her lids to gaze at the stove again, she saw the images of both their faces. In the reflection their gazes locked.

Brian raised an arm, brushing against Wynne. He outlined the reflection of her face on the brazier.

"Beautiful," he murmured. "Very beautiful."

Wynne shivered. He hovered over her, and she unashamedly absorbed his warmth and strength. As in the bower several days ago, as in the orchard earlier today, now here in this austere cell, Brian and Wynne created their own kingdom with only themselves as inhabitants. 'Twasn't the place that was mystical, Wynne decided, but the feeling, the attraction between them.

"These are the pieces we wish to barter," Wynne heard Melanthe say.

Brian leaned into her, nestling her back against his chest and stomach. She made no effort to move. She felt as if she were the coal that burned in the brazier—red-hot and glowing.

"Your eyes," he murmured for her ears only. He touched his finger to one in the metallic reflection and brushed an eyebrow. "They are blue at the moment."

His breath teased one of the curls that whisked around her face. She felt his hand on her shoulder. Spellbound, she continued to stare at their images in the polished metal. She heard Melanthe says something, but the words didn't register.

"Gwynneth," he whispered for her ears alone.

Had she not been leaning against him, she would have melted to the floor. She loved to hear him say her name. Like a silk cloth, it wrapped around her, caressing her, binding her to him.

"Gwynneth!" Melanthe said.

Wynne closed her eyes to break the mystical spell. Through the haze of emotions she heard Melanthe say, "Are you listening to me?" She opened her eyes. "Gwynneth?"

"Aye," she murmured.

"I feel as if I am talking to myself," Melanthe complained. "Here are the pieces . . ." She paused, then sighed. "Gwynneth, please pay attention to me."

Through their mirrored images Wynne saw Brian lift his hand from her shoulder. Oddly it was as if part of her were removed. So quickly he had insinuated himself into her life, her heart. Aye, Brian mac Logan was invading her heart as surely as he had invaded her island. He stepped away from her, and she turned to her stepmother.

Silence hovered heavily. Melanthe gave both Wynne and Brian a measured look. Then she pointed to the casket on Raven's table.

"You are to take these to Sholto, the Ancient of Days and Nights, at the Shelter Stone Cloister."

Moving as if in a dream, Wynne joined her mother at the desk and gazed into the open box. The gold jewelry, lying on a bed of imported silk, glinted golden in the sunlight. Delicate, intricate, unusual, each piece was an example of outstanding workmanship.

Melanthe went to a shelved alcove in the wall and picked up a smaller casket. "This is a special gift for the Ancient of Days and Nights himself."

Returning to the table, she set down the casket and lifted the lid. Wynne gazed at the piece of jewelry nestled inside.

"A bell," she murmured. "A miniature bell."

Embossed on one side were the silver branch and cluster of three apples. The tiny piece of jewelry was so exquisite that Wynne gasped. Brian moved to stand beside her.

"The *craebh ciuil*," he said. "The smith who crafted this—"

"Raven," Wynne said proudly. "I would recognize her handiwork anywhere."

"Aye, 'twas Raven," Melanthe replied. "This is one of the most precious pieces of jewelry ever designed in the cloister, Gwynneth. 'Tis magical. To our knowledge, 'tis the first with the holy symbol since the original bell was cast. It is blessed by the Dryads, and is a holy piece destined only for the Shelter Stone Shrine." Melanthe reverently folded the silk over the bell, then closed and fastened the casket. "Take care of it, Gwynneth."

"Aye, Mother. I will."

Melanthe looked at Brian, then back at Wynne. "Most of all, my daughter," Melanthe added, "take care of yourself."

After the blessing had been given, the goodbyes said, Raven parted from her sister and Brian. Her mother following, Raven entered her chamber.

"My heart is heavy, Mother," she said, removing the cowl from her head as she moved to the open window.

Melanthe sat in one of the chairs closest to the door and picked up her embroidery hoop. "Aye, daughter, so is mine."

A breeze teased Raven's long black hair. Sunlight burnished it until it shone like the coat of a raven—the sacred bird after whom she had been named.

"I knew when I became high priestess that I would have to take the oath of silence one day, but not until today, not until I was talking with Wynne, did I realize the full significance of that decision. I will never be able to speak directly to her again."

"Nay, daughter, you won't."

Melanthe slowly drew the material taut within the hoop, then picked up her needle and threaded it with green floss. Skillfully she wove the needle through the fabric. She understood her daughter's pain because she felt it herself.

"Choosing to come into the cloister was easy," Raven murmured. "Living here is the difficult part."

Green floss flew through the air as Melanthe made the chain of delicate uniform stitches grow.

"I was honored when the Council of the Grove chose me to be the high priestess," Raven continued.

"Well you should be!" Melanthe exclaimed, looking up from her work. "You are the youngest ever to be chosen."

"But at times I find the honor extremely burdensome."

"In all walks of life," Melanthe said, "we each have our share of heavy loads to carry. You would not be without them if you were not a Dryad, if you were not the high priestess."

Raven smiled softly. "You never wanted me to enter the cloister."

"Nay, daughter, I didn't."

"You thought I was running away, hiding from life."

"Your father and I both feared that was why you were joining the order."

"I am of the same persuasion today as I was then."

"I would be happy if you chose to return to your people and to your inheritance." Lowering her head, Melanthe laid down the embroidery hoop. "You are still heir to the High Seat of Ailean."

"I haven't forgotten," Raven said.

"'Twould be nice to know that I have direct heirs," Melanthe said. "Someone to carry on my family's name."

Raven laughed, a lovely sound, one that Melanthe seldom heard.

"You would marry me off, Mother?"

"Aye, daughter, in an eye's blink."

Her daughter was truly a beautiful woman, with dark features—almond-colored skin and golden-brown eyes. As Gwynneth was a child of the sum-

mer, Raven was a child of the winter. She had
been her father's firstborn, his heir by birth. But
she had not been his daughter of choice.

Gwynneth, the daughter born of his true love,
had been his favorite child, the one on whom he
had lavished all his love and affection. Raven too
had adored her baby sister. While the girls were
growing up, Raven had gladly walked in
Wynne's shadow.

Laughter from the courtyard, Wynne's laughter,
caught their attention. Once more Raven gazed out
the window. Melanthe rose and joined Raven at
the window in time to see Mother Barbara, Feich,
and Wynne standing together. After saying goodbye, Feich hobbled into the refectory. The Dryad
priestess and Wynne slowly crossed the courtyard
toward the gate.

"May the gods bless you, my little sister,"
Raven whispered, lifting her hand in blessing,
"and keep you safe."

"And may she bring us back an auspicious message from the Ancient of Days and Nights," Melanthe added.

"We should know soon. 'Twill not take her long
to sail to the Shelter Stone Shrine and back."

"She has other cargo to deliver first," Melanthe
said, moving away from the window, walking
aimlessly about the room.

Raven remained at the window as if she could
not get her fill of looking at Wynne. Finally she
said, "Lord Brian is joining Gwynneth. Who is
he, Mother?"

"Great-Grandmother Feich's adopted son," Melanthe replied.

"Did he hire Gwynneth to sail Feich to the
cloister?"

"Nay."

Slowly Raven turned, her tunic whispering about her ankles.

"What has he hired her to do?"

"He wishes to sail to Ireland." Melanthe spoke quietly.

"Gwynneth cannot go there!"

"She's not going to Sligo," Melanthe said. "She's sailing him to Donegal Bay."

"You have known all along," Raven accused. "You and Gwynneth, yet you did not tell me."

"We didn't wish to prick at old scars."

"That's exactly what they are, and you should not fear them. I don't. I fear the present and what might happen to Gwynneth when she lands in Ireland." Raven paced back and forth. "The O'Illands have sworn to kill her, and they have intensified the hunt since all their heirs to the High Seat have died."

"Gwynneth has been a seafarer for seven years, Raven, and is liege to many valiant warriors. She'll be able to protect herself."

Although Melanthe spoke bravely, she too was frightened for her stepdaughter. But she was old enough to know that she could live no one else's life but her own.

"She can't go to Ireland, Mother," Raven insisted. She raced to the cell door. "I won't let her."

"Nay, Raven!" Melanthe laid her hand on Raven's arm. "You must let Gwynneth live her own life, as you must live yours."

"She is my sister. I must stop her."

"Long ago, my daughter, you made the decision to give up your family and your old way of life in order to be a Dryad of the cloister. Now you have given up still more in order to be the high priestess."

"I can't let her go," Raven whispered. "I can't, Mother."

"You cannot stop her. This is her destiny, and the gods have spoken."

Chapter 13

"**S**et sail immediately," Wynne shouted as she and Brian hurried down the quay toward the *Honeysuckle*.

Frowning, Cathmor leaned over the hull railing. "We won't be leaving for a while, lady." Having long ago abandoned his tunic, he wiped perspiration from his lower face with the sashes of his headband. "The priestesses haven't received all the goods they want us to transport. They're still waiting for several trunks to arrive from a nearby village."

"Surely you can take them another time," Brian said, eager to be on his way.

Cathmor shook his head. "Nay, lord, Mother Barbara said they must go now. They have to reach the Shelter Stone Shrine along with all these other goods." He shook his head. "She was emphatic about it."

"When does she expect them to arrive?" Wynne asked.

"Late afternoon."

"That, lady," Brian said, "will be quite a wait."

"Aye, lord."

Although Wynne had not counted on the delay, and was slightly irritated about it, there was nothing she could do. The cloister was among her regular customers, and they paid her well. Although she meant to give good service to both the cloister and Brian, she must protect her most steady customer.

"We shall wait until twilight," Wynne replied.

"Twilight?" Brian questioned.

She nodded. "If they are not here by then, we will sail without them."

"You're giving them a long time," Brian grumbled.

"Aye, the cloister is one of my valued customers. I shall give them the extra time they need. 'Twill be quite a while before I can return here." She looked up at the Irishman. "Cathmor, arrange for the men to spend some time on shore. Guards will be spelled every two hours."

"Aye, lady."

"What shall we do while we're waiting?" Brian asked.

Wynne gazed at the courtyard where the priestesses were chanting.

Shaking his head, he said, "You may go, lady. I shall find some other way to entertain myself."

Wynne chuckled. "You're not interested in religion or philosophy, lord?"

"Aye, lady, I am, but I feel closer to the gods when I am walking among their natural creations. I think I shall explore the area around the cloister. What are you going to do?"

She smiled. "I shall explore also, lord." When he opened his mouth, she said, "By myself. I would like to be alone for a while."

"I would like to be with you, lady."

"There are things that a person needs to tend to in private, my lord." Her blue eyes twinkled.

He smiled. "Perhaps you will join me later?"

"Perhaps."

Wynne raced back to the ship and rummaged

through her chest. She gathered bathing cloths and a change of clothes, then scooted off again, heading for one of her favorite places, a hidden cove where the women of the cloister bathed. To ensure their privacy, the priestesses had built a small wall around the pool.

Wynne quickly divested herself of her clothing and slid into the warm but refreshing water. With long sure strokes she shot out into the deep, releasing the tension that had built up in her body. Tirelessly she swam the length and width of the pool.

Although she enjoyed being with Brian, reveled in the tension between them, she was glad to be by herself. She had noticed that he was bringing about a change in her. In the past she had vowed that people would accept her as Wynne the seafarer, the warrior woman. She felt differently about Brian. She was eager for him to see her as a woman.

Having worked off most of the tension, she glided more lazily. She rolled onto her back and gazed up at the sky. Then she closed her eyes.

Her desire to appear womanly to Brian also confused her. She felt as if she were betraying herself, betraying the warrior she had worked so hard to be. She had not given in to her father's pleas and arguments when he had begged her to return to the Great Hall of Ailean four years ago. And since then she had rebuffed his proposal of a royal marriage for her. Tenaciously she had held on to her independent life.

She drifted in the water, enjoying the warm sun, relaxing. Every so often she made a few long strokes to pull her through the water.

Now she was rethinking her choices. Since Brian had arrived she had begun experiencing new sen-

sations; they were exhilarating and challenging.
Even thinking about them, she felt breathless, and
her heart beat faster. Only Brian affected her like
this.

Earlier she had questioned him about his relationship with Sorcha. She had prodded and
pushed him to reveal how he felt about a man
beating his wife. Wynne's mother had died when
Wynne had seen only two winters, but she
couldn't remember any anger between her father
and mother. As she grew older, she had become
more aware of Pryse's relationship with Melanthe;
there was always an undercurrent of tension between them, and they regularly argued about what
was best for the girls. Still, they respected each
other. Not once had Wynne seen her father
strike Melanthe.

Last night as she had lain in her sleeping bag,
Wynne had realized that she wanted to mate . . .
and she wanted to mate with Brian mac Logan.
But she was confused. She wondered if she was
truly attracted to the man or to the idea of having
a lover. And out of the mating she wanted a child
. . . someone special to love, someone to love her.

Now, as she remembered the way Brian had
kissed her, she knew for sure that she would let
him be her first lover. Their future might last no
longer than it took him to avenge the shame
brought on his house. No doubt he would accept
his sovereign's plans for a political marriage, and
Wynne would steadfastly refuse to be a second
wife or a bedmate, no matter how kindly she
might be treated or how much Brian might profess
to love her. If she married, she would be the
first wife.

Still Brian would be in her life long enough to
teach her the rudiments of coupling. What a de-

lightful experience it promised to be! She shivered,
rolled over, and pressed for the far shore, where
she treaded water.

"Good afternoon, lady," a masculine voice said.

"Mac Logan!" He had approached her so quietly, she had not heard him. She felt her face flush
and hoped her cheeks did not color as brightly as
she feared.

"I did not follow you," he said, propping a foot
on a large rock. "But I'm glad I found you."

Despite all her brave thoughts and her decision
to mate with him, Wynne was embarrassed by her
nudity. She flipped over, dipping low in the water
until only her head showed. Her hair fanned out
around her.

"I enjoyed looking at you better before," he
said, his eyes suggestive. "More of you was
showing."

"What are you doing here?"

"I had thought to take a swim also," he replied.

"You may swim after me," she said pertly. "I
shall be finished shortly."

"If I wait, lady, I probably won't have an opportunity to bathe until we reach your isle." Grinning
suggestively, he added, "I shall have to join you."

"I think not!"

" 'Tis a large pool, madam, with plenty of room
for both of us."

No matter how large the pool, Wynne knew it
would be much too small for the two of them. She
was irritated that he had discovered her and was
joining her . . . but she was also excited.

He began to undress, and once again Wynne
found herself watching, spellbound. He took off
his mantle and draped it across a nearby low-
hanging branch. Sitting on the rock, he removed
his boots. He rose, took off his armbands and

torque, and laid them carefully on the rock. Then he stood, unfastened his weapon belts and laid them beside the rock. He unlatched his girdle and let it fall to the ground. He stepped out of his breeches.

Swimming to the shallows, Wynne knew she should not watch, but she couldn't take her eyes off him. Alba was the only man she had ever seen totally naked, and she had managed to erase the memory from her mind. She prayed to the gods that she never forgot how magnificent the Highlander looked; he totally captivated her.

Muscles rippled from his chest to his feet. His body gleamed in the afternoon sunlight. Dark hair swirled down his stomach to his erection. Without moving he stared at her, and willed her to continue looking at him. She throbbed at the thought of him taking her, of him introducing her to the thrilling world of mating.

She lifted her eyes to his face. "You promised a gentle mating," she said.

His eyes narrowed. "Aye, lady, but do you fully understand what I can offer you?"

"Aye, Brian," she said, "I understand about your arranged marriage."

Step by step he waded into the shallows, the water lapping higher and higher on his legs.

"I would be honored, Gwynneth of Ailean, if you would become my second wife."

"Thank you for asking, my lord, but I must decline." Putting her feet on the bottom of the pool, she rose and came toward him. "I'm not accustomed to taking second place to anything . . . or anyone. And even if you were to ask me to be your first wife, I would probably decline."

"Much to my regret, lady, I thought that is what you would say." He smiled sadly.

"It gives me pleasure to know that you care for me enough to offer marriage. It will bring tenderness to our coupling."

She held out her hand to him. He arched his brows in surprise. She crooked and wiggled her fingers. "I am releasing you from our bargain, mac Logan. I want you to mate with me."

A smile transformed his face. When he reached her, she caught his hands in hers. They stood gazing at each other as the water rippled around them.

Still holding her hands, Brian bent his head, caught one of her nipples in his mouth, and sucked gently. Desire pierced Wynne's body, taking residence in the lower part of her stomach.

"Wynne," Brian whispered, his voice thick with desire, his warm breath splaying over the sensitized skin of her breast, "I have never tasted anything as sweet as you."

His lips brushed against her heated flesh as he moved to her other breast. His tongue moistly laved the fullness, then he nipped and lapped the areola, before finally he took the taut nipple into his mouth and began to taste of its goodness.

"Oh, Brian," she cried out, "I have never felt like this before."

"How?"

"Like liquid fire."

"Do you want to make me feel the same way?" he asked softly.

"Aye," she whispered, opening her eyes wide.

"Touch me. Love my body as I am loving yours."

Feeling shy, she gazed at him. "I—I have never done so before. What if I do something wrong?"

Brian laughed gently. "There is no wrong, my lady, only loving."

"Kiss me," she whispered.

"You kiss me."

Laughter trembling on her lips, she caught Brian's face in her hands and brought her lips to his. Breathing deeply, she slid her fingers into his hair and massaged his scalp. She settled her lips more firmly on his, tentatively opening her mouth to receive his tongue. But he did not enter her mouth.

With a low groan, Brian pulled her down into the shallows, stretching his lean body along the length of hers. The water cushioned them. As he opened his mouth under her guidance, she touched the tip of her tongue to his; he trembled. She speared hers fully into his mouth.

Suddenly she understood the power of her womanhood. This magnificent warrior was trembling in her arms from her caresses.

A sharp intake of breath lifted his chest, and his grip on her tightened. Their kiss became hungry and urgent, the pressure of their mouths together almost painful.

His hand slid through the water, down her back. She gasped when his hands cupped her buttocks. Caught up in the pleasure, she rubbed her bottom against his hands. He was once more opening up a new world of sensuality for her, and she was entering it willingly.

Brian moved his hand to the warmth between her thighs. No sooner had his fingers touched the sensitive flesh than Wynne murmured and squirmed against them.

"Since this is your first mating," Brian murmured, "would you rather it be somewhere besides the shallows?"

"Nay," she whispered. " 'Tis the right place for me to learn the joys of coupling, my lord Brian."

"Brian." He kissed her.

"Brian," she murmured against his lips.

Whispering endearments, he brushed his mouth down her throat across her collarbone, over the fullness of her breasts; he teased and tormented; he whetted her desire to fever pitch. His hand slid down her stomach, his fingers playing with her navel.

Then he touched the soft triangle of hair. He looked down at her stomach and and through the crystal-clear water saw the golden beauty that beckoned to him like ripe golden apples hanging on the boughs ready to be plucked. His fingers slid deeper, and he touched her secret passage. It was hot and moist, ready for him.

Wynne pressed up against him. Instinctively she wanted to receive his fingers. "Now, Brian," she cried out. "I cannot stand it any longer."

He chuckled softly. "Aye, Gwynneth."

She tangled her hands in his hair and brought his face closer to hers. She arched against him, her breasts rubbing against his chest. When he pressed his erection into the golden triangle, she arched again, determined this time to ensnare him. He pulled back, teasing her with the tip of his manhood.

"Brian?" she whimpered.

"I want you ready," he whispered. "There will be some pain, but I want it to be as little as possible." His fingers slid between them to stroke her again and again, in and out, preparing her.

She moved with him, lifting and falling, her desire intensifying. When he removed his hand she cried out, "No!"

"I'm here," he promised.

He moved over her, lowering his weight. His knee spread her legs apart; his hand continued to stroke her inner thigh. He placed his manhood where his hand had been.

She tensed.

"I will be gentle, Wynne," he promised.

His hands moved reassuringly before he began to tenderly sheath himself in her warm femininity. He felt the tightness, the maidenhood. He stopped and drew in a shaky breath.

"What's wrong?" she asked.

"Nothing is wrong, sweet seafarer," he murmured. "Everything is right."

He was surrounded by her moist warmth; it pulsed around him. Gwynneth of Ailean, Wynne the seafarer—she was his alone. No man had touched her, had made love to her. He would. Brian promised himself that he would wipe away all traces of Alba O'Illand from her memory.

He thrust forward, penetrating a little deeper. She gasped at the size of him, stretching her open.

"Brian—" She was frightened.

He grew still and rubbed his hands up and down her arms. " 'Tis all right, lass," he said.

Then he captured her mouth and kissed her once again. Their kiss grew hotter until she was clutching him. Without releasing her mouth, still caressing her breasts, he entered her fully. She tensed and cried out.

"It's over," he whispered. "It won't hurt again. I promise."

The pain was already gone, she realized, and pleasure was once more warmly spiraling through her body. Wynne closed her arms about him, her fingers digging into his back. She clung to him, moving her hips so that he was forced to move faster and deeper.

Sensation built up so that she thought she would explode. She gasped for breath; her heart seemed to stop beating. She tore her lips from his and arched her neck, then cried out as her body convulsed with pleasure.

Brian tensed as she climaxed. He groaned. She felt him jerk out of her and spill his seed into the water. She shuddered and tightened her arms about him, turning her face into his shoulder. They clung together as their breathing slowed.

"Why did you spill your seed into the sea?" she asked.

"I did not wish you to conceive a child," he answered.

"I want a child," she said.

"I have never made it a habit, lady, of leaving bairns scattered about the land. I don't intend to start now."

"I want your child, Brian."

"Then you shall have to marry me."

"First wife?" she questioned.

"Second."

"Nay, Brian. There must be another way."

Drawing her into his arms and holding her close, the water lapping about them, he chuckled softly. "I'm sure you will find it, my lady."

They lay in the shallows for a long time talking. Then they swam. As the afternoon lengthened, they heard footfalls approaching.

"Wynne," Raven called softly from the other side of the wall, "are you swimming?"

"Aye."

"I thought I would find you here."

"'Tis one of my favorite spots," Wynne replied. Looking at Brian, she smiled and winked.

"The goods have arrived," her sister said and stepped around the wall to see Wynne and Brian in the pool. They were unable to see more than the huge cowl that enveloped her face in shadows.

"You should have told me that you were not alone," she snapped, turning her back to them. "I wouldn't have interrupted."

"You didn't interrupt," Brian said. "We have finished swimming."

Raven's silence spoke louder than anything she might have said.

"We're getting ready to return to the ship," Wynne added.

"Then I shall be on my way and let you dress." Quickly Raven disappeared around the edge of the wall and up the pathway.

"I suppose your family is going to press for an honorable proposal," Brian said.

"They may press for it, sire," Wynne agreed, "but when my father learns of our mating, I suspect he will be so delighted with this proof of my womanliness that he shall forgive you, and begin hunting for a much more suitable husband."

"Do you honestly think he shall find one?" Brian teased.

Wynne thought she detected a serious concern beneath his light question.

"Aye, lord, there are always princes who want to marry princesses."

In silence they returned to shore, dried off, and dressed.

"Now that you have tasted the joys of mating, do you find the idea of marriage more agreeable?" Brian asked.

Clad in leggings and trousers, Wynne dropped her short tunic over her head, her voice muffled as she said, "Now that you have taught me how pleasurable mating can me, I am not as adverse to marriage as I thought I was. Perhaps I shall find a man with whom to wed as the first wife and have a family."

"Aye," he muttered, his visage drawn, "maybe so, my lady." He sat down on the boulder and pulled on his boots. He rose and moved to stand beside her. "Would you find more pleasure in being another man's first wife than in being my second one?"

"Mayhap the pleasure of the wedding bed would not be as great, my lord, but the prestige and sanctity of my position would be much greater. I would be mistress of my own home and children. As second wife I would answer to the first, be subject to her whims and jealousies. 'Twould not do!"

"Nay," Brian said, "I see that it would not." He doubled his fist. "*Damnation!* I hate that Malcolm has involved me in his political intrigues!"

"But he has, Brian," Wynne said softly, sadly, "and he is your liege. His word is law."

They stepped toward each other, into a tight embrace. With a low moan he took her mouth. His arms tightened. The kiss deepened. His tongue fully, sweetly reclaimed her mouth. Knowing how to reciprocate, Wynne welcomed him and teased him back.

Brian's chest lifted with a deep intake of breath, but his mouth never left hers. Wynne clung to his shoulders and pressed against him. Excitement flowed hotly through her, but the kiss was not enough. He had already introduced her to the wonder of fulfillment. And she craved it. As surely as she had received his tongue within her, she wanted to receive his manhood. When he began to retreat, she moaned and clutched him tighter. Her yearnings were not so easily assuaged.

In silent entreaty for him to remain inside her mouth, she gently closed her teeth on his tongue. Again he trembled within her embrace. More daring now, hungry for his possession, she slid her hands to his buttocks and urged him against her pelvis. She alerted him to her needs, to her desire to receive him altogether.

Brian groaned. His hands shifted on her body, finding and stroking her breasts, sending rush after rush of pleasure through her, creating a fevered ache deep inside her. His lips claimed hers once more in a hard and searching kiss. His tongue did wonderful things to her as it stroked her mouth inside and out. He had possessed her completely; she had surrendered her maidenhood. Now with a simple kiss he was demanding her soul.

Turning her face from his, yet feeling the heat of his mouth on her cheek, Wynne drew in ragged breaths. She had gladly given Brian her maidenhead, yet if she gave him her soul, she would be his forever . . . under any conditions . . .

Reeling from this latest revelation, she pulled gently away from Brian. " 'Tis time to return to the ship, lord, if we are to make it to Donegal Bay in record time."

"Aye."

Through narrowed eyes he gazed at her. She forced a bright smile, and started up the path toward the quay. The trip would be good for her, she thought. 'Twould give her time to sort through her newly discovered emotions, and decide what she would do next.

Consumed by passion and driven by the need to satisfy it, she had mated with Brian without fully considering the consequences. Now she began to realize how profoundly he had changed her life. She could never go back to being just Wynne the seafarer. He had made her a woman, with a woman's needs and desires. Yet how could she fulfill those needs without compromising the life she had sacrificed so much to build for herself? How could she remain true to herself and be a woman too?

"Where do you and I go from here, madam?" Brian asked.

"We sail back to the Isle of Cat, change ships, and head for Donegal Bay," she replied with a lightness she was far from feeling.

He caught her by the shoulder and stopped her. "That's not what I meant."

"You and I have no future beyond Donegal Bay, Brian," Wynne said. "Now that I have experienced the wonder of mating, I wish you and I could be together, but we can't. You have a duty to your liege, and I have a commitment to myself."

"You would not regret living with me as my second wife, lady."

"I would soon grow to hate myself and in turn you, lord. 'Twas I who broke my first rule of business, and allowed us to become intimate. I would like to put our relationship back on a business footing. 'Twill be better for both of us." She paused. "At least for me."

"I care for you, Gwynneth," Brian said.

"If you do, lord, please leave me alone." She walked away from him.

"Nay, lady," he muttered, "that I cannot do."

Chapter 14

The sun shone brightly. The wind blew steadily, swelling the brown and black striped sail of the *Honeycomb*. At the tiller, Wynne watched seawater whip against the sides of the ship as they made their way toward Ireland. Since she and Brian had left the Cloister of the Grove and returned to the Isle of Cat, she had once again become a tough woman of business.

She had to protect herself. She knew that Brian cared for her, but she also knew that his caring would not be enough. She would be first in her husband's eyes or nothing at all. On the several occasions when Brian had tried to become intimate, she had reacted coolly to his advances, telling him to leave her alone. Recently he had, and she missed him—his laughter, his warmth, his understanding.

"The gods are smiling on us, lady," Cathmor said.

"Aye," Wynne murmured, her mantle billowing. Inhaling deeply, she tossed her head back and enjoyed the feel of the salty mist on her face.

"It has been a good voyage thus far, my lady," the Irishman said.

A long one, Wynne thought, because she and Brian were closed together in the confines of the ship and were not speaking civilly to each other.

"It will not take long to reach Donegal Bay," Wynne said, "since we have open sea."

"'Tis good," Cathmor murmured, casting a dubious eye at the twenty-odd ponies tethered in the middle and toward the stern end of the ship. "The odor is sometimes more than I can endure."

Wynne laughed. "But the Highlanders are cleaning up after them."

"For that we can thank the gods," he said dryly.

Because Wynne's ships were all trading vessels, her cargo holds were extremely spacious. Since this was her largest ship, its storage area was by far the biggest. Two tents had been erected. One strung over the spar at the midsection protected the provisions. The second one, on the prow platform, gave Wynne privacy. The men had elected to sleep in bags without a tent.

"Most times, my lady, I am pleased with the speed with which we sail to our destinations," Cathmor said, "but not on this voyage. I fear what lies ahead."

Deep down Wynne harbored similar fears.

Leaning back against the hull, she gazed across the ship to see Brian standing on the stern, surrounded by his warriors. The breeze billowed the tartan from his body. His black shirt and trousers emphasized his muscular physique, his handsome features. His gold torque and armbands glinted in the sunlight.

Brian mac Logan was a powerful man, a magnificent warrior. He dominated his surroundings with his impressive height and powerful build. And Wynne was in love with him. Since the day they had mated, her mind had been filled with thoughts of him. Now that he was ignoring her, she wanted him more than ever. She had even considered agreeing to become his second wife or his bedmate.

"My lady," one of the crewmen shouted impatiently, "come get the cat. She's into the provisions."

Wynne turned to see Honey nudging at the tent stays. She was meowing and sniffing, running around the enclosure. She batted the end flaps of the covering, unable to open them because they were too well laced. She leaped up, sheathing her claws as she slid down the awning.

Wynne smiled and teased, "Perhaps we have a rodent aboard ship, Cathmor."

He laughed. "Aye, lady. Let's see what we picked up at the last port that Honey finds so intriguing."

Bracing her feet against the reeling deck, Wynne strode close to the cat. She caught the pet by her collar just before she whisked by. Meowing, the cat struggled to get loose and tried to insinuate her paw beneath the tent.

" 'Tis something here," Wynne murmured.

She caught the rope and unfastened the tent. Cathmor and Brian moved behind her. The minute Wynne opened the tent, Honey dived in. Cathmor and Wynne followed. They pushed aside chests and casks of preserved meat and fish. Sacks of grain. Boxes of bread. Big crocks and firkins of butter and cheese. Hogsheads of water and ale.

"Nothing," Wynne said.

Honey yowled loudly and reared, planting her front paws on top of a tall barrel, knocking it over. It rolled a ways, but Brian stuck out his foot to stop it. Cathmor heaved it up, moved it back to the provisions tent, and set it upright. Honey flew by him and began to brush her shoulder and muzzle against the barrel.

Abruptly Cathmor began to laugh. "Smoked herring, my lady."

Wynne and the rest of the crew joined in his laughter.

He pulled his dagger out. "Well, old girl," he said to Honey, "since you are so determined to have a herring, let me get it for you." He inserted the blade into the top of the barrel. His brow furrowed. "My lady," he said, "this barrel has been tampered with. The lid is not sealed, and I don't smell fish."

He wheeled the barrel to the center of the deck and was soon surrounded by warriors. Cathmor knelt, running his hand around the barrel.

"'Tis strange, my lady. The barrel has holes bored all round it." He pried off the lid and tossed it aside. Then he hunched over the container and peered inside. He laughed softly. "Well, my lady, I think we have found our rodent, and it's not a smoked herring." He sunk his huge arm into the depths and raised it holding a screaming, kicking boy.

"Keith!" Wynne exclaimed.

Cathmor set the boy on his feet. "So we have one less barrel of food and one extra mouth to feed."

"What are you doing here, Keith?" Wynne demanded.

Cathmor chuckled and Brian grinned.

"I think that is self-evident, madam," Brian said.

"This is not a laughing matter, my lord," she retorted, glowering at Brian. "I do not allow stowaways." She turned back to Keith. "And you know it!"

"Aye," the boy said, his voice strained.

"If this were my voyage," she said, "I would

turn the ship around and take you home myself, Keith."

Wynne saw the glimmer of his smile, but he quickly squelched it. "Then I shall have to stay, my lady?"

"I don't know, Keith. The voyage belongs to the Highlander. He is the one who has paid for our provisions and our services. He is the one to decide what to do with you. Does Erinn know you are aboard the ship?"

Keith squirmed beneath Wynne's gaze.

"Does she know, Keith, or have you left her to worry about you?"

"Nay, my lady," he mumbled. "She didn't know that I intended to stow away. I told her you had given me permission to go."

"You lied to her?"

"Not exactly," he said. "You did tell me that you would let me go when my wound was healed. And it is, my lady."

The corners of Cathmor's mouth quivered, as did Brian's. Wynne refused to look at either of them.

"Wait here, Keith, while Lord Brian and I talk and decide what to do with you."

"Aye," he mumbled, his face downcast. He slumped down to the deck, leaning against the barrel. Purring, Honey brushed her shoulder against him, looking quite pleased with herself.

Wynne followed Brian to the stern of the ship. This was the first time they'd been alone since they had mated. Wynne could hardly focus her thoughts on Keith because of the rush of desire through her body. She smelled the herbal water in which Brian bathed. She was close enough to touch him.

By the god of the sea, she wanted to kiss him.

He stared at her, and she sensed he read her thoughts. The corners of his lips twitched.

"Did you bring me here, madam, to talk about Keith or about us?"

Warmth suffused her cheeks. "To talk about Keith."

He shrugged and grinned. "If that were the case, why didn't we do it over there in front of the boy?"

"I wanted him to squirm for a while."

"You like to make men squirm, don't you?"

Ignoring his sarcasm, she said, "Evidently we did not check out stores as carefully as we should have, or Keith would not have been able to stow away." She paused. "He is only a child, and we must take him back to the island."

"I don't like the idea that the boy is here any more than you do, madam, but we won't take him back. We shall be wasting valuable time."

"He can't stay aboard. It isn't safe, and he's not disciplined or skilled as a warrior. He's a child. No telling what will happen to us once we land in Ireland."

"Beathan is my enemy, not yours," Brian said. "Furthermore, I release you from your obligation to sail me back to Scotland. Once I am ashore, you are free to return to your home. You should be in no danger."

She reached out and caught his hands. "Brian," she begged, "please listen to me."

His face hard and set, he pulled his hands from hers. He seemed so different from the man with whom she had made love. He was once more the Highland warlord.

"You know I can't leave you in Ireland," she snapped.

Her heart was overriding her common sense

and reason. She abhorred the idea of leaving him
and his men in Ireland. They were trained, seasoned warriors. They could take care of themselves, and she shouldn't concern herself with
them. But she *did* care for him. She understood
abandonment; he did too. She knew she could
never leave him.

This angered her because it proved she was
weak. It went against all her principles as a seafarer. The safety of her own men should be her
first concern, not the safety of the cargo—or in this
instance Brian mac Logan and his Highlanders.

"You will do whatever I command you to do."
His voice was as brisk as hers. "You are in my
service, Wynne. Don't forget that."

"I won't, lord," she spat back. "But I do not
intend to take Keith with us. He's a child. If I send
Keith back with two of my men in a rowing boat,
we will still have enough crewmen to handle the
ship efficiently." She turned to look at him. "I
would feel much better if Keith were not on
board."

"You're letting personal sentiment cloud your
judgment," Brian said. "Keith is not a child. He's
a young man, the man of his house, and as such
he should be receiving instruction on becoming
a warrior."

"He is," Wynne said.

"More than arm wrestling with his friends and
engaging in small tourneys with his sling."

Cathmor had been telling her the same thing,
but she hadn't wanted to hear it. She depended
too much on the safety of their sequestered life on
the Isle of Cat. Brian had shattered that illusion.

"With your permission, my lady," Brian said, "I
shall be Keith's tutor during this voyage. He will
benefit, and I will keep him out of harm's way."

A champion offering to teach a former slave—it was an honor. For a moment Wynne's anger and frustration abated as she glimpsed the softer side of the man she had come to love.

"Thank you, lord," she replied. "I accept your offer, but as you say, Keith is a young man. 'Tis time he learned the art of sailing as well as fighting. I shall divide his day between you and Cathmor."

Brian nodded, and the two rejoined Keith. His face long, the lad rose.

"I'm disappointed because you lied to your sister," Wynne said, "and if the decision were mine, I would send you home. But since my ship, my crew, and I are in the service of Lord Brian, he has some say in what happens to you."

Keith grew pale and his eyes rounded. Wynne could almost read his mind. The child knew she wouldn't beat him, but he had no idea what the Highlander would do.

"As Lord Brian has pointed out to me, Keith, you are now a young man and should be studying the disciplines of manhood. Rather than punish you, we shall begin those studies immediately."

The lad's face brightened.

"One half of your day will be spent with Cathmor learning how to sail the ship. The other half you shall spend with Lord Brian."

Keith swiped a shock of unruly hair from his face as Brian stepped forward. "For the duration of this voyage you shall learn the ways of a warrior, and I shall be your tutor."

"My tutor?" Dark brown hair slid back over Keith's forehead, giving him a elfin look. A smile spread across his face. "Do you mean it, sire?"

"Aye, lad, I do."

"That smile will soon be wiped away, laddie,"

Cathmor said, his voice gruff but his eyes kind. "You will be working from sunrise to sunset, sometimes longer."

"Aye." Keith beamed. "But I will be sailing, Cathmor, and I will be learning to be a warrior."

"At night, lad, you'll hardly have the energy to crawl into your sleeping bag."

"Sleeping bag!" one of the sailors shouted. "Let him sleep in the barrel, Cathmor. That would be punishment enough."

Keith laughed. " 'Twas worth being stuck in that barrel to be here and 'twill be worth sleeping in it for me to learn how to fight and sail."

As the voyage continued, Brian began to flirt with Wynne, keeping her acutely aware of his presence. Every time she turned around, she found him working close beside her, his hand "accidentally" touching hers as they straightened provisions, as they bailed water from the ship, as they mended sails or performed other chores aboard ship.

He stood beside her at the steering oar, his feet balance on the deck, his arms folded over his chest.

"Aye, my lady," he said one day, "I can see why you love the ship. It gives you a sense of power to know that you are riding the waves."

Although he had his sea legs, he pretended to fall against her, their shoulders brushing, their hands touching. She glowered at him, but he only grinned.

"Pardon," he said but the twinkle in his eyes belied the apology.

She pretended not to notice the way he touched her because she didn't want him to know how keenly she was aware of him, or how much she wanted him. She kept reminding herself that they had no future together. He was destined to marry a Pict princess. The words became Wynne's litany, but no matter how often she repeated them, no matter that she believed them to be true, she still wanted him. With each passing day, her desire had grown until it was a continual dull ache.

Once Cathmor seriously began to instruct Keith, Brian left her and joined the boy and the Irishman. He became more interested in the working of the vessel than in her. Even Honey, the man-hating wildcat—the most ferocious animal in all the Highlands—had shifted her allegiance and now followed Brian and Keith around docilely. Perhaps the cat thought both of them were smoked herring, Wynne thought irritably. As Brian, Keith, and Cathmor worked together, they forged a friendship.

Although Wynne tried to convince herself otherwise, she resented the new friendship because it excluded her. The less attention Brian paid to her, the more his presence on the ship haunted her. He was so near, yet so far.

From daylight till noon, Brian, Keith, and Cathmor moved from one end of the ship and back again, Cathmor teaching Brian and Keith how to sail a ship, Keith and Brian obeying. Over and over again they repeated the drills until they had mastered each task.

Proud of the ship, Cathmor was pleased to explain every detail of its construction. "The heavy oak planking is riveted together and lashed to the ribs by means of cleats," he said. "High King Michael Langssonn of Glenmuir, once a Northlander now a Highlander, taught us to do this."

Brian looked over at Wynne when Cathmor

mentioned Michael's name. Their gazes caught and held. She knew that the two of them were thinking the same thing, remembering the battle of Glenmuir when they had driven out the usurper and restored the High Seat to the rightful heir, Cait nea Sholto and her husband Michael Langssonn, then of Ulfsbaer, Northland.

Cathmor continued, "This construction gives the ship flexibility in rough seas. 'Tis one of the reasons that the Northlanders are better sailors than most. The other is their love of the sea."

Keel. Tar. Mast. Over and over Wynne heard the words, the instruction.

"She has a deep keel, like the ships of the Northland," Cathmor said, "which makes her strong and easy to steer and lets us sail for longer distances in all kinds of weather."

Tiller. Pivot. Rudder.

This was the way every morning went.

The afternoons belonged to Brian and Keith. With Cathmor's help they had carved dummy wooden weapons: sword, dagger, and javelin. They had no wicker with which to weave Keith a practice shield, so they used the lid of the barrel Keith had hidden in.

Brian weighted all of these to make them twice as heavy as the real thing. For the first few days Keith could only drag them around, but he pressed his lips into a straight line and concentrated. He willed himself to do it . . . and he did.

Finally he was wielding his sword against a wooden post set in the deck. When Honey tired of watching him play with the post, she lunged at him and made him play with her. Each day Wynne waited for Brian's impatient cry, "Lady Gwynneth, come get the cat!" Dutifully she did so, knowing that as soon as she dragged Honey away, the cat would return.

After Keith had a romp with the cat, Brian paired him off with one of his warriors to spar with him. When Keith wasn't in the fray of mock battle, Brian had him running the deck, leaping over the provisions, scurrying among them, and jumping over the hull into the water, then climbing back on board, using the rope ladders.

In addition to this, he made Keith practice throwing his sling every day. At first they used a stationary target. When Keith became adept at hitting whatever Brian pointed out, Brian announced that it was time to learn to hit a moving target. This, Brian stated, was the test of a true warrior.

Padding himself in extra clothing, hiding his face behind Keith's barrel-lid shield, Brian ran around the deck while Keith tried to hit him. Pretending he was an enemy, Brian charged the boy and made him fight back. When Keith could consistently hit one moving target, Brian and Cathmor became targets at the same time. A natural slinger, Keith easily mastered each feat.

Wynne smiled when the boy bragged. His greatest delight was snagging Brian, and he became so adept with the sling that he hit Brian every time. Even Brian smiled as Keith told and retold the tale. Aye, Wynne thought, Keith had the makings of a champion—and a braggart.

One evening the wind was high, the sail taut. All had feasted on a meal of smoked ham with tasty bread, butter, and cheese, washed down with tankards of ale. Then they played games. For a while they armwrestled and threw daggers. Finally they settled down, and in the glowing torchlight played board games.

Wynne watched as Keith and Brian played. The

black stones belonged to Brian, the white ones to Keith. Each moved his stones across the squared-off board, Brian collecting the most stones as he deftly jumped Keith's pieces. Then the luck began to turn. Keith began to collect black stones. Wynne listened as Brian gave the boy pointer after pointer, as he allowed him to win several games.

Brian was firm with the boy, but also kind. Wynne could imagine him with his own children . . . with theirs. The thought so jolted her that she rose and walked to her tent. She would be glad when this voyage ended. Brian mac Logan was intruding on every aspect of her life.

Long after the others had gone to sleep, Wynne was still awake. Sitting outside her shelter on her sleeping bag, she huddled against the hull of the ship. The blue-black sky was luminous with twinkling stars and a full moon. Silver shadows filled the ship. Water lapped hypnotically against the hull, and the wind sighed through the rigging.

A sailor stood and walked toward Wynne. Brian. She had no doubt it was he. Towering in height, broad in shoulders, lean in the hips. Aye, he was the Highlander. Much to Wynne's surprise, and to her admiration, Brian rode the tempest of the waves as if he had been born to the sea.

He came closer. Her heart beat faster. He sat down beside her.

"You couldn't sleep either?" he asked.

"Nay."

She sighed and shut her eyes, wishing Brian had not sat so close to her. She could think of nothing but her wants and desires when he was so near her.

"Why are you so deep in thought, seafarer?"

She turned to gaze into his face. Although the moon shone brightly, his eyes were shadowed. But she saw his lips clearly and as clearly remembered the feel of them on hers ... on her body. She trembled.

Brian caught her hand. "Are you cold?"

She shook her head.

He leaned over and lightly pressed his lips to her forehead. "I've missed you, Wynne."

"Aye," she whispered. "I've missed you."

"I've been thinking about us," he said. "And about Lachlann."

"Lachlann!" Wynne exclaimed.

"Aye. He is single, and Malcolm could as easily marry him to the Pict princess."

Joy sang through Wynne's body. Brian twined their fingers together; then he turned her hand over and rubbed the callused top of his thumb over the center of her palm, sending shivers of pleasure through her body.

"I think Malcolm and Lachlann will be agreeable to the marriage."

"But we won't know this, lord, until you speak to your liege," Wynne said, her joy tempered.

He nodded.

"Mayhap Malcolm has already made the marriage arrangements," she guessed.

"Nay, Malcolm will talk to me first."

Wynne pulled her hand from his clasp and brushed it through his hair.

"I want you, lady," Brian murmured thickly.

"Aye, lord, I want you also."

"I have stayed away from you as long as I could, lady, working all my waking hours so that my body and my mind would be rid of thoughts of you, so I could sleep at night."

"Were you successful, lord?"

"Nay." He caught her in his arms, molding his mouth to hers. He guided her lips open and filled

her with the hot demand of his tongue. Without
moving his mouth from hers, he whispered, "I had
not planned to do this, my lady. I had intended
to keep my distance. But I cannot help the wanting
within me, a wanting that only your body can
satisfy."

"Aye, lord, I understand. I feel the same way
about you."

Again his mouth possessed her. His hands
curved around the fullness of her breasts; he
moved his palms over the soft mounds, stroking
and kneading her nipples until they hardened and
swelled to taut peaks. Wynne moaned softly.

"Wynne," he murmured. "I want to mate with
you."

He opened her shirt and moved a finger down
the valley between her breasts.

Wynne knew she should deny his touch. She
wanted to, but unbidden excitement rushed
through her. His callused palm, skimming over
her nipples, ignited a slowly building fire within
her. It swept down into her, to the very center of
her being, into the apex of her thighs and her most
womanly recesses.

Wynne's hand moved down his chest, beneath
the waistband of his trousers. She spread her hand
through the crisp pubic hair. She felt the same fire
in him, the hard shaft of his sex. Tension sizzled
between them.

His lips lifted from hers and touched down
upon them again and again, until her mouth was
swollen and her breath was ragged, until she
clung to him, never to let him go.

When his lips left hers, they traveled a slow,
demanding trail across her cheek to her earlobe,
and she felt the hot moisture of his breath there,
and then upon her throat.

"Let me sleep with you," he said.

"I want to, lord, but I cannot. Nothing has changed between us."

"Aye." He sighed. "You're right, lass."

"I will wait for you," she promised.

He hugged her tightly, then put her away from him. Pushing to his feet, he braced his hands on the side of the ship and gazed into the distance. Wynne straightened her shirt and rose also.

Eventually she asked, "How is Keith coming along?"

"He's going to be a champion one of these days," Brian replied. "I would like to take him back to Scotland with me. Would you agree?"

"You want to take him with you?" she echoed.

"Aye, I would like to foster him."

She was so surprised, she couldn't think. The words hardly registered. "Foster him?"

"Aye, madam," he said patiently. "You are familiar with the custom of fostering."

"I know about fostering," she snapped. "I had not thought of it in regard to Keith."

"'Twould be to his advantage, since I am one of the most powerful headmen in Clan Duncan." He broke off and sighed. "As quickly as House Logan is growing, my kindred shall soon be as numerous as the Duncans, and we shall be a clan unto ourselves. 'Tis one of the reasons that Malcolm has been pressing me to wed again. He wants to unite the kingdoms of Scotland."

Sensitive about the possibility of an arranged marriage for Brian, Wynne steered the conversation back to its original course. "Thank you for offering to foster the lad, my lord," she said. "I shall have to think about it before giving an answer."

He nodded. Still he did not seem inclined to leave her.

"How much longer before we reach Donegal Bay?" he asked.

"Several more days. If the wind keeps up like this and we have no storms," Wynne answered, gazing at the stars. "You're eager to be there?"

"Sometimes, lady, my gut is twisted so tight, I don't know what to do. I am so close, yet so far."

Aye, Wynne thought, she understood that feeling well.

"I fear I shall not be able to find Beathan and reclaim the girdle in time. With each passing night I lose time." He raked his fingers across the rail. "This is so important to Elspeth . . . and to me."

Wynne caught his hand and held it tightly.

"I was a baby and had no way of protecting myself when my father put me out," he said, lifting his head so that she saw his anguish. "But I am a man now, a warrior. I must protect my daughter's heritage."

Wynne squeezed his hand but did not try to assuage his guilt. His heart would not believe it, and the words would sound hollow.

"I don't know what I shall do if I allow my daughter to be shamed."

"We shall be there in a short time," Wynne promised him, "and Cathmor will find Beathan. No ship is more trustworthy or swifter than mine, no warrior better than Cathmor. Neither of us will fail you, sire."

"Thank you, lady." He squeezed her hand.

A mist rolled in from the sea, enclosing them. The air between them changed, and once again Wynne felt as if they were creating a magical world in which no one existed except them. Far away she heard a noise and knew the night crewmen were stirring.

Softly she said, "Morning comes soon, lord."

"Aye."

" 'Tis time for us to go to bed."

He drew her into his embrace. His lips touched her forehead, brushed down her nose, finally settled on her mouth. The kiss was sweetly tentative at first, so fragile that Wynne would have thought they weren't touching. Yet fire swept through her body. She moved closer.

Lost in the beauty of such incredible feelings, Wynne slid her palms up Brian's chest. His skin was warm and moist, his hair crisp and dark.

As he deepened the kiss, his tongue grew more insistent, and his hand began to slip down her back to cup her buttocks. She trembled. She clung to him, pressing her breasts into the hard muscles of his chest. She felt the hard warmth of his erection. She was heavy and aching with desire.

Lifting his mouth from hers, stepping back, both of them breathing heavily, he said, "Good night, lady. Dream of me."

He turned, and she watched him walk across the deck to his sleeping bag. As he moved, the pearly light of the moon played on the material that covered his buttocks and thighs. He never looked back, and she didn't look away until he was wrapped in the sleeping bag.

She eased into her tent and onto her pallet, more restless now than before. Her body was hot, her senses honed to a fine pitch. Her body ached for his touch, for the fulfillment of their coupling.

But underlying all these fiery sensations was a deep-seated contentment. Brian wanted to marry her; he wanted her for his first wife. He was going to speak to Malcolm about it. Somehow Wynne felt sure that Brian would succeed in convincing the king to allow Lachlann to marry the Pict princess.

Smiling, she curled into a ball and fell asleep.

Chapter 15

⌒◯◯⌒

At dawn three days later, they arrived at their destination. Wynne docked the *Honeycomb* in an inlet at Donegal Bay, Ireland. Brian was one of the first to step ashore. Wynne remained aboard. Sailors and warriors scurried up and down the landing plank unloading the cargo and setting up camp in a deserted village of stone houses. All day everyone worked efficiently, talking little.

Honey pressing against her side, Wynne gazed at the rocky shoreline. Donegal Bay, Ireland. She was here ... here in the land she had feared for so many years. A land she had promised herself she would never walk upon again.

With a little disquiet Wynne strode down the landing plank onto the Irish shore. She stood for a moment, rubbing her boot against the dirt, kicking loose pebbles. She looked around, almost expecting some of the O'Illands to leap out of the rocks and attack her. A gust of wind tore at her cloak and whirled her hair about her face.

Through the years she had managed to put thoughts of her deceased husband out of her mind for long periods. But the closer she had come to Ireland, the more often she had thought of him and the horror of their wedding night. She envisioned what could happen to her and her crew now that they were on Irish shores. And since news traveled quickly, she had no doubt that Brian mac Logan's presence would soon be known. Quite possibly no one would connect her with him . . . but one never knew.

She must be on guard at all times. She was on enemy land, and the enemy had sworn a blood oath to kill her. An oath not to be taken lightly. Nay, he had hired a champion to hunt her down. In the past, with the Irish Sea between her and her enemies, she had been able to push the threat aside. She could do so no longer.

Cathmor walked up behind her. "Don't look so solemn, madam. As soon as Lord Brian locates Beathan, we shall be on our way."

" 'Twas not our agreement. He paid me to wait for him and to sail him back to Scotland."

"The Highlander has released you from your original agreement. All of us are witnesses to it."

But she had not released herself! The plight of an innocent girl had compelled her to come, and she had lived up to her end of the bargain. She had safely delivered Brian mac Logan and his men to Eire. She didn't have to stay, didn't have to disembark, but she chose to do so. Aye, she had come because of Elspeth, but she would remain because of Brian mac Logan.

She could not help remembering Great-Grandmother Feich's prophecy and knew that she was about to meet her destiny. Not knowing the future, she was both apprehensive and eager to embrace it.

"I sent both boats out to explore the coastline," she said, referring to the small crafts they always carried aboard ship. "One in either direction. They're to report back by sunset tomorrow."

"I know you are a woman of your word, lady,"

Cathmor said, "but you must not neglect your safety or that of the crew."

"Nay," she murmured, knowing that no matter how endangered she might be, she would not abandon Brian. She loved him and would remain by his side to the bitter or glorious end.

"We have made good time, my lady."

"Aye." She was glad Cathmor had changed the subject.

Truly the gods had granted them favor on the voyage. It had been swift and uneventful. The sun had shone every day, and the temperature had been cool. At night the sky had glowed with moon and starlight. The winds had been the mariners' to command. In record time they had sailed from the Isle of Cat to the coast of Ireland. Even now Cathmor and the crewmen were bragging about their feat.

The gods were still smiling on them. Only now, after they had landed in Eire and were moving into the shelter of the ancient and deserted village, did a storm move in. With the heavens so beautiful, Wynne could hardly believe a storm was imminent. Yet she smelled it in the air, saw it in the turbulent water, and heard it in the wail of the wind. Clouds amassed in the distance and moved steadily toward them.

"I have never heard a mariner boast of having sailed across the Irish Sea in such a short time," Cathmor said. "Bards will sing about it in the mead hall, lady."

Pushing her anxiety aside, attempting levity, she said, "Why let the bards do the singing for us? I shall play the harp, and you shall dance one of your Irish jigs."

"Aye, my lady, you play and sing and I shall

dance." He chuckled. "I will enjoy watching the other seafarers turn green with envy."

The evening breeze gained momentum, whirling dust bowls in the air. Slowly Wynne and Cathmor ambled from the shore up the incline to the ruins of the ancient Irish village, the site Cathmor had chosen for their first encampment. Most of the stone buildings still stood intact. Those that still had roofs would provide shelter from inclement weather as well as fortification against an attack.

Wynne's crewmen and Brian's warriors worked together to set up camp. One of the mariners, appointed cook, moved into the largest building, what had probably been the Great Hall. The walls of the large room were still standing, but those that had formed sleeping chambers along the side had long since crumbled to the ground. Although badly in need of repair, a roof still covered most of the room. Chairs, benches, and tables, though knocked askew, were scattered about the room, and sleeping platforms, jutting from the walls, were still in good shape. The hearth was in excellent condition, and the cook soon had a fire blazing and food cooking for the evening meal.

Brian quickly set up relay groups of mounted scouts to patrol the surrounding area. Each team would be relieved every four hours, so that none became fatigued and ineffective. Other warriors, hidden in strategic places, guarded the immediate camp. The remainder unloaded the ship and stored provisions.

"Come this way, lady," Cathmor said, leading her through the camp. "I chose a special place for you. It's separated from the rest of the camp and grants you privacy to come and go to the nearby lagoon without being seen."

"Thank you."

He smiled at her.

" 'Tis an old village." She studied a few of the scattered dwellings.

"So old that we don't know its history. My father told me that it had been uninhabited for as long as he could remember, and as far back as his father could remember."

In the distance Keith was running about with his wooden sword and barrel-lid shield, hacking and slashing at any object he could find. Wynne smiled. The lad had blossomed since Brian had begun to tutor him. Idly her gaze came to rest on the bell tower that yet stood near the shoreline.

"Is your original home close by?" Wynne asked Cathmor.

"Nay, but when we went on trading expeditions, we often traveled this route and used this place for our camp."

They stopped in front of Wynne's shelter, a round stone house. Cathmor leaned against the door frame.

"The buildings are yet solid, my lady, and the thatching in fair repair. 'Tis a good place for us to camp and to escape the storm."

Wynne entered the house, stepping around the sea trunk and physician's chest that had been deposited there earlier. Although the room had seen only campers for many years, it was surprisingly well furnished. In the center was a round fire pit, curbed with stones. Already a fire burned brightly, and one of the crewmen had stacked wood nearby. A long chain with a cauldron hook hung from the ceiling framework over the fire.

Close to the fire was a table on which had been set a large wooden basin and several wooden tankards and bowls. Benches lined either side of the table, and a filled water barrel had been set at one end. Washing and drying cloths were draped haphazardly. A massive wooden chair with broad arms and three stools were scattered about. Clothing rods were suspended from the ceiling beams by leather thongs. On one rod, a crewman had hooked a sheepskin filled with ale. Corbels protruded from the walls. The remains of torches cluttered the floor.

Kneeling and banking the fire, Cathmor asked, "Is there anything else you wish me to do?"

"Not at the moment." She took off her dagger and sword and laid them across the table.

"Then I shall be on my way to see if I can find news of Beathan."

"Is mac Logan going with you?"

"I have asked him not to. One of us may not stir up as much curiosity as two. Since I am a native, I shall be able to learn more by myself. But—" He shrugged as he picked up the physician's chest and set it on the table. Then he reached for her sleeping bag and began to unroll it.

"Leave without telling the Highlander," Wynne ordered.

"I would like to do that for his sake, my lady." He spread the coverlet over the sleeping platform. "But he will be angry."

"You're not his vassal," Wynne said.

"Nay, but I don't wish to cross him." He straightened and gazed solemnly at her. "During this voyage I have grown to respect him."

Wynne was only too aware of the bond of friendship that had developed between the two warriors, and she was a little jealous of it. She was even more jealous that Cathmor was now deferring to Brian. She made no effort to mask her irritation.

"You would rather cross *me?*"

The Irishman did not flinch.

"I care not whether he will be angry, Cathmor. I am your liege." She knew her voice was sharper than usual, but she felt betrayed. "It is my command that you obey, not mac Logan's."

"I have no intention of disobeying a command you give me, my lady," he said quietly. "I have sworn my loyalty to you. I was thinking only of you. I don't want the Highlander to vent his anger on you."

Wynne sighed, instantly regretting her show of hostility. "I'm sorry too, Cathmor. Mac Logan seems to bring out the worst in me."

"Aye." He walked to the window, pushed aside the wooden shutter, and gazed outside. "The storm will probably hit before I return."

"When will that be?"

"Tomorrow by sunset. The same time you ordered the boats to return."

"That won't be long enough for you to learn the lay of the land and to find the nearest village."

"Lord Brian has loaned me one of his ponies. I should be able to travel fast. He has also sent out his own scouts in what he calls a relay. By the time I return, those outriders, as he calls them, will have scouted as much territory as could be covered in any direction during a three or three-and-a-half-day march."

"He is a wise man," Wynne murmured.

"Always a warrior."

"Be careful, Cathmor."

"I will, lady." He pushed away from the window and went to the door. Stopping, he said, "If I'm not back by sunset, don't come looking for me."

"You are asking the impossible."

"Your word, lady."

She smiled sadly and shook her head. "Nay, Cathmor, I cannot. I am a woman of my word, and I shall not be bound by such an oath."

Ducking, he passed through. Wynne followed.

"May the gods go with you, Cathmor," she said softly.

"I pray they do, my lady. I shall need their help." He looked toward camp. "I pray they are with you when the Highlander learns I have left without him. He is not a man to suffer his wrath quietly."

"Nay," Wynne murmured, "he is not."

Long after Cathmor had ridden out of the encampment, Wynne stood in the door of her lodging and watched Brian's warriors unload their equipment and ponies from the ship. She never had to search long or hard for Brian. He towered over the others, was broader through the shoulders, and was leaner through the hips. She immediately recognized his arrogant gait, the tilt of his head, the set of his shoulders.

She heard ponies thundering up the hill, and turned to see Brian driving them in. Lashing a whip through the air, never touching one of the magnificent steeds, he sat a pony with the same grace that he walked or fought or stood on the deck of a tossing ship. With fluid grace he slipped off the stallion, slapped its flank lightly, and sent it trotting into the large two-room building they were using as a stable.

He had discarded his cloak earlier and now wore only his tunic and black leather trousers. As he shut the stable door, Wynne watched the play of muscles beneath the tightly stretched fabric. Long sleeves were rolled up to reveal firm, muscular, sun-browned arms. The sun glinted off the gold torque around his neck. It reflected on the armband on his wrist as he lifted his hand and brushed it through sweat-dampened hair. Perspiration trickled down his temples and cheeks and stained his shirt across his shoulders and beneath his arms.

He turned and caught her staring at him. He wiped his arm across his forehead and stared back. She smiled hesitantly; he didn't smile at all. He simply stared, his expression so intent that Wynne felt as if he had touched her.

His gaze moved over each feature of her face, her eyes, her lips. She felt the visual caress on her tunic, her breasts. She caught her breath. Her breasts swelled and tightened, thrusting against the soft fabric. He noticed. A smile caught one corner of his mouth, and Wynne's breathing deepened.

One of his warriors called out to him. He answered but continued to stare at Wynne, his gaze moving to her face. Still he did not fully smile. Again he wiped his arm across his forehead, his armband sparkling. Then he turned and walked over to one of the water jars. Muscles rippled through his arms and back as he lifted the jar high and doused himself.

The water sluiced over his head and shoulders. It molded his hair to his scalp and face; it caused the shirt to cling to his muscular torso; it bounced off the leather trousers and splattered to the ground at his feet. Setting the jar down, he tossed his head back, slinging water off his hair. Without sparing her another glance, he strode into the Great Hall where he and his warriors were taking shelter.

Like stormy waves, disappointment tore at Wynne. She didn't know why. He had done everything she had asked of him. She had set the rules by which they had conducted themselves, and he had obeyed. She had told him to stay away from her, and he had. She had told him to refrain from touching her, and he had. Yet his very presence continued to haunt her, as did the memories of their times together.

Honey brushed against Wynne's legs and nuzzled her hand. Wynne looked down. "So Brian and Keith have abandoned you too?" she said. "Keith for his sword and Brian for his ponies."

The cat gave a low meow and arched her head more fully against Wynne's palm.

"Both of us need attention, don't we? But we may not get it anymore. Mac Logan has his battle to fight, and Keith has Brian. But I don't care."

Wynne knelt and threw her arms around Honey's neck. "Aye, I do care." She buried her face in the short, bristly fur. "I'm so confused, I don't know what to do."

Honey leaned into Wynne, rubbing her muzzle against Wynne's nose. Wynne laughed. From the encampment she heard the laughter and raised voices of her sailors. She looked over to see them still unloading the ship.

"Make haste, lads!" she shouted. "Get the trunks into the buildings. We're in for a storm."

"Aye, my lady."

As the crewmen continued their work, Wynne strolled through the camp, examining the old buildings that were yet intact. Several beehive ovens were still standing among the ruins. One, in excellent condition, stood close to the Great Hall. She ran her hand over the top, noting that it was well-built, sturdy, and exceptionally clean. It was in such good shape that they could bake in it if necessary.

She strolled to the far side of the old village.
Honey, making her own exploration, tagged along.
Finally Wynne came to a pile of stones that had
crumbled in front of a small pocket of water next
to the remains of the old bell tower.

The wind biting her face, pressing her tunic
against her body, Wynne gazed out at sea. She
loved it. It had given her a home when no one
wanted to take her in; it had given her a freedom
she had never imagined possible. The water was
gray-green in color, the waves fluffy white. Oddly
the waves did not look so much turbulent as playful; they seemed to be frolicking, as if to welcome
the brewing storm, to invite the thunder and
lightning.

Others might think the seacoast barren and desolate. Not Wynne. Its austerity was as beautiful to
her as the forested coves. She reached down and
picked up a handful of pebbles. Still slashing
imaginary enemies, Keith came running up to her.

"The old village is nice, don't you think?" he
asked.

"Aye, 'tis a fine place to camp."

Laying his weapons aside, Keith started crawl-
ing around and peering into the mound of rocks.

"Lady . . ." He paused. "I see something."

She looked down as he moved closer, squinting
through the cracks.

"I saw something glinting in there."

Walking around the mound of rubble, Wynne
studied it. She kicked lightly at it, spewing pebbles
and stones to the ground. She knelt and also
peered between the cracks.

"I don't see anything."

" 'Twas down here." He yanked several of the
stones out, grunting. "I saw it, my lady. Do you
think it could be treasure?"

"I doubt it," she replied.

"But it may be." Keith grunted. " 'Tis a good hiding place. No one would think to look here."

Wynne suppressed a smile and kept digging.

By now sailors and warriors had begun to circle Wynne and Keith as they pulled away debris. She yanked several more stones out, but they were getting bigger and harder to handle. She broke a fingernail and scratched her hand.

"Raiders hid their booty here, and we're going to find it," Keith declared. "I'm going to be a wealthy man, my lady."

"Aye," she said dryly.

Out of the corner of her eye, Wynne saw Brian push through the circle of onlookers and kneel beside them, blocking out the sun.

"My lord Brian," Keith exclaimed. "I have found a treasure."

"If you have, lad, it belongs to you. 'Tis the law. The finder is the keeper."

Keith's eyes sparked.

Brian moved, and a flicker of sunlight hit the mound. Wynne saw the glint.

"I've found it!" she cried.

Eager comments buzzed through the group.

"She's found it."

"There is something there!"

They tightened the circle, bent closer, and peered more intently.

"It's here, my lord," Keith said. "We've found it!"

Disregarding the size and shape of the stones, Keith began to dig furiously, tossing them aside. The stack in front of him diminished; the pile behind him grew.

"My lady—" Keith's low voice throbbed with anticipation. "I feel something."

An excited murmur rippled through the warriors. They began to clear the rubble from around Keith and Wynne, each wanting to be the first to see.

"Let me see," Wynne said. Keith scooted away, and she slid her hand into the tunnel they had dug.

Tension mounted.

"Can you feel it?" Keith asked.

"Aye," she mumbled. "It is cool and hard. Not coarse like a stone, but smooth like worked metal."

She glanced up to see Brian watching them with cool amusement. That look would be wiped off his face when she and the lad pulled out a worthy prize, she thought. Sliding her hand out, she and Keith carefully dug through the debris.

"Aye," she mumbled, "it is metal."

Honey wedged her face in, sniffed, and meowed her agreement.

Laughing, almost crying, Wynne and Keith worked longer, with more fervor, until finally they had exposed the object. They grunted, they tugged, they sweated. Finally it rolled out.

"A bell, my lady," Keith whispered, falling back. He shook his head. "A very small, very old bell."

A bell!

Could it be the sacred bell of the Cloister of the Grove? Wynne's hands grew clammy. Aye, she thought, it could be. It was so old it was covered in lichen and slimy to the touch. Hadn't the gods of the Grove promised Mother Barbara that they would find and return the bell to the cloister? Surely before summer solstice! Wynne reasoned, before Raven must take the vow of silence.

Honey poked her nose in, sniffing and pawing.

"Nay." Wynne gently pushed her aside. "You tend to your business. Keith and I shall tend to ours."

"Don't be deceived by what you see," Brian warned, as if he had read Wynne's thoughts. "Look at what you have, Keith."

The disheartened child pulled out his dagger, and he and Wynne scraped off the greenish growth. Periodically they elbowed Honey out of the way. They worked for a long time before they succeeded in removing most of the lichen. Finally Wynne leaned back, brushing an arm over her forehead.

"Is it valuable?" Keith asked.

Wynne looked up at Dow, one of her crewmen who also served as a blacksmith.

He was scratching his beard-stubbled cheeks and shaking his head. A thick mop of curly black hair bounced around his long, thin face. "I've seen lots of bells in my lifetime, but this is the ugliest of the lot."

"Aye," Wynne agreed.

Dow ran his hand over the bell. "See how dull it is. Not only is it the ugliest, but this metal is of the poorest grade I've ever encountered." He turned it over, running his fingers around the edges, over the outside, and all around the inside.

"Do you see any identifying marks?" Wynne asked.

The blacksmith shook his head. "Nay, and I can imagine why not. 'Tis a disgrace to the smithy who cast it." He passed his palms over the surface of the bell, up and down. " 'Tis cracked."

Keith leaned forward. "I don't see a crack."

"It's filled with dirt," Dow replied.

"Dow," Wynne said, excitement causing her

voice to tremble, "could there be another bell beneath this base metal?"

Dow pulled out his dagger and pressed the point in the crack, running it up and down. Then he scrapped different places around the surface. Shaking his head, he gazed at her. "Nay, my lady, this is all there is. No doubt it was hastily made to replace a finer bell that was broken or stolen. No wonder the people didn't take it when they left the village. It's not worth anything, and it won't sound good when it's rung."

Brushing debris from his hands, Dow rose.

" 'Tis yours, Keith," Wynne said. She pushed back on her knees. "Do you want to take it with us or leave it behind?"

Disappointed, Keith shook his head. " 'Tis ugly all right, my lady, but it looks so lonely out here." He glanced up at the tower. "Perhaps we could hang it up there where it belongs."

"You're right, lad, it does look forlorn lying out here," Wynne said, understanding his disappointment. " 'Tis not the bell's fault that it is dull and ugly. 'Tis the maker's."

Brian kicked around through the rubble until he found the cylindrical metal rod from which the bell had been suspended in the tower.

"The bell has suffered enough indignity," he said and looked over at the blacksmith. " 'Tis a small bell, Dow. Do you think the tower is sturdy enough to hold it?"

Dow walked around, kicking the stone tower, testing its strength. He ran his hands over it. "It seems strong enough to me, considering that's a small bell. I'd say, sire, that this tower was built for a much larger and heavier one, probably the one this was cast to replace."

"Then," Brian announced, "we shall return the

bell to its rightful home. This will be Keith's first memorial as a warrior."

Keith leaped to his feet. His eyes were bright, his lips split in a big smile. "Thank you, my lord. Thank you."

Smiling, Wynne called to more of her men. Soon they and Brian's warriors were hefting the bell up the nearby tower so that it once again swung on the round bar. As the smithy had predicted, its tone was flat.

Wynne and Keith returned to camp, Keith joining a group of warriors around the fire and telling them about his find. Wynne walked over to a stack of supplies. Tilting over the same water jug Brian had used earlier, she washed her hands.

Afterward she returned to her lodge, Honey at her side. Sitting down against a far outside wall, away from the hustle and bustle of the camp, out of the way of peering eyes, she let herself relax. Honey purred, turning her head and rubbing Wynne's face with her jaw. Weary, she closed her eyes. She would rest for a few minutes before she ate the evening meal.

"My lady!" a deep masculine voice barked.

Wynne jumped and opened her eyes, gazing up at Brian.

"I didn't mean to startle you."

"I must have dozed off," she said, brushing sleep from her eyes.

His legs spread, his hands planted on his hips, he loomed over her. The sun was to his back, and his beard-stubbled face lay in shadow. She didn't like him towering above her. He seemed much too formidable. She pushed to her feet, brushing twigs from her legs and buttocks.

"What do you want, mac Logan?"

He didn't answer, and she looked up, her hands

on her hips. She caught her breath at the raw, unbridled desire that darkened his visage. She knew what Brian mac Logan wanted. Her heart began to pound as she imagined what he would say.

"One of my horses has a deep and inflamed cut," he answered.

Startled, disappointed, she stared at him. She knew he had felt the current of desire running between them. This is not what the two of them were thinking, what they wanted.

"I would like to treat it with the ointment we used on your arm."

They were outdoors, yet his presence reduced the size of the village, made it seem as if it were a miniature crafted for a child's play toy. No matter what they were discussing on the surface, Wynne and Brian were conversing on a more basic, elemental level. The village closed tightly around them.

"Aye," she replied, giving no indication of her true emotions. " 'Tis inside in the physician's chest."

The wind blew her cloak against his arm. His hand fastened around the material. As he removed it, she watched his hands caress the fabric, and her heartbeat accelerated. She remembered him caressing her body.

Pushing her sensual thoughts aside, Wynne said, her voice throaty, "What you did today for Keith was kind."

" 'Twas a repayment."

He fell silent, and Wynne didn't know if he would explain what he meant.

Finally he explained, "All children find prizes like the bell that have no bartering value. Yet to the one who finds them, they are worthwhile."

Again he paused, and Wynne could tell that he had gone back in time and memories. "Once I found an old chest. Like Keith, I was sure my prize was booty. 'Twas filled with nothing but old clothes set out during the spring cleaning. My mentor laughed and made fun of me. He described the incident to my father, who ridiculed me in the mead hall in front of all the other warriors. I promised then that I would bring home more booty than any of my father's men. And I did."

"Tonight my men will jest with Keith," Wynne said. "They will not be cruel. 'Twill all be light-hearted fun."

"I know that, lady. And from this day forward Keith will always remember this bell. When he is assailed by doubts and fears he will gain strength from this moment of triumph."

"My lord," Wynne said, "I have been giving thought to your request to foster Keith."

He looked at her.

"When I return to the isle I shall speak to both Keith and Erinn. If they are agreeable I shall give my approval."

"Thank you, lady."

"But, lord, I want you to let Keith stay with us some portion of the year so that he knows his kindred family as well as his fostered."

"That can be arranged."

They heard Honey's playful growl from above. Both looked up toward the roof at the same moment that Honey leaped down. Wynne felt the cat's weight brush against her back as Honey flew through the air, bumping Wynne against Brian and toppling both of them to the ground. Honey fell between them, but with a deft twist was on her feet, yowling, ready to play.

"Damnation!" Brian pushed to a sitting position and glared at Wynne over the cat. "Gwynneth, I swear I have never hated anything more than I hate this cat."

"Nay, lord, you don't. She may irritate you at times, but when you think no one is watching, you feed and play with her." She smiled. "Between you and Keith, our smoked fish is quickly disappearing into Honey's tummy."

Disentangling himself from paws and tail and abrasive tongue, Brian stood. Honey raised up on her hind paws, placing the front ones on Brian's chest. He stumbled back, fighting for balance as she leaned into him, thumping her nose against his. He caught the wildcat's paws in each hand and pushed her away from him. But Honey wouldn't budge. She brushed her muzzle against his cheek. He sneezed. Wynne caught Honey and tugged her away from him. He sneezed again.

"I've been looking for Cathmor." He blinked his watering eyes. "Where is he?"

"Gone," she answered.

"Gone," he repeated.

She nodded.

"He left without me!" His lips thinned.

"Aye, I told him to."

"You countermanded one of my orders, madam!" Fury blazed in Brian's eyes; it contorted his features. The warlord had replaced the tender lover. He moved slowly toward her. She backed up.

"When we were on your island, madam, you were the mistress, but here on this voyage I am the master." He caught her wrist, his fingers biting into her flesh. "You will not dishonor me in front of my men or yours, Gwynneth. Do you understand me?"

Wynne stared into his eyes, glazed with anger directed toward her. She was frightened. She had witnessed Brian's temper and knew how black it was, how dangerous he could become.

But she wasn't thinking about Brian or his anger. She was remembering Alba, the way he had screamed at her. She was brutally being carried back in time. Yet she refused to cower as she had done when she was sixteen. Long ago she had promised never to let a man beat her again. And she hadn't.

"Turn me loose!" She twisted her arm from his grasp and glared angrily at him. "Don't ever speak to me in that tone of voice again, and don't touch me in your anger."

Brian stepped back, his face still contorted with fury but his voice calmer. "I didn't intend to frighten you."

"I wouldn't allow you to," she said. "I promised myself, Highlander, that no man would take advantage of me again."

"You countermanded my orders. What happens here in Ireland, lady, is my business, not yours. You had no right to send one of your warriors to tend to my business."

"You're right, lord. I overstepped the bounds of my authority."

He stared at her.

"But I would do it again," she added softly, firmly.

"Aye, lady, I know you would, and that knowledge makes me even angrier." He paused. "But I would never strike you. I would gladly kill the man who hit you and put a fear of all men into you. At the moment I regret that he is dead, and I am denied the pleasure of killing him."

In the same breath with which he assured her

that he would never hurt her, he reaffirmed the wild, primitive side of himself, the barbarian warrior. For all their brutality, his words excited her, because she felt for the first time that someone cared enough about her to lay his life on the line.

"I didn't countermand your order with the intention of belittling you," she said. "I am Cathmor's liege."

" 'Tis my duty and responsibility to avenge my shame, lady. I should be the one who gives the orders, the one who enjoys the glory or endures the defeat."

"Aye."

"The respect and honor that you ask for yourself, you are refusing to give to me."

"I sent Cathmor alone because I want both of you alive, my lord," Wynne said. "Because I care for you."

His face softened. "I'm glad that you care, lady, but do not interfere again. I am capable of taking care of my responsibilities."

"Aye, lord, you are. But I figured that one person making inquiries about an Irish raider would be less conspicuous than two. And more likely to find the information you are seeking, thereby saving us time, my lord."

Silence lengthened between them. Wynne thought she detected a slight twitch at the corners of his mouth. He lowered his lids, hiding his eyes.

"Any man who gets you, Wynne, will have his hands full," Brian said.

"Aye, lord, he will," Wynne replied. "Let's hope that his hands are big enough to hold me."

"Not only hold you," Brian said, "but control you."

"No one's hands are that big."

"Nay, lady, I suppose not."

Feeling a little better now that Brian was teasing her, Wynne said, "Cathmor will be back by sunset tomorrow."

The wind, gaining momentum, whipped her cloak. Thunder cracked in the distance, and both of them looked up at the sky. The bank of dark clouds had moved closer.

"The storm," Wynne said as she led him into the shelter. She walked over to the physician's chest in front of the fire pit, unfastened the leather straps, and lifted the lid. " 'Twill be a bad one, my lord. Make sure the beasts are tucked in safely so they don't take fright and run."

He nodded as he took the jar of ointment from her, his fingers closing over hers.

"Are you frightened of storms?" he asked.

"Nay," she replied, breathless.

Only of my emotions where you are concerned. Only of being alone after you have left my life!

Wanting to be with him, she said, "Although I have never treated ponies, I'm a good dresser. Melanthe taught me well."

"I'm sure you're a good dresser," he murmured, a lazy smile tugging at his lips. "Certainly you're a good *un*dresser."

Pleasure flushed Wynne's face, and from the way his gaze settled on her cheeks, she knew he was aware of her state of anticipation.

"Would you like me to examine your pony?" she asked.

His smile widened; his voice lowered. "Aye, I would."

Chapter 16

⟡⟡⟡

The wind gushed around them, whipping up dust and pebbles. In the distance lightning speared the sky; thunder rumbled.

Wynne looked at Brian's profile as he gazed up at the sky, and her heart skipped a beat. He was the handsomest man she had ever seen, mature and rugged. Aye, he would always be a Highland warrior, but he was not unkind or unjust in his treatment of others. He turned at that moment. Their eyes locked. He smiled; so did she.

"A storm is rather like a person, don't you think?" she murmured.

"Aye, lady, like lovers."

Twin blades of lightning zigzagged up the sky, intertwining to become one brilliant flash of silver. Lovers, Brian had said. Wynne agreed. Truly the elements were mating and would give birth to new life on earth. She shivered with anticipation.

"Many people are frightened of storms, lady, because they wreak great havoc and leave damage in their wake."

"Aye," she admitted, "but they are also a necessary part of nature. They are exhilarating, lord, and wonderful."

He stopped walking. So did she. They gazed at each other without touching. No words were necessary; they were communicating fully. He

held out his hand. She placed hers in it. Both
looked down as he closed his fingers around hers.
At the same moment they looked up at each other.

By mutual and silent consent they resumed
walking. When they reached the two-room building used as a stable, they heard the ponies whin-
nying. One of the Highlanders, a young warrior,
pushed away from a porch pillar and sauntered
toward them.

"How's the stallion?" Brian asked.

Albert was a large man, but Brian dwarfed him.
Albert's eyes, a deep blue, moved toward the stallion, then back to Brian. "He's restless, more so
than the others."

"Aye," Brian said, looking at Wynne. "I am too.
'Tis the storm."

"You have the ointment?" Albert held out his
hands.

"Aye, but my lady and I shall examine the stallion. She is a dresser."

Placing his hand in the middle of Wynne's back,
Brian guided her into the smaller room. Albert followed. At one time the space had been used as
either a sleeping chamber or a kitchen. A fire
burned brightly and a bedroll had been spread
over the frame of an old bed.

There were several tables, one of them pushed
against a far wall. On it was a wooden basin filled
with water, some wooden tankards, and a large
leather wine bag. Lying on the floor were several
satchels, the kind used by Brian and his men. Constructed of soft, worked leather, they held supplies, a change of clothing, and mail and helmet.
They could be rolled up and tied to the backs of
their ponies.

Still guiding Wynne with the light touch of his
hand on her back, Brian led her across this cham-

ber into the larger one, where the ponies were stabled. Although lighted torches hung on columns in both rooms, Albert followed with a burning one.

Reassuring the ponies with soft words and gentle pats, Brian and Wynne moved slowly until they reached the gray. The warrior dipped the torch close to the pony's flank. Brian spoke in a low voice to the stallion and ran his hand down its back in soothing motions while Wynne examined the wound. It was deep into the muscle. Worse, it was inflamed. She moved to the front of the horse, examining its eyes, muzzle, and teeth.

Brian muttered, "The flesh is red and swollen, lady."

"He's feverish to the touch." She returned to Brian, again running her hand down the pony's leg, up and around the wound. The stallion flinched.

"For a verity, lord," Albert said, "he is getting worse."

"Will he make it?" Brian asked.

Wynne looked up at him. Torchlight cast dancing shadows across his craggy features, emphasizing the strength of his chin, playing off the black beard stubble. The eyes were dark with concern.

"Cathmor believes the gods have blessed this ointment," she said. "Let us hope that is so."

She opened the jar, curling her fingers through the thick, dark paste. Talking in low tones to the stallion, she carefully smeared the medicine over the wound. When she was finished she took strips of cloth from Brian and wrapped the leg. After she tied off the bandage she straightened.

"There, lord." She wiped her hands on a remnant of the cloth. "We have done all we can."

"Shall I sit with him tonight?" the warrior asked.

"Nay, 'tis my stallion," Brian replied. "You get some rest, Albert. I'll sit with him." He paused. "If he's worse tomorrow, I shall have to kill him."

"Aye." The warrior hooked the torch on a holder on one of the center pillars. "Shall I bring your satchel over?"

Brian nodded. As Albert left the building, Wynne moved into the smaller chamber. Stopping at the rickety table, she washed her hands in the basin and dried them on a nearby cloth.

Brian might have to kill his pony. When he had made the announcement, his words had been devoid of emotion, but Wynne knew he was suffering. A highly trained, disciplined pony was part of a warrior's necessary equipage and weaponry, and such a pony was hard to come by. Training a pony so that it and rider worked together as one took a long time, and required a lot of patience, and produced a strong bond between man and beast.

"I would rather not have to embark on this quest with an untested steed," Brian said, wandering into the room where she stood, "but if I must . . . I must. I have brought several extra ponies with me."

"Aye." She remembered. "Cathmor said you loaned him one of yours."

He nodded. "I'll be glad when he returns. Since he's a native, he may learn more than my scouts." He rubbed a hand over his forehead in a weary gesture. "Have you received any news from the scouts that you sent out?"

"Nay, they have until sunset tomorrow."

"Brian," Albert called from outside.

"Enter," Brian replied.

The Highlander strode to the table. He picked

up one of the satchels, evidently his, and replaced it with Brian's.

"Do you want anything else before I return to the Great Hall?"

"Aye. Escort Lady Gwynneth back to her quarters."

"Thank you, lord," she said softly, "but I wish to remain here. The stallion will need my care as well."

Brian opened his mouth to say something. Albert looked from Brian to Wynne, then back to Brian. Brian waved Albert out. The warrior disappeared into the darkness. A gust of wind blew through the open window and set to dancing the torches and the flames of the central fire.

"I didn't want to call you a liar in front of my kindred," Brian said, "but there is nothing else we can do for the stallion."

"Nay. I want to wait with you and did not wish to make my announcement in front of your kindred."

Brian and Gwynneth stared at each other, the tension between them building, stretching . . . almost at the breaking point.

"You know what you're asking, lady?"

"Aye."

"By all that is holy, Gwynneth." Brian shook his head in exasperation. "I can barely hold myself in check. If you stay here tonight with me, both of us together in these close confines—" He broke off, shrugging, running a hand through his hair.

She laid a hand over his mouth, but he wouldn't be silent.

"I have tried to honor our agreement and keep our relationship on a business footing, but if you remain here, lady, I shall not be thinking altogether of the stallion."

"I hope not. I want us to be thinking about each other."

She lowered her hand and touched his arm.

"Until tonight, lord, I have been imprisoned by the future. I was letting it tell me what to do. In reality, all we have is now. This moment. And I want to take it."

Light was her touch, but it burned through his body. "Then, madam, I must do the thinking for both of us." He pulled away from her and smiled grimly. "During this entire journey I have kept my mind occupied with other matters so I would not have time to think of you, but it has not worked. Thoughts of you interrupt everything I do or say. During my waking hours I see you in those tight-fitting leather trousers, the wind blowing your tunic against your breasts." His voice was low and throaty. "At night I dream that you are mating with me, that you have agreed to become my bride. Then I awake to find myself alone."

Wynne took heart. He dreamed of her . . . not another, but her.

"You shall not awake alone tomorrow, my lord. We shall be together."

The fragrance of her herbal water wrapped around him; it filled his nostrils, tantalized his senses. His hand fastened around her cloak, and he pulled her closer. He wanted to believe her . . . he had to believe her. That was how much he desired her.

"I kept telling myself that any woman could fulfill my needs, but then I realized, it wasn't *needs* that haunted me, my lady. 'Twas desire for a particular woman. You."

She unfastened the gold brooch of her mantle, sliding the material aside, letting it fall to the floor. She closed the distance between them.

"And then, lady, I thought perhaps I could please my liege by honoring a political marriage and by taking you as my second wife."

She laid her hand over his mouth. "Perhaps, lord, that is all the gods will allow us to have."

He shook his head. "Nay, lady, I shall not marry the Pict princess."

"What will Malcolm say?"

"I don't know, and I don't care," Brian answered. "You are the most important person in my life, lady. I shall fight any who tries to come between us. I want you to be my first and only wife."

"Aye, my lord," she murmured, letting him hold her closely, laying her cheek against his shoulder.

Gently pulling back from her, he touched her face with the tips of his fingers. "I meant what I said, Wynne."

"I know you did, lord."

He unfastened the thong that tied off her braid and unplaited it. He drew his fingers through her hair. Like silk it caressed him.

"Your touch is gentle," she said. "Like the spring breeze on my face in the apple orchard. Yet it's hot, Brian, hot as the touch of summer's sun when I'm on the deck of my ship."

"I want you, Gwynneth, as I have never wanted another woman."

"Not even Sorcha?"

"Nay." The anguished whisper came from his innermost being. "I am insane with wanting. Sometimes I cannot think straight, my lady." He traced the contours of her face.

"I want you too."

Aye, she desired Brian mac Logan. He had not yet said he loved her, but she knew he did. He wanted her for his first wife and was willing to go against his liege to have her. She still didn't know if they could have a future together. Too much was at stake. But she loved him, and she would take what this night offered.

He claimed her lips in a warm, sweet kiss. Their embrace tightened, and the kiss deepened. Desire splintered through her to settle in the core of her femininity and to build an ache that intensified.

Holding her face in his hands, his lips hovering above hers, he whispered raggedly, "I will give you pleasure. I promise."

"And I, Brian, shall do the same for you."

He looked down at her breasts, and she felt them tingle to life. He released her face and touched their fullness. The buds tightened. With his thumbs he stroked and kneaded the sensitive peaks. Through the fabric she felt the heated touch and moaned.

"I shall love you," she whispered.

She tugged his tunic from his trousers and slid her hands up his chest to the gold torque, then down to his waist. His body burned beneath her touch. Aye, they were like lightning. Both of them were fire. Pulling the material over his head, she dropped it at their feet. She kissed across the torque, across his broad chest, down the trail of black hair to his navel. She basked in the feel of his sinewy muscles beneath the taut bronzed skin.

Intermittently flashes of light illuminated the shelter; wind caused the central fire to sputter, the flames to dance. A wildness permeated the room, a blending of the storm outside and the storm between them.

"You said I brought the storm to you," he murmured, running his hand through her hair, "but you are the storm."

She laughed. "I have always been called the Lady of Summer."

"A summer storm."

Again she laughed.

"But you are also the golden glow of lightning as it magically turns the storm-darkened night into day."

At that moment lightning flared through the sky and seemed to stand still. Light illuminated the room.

"I can see you so plainly." He touched each feature of her face.

Thunder bellowed, followed by smaller flashes of light, then a glorious, mystical darkness.

In the shadows that moved from silver to blue to black, she undressed before him. Sometimes she could see the wonder on his face; other times he was obscured by the darkness. Sitting on the bed, she removed her boots, her tunic. She slipped her medallion over her head and laid it on the table. Off came her trousers and leggings. His eyes never left her, his gaze as poignant as a touch.

When she was undressed he began to strip off his own garments. As unashamedly as he had watched her, she watched him.

His body gleamed in the firelight. His calves, thighs, and flanks were all darkly hewn in hard, sleek lines. Visually Wynne traced the dark line of hair that ran from his chest, to his navel, to his taut, flat abdomen ... lower to the thick nest of curls. As she gazed at his jutting manhood she swallowed hard. She felt a burning sensation in her lower body. Desire washed over her like torrents of rain, taking away every other sensation except her powerful need for him.

He had told her many times that she was beauti-

ful. So was he. And she was going to make love
to this magnificent man.

He caught her by the shoulders and drew her
into his embrace. His arms pressed her hips close
to him. With a groan he lowered his head, his lips
touching hers at the same time that she thrust her
breasts against his chest. She savored the feel of
the crisp hair against her sensitive nipples. His lips
opened hers with the driving force of his tongue,
and his hands moved over her back.

They glided to her waist . . . below. As his warm
fingers kneaded the soft roundness of her buttocks, as the weapon-callused palms gently rubbed
them, Wynne shivered and wrapped her arms
around him.

"You fit into my arms so perfectly," he muttered. "I love holding you." He pulled her closer.

She loved having him hold her.

"You're soft and warm. You smell good." He
punctuated each word with kisses. "And you
taste good."

She captured his mouth, her lips moving against
his. She teased him for a while with her tongue;
then he teased her. His fingers played havoc with
the sensitive skin of her buttocks, causing her to
wiggle closer to him, to feel his erection against
her pelvis. Each touch, each discovery heightened
her excitement and whetted her desire to experience the intimacy shared between a man and a
woman during mating.

Thunder rolled. Lightning flashed. The wind
whipped against them.

Again her mouth claimed his. She leisurely explored his lips with gentle strokes. She coaxed him
to open and receive her. With the drugging kiss,
she asked for an even hotter invasion. When the
kiss ended, he pulled back and gazed at her in

the flickering light. She brushed her hand through his hair.

"I wish we were back in the luxury of your bower, lady, on your thick mattresses and the beautiful linens."

"I love my bower," she admitted, "but it seems fitting for you and me to mate here in the wild."

"Since I am the barbarian?" His warm breath spread across her already flushed flesh.

"Since both of us are, my lord," she murmured. "The bower is a magical world that you and I have created. This is real, Brian. This is you and I."

She slid her fingers down his face, enjoying the abrasive brush of his beard stubble against her palms. He caught her hand in his and brought it to his mouth. He kissed each of her fingers, then her palm. He lifted his head, his mouth capturing hers in long, hot kisses. His hands gentled and soothed her; they brought her newly aroused sensations to fever pitch. His lips burned a trail down her throat and over her breasts.

She arched her back to offer more of her neck, her breasts. She wanted him to caress all of her body. Mouth. Chin. Throat. She panted. She wanted him to . . .

In answer to her silent plea, his hands slid up to cup her breasts; his thumbs rubbed her nipples until they hardened. His hands slid down, over her hips, the outside of her thighs. He touched the juncture of her thighs.

They slid to the floor together, their caresses becoming more desperate. He bent his head, moving to the musky sweetness between her legs. When he kissed her, she gasped and tangled her hands in his hair.

She tried to pull him away, but once he had tasted her, he would not be stopped. The whisper-light strokes of his lips and tongue pushed her to new heights of passion. She was moving with him, opening her legs to receive him, crying from sheer pleasure.

When she thought she could endure no more, he raised his head and stretched his body over her, one knee keeping her legs apart, his hand stroking her thigh. He moved, and she felt his thick erection against one leg, his hand against the other.

"I shall be gentle," he promised.

"I don't want gentleness," she cried. "I want your fire. Your wildness. I want Brian mac Logan, the barbarian."

She arched her hips, and her sheath closed tightly around him. Wild with yearning, she moved to take him more deeply.

"Wynne!" Brian cried. He was almost out of control, thrusting into her with frenzied need, again and again. When he groaned, she laughed softly, exultantly. He wanted her with the same desperation that she wanted him. With a tortured groan, he held her close and claimed her lips in a hot, wet kiss. His rhythm matched hers as he thrust in and out of her.

His blood surged with a pounding fury as his body grew tense and clamored for release. But he wanted the pleasure to last. He slowed their rhythm. He withdrew almost entirely, then filled her completely. It was like being sheathed in hot silk, and Brian trembled with the intensity of the sensations.

Tension spiraled higher and higher. Their groans of desire blended with the lightning and thunder; their whimpers joined the sound of the wind. Their passion was the wild dashing of the waves against the shore.

Wynne's eyes clenched shut. The thick, rhythmic tremors began, arising from deep within her secret core and spreading outward in delicious, shattering vibrations. With a strangled cry, she flung back her head, arched against him, and sobbed out her release.

She heard Brian, his muffled sound somewhere between a moan and a sob. He went suddenly rigid, then shook with uncontrollable spasms. With a tremulous sigh, brave and powerful warrior that he was, Brian collapsed to the sleeping bag, shifting the bulk of his weight to one side. With a final shudder, he buried his face in the sweet hollow of her neck, breathing in the scent of her.

Wynne snuggled close and clasped her arms about him. He had taken care of her, had promised to defy even his liege to have her as his first wife. Now she would take care of him. Her fierce warrior was sated, like a young boy. She would give him solace.

Later they would talk.

The full fury of the storm broke, but Wynne was only aware of the man who held her, of the warmth and security in which he encased her. Long since dressed, they lay together on the bed in their own special world.

The fire burned brightly, removing some of the chill and dampness. The only sounds were the crackle of the flames, the drumming of the rain against the thatched roof, and the intermittent boom of thunder moving farther away.

"We shall be married as soon as possible," Brian said.

"I wish we could, my lord," she whispered, "but we can't."

"I have made up my mind, Wynne. You are the woman I want as my first wife."

"And I want to be your wife, but we have more to consider than ourselves. First, my lord, I have nothing of value to offer you. I know that your liege will not be pleased with me as a prospective bride. I inherit no kingdom, and no one wants the Isle of Cat. That's why I have been left to myself."

"I don't care what Malcolm thinks," Brian answered. "I care only what *we* think."

"He may not force you into marriage with the Pict princess," Wynne said, "but neither will he bless a marriage between us. You won't be treated as an outcast, but you won't enjoy his favor as you do now."

"I would like his blessing," Brian said, "but I don't have to have it. House Logan is large and strong. I come and go as I please."

"Aye, lord, in that you and I are alike. And that is another reason we cannot marry. Each of us goes his own way." Propping herself up on an elbow, she brushed hair off his forehead. "You have your liege, and I am my own."

"For once, Gwynneth," Brian said, "can't you think like a woman instead of a warrior?"

The words smacked of arrogance, but Wynne didn't recoil from them; neither did she retaliate in anger. She hurt, and she was confused. Brian must be suffering similar emotions.

"I can no more separate the woman from the warrior than you can separate the man from the chieftain," she replied quietly. "As you once told me, lord, you are not a young warrior in the first rush of manhood. I am not a maiden. Thus our coming together will be different." Her voice softened. "You are of the land, Brian. I am of the sea. We would not be happy in each other's worlds."

Sliding off the bed, he paced back and forth, reminding her of a caged animal. Agitated. Confined. With no escape. Is this how he would feel several winters from now if the two of them married?

"Like the thunder and lightning, Brian, you and I shall come together from time to time."

"I won't accept that! I want us to be together for all time."

He moved to the table and filled two tankards with ale. One he kept; the other he brought to her.

"What about your reputation?" he began.

"Don't be concerned about my reputation, sire. I am a woman of divorcement." She rolled the tankard between her hands. "No one will know the difference. And no one will care."

"I will! I know you were a virgin, and I care that—"

"Aye, Brian mac Logan, you care."

"My lady, we can no longer think only of ourselves. We must consider the child we might have made together."

Smiling sadly, Wynne said, "Perhaps we don't have to worry, my lord. We didn't use the flower pollen."

He returned her sad smile as both remembered that beautiful morning on the Isle of Cat.

"My lord," she said, "I wish we could have a future together—"

"We can, Gwynneth." He sat on the edge of the bed. "We shall be wed as soon as I avenge the shame brought on House Logan."

"Nay, Brian," Wynne said. "You came here to get your daughter's girdle. You'll get it, and we'll sail back to Scotland. You are headman of House Logan, bestman to High King Malcolm. You are a warlord and have sworn allegiance to your king and your house. You have been signified for a political marriage. That's what you will do, Brian mac Logan, and I shall return to my isle and live my life as a seafarer.''

''Nay, by all the gods of land and sea!'' He leaped to his feet and slammed the tankard on the nearest table. ''How can you suggest this, madam? We are not negotiating a business agreement. We are talking about our lives, about a child we may have made.''

''You have spoken of marriage frequently to-night, my lord,'' Wynne said. ''And you have said you care for me, but do you love me?''

He gazed at her.

''I thought not,'' she said softly. ''Custom de-crees that a woman may have a voice in her choice of husband. The one thing I have always wanted, still want, is love. My father and my stepmother devoted their lives to their houses, clans, and king-doms, and lived without love. I do not intend to do so.''

He returned to the bed and leaned over her, pushing her down until she was flat on her back. He pinned her to the bed by bracing his palms on either side of her. Their faces were almost touching.

''I would to the gods that love was a piece of fruit I could pluck from a tree, madam. I would pluck it and give it to you. I would fight all the monsters in the world if I could find love to give you. But it doesn't grow on trees, Gwynneth. Only in hearts. With the gods as my judge, I care for you. I want you to be my first wife. But I don't know if I have love to give to anyone. If I do, I shall give it to you. But I fear I don't.''

Wynne eased the furrows out of his forehead.

"Perhaps, lady, all I have left is my code of honor. Will you strip that from me?"

"I don't want you to marry me because of honor."

"Nay, lady, I want to marry you because I want you by my side from now on. I want you to share my life and my bed." He straightened. "If you won't marry me for our sakes, madam, at least consider the child we might have created."

"If we are not married," she answered, "the responsibility of a child will be mine."

"Whether we are married or not, any child you conceive from me is my responsibility also."

"Not by law or custom."

"I'm not speaking of law or custom, madam. You know that I do not follow custom unless it pleases me. I know custom lets the woman choose whether she will carry the baby to full term or not."

"Don't worry," she replied softly. "I won't abort any child of mine."

"I wouldn't let you abort a child of *mine*."

"If we do not marry and I have a child, Brian, I shall tell you about him, and he shall know that you are his father. When he comes of age, I shall allow you to foster him."

He regarded her incredulously. "I shall not be a foster father to my own child, lady. I would wander this earth a lost soul forever rather than do that."

"Aye," she whispered, "I believe you would."

"If . . . *when* the baby is born, madam, I shall be present. I shall take it into my arms, baptize and name it. That, lady, is a promise I make to you this day, and only death shall keep me from keeping it."

The resolute words vibrated in the air between them.

"Brian, would you agree to a handfasting?"

"Why?"

"We would be legally bound together for one year and a day. You shall be known as the father of our child, and it would be called by its father's and its mother's names. We also would have time in which to see if we can have a future together."

Slowly he moved to stand in front of the window, gazing into the darkness. Eventually he turned, piercing her with his gaze.

"Aye. I agree to a handfasting. On the morrow?"

She smiled. "Can we hold the ceremony on the landing plank?"

"The landing plank?" he stared at her as if she were daft.

"At the bottom, so that we are both on land and at sea."

He smiled. "Aye, lady, we shall do that."

Brian held out his arms, and Wynne raced into them. She loved him more than she could ever say, and knew that she didn't want to give him up . . . not to death, not to separation at the end of the handfasting.

She had argued with Brian, had pointed out all the disadvantages of their marrying. She had meant what she said, had known what custom demanded, but deep in her heart she wanted Brian to defy all for her. To want her as much as she wanted him. She was determined to make Brian mac Logan love her.

She laughed softly. " 'Tis a good thing I brought a long tunic with me. I shall be married in it." She tilted back her head. "I never bring a tunic with me when I sail. I wonder why I did this trip?"

" 'Tis your destiny," he whispered, lightly kissing her.

Outside they heard a pony gallop up, and a man called, "Brian!"

"One of my outriders," he muttered, separating from her. Wynne followed him to the doorway just as the scout slid off the pony.

"We have a visitor," the rider announced. "An Irishman by the name of Siad."

"Where is he?" Brian asked.

"At the old Great Hall. He travels under a white banner, lord, and has asked to see Lady Gwynneth. He says he has information for her."

"You know him?" Brian asked.

"I met him once," she answered. "He's the young man who brought me news of Alba's death four winters ago when we were fighting in Glenmuir."

Brian nodded. To his warrior he said, "Did you see signs of others traveling with him?"

"Nay, not as far as we could see. We were scouting out the territory, sire, as you ordered. By tomorrow evening we shall know what lies around us that can be reached in two to three days' journey."

"Return to your post and keep me informed," Brian commanded.

With a quick nod the outrider mounted and nudged his pony forward. Soon the darkness enveloped him.

Brian held out his hand to Wynne. "Let us see if Siad brings you good news or bad, lady."

Chapter 17

Brian and Wynne entered the Great Hall and crossed to the central hearth where a fire blazed. Grouped around it were warriors and seafarers awaiting their evening meal. They gazed curiously at their visitor, who stood at the head of the fire pit.

The young man lifted his left arm in greeting. The right one, the sleeve hanging low over his wrist, he kept to his side. "My lady, my lord, I am Siad, outcast of Clan Illand. I travel alone and come in peace." He smiled at Wynne. "I don't know if you remember, my lady, but it was I who brought you news of your husband's death four winters ago."

"Aye, Siad," Wynne said, "I remember. Did you find your way to Athdara?"

"I did, lady, and I would be there this night if one of my men had not betrayed me." Siad turned to Brian. "My lord, are you Brian mac Logan, headman to House Logan of Northern Scotland?"

"Aye."

"Then, lord, you and I are searching for the same man, Beathan, a thief and a raider, and an outcast from Clan O'Illand."

"Are you searching by yourself or do you have others with you?" Brian asked.

"I came here alone," Siad answered, "but I left

my men hidden in a cave not far back. I wasn't sure of your reception."

Brian nodded. His guards were keeping watch around the village, and Brian knew they would sound an alarm if Siad were trying to entrap them. However, Brian was a good judge of people, and felt he could trust the Irishman.

"Do you know where Beathan is?" Brian asked.

"Aye, lord. He and his band raided your village, then came to ours and did the same. We have followed him and his men here, and believe he is making his way to the O'Illands in hopes of buying his way back into the clan."

"How did you know we were here?"

"After we heard about the raid on your village, we suspected you would be pursuing Beathan. Since we've arrived, we've been keeping watch on the ruins. This is where most travelers land." Siad smiled and waved his hand. "Travelers have taken refuge in these ruins for as long as anyone can remember. They provide excellent shelter in bad weather."

Brian waved his hand to the nearest trestle table, cleaned and ready for use. "Please sit down and join us for the evening meal. I'm sure you're weary."

"Aye, my lord, that I am."

Wynne slid onto the bench, and Brian settled next to her.

Shrewdly Siad studied Wynne. "It seems to me, lady, that you would stay far from the shores of Ireland. What is of such great interest to have brought you here?"

"My lord's interest," she returned.

Brian caught her hand in his. "Lady Gwynneth has consented to be my handfasted bride."

Since handfasting, or trial marriage, was an es-

tablished custom among the Scots, neither Brian's
nor Wynne's warriors seemed unduly surprised
by the announcement. Yet Wynne knew the sud-
denness of it had to be a shock. Still no man revealed his surprise by so much as a look or a
word.

Brian rose, bringing Wynne to her feet as well.
He held their entwined hands high. "Lads, Lady
Gwynneth has agreed to handfast with me shortly
after sunrise on the morrow. I know you wish the
lady and me well."

Huzzahs sounded throughout the ancient hall.
Weapons clanged together. Hands slapped tables.
Spears rang against shields. Ale was served.

"A salute, laddies," called out Dow the blacksmith, holding his tankard aloft. "To our lord and
our lady."

"Our lord and our lady," rang out many times
and through many refills of ale.

Finally Brian said, "Now 'tis time for the evening meal."

Laughing among themselves and mellow from
the ale, everyone settled down.

"Dow," Wynne ordered as if they were sitting
in her Great Hall on the Isle of Cat, "serve the
food. Our guest is hungry."

"Aye, lady." The blacksmith bobbed his head,
curls bouncing around his lean face. "Certainly it's
not the fare served at Mistress Sheila's table, but
it is better than that served aboard ship."

"Aye," several of the warriors and crewmen
agreed, and more laughter followed.

While the other men served themselves, Dow
and Keith waited on Brian, Wynne, and Siad. Dow
set a wooden platter holding a loaf of dark bread
in the center of the table. Next to it he placed a
crock of butter, another of cheese. In front of the

diners he set three bowls filled with a steaming stew, thick and rich with meat and vegetables.

Siad leaned over his bowl and inhaled deeply. "Ah, lady, this smells so good. Like you, it has been a long time since I have eaten freshly cooked food."

" 'Tis venison," Dow announced. "We killed it this morning."

After they blessed the food, they ceased talking and ate. When all were finished, Brian pushed away his plate and accepted a tankard of ale from Dow.

"Why did you seek us out, Siad?" Brian asked.

"I need your help," the man replied. "I could have dealt with Beathan and his band easily enough. But if he has joined the O'Illands, which I think he has, I will not have enough men."

"That means I shall be fighting the O'Illands as well as Beathan's beggarly band?" Brian said.

"And Folloman, the O'Illands' champion," Siad added.

Wynne stiffened. Brian reached beneath the table and caught her hand, squeezing it reassuringly. She had known the danger of coming here. This anxiety had been a part of her life for seven years, but now, sitting here in this dilapidated old building, listening to Siad talk, she realized that she no longer feared death. Her greatest fear was losing Brian.

"Folloman is an O'Illand?" Brian asked.

"Aye, sire, he was. Now he's an outcast," Siad said, explaining the agreement between Folloman and High King Triath in regard to Wynne and the blood oath.

"I came here to find Beathan and reclaim the sacred girdle, but it seems that he is not my sole enemy," Brian said.

"Nay, lord," Siad replied. " 'Tis Folloman. He intends to have Lady Gwynneth. She has a great deal to offer to him. She is wealthy beyond description and has several ships. Folloman desires to become a sea trader. Also, my lord, if a child is born to Folloman and Lady Gwynneth, it will be second heir to the High Seat of Ailean, giving Folloman ties to both Ireland and Scotland."

"Does Beathan have the girdle?" Brian asked.

"Aye. Being from Ireland, he recognized it immediately. He felt that if Triath never found Lady Wynne, he could reestablish his ancestral line through the sacred Mayo Girdle."

"Is Clan O'Illand large?" Brian asked.

" 'Tis small compared to most, but it has grown since Folloman added his raiders. They have several hundred warriors."

"How many warriors do you have?"

"Twenty."

"The same as me," Brian answered. "We're clearly outnumbered." He rose and formally addressed his warriors. "Kindred, when we set sail from the Isle of Cat, I did not know we would be forced to fight an entire clan of Irishmen for the girdle. We are considerably outnumbered, perhaps by five to one. Does anyone wish to speak on the subject?"

"Aye, lord." One of Brian's warriors rose. "Our strength does not lie in numbers, Brian, but in our cunning, courage, and knowledge of battle tactics. Let's finish what we have begun."

In unison the warriors rose, yelling "Hear! Hear!" and rapping their weapons against their spears.

"The matter is settled," Brian declared.

They returned to their seats.

"How far is the O'Illand village from here?" Brian asked.

"Sligo Bay, a short journey by sea, a longer one by horse."

"Will you guide me there?"

"Aye, lord, 'twill give me great pleasure to do so." Siad held up the stump of his right hand. "I have waited a long time to avenge myself of this." Siad glanced at Wynne. "What about you, my lady?"

"She will leave Ireland immediately," Brian said before she could answer. "I want her away from Folloman and the O'Illands."

Siad nodded.

"I'll not leave without you," Wynne said.

"You must, lady," Siad said. "The family will stop at nothing to find you. Not only have they brought in a champion and promised him great wealth and social position if he captures you alive, they have also offered a bounty of five pounds of gold to anyone who brings you to them. You are a valuable prize indeed."

"She is leaving," Brian said. "Folloman will never know that she has been here."

This time Wynne did not protest out loud, but she had no intention of doing as Brian said.

"So far, my lord," Siad said, "we have the element of surprise on our side. The O'Illands know that I am chasing Beathan, but they do not suspect that you are also. No matter how few men we have, surprise can be a definite advantage."

"Aye." Brian pushed back from the table and studied the Irishman through narrowed eyes. "I have no choice but to travel with you," he said. "You know the terrain and the people; yet I don't know that I trust you."

Siad rose. "Present your sword, sire."

Brian stood and withdrew his sword, holding it flat on his two palms. Siad cautiously caught the flat of the blade and kissed it. Kneeling, he said, "I, Siad, formerly of Clan O'Illand of Sligo, Ireland, do pledge fealty to Lord Brian mac Logan of Northern Scotland. If I speak not the truth, may the gods of the forest smite me."

"If you speak not the truth," Brian said, "I shall smite you. Now rise."

Brian resheathed his sword, feeling reassured now that Siad had sworn loyalty to him.

"I trust you have a plan," Brian said.

Siad grinned. "I know how to get you to the O'Illands' village from several directions, lord, but I shall leaving the planning up to you."

Brian returned the grin. "Tell me where your men are hidden, and I shall send one of my outriders to get them. While we are waiting for them, you and I shall devise a scheme."

Wynne rose and drew out her own sword. Brandishing it, she shouted, "To victory, Highlanders and seafarers!"

"Hear! Hear!" rang out through the camp as tankards were raised.

Glasses were filled. Salutes given.

Throughout the evening the outriders had been slipping into camp and making their reports as others rode out. Relaxing, knowing that Brian had matters under control, everyone stretched out around the fire, waiting for the arrival of Siad's men.

"Do you know the history of this ancient village, Irishman?" someone yelled.

"I have heard legends of it all my life," Siad answered. "These ruins used to be a monastery of learning that belonged to an order of bards. They've been gone for a long time. Since their departure many tales have circulated about this old place. So many that it's difficult to separate myth from truth."

"If this was a religious monastery," Dow said, "why did they not have a better bell? This one is cast out of such a base metal that it has already cracked."

Siad glanced through one of the open windows, as did Wynne and Brian. The storm had blown over, and the sky was aglow with stars and moonlight.

"From what I hear," Siad said, "at one time they did have a beautiful bell. 'Twas long, long ago."

Brian leaned back against one of the pillars and pulled Wynne into his arms. As the evening grew chilly, he wrapped her in his mantle. She snuggled against him, glad for the warmth and protection. She was a strong woman who had proved her independence, but she was grateful to have him to lean on. She didn't like being patronized, but she enjoyed being cherished.

"Aye," Siad said, "the bards had a bell. 'Twas a grand one, golden, brought back from Scotland when this was a monastery. It hung here for many years. It was embossed with—"

"The *craebh ciuil*," Wynne whispered, as all at once the realization came to her. There must be more to the old bell than the naked eye could see.

"Aye, so the stories say," Siad continued.

"The sacred bell of the Cloister of the Grove," Wynne murmured.

Brian gave her hand a knowing squeeze.

"Beg your pardon?" Siad said.

" 'Tis nothing, lord." Wynne shook her head. "Continue your story."

"When the Irish priests heard that Scots raiders were coming to steal the bell, they hid it. In their greed and stupidity the Scots killed all the priests who had knowledge of the bell."

Just then a gust of wind tore through the village with such vengeance that the old bell tolled. The dull tone hung on the air for a moment before it was lost.

"The bell was never found again, though many have hunted for it," Siad murmured. "All that remains are the stories that have grown through the years and the ancient riddle."

Wynne leaned forward with interest.

" 'Seen by a few, the bell is gray turned to gold,' " Siad quoted. " 'Seen by all, it is gold turned to gray.' "

Wynne repeated the words to herself, then said, "What does the riddle mean?"

He laughed softly. "If anyone knew, my lady, we would have already located the bell."

Maybe they *had* found the bell, Wynne thought.

"The one we found today is mine," Keith announced proudly. Siad listened kindly while the boy told about finding it.

As Keith spoke, Wynne laid her cheek against Brian's breast, listening to his heart beat, feeling the rise and fall of his chest. Growing drowsy, she thought about the bell. She had wondered if it really did exist. Siad's tale had confirmed to her that it did. And they had found a bell. Dow had said that there was no metal beneath the base one, but Wynne felt sure there was. She intended to search a little harder.

"My lord," Siad said, jarring Wynne out of her ruminations, "I am weary. Will you show me where I am to sleep?"

"Come with me," Brian said.

He and Wynne rose, and Brian kept his arm around Wynne's shoulder. The warriors, having already selected their sleeping areas and laid out their pallets and sleeping bags, dispersed to their separate places. Siad followed Brian and Wynne from the Great Hall.

"My lady." Keith tugged on Wynne's hand. "I want to talk with you, please."

She stepped aside. He swiped the errant lock of hair from his face.

"Does this ... uh ... your handfasting, does it mean that you will be leaving the Isle of Cat and living with Lord Brian?"

"I'm not sure what it means," she answered, "but I won't desert any of you, Keith. That's a promise. Don't you like Lord Brian?"

"Aye, lady, I do. But I was wondering what was going to happen to Erinn and the others."

"I shall take care of them."

He nodded.

"What would you think about being fostered by Lord Brian?"

Keith's eyes rounded. "Are you jesting, lady?"

"Nay, but I must talk first with Erinn."

"Aye, my lady."

"Come along, Keith," Dow called. " 'Tis time for bed."

Casting Wynne a last glance, Keith ran over to the blacksmith, Honey slinking beside him. Then he, Dow, and the cat reentered the building.

Wynne and Brian escorted Siad to a small foodstore located in the center of the village, one that his men would watch all through the night.

"My lord," Wynne said as she and Brian returned to the encampment, "let us sleep in my shelter."

"Sleep?" Brian teased her. "That wasn't what I had in mind, lady."

Happiness, like warm honey, sweetly coated

her. "Whatever you have in mind for us, lord, can
be better done in my shelter."

"Then, lady, after we check on the stallion, we
shall go to your lodging."

Now that the men had gone to bed, the camp
seemed deserted, the fires burning low. Wynne
and Brian briskly made their way to the stables.

"Do you think the bell we found is the holy one
of the Cloister of the Grove?"

Brian shrugged.

"I think so, lord, but even if it isn't, I'm glad
Siad told me about the riddle. Mother Cordelia or
Grandmother Feich might be able to unravel its
mystery. Maybe I am destined to bring this knowledge back to the cloister, rather than the bell,"
Wynne murmured. "The Dryads will be pleased
to hear the riddle."

They entered what had once been the portico of
the building they were using as a stable, and Brian
called softly, "Albert."

A smile on his face, the young warrior appeared
at the door. "Sire, the stallion seems to be better.
He's not as restless as he was earlier."

"Good."

Wynne and Brian moved into the larger room,
where both of them examined the stallion.

Straightening and walking over to retrieve his
satchel, Brian said, "Well, lad, I shall let you watch
the ponies tonight."

Blue eyes twinkling, Albert nodded. "Good
night, Brian. May you and your lady have a pleasant evening."

"We shall." Brian winked down at Wynne.

After they had departed the stables and were
cloaked once more in darkness, Brian whistled, the
sound a soft birdcall. Immediately a man appeared

at his side. They stepped away and spoke together in low tones. Then Brian returned to Wynne.

"What was that about?" she asked.

"I don't want to be taken unawares during the night."

"You don't trust Siad?"

"He has to prove himself."

"Considering the O'Illands, and Folloman's large army," Wynne said, " 'tis good that you have me and my warriors to fight with you."

"Nay, my lady." His voice was soft but resolute. "You and your warriors will not fight with me. The longer you remain on Irish soil, the longer your life remains in danger."

"We knew that when we sailed."

Brian caught her face in his hands and gazed into her eyes. "If I had known then what I know now, my lady, we would not be here together."

"And we would not be handfasting on the morrow."

Silence enshrouded them.

"Does my being a woman affect your decision?"

"Your being the woman I care for affects every decision I make, lady." His stroking fingers were like flames dancing on her cheeks. "Earlier I gave the command to start loading your ship. When we march out, lady, you are to sail away from this harbor."

"I command the ship," Wynne whispered. "It doesn't sail unless I give the order."

"Give the order for me," Brian said.

"Cathmor and my two boats have not yet returned."

"If they are not back by the appointed time, I'm asking you to leave without them. Stay in waters close by, and give me five days," Brian said. "If we are not back by then, you are to sail for home."

She hesitated.

"For your own good, my lady, but also for our good."

Still she said nothing.

" 'Twas the original bargain that we struck, lady. The one you have been stubbornly insisting on."

She nodded, acknowledging that it was their bargain, but not that she would comply with it. She would never set sail for Scotland without him or his men. But she didn't say so. She didn't want him to worry unnecessarily. She smiled. "Now, my lord, seeing that we have the night, how about doing something for our own good?"

"What would that be?"

"Come into my bower, sire, and I shall show you."

"I'm beginning to like the sequestered life, my lady."

Naked, Brian and Wynne stood in the dim glow of the firelight. She was still surprised by the contrasting qualities that were Brian mac Logan. The consummate warrior, he had learned to take with authority and to conquer by force. But because of her, the warrior had given way to the lover. She felt a tremor of vulnerability and a surge of power.

She touched his cheek with the tips of her fingers. "You're a handsome man."

She kissed his forehead, then trailed her lips down his cheeks and felt him tremble against her. She brushed her fingers through his hair, lingering at the temples.

"The white hair," he said.

"Silver," she whispered.

"Does it offend you?"

"Nay."

"One day I will be completely white-headed, lady, and wrinkled. Will you think me handsome then?"

"Aye. No matter what the color of your hair, my lord, no matter how wrinkled your face, you will always have beautiful, expressive eyes. No matter how old you are, you'll always be a formidable warrior." She smoothed his eyebrows. "Beneath it all, you're a kind and gentle man whom I love."

He smiled. "I will appreciate your not spreading word of my beauty and kindness, else my reputation as a warrior will never recover."

Heady on love, she laughed. " 'Twill be our secret, my lord."

She curled her hands around his upper arms, tipped her head to one side, and drew him down to her soft, welcoming lips. Just before their mouths touched, he saw her dark lashes lying against her creamy cheeks, glowing from exposure to the wind and sun. Her hands began a loving offensive on his body as they kissed. Desire took on a new and deeper meaning for both of them.

She drew her mouth from his. "I have never felt like this before." She nestled her cheek against his chest, once again savoring his strength, his warmth, taking them into her so that they became hers. She closed her eyes and inhaled deeply, breathing in the fragrances that belonged to him. Her senses were inundated, but she would have it no other way.

"My entire body is on fire for you. I shall never have my fill of you."

"I hope not."

She slipped her hand between their bodies, slid it down his stomach through the pelt of hair to rest over his arousal. She teased him; he sucked in his breath. The muscles drew; they tightened.

He removed his hands from around her. Bereft, she swayed, then looked up. He laughed huskily, and they gazed into each other's eyes.

"In mere days you have become part of my thoughts, Gwynneth, my breath—"

His mouth came down on hers, heavy and hard. She ground hers against his in return. Neither wanted gentleness tonight. They were desperate, driven to a frenzied need by lack of time, by fear of never seeing each other again.

Although they had only recently mated, Brian was shaken by the passion that ignited between them. In the space of a heartbeat everything was forgotten—the stolen Mayo Girdle, the coming battle against the O'Illands, Folloman, and Beathan. All he knew, all he wanted to know, was the feel of Gwynneth in his arms.

Easily he lifted her, crossed the room, and laid her on the sleeping platform. For a moment she lay on her back, gazing up at him. He touched her face with the tips of his fingers, brushing the strands of hair that pooled golden on the fur lining of the leather sleeping bag. Even in the firelight he saw the sheen of perspiration on her skin and smoldering desire in her eyes.

"Don't keep me waiting," she said. "I have many winters of loving to make up for."

She caught his hand in hers and tugged. He eased onto the bed beside her; she turned to meet him. He stroked the line of her waist, her hip, her planes and curves.

"You are soft and smooth, like silk. So fragile. So delicate." His touch was almost reverent.

She hungered for more. "I'm a woman burning with need," she whispered.

She twisted, slipping beneath him and opening her legs to accommodate him. She locked her ankles over him, hugging him with her body. Sliding her hand between them, she clasped his swollen manhood and drew him forward until he rested against her dampness.

"This is what I want, Brian mac Logan," she whispered fiercely, her hips rising. "You, my love. All of you. Lightning and thunder."

When her moist warmth touched him, sensation burned Brian. He caught his breath and slid into her. She rose to accept him, surrounding him with her softness, enfolding him with the sweetest yet hottest of embraces.

"Lady." He breathed the word as if it were a prayer. "I have never known such pleasure." Intense joy coursed through him in flashes of hot and cold, dark and light. He pressed his forehead to the fur lining beside her head.

Wynne's need was wild, furious. She was battling time and the elements, both of which seemed relentless in their determination to separate them.

She arched her hips, tightening her legs so that she could receive him more deeply. She trailed her fingers along his spine from his shoulders to his buttocks.

Perspiration moistened Brian's entire body. The musky odor that accompanied mating enveloped him. His heart was beating erratically, his blood rushing.

Wynne planted soft kisses across his chest as she sought and found his nipple. She nipped it with her tongue; she scored it lightly with her teeth. He caught his breath, quivered, and sighed.

Making the ultimate surrender to passion, he thrust deeply into her again and again. He reveled in her sighs of pleasure, her moans of delight. He stroked in and out, his pleasure building until he knew he could no longer contain himself.

She whispered his name. He chanted hers.

Her fingers dug into his shoulders. He pressed into her; she arched against him. Higher and higher they climbed. Then he tensed ... gasped. She moaned. He collapsed, and they clung together. The intensity of their release was made more wondrous by the knowledge that they had reached it together.

She unwrapped her slender legs and released him.

He held her in his arms. "You're so wonderful," he murmured, sated. "So precious."

He had never felt so replete. So rested. Wynne was his equal, and in her he found fulfillment, a complete fulfillment he had never before experienced.

The thought ... nay, the recognition ... shattered the beauty of the moment. He had not shared passion like this with Sorcha.

"What's wrong?" Wynne pushed up on an elbow and gazed down at him. Her face was glowing softly, her eyes large and luminous. "You were startled."

"Since Sorcha died, I have been feeling like an old man—"

"My lord," she interrupted, "when I commented on the silver strands in your hair, I did not mean it as a criticism."

He shook his head. "I did not take it that way, lady. It's just that when Sorcha died, a part of me died too. I thought I would never feel fully alive again."

"And?" she breathed.

"With you I feel young and wonderful, lady. As if life has begun again."

"It has for us."

"Not for me. I can't forget Sorcha. She was part of my life; she gave my children to me."

Brian remembered Sorcha, their years together, their happiness. He was confused, as if he had just betrayed her. He pushed up on the bed, slinging his legs over the side of the platform.

"Your life with me has just begun," Wynne pointed out. " 'Tis true Sorcha was part of your life, a wonderful part, Brian. Nothing can take that from you. But she's gone. And memories cannot replace life. She is your past. I am your present."

In the muted light of the waning fire, he studied Wynne. Her soft smile did wonderful things to his insides.

"Would you like to reconsider the handfasting, my love?" she asked.

"My love," he echoed pensively. "Are you so sure you love me, lady?"

"Aye, lord, I do."

He drew her onto his lap and into the circle of his arms. She placed both of her hands on his chest and gazed into his face.

"And, lord, I pray that someday you shall love me."

"I pray that I do too, lady."

A long, satisfying kiss later, he rose with her still in his arms and walked out the door. The night air was cool and fresh, the sky aglow with stars and moonlight.

"Where are we going?" she murmured.

"To the lagoon."

She laid her cheek against his chest as he walked. She felt the rise and fall of his breathing, the movements of his powerful body as he stepped into the pool with her, deeper and deeper until she felt the cool wetness lap against her buttocks, her back, her shoulders.

He sank beneath the water, carrying her under with him. When they shot up, both were gasping and laughing. She brushed her hands through his wet hair. Between kisses they washed each other's faces. She rubbed his chest in slow languid movements, loving the moans of pleasure that rumbled from his chest when she kissed each of his nipples. He loved her breasts, kissing the nipples until she moaned also.

Gazing into her eyes, drawn by the promise they held, Brian brushed the hair from her face. Her lips trembled; her eyes shimmered.

A freshening breeze sent droplets of water splattering on them. Both looked up to see they were beneath a tree limb, the leaves and branches laden with rain.

"If we don't move, lord, we're going to get wet." Wynne giggled.

"I don't mind," he replied. "Do you?"

They laughed together as they melded into an embrace. He reached up, caught the tip of the branch, and gave it a tug. Water sluiced down on them. They laughed longer and louder.

Their lips touched, softly, warmly, in another glorious kiss, filled with passion and a silent promise of commitment. It transcended time, returned Brian to youth and wistfulness, infused him with the courage to dream and to conquer.

"Wynne," he murmured, "maybe we can—"

"Aye, lord, we can."

Her hand slipped down his stomach, lower to touch his manhood. Her fingers curled around it.

"Lady, do you fully understand the consequences of your actions?"

"Aye," she whispered, "but show me again, lord. It may take me a lifetime to learn."

Chapter 18

After a night of sweet, wild love in Wynne's cottage, Wynne and Brian lay on her sleeping platform in each other's arms and talked. He described his life with Sorcha, the children and his dreams for them, his plans for rebuilding his village and for their life together. He talked as if Wynne would be a part of his world, and she pretended that she would be. Although foremost in their minds was Brian's coming battle with the O'Illands, Beathan, and Folloman, neither discussed it. They wanted a few more hours alone in their magical world, a few more hours to discover each other, to bask in the wonder of their feelings.

Finally dawn began to shade the horizon in soft pastel colors. Brian rose and moved to his satchel. He opened it and pulled out clean clothes: leggings, black trousers, gray tunic, and an ankle-length cloak made of soft worked leather. He laid them on the table next to the wooden washing basin, which they had shared between bouts of lovemaking during the night. Now the basin was empty; the drying cloth lay negligently to one side; the partially filled water barrel sat on the floor, the lid propped against it, a dipper bobbing.

Her heart growing heavier by the moment, Wynne watched as, piece by piece, Brian dressed. After tying off his second boot, he rose and slipped his gold torque about his neck and a gold armband over each wrist.

Still the magic of the moment was not broken until he placed his chain mail and helmet on the table. The sword and dirk he wore every day. Not so the mail and the cloisonne bronze helmet with the hinged cheek guards. The bloodred enamel mocked her. Lying next to it was her medallion, the red gemstone twinkling in its bed of gold filigree.

Wynne rose and dressed in a short tunic. She moved to the table, picked up her necklace, and gazed at it as she rubbed her hand over the medallion and outlined the gemstone. She handed it to him. "I want you to take my talisman with you."

Brian held it on his extended palm. The red gemstone glittered in the morning light. He touched it with the tip of his finger.

" 'Tis a beautiful piece, my lady. Quite valuable."

"It's magical, lord. Raven made it for me many years ago." She picked up her sword. "She also designed and crafted the hilt of my sword. It too has the red gemstone."

"And an inscription," he murmured, running his fingers over the *ogham fedha*. "What does it say?"

" 'To the Lady of Summer.' " She replaced her sword on the table.

He continued to rub the stone on the medallion.

" 'Tis the same color as the enamel on your helmet," she said.

"I can't take it, Wynne. 'Tis your talisman."

Her gaze fastened on his. "You can take it, lord, because I am giving it and its magic to you. As long as you wear it, part of me will be with you."

"Thank you for your thoughtfulness," Brian

said, "but whether I take it or not, Wynne, I shall forever have you with me. You're in my heart, my lady, where no one can touch you."

Brian's admission moved Wynne. Although he had not used the word *love*, he had confessed to loving her. Carnal desire was of the body only, love was of the heart.

He caught her hand and curled it around the jewelry as he pulled her into his arms, and they hugged tightly, possessively. He drew back and smiled down at her.

"Thank you, my lady." He dangled the chain on a finger. "Please put it on me."

Wynne took the amulet as he lowered his head. She slipped the chain over it, pressing the talisman against his chest with her palm.

"May the gods protect and keep you, my love."

She kissed the talisman, then raised her face. He lowered his, and their lips met in a warm, lingering kiss filled with promise.

Brian returned to the table, rummaged through his satchel, and returned with a gold brooch. "I give you this, my lady. It will protect you from all harm."

Accepting the piece of jewelry, she turned it over in her hands.

" 'Tis crudely made," he said, "but it means a lot to me, lady."

"It's beautiful, lord."

"Elspeth crafted it for me before we marched to Glenmuir."

"It holds great value for you," Wynne said. "I would feel better if you were wearing it, lord. You are the one who is going to battle."

"You have given me your talisman, lady. I shall be worried unduly if you are wearing no amulet at all. This one has great magic. Feich told me that children can often commune with the spirits better than adults. Elspeth's magic is strong."

Wynne smiled. "I shall wear it with honor, my lord." She pinned the brooch to her mantle. After a moment she said, "Brian, I would like to return to you the measures of gold and silver you paid me for bringing you here."

"Nay, lady," he replied. "You and I had an agreement."

"When we bargained, this journey was solely for you," she pointed out. "As it turns out, lord, I have become as involved in it as you have. 'Twould be wrong for you to pay for services that benefit me."

"Lady, I gladly pay for services that benefit you. And I shall not take back what I have given you. According to our custom a woman is entitled to her own wealth."

She nodded but was not pleased.

"Let us consider the measures my dowry," he said.

"*Your* dowry?" she asked in surprise.

He smiled. "Aye, Lady Gwynneth nea Pryse, I bestow on you these measures of gold and silver as my dowry, given to you as we handfast this day."

Wynne laughed. "I shall hold them, lord, for safekeeping. Perhaps we shall have need of them one of these days."

The matter settled, Brian resumed fastening his weapon belts about his waist.

"If I should die, you will inform my family, won't you?"

"I shall also avenge your honor." She forced back tears.

"Lachlann has already given his word to do so, lady." The lover was gone now; the warrior stood in his place. "If you have conceived a child, I would like it to be born in my village. If I'm not there for the birthing, I want my adopted mother, Feich, to accept the child, to baptize and to name it."

"I will do as you wish," she promised. "I shall take care of your children as if they were my own."

"Thank you," he murmured, and kissed her forehead.

A selfish part of Wynne wanted to beg him to leave Ireland, to set sail immediately for Scotland and safety. But she did not put these thoughts into words. She loved a warrior and understood the code by which he lived. To avenge a shame brought on his house was his duty, his responsibility.

He drew back from her, looked down at her short tunic, and smiled. "Is this what you intend to wear to our handfasting?"

"Nay, lord."

"Then hasten your dressing," he said. "I need to be on my way."

"Go meet with your men and ask about your stallion, lord," she said. "I shall join you soon."

"I don't mind waiting." His eyes twinkled. "I rather like watching you undress."

"I want to surprise you," she whispered, ducking her head so that he couldn't see her tears.

He caught her chin and lifted her face. Touching a knuckle to an errant tear that slipped down her cheek, he said, "None of this, my lady."

She sniffed. "I'm only doing what you asked, lord."

"I asked you to cry?" He hiked a brow.

She tried to laugh, but the sound was a strangled sigh. "You asked me earlier to be a woman for once in my life, and I am. A warrior can't cry for the mate who is going to battle, but a woman can."

Brian hauled her into his arms, the metal latches of his girdle biting into her skin. She welcomed the abrasive touch. It chewed through the numbness and sorrow, reminding her that they were alive. They clung together until sounds from the camp harkened and announced that day had fully arrived. There was work to be done. Reluctantly they pulled apart.

"When we return home, lady, we shall have our handfasting blessed," he promised.

"Will you feel any less a bonding if we aren't blessed?"

He smiled tenderly. "Nay, lady, as far as I am concerned we are already married and blessed by the gods."

" 'Tis enough for me," she whispered. "Now go lord, or I shall never get dressed."

Gwynneth's father, Pryse of Ailean, marched back and forth in Melanthe's cell. He plowed his hand through his thick, dark hair. "You gave my youngest daughter your blessing?"

"Aye, Pryse," Melanthe replied.

"Why didn't you wait?" he asked. "You knew I would be here shortly."

"She wouldn't have waited," Melanthe replied. "Brian mac Logan was in a hurry to reach Ireland."

Wearing her long white tunic, the waist cinched with a delicate gold girdle, Melanthe sat in a cushioned chair in front of the open window. She would have been more comfortable without her cowl, but she wanted it as a reminder to Pryse—and herself—that she was not his wife.

She held her embroidery hoop and needle in hand, but her thoughts were too chaotic to concentrate. She had seen Pryse several times since Gwynneth had married and subsequently divorced Alba, but the two of them had not had a long private talk in many years. He had surprised her this morning by swaggering arrogantly into the cloister courtyard and into her private chamber.

But that was characteristic of Pryse. As a young warrior he had quickly gained the reputation of treading fearlessly on the gods' toes.

Although Pryse mac Ross was not a tall man, he was broad-shouldered and muscular. Because his hair had not turned gray with the passing of the winters, and he had stayed in excellent health, he looked younger than most men of fifty winters. He ruled his kingdom with an iron hand and was still the champion among his warriors.

He paced the cell, the rough leather soles of his boots clipping against the planked floor. His mantle, slung over both shoulders, trailed behind him, fanning Melanthe's legs as he passed by her.

"By the blood of the gods, Melanthe!" He stopped before her, yanked the embroidery from her hands, and tossed it aside. "Pay attention to me when I'm talking."

Inwardly Melanthe was shaking. She had not only defied one of the most powerful kings in all the land, but she had defied him in regard to the love of his life—his younger daughter.

"Ireland, Melanthe!" He resumed his pacing. "Gwynneth has sailed to Ireland."

"Please sit down, my lord," Melanthe said in the voice she used when placating young novitiates.

"Don't speak to me in that superior-mother

voice," he snapped. "I'm not one of your students."

Looking over his well-muscled physique, Melanthe smiled. "Nay, Pryse, that you are not."

"And get that damned thing off your head." Two long steps brought him directly in front of her. He grabbed the cowl and flung it back, stirring wisps of curls around her face. "I hate glaring into the shadows of that headpiece. It's like looking into the face of—" He shrugged and slapped his hands against his legs.

Rising, Melanthe went to a narrow table set against the far well. Lifting a pitcher, she asked, "Would you like some imported wine, my lord?"

"Imported wine," he mocked. "Aye, lady. You have many luxuries in your cloister, do you not?"

"Aye," she answered, determined not to let him goad her into anger. "We are a wealthy cloister."

Having filled the glasses, she handed him one. As he took it he clasped his hands around hers. She gazed at them. Hers small, soft, and whiter. His big, callused, and sun-darkened.

"Melanthe, what happened to us?" Pryse asked, and she knew his thoughts were traveling the same path as hers. But she said nothing.

"You are beautiful."

"I'm an old woman."

"Age has nothing to do with beauty, madam." His ebony eyes twinkled. "Besides, I'm an old man."

The soft words touched Melanthe, and she didn't want to be touched. Not after all these years, all these hurts. She had found peace away from him, and she was not going to let him ruin her life a second time. Gently removing her hand from his, she went to the window and gazed out onto the courtyard.

"You've always been beautiful," Pryse said. "I'll never forget the first time I saw you, sitting on the canopied platform watching the tourney."

Melanthe laughed. "You were the champion, my lord. The best."

Pryse quaffed his wine in one long swallow. "But I was never good enough for you, was I, Melanthe?"

She didn't answer, because in part his words were true. Unlike many of the people of her kingdom, she had been allowed to go to Eire to study. She had learned the power of words, stones, and herbs; she had learned the songs to carry people from this world to the other. Blacksmithing. Goldsmithing. Writing the *ogham fews*.

"I was a man of the forest, unlearned according to your standards. I excelled only in fighting."

"You are a warrior, my lord," Melanthe said, regretting that she had never seen beyond the leather trousers and sleeveless tunic he had worn, that she had thought him a ruffian.

Even today he wore similar clothes, only slightly more refined.

He set the beaker on the table and walked closer to her. "Melanthe, do you think—"

"Nay, Pryse, too much time has lapsed and too much has happened." She moved away from him. "I'm happy here."

His hand balled around the fabric of her robe. "You always were happier being a priestess," he declared bitterly. "You should never have agreed to marry me."

"I had no choice," Melanthe snapped, knowing that the failure of their marriage rested in large measure on her. But she did not like him to remind her. "Our houses had been fighting each other for years. We were the only hope for peace.

And we succeeded in obtaining it—between our kingdoms if not between each other."

"Aye, Melanthe, we did an excellent job, did we not? One of my daughters is a Dryad, the other a seafarer, neither of whom I have seen more than twice a year during the past four years. And if I see them, my lady, I come to them. Neither of them shows any sign of getting married and having children. Both of them hate and blame me for their lonely lives. The one who will inherit the High Seat of Ailean wants only the High Seat of a silenced cloister. The other cannot inherit." He laughed bitterly. "Aye, we succeeded."

"We married," she said.

"Nay, lady. Words were said over us, and you endured mating with me several times, but we were never wed!"

"How can you say this?" Melanthe whispered.

"After you conceived our daughter, you didn't want to mate with me again."

"I grew so heavy when I was with child."

" 'Twas only natural that you would grow heavy, madam. You were nurturing a new life."

"I did not lose the weight once Raven was born."

"I never criticized you, madam. I did not care. I was glad that you were healthy, that you did not die during the birthing like so many women do."

"You had eyes for all the lovely women you saw."

"Lady, had I looked at all the maidens you accused me of looking at, I would have been nothing but a body of lecherous eyes!"

"You did letch for one of our slaves in particular."

She was referring to Gwynneth's mother.

"Melanthe, don't blame me altogether for that

choice. No matter how large you had grown, I thought your body was beautiful. I would never have looked at another woman if you had not refused to mate with me."

"After the baby was born, our mating was painful for me."

"I did not press you." He paused. "I asked you to see the healer. Instead you went to the assembly and asked for a divorcement. You publicly humiliated me, and I never knew why."

"I realized that I was not the woman for you," she whispered. "You were a lusty man, Pryse."

"Was it I who hurt you, lady?"

"Nay." She blinked back tears. 'Twas her own foolishness, she now realized, her idea that she was a better woman than he was a man ... because she was learned and he was not. And she had been too frightened to let him know that she reveled in his sexuality. She had been unwilling to abandon herself to him.

"You went to seek peace with the priestesses," he said, "and you took our daughter with you."

"It didn't take you long to find a replacement," she retorted.

"Lady, after years of living with a woman who despised me, I wanted a woman who didn't find fault with everything I said or did."

His words pricked her. "Did I do that, lord?"

"Aye, lady, you are a smug, arrogant female. In some ways learning has not been to your advantage."

"And you, lord, took pride in your ignorance."

"You infuriate me, Melanthe."

"You don't always make me laugh, Pryse!" She glared at him.

"But I have always wanted you. I still do."

He walked across the room and picked up her

embroidery. He carried it to her. His voice was gruff but the anger was gone. "I apologize, lady, but I'm jealous of this piece of material. I used to watch you sew and wished you would touch me like that." He laughed bitterly. "Would it interest you to know, lady, that I often wished I could be one of your students, that I could receive the attention you gave them?"

Melanthe swallowed the knot that had formed in her throat. Nervously she unfastened the hoops and restretched the fabric.

"I dreaded Raven's thirteenth birthday, my lady, because it marked the end of her formal education. You left her in charge of Gwynneth, and you returned to your cloister."

"You did not ask me to stay longer."

"Nay, 'twas custom for the older daughter to teach the younger children."

"You didn't ask me to stay because you wanted me."

"Nay, lady, I did not wish to suffer another rebuff." He paused. "Melanthe—"

She looked up at him.

"The morning sun is glinting in your hair."

She reached up and touched it.

"Black," he murmured. "So rich and black."

"Now streaked with white," she answered. "Not so yours."

"I wish I had made you stay with me."

"I wish I had stayed, lord," she answered, "but we have walked different paths for so many years, it is impossible to return to where we were and pick up the same route once again."

"Aye, 'tis so."

Melanthe was disappointed when he did not press the issue.

He refilled his glass with wine. "Do you think Raven will ever leave this cloister?"

"I fear not, lord."

"What in the name of the gods are we going to do, madam?"

They gazed at each other in mute helplessness.

Chapter 19

Carrying a bouquet of white blossoms in his hand, Brian strode through the village toward the ship where Wynne awaited him. At her request they would be married on the gangplank. With each of Brian's footsteps, the group of warriors and crewmen following behind him grew.

They looked at the flowers and grinned, but his stern countenance forbade any of them to say a word. They did, however, continue to grin broadly. He knew they shared his happiness.

From the ship Wynne watched. Her hair hung in deep waves over her shoulders and down her back, like strands of pure sunshine, glowing and radiant. She had darkened her lashes and added soft color to her lips and cheeks.

The morning breeze blew, stirring her hair. Her long tunic—the same shade of blue as the sea—rustled about her ankles; the wind caused it to hug her hips and legs. Sunlight glistened on the delicate gold girdle that encircled her waist.

By the time Brian stepped onto the foot of the landing plank, she stood at the top. She was beautiful, Brian thought, looking up at her. The most beautiful woman he had ever seen. He walked up the plank and held out the bouquet. She gazed at the flowers, then lifted her head to smile.

Brian and Wynne felt as if they had been swept away to their own special place.

"Thank you, my lord." Taking the flowers, she buried her face in them.

When she lowered the bouquet Brian laughed. "Pollen dust, madam, is glittering on your face."

"Aye." She laughed. "I would wallow in it if I could."

"According to the legend this is a sure way to conceive a baby."

"Not *a* baby, Brian," she whispered. "*Our* baby. I want to conceive our child, lord."

She held open her arms, and he went into her embrace. They held each other tightly, protectively.

"You have brought me great happiness," he confessed. "A joy I thought I would never again experience. I too want you to conceive our child, lady."

"Then, my lord, we had best finish the handfasting so we can get on to weightier matters."

He pulled back and kissed the tip of her nose.

"Come on, Brian," one of the men shouted good-naturedly, "can't you kiss her any better than that?"

Remembering where they were, and their purpose in being there, Brian and Wynne joined their warriors and kindred in laughter.

"Let me show you how it's done, lads," Brian shouted. He folded her into a deep embrace and kissed her, long and fully.

The men shouted and cheered.

When Brian and Wynne parted, pollen lightly dusted both of them.

Letting out a deafening squall, Honey broke away from Keith. She raced through the water, looking as if she were skimming the surface, bounded up the gangplank, and wedged herself between Brian and Wynne.

Rubbing the cat's head, Wynne murmured, "So you're jealous of me, old girl." She looked over at Brian and smiled. "You've stolen not only my heart, my lord, but that of my cat."

"Yours I want, lady," Brian replied on a teasing note. "The cat's I hadn't bargained for."

Honey brushed her cheeks against Brian. He shook his head in mock disgust, and Wynne grinned.

"I've witnessed many handfastings," Dow called out, cupping his mouth with his hands, "in which the groom has a wildcat on his hands, but this is the first time I've seen him with *two* of 'em."

Brian laughed. "Good blacksmith, I can handle the one wildcat. 'Tis the other that has me worried."

Dow scratched his head. "Aye, my lord, I'm afraid of Honey myself. I haven't slept too well since she first attached herself to the little master."

Laughing, Brian said, " 'Tis the two-legged one I'm talking about, lads."

More laughter resounded.

"It will do you good to remember that, lord," Wynne teased.

"I'll forget nothing about you, lady," Brian promised. He caught her hand in his once more, bringing it to his mouth. "Nothing."

As their mood became more somber, so did the attitude of the bystanders. Water lapped gently against the bottom of the plank as they gazed deeply into each other's eyes.

"Lady Gwynneth, will you handfast with me?" he asked.

In their hearts they were already married. Now

they performed the ritual that publicly declared their union.

"Aye, my lord Brian mac Logan."

He raised their entwined hands; Wynne clutched her flowers in the other. They faced the crowd.

"Warriors and kindred, with you as my witnesses, I, Brian mac Logan, do this day handfast myself to Gwynneth nea Pryse in marriage to be binding for a year and a day."

He looked down at Wynne, at the sunlight glinting in her long tresses. At her sparkling blue eyes. At her tremulous lips.

"After the year and one day, either party of this wedding shall be free to go his or her own way," Brian said. "If at that time one party disagrees with the marriage, that party takes custody of any child born of the marriage."

They lowered their hands, and the crowd looked at Gwynneth.

This time she raised their hands. "I, Gwynneth nea Pryse ..." As she pronounced the same words, Wynne knew that her life was changing, never to be the same again. It was thrilling, but also troubling. So much was unsettled between her and Brian. "I do handfast myself to Brian mac Logan in marriage for one year and the day."

"We stand witness to this handfasting," the warriors called out in unison, then they burst into cheers and clanged their weapons together.

The ceremony was sealed.

Evidently losing interest, Honey leaped off the landing plank, splattering Brian and Wynne with water as she gracefully raced back to shore.

"Now to the morning meal!" Dow shouted. "A marriage feast if ever a lord and lady had one!"

Dow and Cook had indeed prepared a feast, and

Wynne couldn't deny the warriors their pleasure. Nor would she take the day away from Brian. She wanted him to ride off to battle with happy memories.

They ate. They talked. They told tales of valor. The ancient ruins became a magical world that closed out reality, keeping war at bay.

When the meal was over, Wynne leaned over to Brian and said, "My lord, may we be by ourselves for a little while?"

"Aye, lady, I know where to take you." He rose. "Lads, thank you for a wonderful marriage banquet. My lady and I are going for a short walk toward the lagoon. All of you know what to do."

Hand in hand, Brian and Wynne strolled out of the building, across the encampment, and beyond the lagoon. When they stood at the edge of a clearing, Wynne saw that the meadowland was filled with white flowers, the ones Brian had picked for her.

"You wanted to wallow in them, lady." He waved a hand. "Do so."

Laughing, exhilarated as only those in love can be, they raced to the clearing. Brian threw his leather mantle onto the ground, and both of them sat down.

A gentle breeze ruffled his hair. Wynne saw the bronzed texture of his skin, felt the heat emanating from his body. She looked at his lips, so expressive and finely shaped, so masculine. She remembered the feel of them on hers.

She gazed down at her bouquet of flowers. She had been overwhelmed by his gesture. In the privacy of her island he had picked her a harebell, but here in front of all his warriors? She still had difficulty reconciling the warrior with the lover.

He was a complex man who continually surprised her.

"Thank you for the flowers, lord."

He gazed at her.

"Do you believe in them?" she asked. "In the magic of the pollen dust?"

A smiled touched his lips, his eyes. "Aye, lady, I believe."

She flung her arms around him and pressed her face against his chest. "I love you, Brian, and I don't want you to leave me. I'm not begging you to stay," she hastily corrected herself. "I know you can't do that, but—" She drew back her head. "Take me with you, Brian. Let me fight by your side."

"Much to my regret, my lady, you are fighting by my side."

She looked at him, not understanding.

"Without your ship, my men and I have no immediate hope of returning home."

"Aye," she murmured. "I'm sorry, lord. I know better."

"Don't," he whispered, bringing her back into the safety of his arms, laying his cheek on top of her head. "I have the same feelings you do, Wynne, the same fears."

"You do?"

"I am frightened that we may not be together, that last night and today are all we shall have."

"Aye."

"I would love to take you and run away and hide from everyone, never to be found."

His mouth, warm and soft, claimed hers. Flames of desire ignited between them. His hand skimmed her body until his fingers pressed gently against her secret place, intensifying her longing. Even through her clothes Wynne felt his hot flesh.

His mouth touched her forehead, her eyelids. His breath splayed over her.

"I must confess, madam, that I want you again. Right now."

"'Tis your right."

"According to custom." He pulled back to look at her. "Do you want me too?"

"I do, my love. Willingly I come to you."

She dissolved against him. He snagged the hair at the back of her head with one hand and banded her waist with the other. They looked deeply into each other's eyes. Brian's lips touched her; she opened in welcome. He pulled her closer; she clung. She pushed her fingers through his hair, loving the feel of it against her palm.

His hands, both gentle and urgent, moved over her. She let him have his way, for his way was her deepest pleasure.

He undressed her, tantalizing her with touches of his hands, brush strokes of his lips. When she was naked, he sat back and looked at her, taking in every detail and adoring her with his eyes.

"I want to see you," she said.

"Then you shall."

He rose, and with the same methodical and tantalizing slowness with which he had dressed earlier, he now undressed. He reached over and plucked one of the flowers, then daubed it against Wynne's face, leaving a trail of pollen across her cheeks and nose. Without touching her elsewhere, he kissed the trail of flower dust.

"Surely we have caught the eye of the gods," Brian whispered, "and shall conceive, Wynne."

"But to make sure—" She also picked a flower and blotted it against Brian's face. As he had kissed her, she now kissed him.

And then their naked bodies came together, re-kindling the fire that burned between them.

She explored his hair-covered chest, the smooth ridges of muscles and warm flesh, until he moaned and murmured his delight. She scattered soft kisses down the strong column of his throat, across his chest.

Then she was lying on her back and he was leaning over her. He made love to her with his mouth, his hands. His lips grazed the tips of her breasts. They were swollen, tender, needy. He brushed his hands against her pelvis. She opened her thighs, welcoming him, begging him. He teased and stroked. She cried out with pleasure.

"More." Her voice was thick; she could hardly speak.

She closed her fingers around his warm, rigid manhood. She began to tantalize him, to push him over the edge. She teased and stroked him, matching his rhythm. His hips rose and fell; he groaned softly against her breast, caught her nipple, and suckled greedily.

Her breathing was ragged, her skin flushed. His eyes blazed with need. Their yearning for total fulfillment became an ache that kisses and caresses could no longer assuage.

"Now, Brian," came her ragged plea.

"Aye, my lady wife."

He covered her with his body and claimed her lips with a searing kiss as he sheathed himself deeply within her.

Pleasure, like a streak of lightning, flashed through her entire body. She gasped, holding him against her, then moving with him. She rubbed her hands up and down his back. She nipped his shoulders, dug her fingers into them. He pierced her with deep, demanding strokes. Her hips rose to meet him.

Hotter and hotter grew the fire; higher into the morning sky danced the flames. Together they became one in ultimate pleasure. Their bodies locked together, they cried out their completion and collapsed. Rolling to one side of the mantle, Brian drew Wynne into his arms, pillowing her head on his chest. Gradually their breathing evened, their heartbeats slowed.

Wrapped in the mantle, Brian and Wynne lay quietly in the meadow until the sun was directly overhead. Brian stirred. With a sigh of regret, Wynne knew they must depart from their magical bower. They might never return . . .

" 'Tis time to go, lady. My outriders will be returning soon with Siad's men, and we shall be off."

After they dressed, Wynne gathered her flowers, still immersed in the magic of their shared world. She smiled as she remembered the pollen dust, and prayed that she and Brian had conceived a child.

As soon as they returned to camp, they were rudely caught up in the tension and activity of the imminent battle.

A guard shouted, "Two riders approach. A third horse without a rider! They're flying the black banner."

Wynne and Brian raced to the top of a small incline and watched the riders gallop toward camp.

"Ours?" she asked.

"Aye."

Danger loomed large and heavy. The three lathered horses spewed up gravel as they came to an abrupt halt near the main campfire. One rider led his pony and a riderless horse toward the stables. The other, a limp body lying across his mount, rode up to Brian.

"We found Cathmor!"

Chapter 20

"Cathmor!" Wynne cried out, tearing away from Brian, dropping her flowers in her haste.

She ran toward the outrider, Brian beside her. Warriors gathered around them.

"Is he alive?" Dow shouted.

"Barely." The outrider carefully slid to the ground. "He's taken a spear in the shoulder."

"Hunting or battle?" Brian asked.

The answer was important. A hunting spear, with its barbed blade, nearly always proved fatal.

"Battle."

Brian's anxiety lessened by a small degree.

The outrider and Brian eased Cathmor's huge body from the pony, and together they carefully heaved him over Brian's shoulder. Cathmor was covered in blood, his garments soiled and torn. He groaned as they jostled him.

"Take him to my shelter," Wynne ordered, running ahead.

Brian followed briskly, moving into the room he and Wynne had shared that night. Dow, Albert, and the outrider were right behind them. Brian deposited the Irishman on the sleeping platform, and he and Dow straightened him out and removed his empty scabbards and boots.

Wynne dragged the table close to the sleeping

plattorm and quickly refilled the bowl with water.
She gathered washing and drying cloths, and un-
hooked the sheepskin of ale and set it on the table.
She laid out cloth to be cut into strips for
bandages.

"He's ready," Brian said.

She moved to the bed and for the first time really looked at Cathmor. He had endured a severe
beating. His eyes were swollen shut. His lips were
cut, discolored, and swollen. Dried blood smeared
his face, hair, and beard. There was a huge purple
swelling on his forehead.

No matter how battle-hardened Wynne was, his
condition disconcerted her. Unmindful of her
tunic, she knelt beside him and gently stroked the
matted hair from his forehead. With her knife she
cut off the blood-soaked tunic, sliding back the
material on either side so she could examine him.
Serrated and puffy flesh surrounded a yawning
and jagged hole.

"The wound is bad," Dow murmured, leaning
over Wynne's shoulder."

"Aye, but 'tis clean," she said. "We can be glad
that it was a battle spear."

"Aye," the blacksmith agreed softly. "If you
don't need me further, lady, I'll see to the lads.
They're going to be wanting to know how
Cathmor is doing."

She nodded, and he slipped out of the room.

"My lord," she said to Brian, "I need your
help."

Between them they eased Cathmor onto his side,
and she examined the entry point of the wound,
then gently laid him back down. Brian lifted the
trunk and set it on the table. Without Wynne's
asking, he opened the lid and began to take out
her vials and pouches, her bowl and pestle. After

stoking the fire with what wood remained, Albert
sent the outrider out to get more. Then he filled
the cauldron with water and hung it over the fire.

Cathmor stirred, groaned. His face twisted in
pain. His lashes flickered, and he regarded Wynne
through narrow slits.

"Lady . . ." His voice was scratchy.

"Aye."

He reached out a big hand, swollen and lacer-
ated, fumbling until he touched her face. She
pressed his palm against her cheek.

"Lady." He seemed relieved. "Grave . . .
danger."

She dipped a cloth in a basin of water and gently daubed his wounds.

"My . . ." He licked his lips; Wynne twisted the
rag, letting several drops of water fall on his lips.
"Lord Brian."

Standing beside the sleeping platform, Brian
lightly touched the man's uninjured shoulder.
"I'm here, Cathmor."

The Irishman struggled to speak. "I rode deep
into the countryside, crossing from Donegal into
Sligo. I came upon the chief village of the O'Illands." He paused, breathing deeply. "I had
dressed as a local peasant and was able to slip
into the village without arousing suspicion. The
warriors guarding the village were so unwary, I
made my way into their very midst and wandered
freely around the camp without attracting any notice. I found the leader of the camp himself—just
as another man, who was obviously under his
command, gave his report. He told his liege that
Brian mac Logan and Lady Gwynneth had joined
forces and were camped in this very village. I
slipped away and was returning here when two
men stopped and questioned me. I ran. When I

was well away from the village, deep in a forest, they caught up with me. One of them threw his spear and brought me down." Cathmor paused, struggling for breath, clearly exhausted by his tale. Still he struggled to get more words out. "My lord, the leader of the camp was Folloman."

Brian gasped. "Are you sure it was he?"

"Aye." Cathmor closed his eyes, his face drawn in pain. "I recognized him from long ago."

"But you never told me you knew him," Wynne said.

"I knew him by the name of Forba," Cathmor replied. "Many long years ago, we were Druid priests together. Then the Christian church began to persecute us. We disguised ourselves and hid. Soon we forgot our spiritual ideals and became brigands. Forba in particular seemed to lose all sense of right and wrong. It was he who left me to die after the hunting accident, all those years ago. Yesterday he recognized me as I lay wounded on the ground. He laughed as he rode away, once more leaving me to die."

"He doesn't understand your tenacity to live, does he?" Wynne whispered.

"My tenacity to protect you," Cathmor said. "I had to warn you."

"Did you clearly see the man who told Folloman about us?" Brian asked.

"Aye, lord, I did, and I'll recognize him if I see him again."

"There is a traitor among us," Brian said.

"Nay, not among our warriors," Cathmor said. "He was a stranger to me."

"Do you think it is Siad?" Brian asked Wynne.

"I don't know," she replied. "I had thought we could trust him because we have a common enemy, and he did swear fealty to you."

"Maybe the bounty was too much for Siad to resist," Brian said. "And swearing fealty doesn't mean much when one is a brigand."

"But someone cut off his hand," Wynne pointed out.

"Perhaps he only wanted us to think that," Brian replied. "He could have lost it in an accident."

"Aye," she murmured.

"Albert," Brian called to the warrior who stood near the door, "bring Siad here. When his men arrive in camp, make sure they are put in the Great Hall under guard. Don't trust any of them."

"Aye, sire." He hurried off.

Moments ago Wynne's anxiety had been centered on Cathmor; now she was worried about the traitor in their midst. She turned to the chest and sorted through her instruments, vials, and caskets of medicine, pouches of dried herbs and roots. She picked up a flagon of dark liquid and measured a spoonful into a bowl.

"Is there anything else I can do to help you?" Brian asked.

When she shook her head, he went to put more wood on the fire.

As Wynne filled a tankard with ale, she noticed that Cathmor had fallen into a deep sleep. " 'Tis good that he is unconscious. I'm going to clean his wounds with the ale, and it will burn."

She talked to remind herself that this was really happening. It wasn't a bad dream that would go away. She talked so she wouldn't think about what might happen to her friend.

"Mother Barbara said that in her experience ale keeps the inflammation from spreading."

With Brian's help she raised Cathmor and poured the ale into his wound, first at the point of entry, then at the exit point. After they laid him down again, Wynne returned to preparing her herbs and medicines.

A guard called out to announce the arrival of Siad, who entered the shelter and stood at attention. "You sent for me, lord?"

"Yes, Siad," Brian answered. "Folloman and his men have learned of our presence here at the ruins."

Siad's eyes went wide, and he shook his head. "How could he know?"

"Before you joined us, Cathmor set out on horseback to obtain what information he could as to the whereabouts of Beathan, Folloman, and their men. He rode as far south as the chief village of the O'Illands. In hiding, he overheard a man telling Folloman about me and Lady Gwynneth." Brian went to the window and gazed out. "I'm sure that even as we speak, Folloman is amassing his army and preparing to attack us."

Puzzled, Siad looked from Brian to the man on the sleeping platform, then back to Brian. "Who would have betrayed you?"

"That is my question for you," Brian replied.

"You think it is one of my men?" Siad asked. "I trust my warriors. We have ridden together for the past four years." Looking affronted, he added, "I have sworn fealty to you, lord. Does that count for naught?"

"As if there can be trust among brigands," Wynne said sarcastically.

Siad turned to her, speaking quietly. "We're outcasts, madam, not brigands. That is why we were hunting Beathan."

Wiping her sleeve over her forehead, she said, "I apologize, Siad. I'm so worried."

"I am too, madam." Siad turned back to Brian. "What are we going to do?"

Brian shrugged, not wanting to share any more information with the Irishman until he knew he could be trusted.

"My lord," Siad said, "earlier I told you I had a favor to ask of you, that I would request it after the battle. Perhaps now is the appropriate time. I want you to know how greatly I desire your trust and admiration."

Brian waited.

Siad straightened his shoulders and stared directly at Brian. "We are a small group of outcasts, sire, without a name or a clan family, but we are not thieves or murderers. We had hoped to return the girdle to you for a bounty, and hoped you would extend your graciousness to include us as broken men in your house."

Brian rubbed his chin. The request sounded legitimate and sincere. All clans consisted of native men and broken men. The native men were those related to the clan chief and each other by blood ties. The broken men were individuals or groups from other clans who sought and obtained the protection of a powerful house or clan.

"I did not betray you or the lady," Siad swore. "But my word is all I have to give you, sire."

"I believe you," Brian said.

"I hate to think one of my men betrayed us, but I did leave them alone when I traveled here to join you." He shrugged. "When they arrive, we shall ask Cathmor if he recognizes one of them." Brian nodded, and Siad went to the door. Catching the frame with one hand, he looked over his shoulder. "Will this keep you from allowing us to become part of your clan?"

"I shall consider your request," Brian replied.

"If you and your men have behaved honorably, and if they swear fealty to me, I shall be inclined to accept you into House Logan."

Siad smiled. "Thank you, lord."

He walked out of the shelter, leaving Brian and Wynne alone with Cathmor.

Wynne opened several pouches and extracted herbs, which she ground into powder, then measured into a small bowl. She lifted a vial of amber liquid, and measured out two drops. She stirred, added more liquid, and stirred some more. Finally she had a brownish paste. She coated this over Cathmor's shoulder, then bandaged it. She spread ointment on his cuts and placed a medicated dressing on his forehead, an ointment that would keep evil spirits from entering his body, causing him to have bad dreams and to see the demons and monsters that often accompanied a wound of this sort.

When she was finished, she rose and went to the window. She leaned against the casement and rubbed her forehead.

"I am only a dresser of wounds, not a healer," she whispered. "I've done all I can for him. I hope it's enough."

"When you've given all you can," Brian said, "you've done more than enough."

Standing behind her, he clasped her shoulders and kneaded the tense muscles. Slowly he massaged her, his hands moving up her neck, back and forth across her shoulders, his thumbs pushing into the flexed muscles.

"Inflammation has already set in," she murmured, letting her head loll forward. "Its poison is spreading through his body."

Then she could no longer stem her thoughts or push her anxieties aside. Abruptly she turned and pressed herself against Brian. She slipped her arms around his waist and laid her cheek against his shoulder. She needed his strength, his warmth, most of all his faith. His arms closed around her.

"Now, my lady wife, you must leave," Brian said after a few moments. "Is the ship ready to sail?"

"As soon as we get Cathmor aboard," she replied, "and my scouting boats return."

"They're supposed to be back by sunset, so they should be in the vicinity," Brian said. "It won't take you long to find both of them, even if you have to sail first in one direction, then the other."

"Keep some of my men with you," she said.

"What about you?" Brian asked, tilting her head back. "What if the O'Illands have a ship and attack you?"

"No one has a ship like the *Honeycomb*," Wynne said, forcing a bright smile. "She can outsail anything on the sea."

"I hope so, lady. You're going to need an advantage of some kind."

"What about you, lord?"

"Do not worry about me, lady."

"I do. You were depending on Cathmor to lead you through the countryside, and if not him, then Siad. Now we're not sure if Siad or one of his men has betrayed us."

"I trust Siad," Brian said, "but I haven't met his men." He rubbed his chin. "We may still have the element of surprise on our side. Folloman does not know we are aware that he has knowledge of us."

"Perhaps," Wynne murmured, breaking out of Brian's embrace.

"Now, wife, move with haste. Load the ship, move Cathmor, and sail out. Remember to—"

"I know." She laid her palms against his chest.

"Sail up and down the coast, always returning to this spot. If in five days you and your men have not returned, I am to set sail for Scotland."

"Aye."

Giving her a quick kiss, Brian strode out of the shelter and called for all of his men to come together in the Great Hall.

Sunlight streamed through the front door and the open window; it slipped through cracks in the thatched roof and poured through the large smoke hole. Brian stood by the blackened central hearth, his warriors around him, some sitting on the floor and on sleeping platforms, others on benches.

While Brian spoke to them, explaining what had happened, several of his outriders rode into camp with Siad's men. The brigands joined the mac Logan kindred in the old building, standing to one side. Tension between the two sets of men rose as they eyed one another warily. Since the newcomers were Siad's men, Brian let Siad address them.

The young warrior marched back and forth in front of his men, staring into the eyes of each as he passed by. His left hand rested on the hilt of his sword. He repeated for them the charges Cathmor had made. Everyone remained silent. Then the men looked at one another.

"Beathan could have guessed that we would follow him," Siad said, "but he wouldn't have known for sure. And if it had been us they suspected, both Beathan and Folloman would have known that we would sail directly into Sligo. I know the coastline so well, I could easily hide there from them." His voice rose in anger. "How does Folloman know that Brian mac Logan and Lady Gwynneth are here?"

"Spies," one of Siad's men yelled. "Like us, Folloman has sent out spies."

"Spies here in Donegal country?" Siad said. "Nay, I think not. Donegals would not take kindly to O'Illands on their territory." He paused. "Nay, my friends, the spy is one of us, or one of mac Logan's men."

"Aye," one of the younger warriors shouted, "it could have been one of mac Logan's men, or the seafarer's."

Siad's men nodded and shouted their ayes.

"Aye, Rus," Siad replied, responding to the young man, "it could have been any one of us. And we shall soon find out. Lord mac Logan has sent out spies as well, and one of them can identify the man who betrayed us."

Rus squirmed nervously, his gaze darting about. He plowed a hand through his hair.

Brian rose. "We shall take you to the shelter where Cathmor is lying. One by one each of you will march by him until he identifies the man who betrayed us."

"If you think you're safe," Siad said, "you're wrong. Cathmor was left for dead, but one of Lord Brian's outriders found him. He's critically wounded, but he's alive."

"Nay!" Rus leaped to his feet. "I saw them kill him. They threw a spear into his back and hacked him with their daggers. The old man couldn't be alive."

Sadly Siad said, " 'Twas you, Rus?"

He shook his head. "Nay, Siad, I didn't betray you. 'Twas him!"

He pointed to an outcast, a surly fellow who growled, "Don't say nothing, lad. They don't know anything. They's guessing."

Frightened Rus looked from his companion to Siad.

"This man Sedlang was supposed to be keeping

guard at the cave where you left us," Rus said. "But when I left the cave to relieve myself, he was gone. I thought something had happened to him."

"Shut your mouth!" Sedlang shouted.

"I followed his trail," Rus went on. "He headed to the chief village of the O'Illands." Again he pushed a hand through his hair. "But when I got there, I saw several men outside the village walls beating an old man. I was frightened and started back to the cave. That's when I ran into Sedlang. He told me he had been spying out the land. He swore he had just gotten there in time to see them beat the old man." Rus took a deep breath. "We rushed back to the cave and didn't let anyone know we had been gone."

"You betrayed Lord Brian and Lady Gwynneth?" Siad said.

"You can't prove it was me," Sedlang taunted. "That old man couldn't have lived through that beating."

"He did," Brian said.

Using his dagger, Siad cut Sedlang's weapon belts, and his sword and dagger dropped to the ground. One of the brigands caught the traitor by the nape of the neck.

"Where shall I take him?"

"Follow me," Brian said.

Within minutes it was all over. Cathmor made the identification, and Siad and his men executed the prisoner; when they returned to the Great Hall, all of them swore fealty to Brian.

Standing, Brian addressed the men. "Highlanders and kindred, when I handed out my war dagger, I told you that we were coming to Ireland to avenge the wrong Beathan had brought upon my home."

"Hear! Hear!" his warriors shouted.

"Cathmor has now told us that the O'Illands know we are here. We have been robbed of the element of surprise. Yet Folloman doesn't realize we have been warned. He won't expect to encounter an army marching toward him."

Brian unsheathed his dirk and held it aloft. "The war dagger, lads!"

Blood-curdling war cries, accompanied by the vicious clanging of spears and swords, filled the air. Albert raced to Brian, grabbed the dirk, and held it aloft, signifying his willingness to fight with his liege. When he brought his hand down, another man took up the dirk and raised it high, then another and another, until all the Highlanders had volunteered.

Dow seized the dirk. "What about us, sire?" he cried. "Since our lady's life is threatened, we have a stake in this battle too."

"Aye, sailors," Brian shouted, "you do. Your lady has given you permission to fight with us."

One by one they volunteered in the same traditional manner.

"And I, sire," Siad shouted, "I take up the war dagger of Brian mac Logan."

All of Siad's men swore their battle allegiance.

"Thank you, lads," Brian said, his gaze sweeping over them. Turning to the sailors he said, "Enough of you must remain on the *Honeycomb* to protect my lady and Cathmor."

"I shall stay with my lady," Keith announced, hooking his hand on his stone pouch. "She is my liege, sire, and I shall protect her with my life."

"I know you will, Keith."

"Thank you, sire." His chest swelled, and he drummed his fingers over the leather purse.

"I shall stay with her also." Dow laid a hand

on Keith's shoulder. "With Cathmor wounded, she will need me to help her sail as well as fight."

Brian nodded. "Make haste and decide who will go with me and who will remain with Lady Wynne."

While Brian instructed his men, Dow separated the sailors into two groups, one joining Brian, the other moving toward the ship to prepare to set sail.

ot wanting him to send her back, she stayed to-
ard the rear of the group, moving through the
nks only when they reached a flat stretch of
eadowland.

In the far distance she saw a massive group of
pproaching warriors. Their outrider, galloping far
head of the others, stopped and stared at their
own army, then spurred his horse around and returned. As the distant cloud of dust settled,
Wynne surmised that Folloman had halted his
troops while he received his scout's report and
decided how to proceed.

Wynne nudged her horse forward until she finally reached Brian's side. "They must have two
hundred warriors, my lord," she said.

"Aye," Brian answered, his preoccupied gaze
pinned on the body of men who were about a mile
and a half from them. The distance between the
two groups closed as Brian and his men continued
to ride. Then Brian turned and gazed at Wynne,
squinting at the helmet that covered the upper
part of her face.

"Wynne?" he demanded, "is that you?"

"Aye, my lord."

His face hardened. "I told you to leave."

"I couldn't, lord." She kept her gaze straight
ahead. "I thought you might have need of me,"
he added, "And my bow."

"This is man's work, lady."

"'Tis a warrior's work, my lord," she softly cor-
cted, turning her head and looking at him. "And
ou married a warrior, one who loves you very
uch."

"I love you and want to protect you." His voice
ftened. "I recognize that you are a warrior, my
fe, but your duty lies with your ship."

"For the first time since I became a seafarer, my

Chapter 21

Wynne had remained in the shelter where she
had changed into trousers and a tunic, and
had plaited her hair. Over her mail she strapped
her weapon belts about her waist. Wynne the seafarer was ready for battle.

Dow reported to Wynne what had transpired in
the Great Hall.

"Have Cathmor placed on the ship," she
ordered.

Emerging from the shelter, she glanced across
the ruins. As quickly as the camp had been
erected, it was being dismantled. Her handfasting
seemed to have happened in another lifetime. Sad-
dened, she stooped and picked up the bouquet of
flowers she had dropped earlier. She touched the
bruised petals, and breathed in their fragrance.
With a small sob she pressed the flowers against
her cheek, wondering if this crushed bouquet was
a portent of things to come.

Pushing away such thoughts, she called her men
together and directed the reloading of the Honeycomb, ordering the cargo to be placed in such a
way as to allow plenty of room for battle, if it
came to that. While they were loading, her first
scouting boat returned. The crewmen described
the southern coastline in detail and reported having seen no warriors on the march.

She joined Brian at the edge of camp where his men were preparing for the coming battle. They had donned their mail and helmets, polished and prepared their weapons, and were now dressing their horses with gold bridles, choice leather reins, and saddle skirts woven in the colors of House Logan. Many braided colored sashes into their horses' tails and manes; each painted his talisman on the flank of his mount.

Siad rode up to him. "My lord, are you ready?"

"Aye," Brian said. He gave Wynne a long kiss, held her tightly, then set her away. "Goodbye, wife. Take care of yourself. I shall return shortly."

"Aye, husband."

"Protect her, lord."

Keith came running up to Brian. "My lord," he shouted, "Cathmor begs to speak with you before you leave."

With Wynne at his side, Brian strode across the camp, up the plank, across the deck to Cathmor's sleeping bag.

"My lord—" The old man's lids twitched. Through swollen, discolored flesh, he peered at Brian. "Protect my lady, mac Logan."

"I shall," Brian promised. "She is now my lady wife."

Cathmor gazed at Brian, then at Wynne. She nodded. The old man's lips trembled as he tried to smile.

Brian said, "We were handfasted this morning."

Cathmor nodded. "She must leave, sire. Sail now."

"She will," Brian said. But when he turned to Wynne, she looked away.

Just then Dow raced up the landing plank, and across the deck. "My lady," he called, "the second scouting boat has returned."

In a short while Wynne's scout was ab[...] He reported a large army marching towa[...]

"Secure the smaller boat," Wynne order[...] prepare to sail."

She raced to the hold, where she knot[...] plait atop her head. Aye, she thought, the [...] comb would be sailing as Brian had comma[...] as she knew it must. But she would not be [...] She belonged by her husband's side, not a[...] ship. Dow was a seasoned sailor and pilot. [...] him in charge, Wynne need not worry about[...] safety of her men. Freely she was surrendering [...] position as captain, so that she could be with [...] husband, her love. She felt no regret.

She settled her helmet on her head, slid her b[...] and quiver over her shoulder, and walked [...] onto the deck.

"Dow," she said, "I am leaving you in char[...]

Surprised, he whirled around. "Where are [...] going?"

"To ride with my husband."

"My lady!" Dow exclaimed.

"I have never abandoned my ship before[...] said, "but I have never had just cause to [...] You and Cathmor are able seamen. Make su[...] follow the coastline for five days as Bri[...] structed, and—"

Dow nodded. "I know, lady."

"Send out runners to keep you posted."

"Aye, my lady."

"Take care of my ship," Wynne said.

"As if she were my own. May the god[...] land and wind ride with you, lady, to pr[...] keep you safe."

Wynne quickly disembarked and hurr[...] stable. It wasn't long before she had sa[...] of the remaining horses and was riding a[...]

lord, I have stepped down from the steering oar. But I have left it in capable hands," Wynne said. "I wanted to be by your side, husband. This is where I belong."

For a moment they stared at each other through visored helmets.

"Lady, since you have hidden yourself among us, and we have ridden a far distance, I am not going to send you back. But in the future I will not tolerate your disobeying my orders."

"Aye, my husband."

He stared suspiciously at her and sighed.

On they marched until they reached the long line of O'Illand warriors. Brian held up his hand and halted his men. Mounted warriors, clad in mail and visored helmets, faced each other. Their banners fluttered from wrought-iron standards. Brian trotted his stallion into the barren area that lay between the two armies. One of his warriors started to ride out with him as his second, but Wynne moved more quickly and joined him first.

An O'Illand warrior galloped out to join them.

"I am Brian mac Logan, headman of House Logan of Clan Duncan, of Northern Scotland."

"I am Folloman of Clan O'Illand," the other man answered. "Why are you on our land?"

Wynne's stomach tightened when she heard Folloman's voice. It was he who had sworn to return her to Clan O'Illand, to marry her and conceive a baby with her. The thought of his touch nauseated her.

"My quarrel is with one named Beathan," Brian continued. "He raided my village and stole a sacred girdle from me."

"Beathan is dead," Folloman replied. "We had a difference of opinion. Now I have the girdle."

Folloman looked beyond Brian at the sixty or so warriors who rode with him.

"The girdle is mine, and I want it returned," Brian said.

"Aye, I understand your feelings. You see, you have something of *mine*, and I want *it* returned. You have my betrothed, Lady Gwynneth of Ailean. I shall gladly give you the girdle in exchange for her."

"Lady Gwynneth is not a possession to be bartered," Brian said.

"She is all I will take in exchange for the girdle." Folloman laughed. "Mac Logan, you disappoint me. You know that women are nothing but chattel."

"You couldn't be more wrong, Folloman."

"Do you have soft feelings for the woman?"

"She is my wife. We were handfasted this morning."

"Such a shame, my lord. You have defiled my betrothed," Folloman said. He opened the leather purse he wore about his waist and pulled out the Mayo Girdle. Holding out his hand, he dangled it before him. "Beathan immediately understood the value of the belt when he stole it from your home. He brought it to me in hopes that he could become a part of Clan O'Illand once more. But he and I did not agree, so I thought it best to kill him." Folloman tossed the girdle into the air and caught it deftly. "It is so delicate, it could easily tear. All you have to do to get it back is give me Lady Gwynneth."

Folloman moved his horse closer to Wynne. He smiled. "I do believe the lady we are discussing is riding with you, mac Logan."

"Aye, Folloman," Wynne said, "I ride with my husband."

"I've heard much about your prowess as a warrior, madam, but I don't believe it," he taunted.

Brian laughed. " 'Twould serve you well if you did, Irishman."

"Do you still have the cat, madam?" Folloman asked. "The one that maimed Alba?"

"Aye. She's aboard my ship."

"She's an old cat."

"Not too old to scar anyone who tries to harm me." Wynne returned his gaze, the truth of her words blazing in her eyes.

"I need you, lady, to redeem my honor and my name. Since the O'Illands are declining in power, they agreed that if I bring you to them, my men and I shall no longer be outcasts, but shall become members of their clan. Only you, my lady, can lift the curse from Clan O'Illand. No other woman will do. You and I, Folloman, champion of Clan O'Illand, shall marry, and you shall produce a child who shall inherit the High Seat of the clan. Once the child is born, I shall have custody of it and the High Seat, and the clan can do with you as they wish." He laughed. "Their revenge will be complete, and they shall save their clan. Forever the name O'Illand will be recorded in the annals of Irish clans."

Brian moved closer to Wynne. "I shall see you dead and beheaded and your soul roaming this land for all eternity before I let you have Wynne," he declared.

"And I, mac Logan, shall be forced to destroy this belt and you." Looking at Wynne he added, "My lady, I appeal to you to see reason. If you come to me, I shall return the girdle to mac Logan, and shall request that the O'Illands spare your life once you have taken the necessary steps to lift the curse from their name. Before the gods, my lady, I swear."

"I spit on you," she hissed.

Brian urged his horse closer to Folloman. Taking off his glove, he slapped the Irishman across the face. "I am a man of *enech*, Folloman, a man of honor, and I'll do what I must to preserve the *enech* of my house." He paused. "I, Brian mac Logan of House Logan, call you out, Folloman, outcast of the O'Illands."

Folloman's lips curled derisively. Brian saw the hatred in the depths of his eyes. The Irishman knew there was no honorable way he could escape the challenge. He crushed the belt in his fist. "I accept, Highlander."

"You have the choice of weapon," Brian replied.

"Sword," Folloman snapped. "Will Lady Gwynneth be your second?"

"Aye," Wynne called at the same time that Brian shouted, "Nay."

Shaking his head, Brian turned to her. "Nay, lady."

She knew he meant what he said.

"Albert!" he shouted, and the young warrior hastened to join him.

Both men dismounted, and Brian unsheathed his sword, holding it up so that sunlight glinted on the long silver blade. Folloman withdrew his own sword and brandished it, his face twisted into an ugly frown of fury. His stance and gaze radiated his hatred and contempt.

"When I am through with you, Highlander, you will crawl back to your own land in shame. You'll never redeem your *enech*." He laughed. "I shall double your shame by letting you live with the knowledge that I, Folloman of Eire, a man older than you, defeated you and took your woman. Yet

I, an Irish chieftain, will allow you to live. I shall cripple you for life. And if your woman has conceived your child, I shall kill it myself."

Fury rushed through Brian's veins. Nothing pushed him beyond control faster than threats to innocent children. He cared not if he became a barbarian, if he fought like a berserker. He would die before he let a child be murdered by this lunatic.

He took off his helmet and handed it to Albert. "Call your man, Folloman. This one shall stand for me."

Folloman spun around and moved among his warriors, speaking to several.

Wynne slid off her horse and joined Brian. "You are protected, my lord, by my magical talisman." She slipped Elspeth's brooch from her mantle and fastened it to the neckline of his tunic beneath his torque. "And you're wearing Elspeth's. No one can defeat you now."

"Aye."

Brian stared into the beautiful depths of her blue-gray eyes. He smiled tenderly at her.

"I love you, Wynne the seafarer," he said.

"I love you," she whispered.

"My lady, I have never loved another woman as I love you. Whatever happens, I want you to know that in my heart I am joined with you for all time."

"My love," she said, her eyes glowing, her lips trembling. "What about the Pict princess?"

"Malcolm shall have to find another headman for that union. I want you and intend to have you, even if I must live on a boat with you and sail the seas."

Wynne laughed. "My lord, I have a similar confession to make. I too want be a family, but I am willing to try village life again."

"We can have both," he murmured.

"Aye." She stepped away and remounted her horse. "I wish you well, my love, my husband."

Folloman, having designated his bestman, returned. He and Brian took their places opposite each other. Brian studied Folloman's eye movements, the way he held his sword and distributed his weight on his feet.

Folloman studied him with the same intensity.

Brian had the advantage of fewer years over Folloman, who was past forty, but the Irishman was strong and had the body of a much younger man. He was a hardened warrior, accustomed to winning.

Still, Brian was known for his endurance. That and patient intelligence had often brought him victory against far stronger men.

"Warriors," Albert shouted, "are you ready to begin?"

He leaped out of the way, and Folloman and Brian began to circle each other. Brian lifted his sword and brought down the blade with a tremendous crash as Folloman deftly feinted the blow. The clang signaled to the warriors that combat had truly begun.

Amid the cheers and taunts of their respective warriors, Brian and Folloman fought blow for blow. Both were well matched. Although Folloman's experience far outweighed Brian's, Brian was the younger, the quicker, and the lighter of the two.

Both men were cool and composed. It was difficult for Brian to read Folloman, to figure what he was going to do next. Brian quietly moved about, dodging blows, lunging, his eyes never leaving

Folloman. Always he measured his adversary's
moves and calculated his own accordingly. From
the beginning he had known that he would be
fighting one of the most formidable foes of his life,
and that he would win only if he could outwit
and outmaneuver the Irishman.

As the two men circled again, Brian saw Wynne
out of the corner of his eye. Her face was pale and
drawn, her fingers twisted together.

As a warrior, Wynne should have been accustomed to watching men engaged in single combat,
but she wasn't . . . not when the man she loved
was involved. She could not remember a time
when she had been so anxious.

Once again the two men circled warily. Folloman rushed in. Brian backed up, but he was not
quick enough. Folloman drew first blood when his
blade slashed into Brian's thigh.

Brian was in retreat. Folloman pressed his attack. Blow by blow, he pushed Brian farther and
farther back, then forced him against a large
boulder.

Brian pushed forward with a few well-placed
thrusts, turned, and cornered Folloman.

The meadow echoed with the sounds of steel
against steel, with the cries and grunts of the battle-weary warriors. With a yell and a fierce lunge,
Folloman pierced Brian's shoulder. The wound
was deep. Blood gushed out to stain his tunic beneath his chain mail.

Wynne drew in a sharp breath.

Folloman, a malicious grin on his face, rushed
in for the kill. Brian rallied his strength, deflected
the blow, and landed a hard, clean one himself.
Bleeding from the side, Folloman pulled back.

But the Irishman was not down. He whipped
his sword through the air, the sharp edge again

catching Brian's fighting arm. Blood dripped off his wrist and fingers and splattered to the ground.

Backing up from Folloman, Brian stumbled over an exposed root. But even as he fell, his confidence returned. By now he realized that Folloman had a few basic moves which he used time and again—well-placed blows, followed by hasty retreats. Above all, his arrogance would be his downfall.

A second time Folloman came in for the kill, but this time Brian was prepared for him. He dived to the ground and rolled out of the way, quickly leaping back to his feet on the other side.

Angry, scowling, Folloman advanced, his sword swinging from left to right. The blows were coming so fast and furiously that all Brian could do was hunker and ward them off. Folloman's laughter rang louder than the clang of metal. His men shouted and beat their weapons together.

He pressed forward. Brian reeled from the fast and heavy assault. Then gathering all his strength, he thrust. Again. And again. His furious offensive startled Folloman. Folloman stumbled back.

Gasping for air, blinking sweat from his eyes, Brian rallied new strength. He rushed toward the still shocked Folloman and landed a blow that sent him reeling backward. Folloman crashed on to his back, his legs flailing. Before Brian could strike again, the chieftain rolled over and leaped to his feet, once again assuming battle stance.

Wynne watched Brian's chest heave as he dragged air into his lungs. He wiped perspiration from his forehead with the back of his hand. Yet he never took his eyes off Folloman. She prayed to the gods of the Grove to help him.

Brian and Folloman were slowing down. Their blows came not as hard, as quick, or as smooth. Both had sustained numerous cuts and bruises, and the ground around them was stained with their blood.

Folloman moved forward. Brian stepped backward, but not quickly or far enough. The Irishman raised his sword and brought it down with all his strength. The blow, one too many to Brian's bruised and wounded arm, sent excruciating pain through his body.

Barely able to maintain a grip on his sword, Brian fought to keep from losing consciousness. He drew in deep breaths and kept retreating, moving backward, sideways, always away from the pounding blows of Folloman's sword.

In the fray of repeated impacts, the flat side of Folloman's sword walloped Brian again, hitting him fully on one of his open and bleeding wounds. Dizzy with exhaustion and pain, Brian could no longer hang on to his sword. It spun through the air, landing close to Wynne's feet.

She gasped.

Cheers went up for Folloman.

He shouted his victory. His sword poised, evil purpose etched in his face, he advanced slowly toward Brian. Wynne's heart pounded, her breathing shallow and painful.

Brian tottered on his feet. Folloman circled him slowly, teasing him.

"The victory belongs to me, Highlander," he taunted.

"Don't brag too soon, Irishman."

Brian couldn't distinguish Folloman's features. He laughed, the mocking sound echoing through the clearing. Brian took several more deep breaths, and his vision began to clear.

Folloman advanced. Again he laughed. He was getting cocky and overconfident, letting down his guard. It was what Brian had been waiting for.

His eyes pinned on Folloman, Brian dived in low, encircling Folloman's ankles with his arms and toppling him to the ground. Folloman's sword clattered out of his hand.

Brian picked it up, holding the mighty chieftain at blade point with his own sword. "I am the winner, Folloman, you the loser. I could take your life."

"Take it!" Folloman shouted.

"Nay." Brian stepped back.

"Coward!" Folloman taunted.

"You shall live to bear the full force of your shame."

Dishonored, disgraced, Folloman's warriors began to back away.

"You wanted me to suffer double disgrace, Folloman. 'Tis you who shall suffer instead. You have lost a duel to the death, and I, your adversary, have spared your life." Brian laughed. "Clan O'Illand will not be pleased with you." He turned and headed toward his warriors.

Folloman pushed to his feet, his visage sinister. "The battle isn't over yet, mac Logan!" He pulled a dagger from its sheath and charged at Brian's back.

"Watch out, Brian!" Wynne shouted.

As if in a single stroke, she nocked an arrow and sent it flying. As Folloman bore down with the dagger, her arrow hit true, thudding into his chest.

Grunting, bending over, he grabbed it and tugged. He coughed, and blood dribbled from his mouth. He collapsed in the dirt.

Unmindful that Brian was soaked with blood and perspiration, Wynne slid off her horse and ran into his arms, pressing herself against him. He was alive, and he was her love. They were married for all time.

With one arm encircling his ladylove, Brian held his sword high in the air. His men cheered. He caught Wynne's hand and raised it. The warriors cheered more loudly and beat their weapons together.

"My lady," Brian said, "I was angry at you for following me, but I am grateful that you were here to save my life once again."

"If need be, my lord, I shall spend the rest of my life keeping you safe," she promised. And she brought her mouth to his.

Chapter 22

Sunshine spilled into Wynne's shelter at the ancient ruins. Sighing deeply, contentedly, she slid deeper under the blankets on the sleeping platform. Yesterday her world had been turned upside down. Today it was right side up. Folloman was dead, and Triath, high king of Clan O'Illand, had renounced the blood oath against her.

Brian had once more claimed possession of the sacred girdle. They would be returning to Ireland with Elspeth at summer solstice so that the Court of the Yew could officially present the girdle to Brian for safekeeping until Elspeth reached her sixteenth year. Brian had promised Siad and his men that they could become broken men in House Logan. The ceremony would be performed as soon as they arrived in Northern Scotland.

The morning breeze blew against Wynne's face, bringing the scent of the sea. Smiling, she opened her eyes and turned her head. Brian was not in bed with her. She bolted up. Fully dressed, he sat in the chair watching her.

"Good morrow," he said, a leisurely smile curving his lips.

"Good morrow," she murmured.

She could not get her fill of looking at her handsome husband. Even with a few cuts and bruises on his face, he was still a man set apart from all others—her lover, her husband, her champion. Yesterday he had challenged Folloman and had won, leaving High King Triath a shamed man. Wynne was a free woman, forever out from under the shadow of the O'Illands.

"How are your wounds?" she asked.

"Sore," he answered.

"Did you rest well?"

"As well as can be expected."

Unmindful of her nudity, Wynne slipped out of bed and moved to where he sat, kneeling between his legs. She ran her fingertips over his face. Her lips met his softly as he filled his hands with her breasts. On his face she saw the deep enjoyment of a man who was holding something precious.

"We begin our journey home today," he murmured.

"Aye," she agreed. "We're going home."

Both of them knew they had a home together, but they weren't sure what form that home would take. During the last few hours Wynne had realized that home was more than a place to live. Rather it was an idea, a feeling, a relationship with those she loved. Although she enjoyed the sea and her island, and had once considered them her whole world, she knew now that she would be at home with Brian wherever he was. Both of them together, with their children, made a home.

She moved to her sea trunk, opened it, and pulled out clean leggings, trousers, and a tunic.

"Without an heir to the High Seat," Wynne said, "the O'Illands will become a sept or a branch of Clan Donnal."

"Are you sad that Cathmor won't be returning with us?"

"Nay, he'll be here for only a short while." She stepped into her leggings, then her trousers. "Then he'll return to the Isle of Cat to become Lord Cathmor of Cat."

"My lady," Brian said, "I would be content to move the Logan kindred closer to the coast where you could dock your ships. Would that make you happy? Could you leave the Isle of Cat?"

"Aye, lord, I'm ready to leave. It has served its purpose for me. As you said, I built a cloister out of it, and I no longer need or want it. I'm eager to build our village and to be with our family."

Brian grinned. "Lady, I must warn you, my children are rather . . . spirited."

"A necessary trait in a leader, my lord."

Brian chuckled.

They were quiet for a few moments while Wynne finished dressing. Then she said, "Cathmor is happy, lord, now that his honor has been restored."

She crossed to the window. "Come look, lord. Keith is acting like cock of the walk."

Brian joined her, putting his arm around her. They both laughed at the sight of the overconfident young man swaggering through the village.

"He's a good lad, lady," Brian said. "I shall be proud to be his foster father."

Standing to one side of the bell tower, Keith caught the lower edge of the bell with both hands and gave it a great shove. Its doleful tone reverberated through the village. Again and again he swung it.

" 'Tis such an ugly bell," Wynne murmured. She was so disappointed it wasn't the sacred bell of the Cloister of the Grove.

When Keith had first discovered the bell, and she had learned that this place had been an old monastery, she had felt sure the gods had brought her to the sacred bell of the Grove. She had persuaded Dow to examine it again, but he had made the same pronouncement. It was a miserable bell made of a base metal. A more precious bell was not hidden beneath the dross.

Wynne's gaze swept over the ruins she had come to love—the Great Hall, the building Brian and his warriors used as a stable, the foodstores, the ovens. She fixed her gaze on the newest-looking oven outside the Great Hall. Perhaps today in celebration she would have the fire lit in it and some bread baked.

Then she heard Grandmother Feich saying: *You are going to sail beyond the sun and stars, past everything you know and can see to an arc of golden light that stretches as you get closer and becomes a great shining circle.*

As the words rang through Wynne's mind, her gaze returned to the bell tower. Now that her past had been resolved, her future ensured, she wished she could find the bell of the *craebh ciuil* so that she could return it to the Cloister of the Grove and present it to Raven before she took her vow of silence at the summer solstice.

The sun climbed higher in the morning sky, its rays fanning out in golden radiance to form an arc over the tower. Wynne was blinded by its brilliance.

"Careful, lad," Dow shouted to Keith, "the crack is going to worsen."

The light will expand and cover everything, extending to the farthest heavens and earth. As it shone in the beginning, it will shine again. Forever.

The brilliant light hovered over the Great Hall; and she knew.

"Brian!" she shouted, running out of the shelter. "I've found the sacred bell of the cloister!"

Brian followed, calling out, "Wynne, Dow examined the bell twice. It's not the sacred one."

"Nay, but I know where it is."

Wynne ran toward the Great Hall. "The oven," she said, kneeling and running her hands over it. "I never noticed that it has a different shape from the others. And it's cleaner, as if it has never been used. And it has not been! Hand me your dagger."

Brian took out his dirk but did not hand it to her. He began to dig away the stone that formed a shell over the beehive-shaped oven. "I hope you're not in for another disappointment, lady."

"Nay," she said. She hovered over Brian as he dislodged stone after stone.

Soon Dow and Keith were helping.

"Look, Brian." Her voice was animated, her face glowing. "I see something gleaming." She rushed on. " 'Tis gold, Brian! 'Tis gold!" She pointed. "Look."

"If this is the sacred bell, lady," Keith said, "is it valuable?"

"Aye," she said, then murmured, " 'Seen by a few, the bell is gray turned to gold'. The mold used to cast the bell was gray clay," she muttered. "The bell itself gold. Gray turns into gold."

Brian pushed closer, as did Dow and Albert. Not to be left out, Honey squirmed her way into the circle.

" 'Seen by all, it is gold turned to gray.' To disguise the bell, the Irish Druids built an oven of gray stone over it. Gold turned to gray!"

"Aye, lady," Brian said as he removed even more stones, "it looks as if you have found your bell."

"Not *my* bell," Wynne said. "If it's the *craebh ciuil*, it belongs to the Cloister of the Grove."

Slowly the pile of stones around Brian grew as he uncovered a golden dome. Wynne gasped.

Quickly they removed more stones until the bell was totally uncovered.

"Here, lady," Dow exclaimed, tipping the bell, "the embossed apples."

Wynne touched the apples, running her hands over them again and again. " 'Tis the bell," she murmured. " 'Tis the bell."

At Wynne's insistence, Dow tipped the bell over, and she looked inside for the caster's sign. Up at the top she found the sacred three-pointed knot and the three circles of existence.

Aye, it was the sacred bell of the *craebh ciuil*, and she would return it to the Cloister of the Grove before summer solstice. Raven would not have to take the vow of silence.

Several weeks later, after they had stopped by the Isle of Cat to drop off Honey and gone on to the Shelter Stone Cloister in Glenmuir, Wynne and Brian strode through the village of the Cloister of the Grove toward the courtyard of the Inner Sanctum. A group of their warriors, Dow and Albert among them, pulled a large cart, the contents of which was covered with a large cloth.

"Gwynneth!" Mother Barbara protested. "You know you cannot enter this area unless you are invited."

"I have been invited, good mother," Wynne replied.

"Aye, Melanthe and Raven have always been too easy on you." The smile in Barbara's eyes took the bite out of her words. "Do you bring word from the Ancient of Nights and Days at the Shelter Stone Cloister?"

"I do," Wynne replied. "Please get the high priestess. I should like to present her with a gift."

"Raven is in the orchard," Barbara replied, "saying her morning prayers. She'll be back shortly. I'll get Melanthe."

Although Barbara was slightly crippled, she could move quickly when she deemed it expedient. Today was such a time. She knocked on the door to the advisory ovate's cell.

"Melanthe," she shouted, "Wynne is here. She has a gift and a message from the Ancient of Nights and Days."

Before the door opened, Barbara shuffled on to the bell tower. Grabbing the rope, she gave it several vigorous pulls. As Wynne heard the tolling, she shivered with anticipation.

Brian looked down at her and smiled. "You're glowing, my lady. Are you enjoying your victory?"

"Aye, my love, I am. So often dreams and fantasies are better than reality, but not this time. I can hardly wait to see Raven."

The door to Melanthe's chamber opened, and she emerged wearing her cloister robe, but with the cowl shoved off her head and draped down her back. Unaccustomed to seeing her stepmother so revealed, Wynne stared at her. Something was different about her.

"Gwynneth," Melanthe exclaimed, and rushed across the courtyard. She threw her arms around her stepdaughter, hugged her tightly, then pushed back. She touched Wynne's face. "I'm so glad you're home."

As if unable to believe Wynne were there, she drew back and gazed at her. "The Mayo Girdle?" she asked. "Did you get it?"

"Aye, Mother, we did," Wynne replied, "and I

am forever freed from the curse of the O'Illands' blood oath."

"Free from the blood oath," Melanthe murmured. "By the blessed gods of the Grove! Tell me how."

"I shall, but it's a long story. Let's wait until you and Raven are together."

"*Gwynneth!*" a male voice bellowed.

Stunned to recognize that voice, never having expected to meet her father at the cloister, Wynne whirled around.

"My lord father, what are you doing here?"

It had been only half a year since Wynne had last seen her father, but he too seemed different. Pryse of Ailean strode through the wrought-iron gate and across the courtyard with a spring in his step that she hadn't noticed before. His face, though still rugged, seemed less harsh. He moved to stand beside Melanthe.

"What do you mean by sailing off to Ireland, daughter?" he demanded.

"Lord mac Logan hired my services," she retorted, irritated by his authoritarian tone.

"Do you realize that your mother and I have been worried about you?"

Still wondering at the difference she noted in him, Wynne looked from her father to her stepmother. Again she noticed that Melanthe wore no cowl. Her eyes were glistening, her face glowing. Her father looked happier, more content.

"Is this the man who hired your services?" Pryse fixed Brian with a glower.

"Aye, my lord father," Wynne replied. She curled her hand around Brian's arm and drew him closer. "He is also my champion and my lord husband."

"Your lord husband!" Melanthe and Pryse

echoed in unison, looking from Wynne to Brian, then at each other.

"Aye, the man I love. My lord father, this is Lord Brian mac Logan of House Logan. He defeated the champion of Clan O'Illand and has released me from the blood oath that Alba's family swore against me. We are handfasted, but wish to have a wedding ceremony."

Wynne couldn't remember when she had seen such a wide smile on her father's face. "I have heard of your exploits, my lord mac Logan," he said. "I'm pleased to welcome you into our family, to give my daughter to you in marriage. Later we shall discuss a dowry."

Because a dowry was customary and part of the woman's settlement if she and her husband divorced, neither Brian nor Wynne demurred.

Pryse moved closer to Melanthe, the two of them smiling at Wynne. Priestesses as well as Wynne and Brian's warriors gathered around. As the group fanned to the side, forming an aisle, Wynne looked up to see the high priestess moving toward her. As usual she wore a sleeveless green robe over a white tunic, and her head was covered with the green cowl.

"Superior Mother," Wynne said, her heart beating so fast she could hardly speak, "on my return trip to the cloister, I sailed by the Shelter Stone Cloister. The Ancient of Nights and Days was happy with the jewelry you chose to barter with him, and he was grateful for the replica of the *craebh ciuil* bell. He's most desirous to have you and your council visit with him," Wynne went on. "He wanted me to relay to you that indeed a runestave such as you inquired about is at the shrine. All of you may examine it in person."

Barbara was so excited that she clapped her

hands together. The young novitiate, Agnes, grinned and joined Barbara.

Wynne continued, "My lord high priest of the shrine also instructed me to tell you that the mark is indeed the three-pointed knot and that it is located at the inside top of the bell on the opposite side from the *craebh ciuil.*"

"Thanks be to the gods of the Grove!" Barbara exclaimed. "We shall soon have our bell." She closed her eyes. "Aye, one of these days it shall be returned to us."

Peering around Wynne, Melanthe said, "What's in the cart, Gwynneth?"

"A gift from the Shelter Stone?" Barbara asked.

"I said I brought you a gift," Wynne said, "but it did not come from the shrine, good mother. 'Tis a gift from me."

Wynne stepped aside, grabbed the cloth, and tugged. It flew through the air, falling to the ground at her feet.

Waving her hand, she announced with a flourish, "The sacred bell of the cloister. The *craebh ciuil.*"

A gasp went up from the onlookers. Several of the women clapped their hands over their mouths. Barbara swooned and would have fallen if Dow did not rush to her aid.

"The bell," Raven whispered.

"Aye," Melanthe said. " 'Tis the bell."

Sunlight hit it, and a golden rainbow arced over them. Raven reached out and touched the bell. As she traced the outline of the apples, Wynne told how they had discovered it. Raven was still touching it when Wynne finished her tale.

Wynne motioned to Dow and Albert, who tipped the bell. "If you'll look, holy mother, you'll find the caster's mark where the Ancient of Nights and Days said it would be."

Raven knelt and looked at the mark. Then she rose and stepped back. "Ladies of the Cloister of the Grove"—her husky voice trembled—"my sister Gwynneth nea Pryse presents us with the greatest gift we could ever receive. All of you come look at our bell. We shall hang it today."

She stepped aside and held out her arms to her sister. Wynne rushed into her embrace.

"Now you don't have to take the vow of silence," she said.

"Nay, little sister."

Wynne reached up and pushed the cowl from Raven's head. "I've wanted to do that for a long time."

For the first time since Raven had joined the cloister, Wynne looked upon her sister's beautiful face. It was framed by thick, straight black hair, parted in the middle and burnished to a high sheen. Her eyes, a startling shade of brown flecked with gold, glowed. They were filled with love, and Wynne stared into their depths. Tears ran down Raven's cheeks.

"Little sister." Raven held her tightly.

They cried; they laughed; they talked, both at the same time. They stopped; they started again in unison. Melanthe cried, and Pryse put his arm around her shoulders and pulled her against him. The sisters pledged their love and promised a new beginning. Both women turned to their parents and included them in the celebration and forgiveness.

Later the family moved away from the priestesses and warriors to stroll through the orchard. Brian held Wynne's hand; Pryse walked between Melanthe and Raven.

"Now, Raven," Pryse said, "we can return

home. 'Tis time you learned how to govern your kingdom."

"I have been giving a great deal of thought to that lately," Raven replied. "I cannot, my lord father. This is where I want to be. For now this is where I belong."

He looked at Melanthe. "Just like your mother. She won't leave the cloister either. But I haven't given up trying to persuade you."

So that was the way it was, Wynne thought. She looked at her stepmother and smiled. Soft color shaded Melanthe's cheeks as she returned the smile.

"Perhaps someday I shall leave," Raven said, "but until then, my lord father and lady mother, I have a suggestion to make." She paused. "If Mother were to adopt Gwynneth, she would also be an heir to the High Seat of Ailean."

"Aye," Pryse drawled, his eyes flashing, "and she is married."

"And closer to conceiving a baby," Wynne added, looking up at Brian with a grin.

Much closer, Wynne thought.

Melanthe agreed. " 'Tis the right thing to do."

The marriage of Lord Brian mac Logan and Lady Gwynneth nea Pryse was solemnized in the apple orchard at the Cloister of the Grove. The morning sun was radiant, its rays glowing through the branches and blossoms of the apple trees. The sacred golden bell tolled, and Raven nea Pryse, high priestess of the Grove, officiated at the ceremony.

When she finished speaking the sacred words, she said, "You may seal your promises with a kiss."

Willingly Brian and Wynne melded into each

other's arms. When they parted, they held hands and turned to face their guests, who all cheered. Then Wynne saw Lachlann mac Niall shoving his way through the crowd, a big grin on his face.

"I see that I arrived in time." He caught Brian in a loose hug and dropped a kiss on Wynne's cheek. "I have a gift for you, my lord."

The crowd fell aside, and four children—three girls and a boy—stood there staring. Wynne stared back at them. This was her family, and it was the most beautiful sight she had ever beheld. Brian knelt and opened his arms.

"Papa!" all of them called, and raced into their father's embrace.

Secure in her love for Brian, Wynne waited patiently while he explained to them that she was their new stepmother and that she was going to live with them, to love and take care of them.

Brian introduced them. Elspeth, the eldest, looked like Brian, with dark hair and gray eyes. Lucy, the second eldest, was tiny and dark. Wynne supposed she looked like her mother. With the exception of those beautiful gray eyes, Maggie didn't favor any of the others. Her arms folded across her chest, she never took her gaze off Wynne. Calum, the youngest at five years old, was beautiful. Like Elspeth, he looked like his father.

"And this is Lady Gwynneth nea Pryse, your stepmother," Brian said. "As she is going to take care of you, you're also going to have to take care of her." His eyes twinkled. "She's never been a mother before."

"Never?" Calum asked solemnly, his gray eyes fixed on his father's face.

"Nay."

All four of them looked at Wynne.

"But she does have a cat—a Highland wildcat."

"She does?" Calum's eyes rounded. "A real wildcat?" Holding up his arms, he curled his fingers and snarled. "That kind of wildcat?"

"Aye," Wynne said, "but she's friendly, and she loves your father."

All four of them whooped, then sang, "She loves Papa."

"Aye," Brian answered dryly.

"Where is she?"

"She's on the Isle of Cat, our old home. After a long trip like your father and I have just completed, I wanted to let her rest."

"Are you going to bring her to our house?" Lucy asked.

Wynne nodded.

Elspeth reached up and touched the brooch that Wynne wore. "I crafted that for my father."

"Aye," Wynne said. "He gave it to me because it has great magic and will protect me. Shall I give it back?"

Elspeth thought for a moment, then said, "Nay, you may keep it. You're going to need as much magic as you can get to keep up with Maggie, Lucy, and Calum." Gravely she added, "Lachlann says they are a handful."

Lachlann chuckled. "That they are, Elspeth."

"I am *not* a handful," Calum exclaimed. He reached for his father's hand. "See, my lady, my father's hand is not large enough to hold me."

"Aye, 'tis true," Wynne agreed.

"Are you going to be my mama?" Calum asked.

"Aye, if you wish it."

"I do, lady," he said, "and I want you to tell my sisters that I'm a warrior. I don't like them giving me orders."

Lucy reached over and brushed a lock of hair from her brother's head. He swatted her hand away. In a solemn adult tone, she said, "I've told Calum that when he gets older, he can give orders, but now he's too little."

"You're tall," Maggie said without preamble. "So is Elspeth. And you have freckles like Elspeth."

Grinning, Lachlann said, "Well, lady, here you have it."

"Aye, here is part of my family." She smiled. "And this is your lady grandmother Melanthe and your lord grandfather Pryse."

Melanthe walked over to join them. "Come with me," she invited. "I have a treat for you."

Four sets of eyes became fixed on their father.

"Aye, go along," he urged.

Soon Wynne and Brian were alone. They strolled slowly through the orchard. Brian stopped and picked an apple blossom. Laughing, he blotted it against her face; Wynne did the same to him. They continued down the pathway to the brook, where they stopped. She raised her head as he lowered his. They kissed, fully, thoroughly. When she drew her lips from his, she leaned back in the circle of his arms.

"Now, my lord husband, shall we retire to our chamber and finish what we began so long ago?"

"Aye, my lady wife."

He swept her into his arms and walked along the low wall to the pool where they had first consummated their love. He moved along a pathway until he reached a bower canopied with tree branches and decorated with flowers. A pallet had already been laid out on the ground.

Smiling, Brian said, "I came earlier to make sure we would be comfortable, my love."

"And have plenty of pollen dust," Wynne added.

"Aye," he said, and kissed her long and deep.

Avon Romantic Treasures

*Unforgettable, enthralling love stories,
sparkling with passion and adventure
from Romance's bestselling authors*

LADY OF SUMMER *by Emma Merritt*
77984-6/$5.50 US/$7.50 Can

TIMESWEPT BRIDE *by Eugenia Riley*
77157-8/$5.50 US/$7.50 Can

A KISS IN THE NIGHT *by Jennifer Horsman*
77597-2/$5.50 US/$7.50 Can

SHAWNEE MOON *by Judith E. French*
77705-3/$5.50 US/$7.50 Can

PROMISE ME *by Kathleen Harrington*
77833-5/ $5.50 US/ $7.50 Can

COMANCHE RAIN *by Genell Dellin*
77525-5/ $4.99 US/ $5.99 Can

MY LORD CONQUEROR *by Samantha James*
77548-4/ $4.99 US/ $5.99 Can

ONCE UPON A KISS *by Tanya Anne Crosby*
77680-4/$4.99 US/$5.99 Can